The Last Resort

The truth was, Bentley couldn't cut so much as a twig from a tree without feeling uneasy. Cutting vines was particularly disturbing for him because of the way they cast about for something to hug.

Published by
Berkeley Hills Books, PO Box 9877, Berkeley CA
94709
www.berkeleyhills.com

Distributed by Publishers Group West

ISBN 1893163687

Designed by Nik Eakle Graphics, nikone@gmail.com

Illustrated by Nancy Gorrell

Printed in Canada

1 3 5 7 9 10 8 6 4 2

For Dandy, Süsse, Wolf, Pudge, Madeline, Nick, Gelse, Noah, Baku, Buddy and Ninja.

The Last Resort

Natasha and Emmett Eiland

•

Berkeley Hills Books

Berkeley, California

Part One

Chapter One

[Spring 1960]

In the early spring of 1960, Lenore Holt posted a wanted ad on the bulletin board at a Co-Op grocery store in Berkeley.

Wanted: A few good people
for wine-tastings and discussions about gardening.

Responses straggled in during the month, and when she had a sufficient number of interested people, Lenore set up a meeting at her house on Josephine

Street in the Berkeley flats.

Six people showed up—seven including her—and they tasted red wines from Burgundy and nibbled on bread and cheese. About an hour into the tasting, when the wine tasters had grown jolly and were laughing unguardedly, Zoë Androtti, one of those who had answered Lenore's ad, noticed that her fellow wine tasters' tongues had turned purple from the rich red wines. She kidded the tasters about it, and that's how The Purple Tongue got its name.

On that first night, after they had tasted the wines and identified their favorites, they migrated to Lenore's living room and shared information about gardening, such as where to buy the best perennials and what to do about the poorly draining, clayey garden soil of Berkeley. Zoë was one of those people who seem to notice everything, and she made her second observation of the evening: She and all the others in Lenore's living room that night were about the same age: around forty-five.

[February, 1975]

Fifteen years later, the Purple Tongue was still together and the members were now about sixty years old. Though they didn't yet know it, they were on the verge of doing something about which most people merely fantasize.

They had gathered to taste Burgundies once

again.* After the formal wine tasting, the seven members left their places around the dining room table and repaired to Lenore's living room to talk about gardening. Comfortable in each other's presence after fifteen years of friendship, they sipped from glasses of Lenore's house-zinfandel, and huge, gentle Tucker Calhoun made an announcement: "This week Weezie and I had to place my father in a nursing home." His voice broke with emotion. The others shifted in their chairs, unsettled. Knowing that their friend Tuck tended to plunge into deep depressions, they searched for ways to divert him before his thoughts turned completely dark. "Dad finally just went over the top. I mean, he became so hard to deal with and so grouchy that we couldn't stand having him live with us anymore. What else could we do...?" Tuck held his palms up as if asking his friends for forgiveness. The gesture looked at once pathetic and hilarious in one so large.

"You put your father in a rest home because he's grouchy? There's more to it than that, isn't there, Tuck?" Tina Boatman, a member of the Purple Tongue from the beginning, was a clinical psychologist with legs as long and shapely as Tina Turner's and skin the same glossy brown color. Hoping to engage Tuck before he spiraled downward into depression, she had intervened with a tried-and-true line that, spoken with sympathy, almost always elicited deep, healing insights in her patients: "There's more to it than that, isn't there?"

* See appendix for details of the tasting. [Ed.]

3

"No Tina, you don't understand. My dad is *really* grouchy." Tuck's voice had regained some conviction.

"Like how?" she asked.

Suddenly Tuck made a huge, snarly face and he growled fiercely. His jowls shook like a bulldog's. His friends recoiled. "Grouchy like that," he said.

When Tuck showed his teeth, Tina threw up a hand, thinking for a split second that her old friend might bite her, but she soon collected herself. "I see. Could you put that into words?"

"No. I don't want to think about it." With his bald crown and broad face, Tucker Calhoun looked like an oversized medieval monk.

Zoë Androtti, who sat beside Tuck, reached over and patted his round shoulder. She was so tiny that she probably could have stood on Tuck's foot without his noticing.

Tuck seemed to be deflating like a leaking blimp despite everyone's concern. It looked to some of the friends as if he might already have descended a step deeper into one of his famous blue spells. His big head was beginning to slump. "My dad can hear me put my hand on my wife's knee from three rooms away. If a carnal thought crosses my mind, he instantly knows and finds some way to put a stop to it."

"I guess *so*," Zoë said. "At your age carnal thoughts are embarrassing, don't you think?" Tiny Zoë had a good heart but a notoriously wicked sense of humor.

Tuck, speaking now in a flat, depressed monotone, went on. "At any moment, night or day, he is liable to charge into our bedroom to show us that he has just wet himself."

"I don't think we need to hear that," Pamela Noonan said, glaring at him. "This is a wine-and-garden meeting and not group therapy." Pamela was the group's one true socialite, born to a wealthy family of the old school. She ended her protest, as she often did, with her thin nose high in the air.

Lenore Holt hosted the night's meeting of the Purple Tongue. It was she who had brought the group to life fifteen years earlier with a "wanted" sign she posted in a grocery store. Since that first meeting, she and her husband had made an upward move to a nice old home in a Japanese style in the Berkeley hills. Lenore had been a full professor of English at Cal for many years and a certain aura of authority clung to her, enhanced by her commanding height of six feet and one inch. Over the years she had been the member of the group most likely to call the group's wandering attention back to wines or to gardening. But she had mellowed and was as inclined as the others to let the conversation take its natural course. So, even though Pamela was right and this *was* a wine-and-garden group and not group therapy, Lenore let the conversation go where it would. She listened with sympathy to Tuck's story about his father and heard in his voice the same, familiar sound of guilt she had heard in the voices of her many other friends who had had to intervene in their parents' lives. Her own mother was slipping deeper and deeper into Alzheimer's disease, and Lenore was tormented by the feeling that she had to do something to stop it.

"Remember the early days of this group," she asked the others, "when we used to talk about our children? Those were the years when none of them would leave home after college."

"That went on for a long time," Zoë said with a laugh. "It was all we talked about at these meetings except for wine and gardening." The group had been together so long that they had passed many of life's milestones together, including the important one of finally booting the children from the family nest.

Lenore thought for a moment and then went on. "After they finally left, bless their hearts, and we began to have a little more money, we used to compare notes about our remodeled kitchens and our new houses." Tina and the others smiled and nodded, recalling the years when they had been so thrillingly upwardly mobile. In their fifties, several of the members had even moved to Piedmont, a lofty old enclave of high status and good schools near Berkeley and Oakland.

"And now?" Lenore continued. "Now we talk about our failing parents." Confessions like Tuck's tonight, rather than garden talk, had become the common fare after The Purple Tongue's wine tastings.

"You know, it's not just us," Sophia Fletcher said. "Everyone our age seems to be telling sad stories about their father's incontinence or their mother's dementia." Sophia, a member of the Purple Tongue from the beginning, was an over worked co-owner of a book distribution business. For years she had dreamed that someday soon she would throw her career aside and bake pies, but she was trapped by success. Despite the stress she lived with every day, she had the most beautiful smile anyone in the group could remember seeing. When Sophia smiled, all of the tiny wrinkles in her face made perfect sense: They were the result of decades of smiling at the world. She showed no signs whatever of knowing just how delightful looking she was.

All the old friends sipped from their wine and thought about their own parents, gone now or still living.

"We're doing the best we can for our parents," Lenore said. "But is that what we want for ourselves when the time comes? Nursing homes?"

Tuck looked around. "Hey, everyone, I don't know what else I could have done for my father except the nursing home."

"Don't worry, Tuck," Bentley Fairbanks said. "Just because you got your father into a nursing home doesn't mean he's going to stay there." Bentley finished his wine and stood his glass on a coffee table. He moved with a supple grace that often kept new acquaintances from noticing, at first, his lined face and the silver curls at his temples. Bentley, sixty years old just like the others, looked as if, in a pinch, he could sub onstage for Rudolph Nureyev.

"Wait," Tuck said, raising his head, "you mean he might escape?"

"Well, that too," Bentley said. "But I was thinking of my mother. She was kicked out of a whole succession of nursing homes. I would get her into one and then, *ring!* They were calling me up and telling me to come pick her up."

"Oh no, they might kick my dad out?"

"I'd lay odds on it. He's a champion grouch, right? Tuck, this is the 21st century. To stay in a nursing home, you have to qualify."

"What do you mean?"

"I mean it's not like you can just plunk down your money, move into a nursing home and start annoying the staff. *Au contraire!* Your father will have to 'fit in.' He will have to 'contribute.' Joining a nursing home these days is like getting into a fraternity. You damned near have to be asked."

"No one would ever ask my father!" Tuck said. "I know that." Tuck laid his big head on the coffee table before him. Wild tufts of hair stuck out over each temple, but some of the friends could not help but observe a sizeable halo of bare scalp at the crown of his head.

"Well then, expect to see him back home by April Fool's Day," Bentley said. "April one."

Tuck, a garden writer, and Bentley, a nurseryman, had deep interests in common and were good friends even outside the group. But even the nicest people,

such as Bentley, couldn't resist teasing Tuck a little
when he became despondent. Maybe it was because
of the comic figure the big man cut when he began
to droop. Or maybe it was because he was such a
good fellow and he forgave everything. Besides, he
was apt to spring back just minutes later and bubble
with cheer.

*"I mean it's not like you can just plunk down your money,
move into a nursing home and start annoying the staff."*

Lenore opened another bottle of wine and started it around the group. Bentley spoke: "We're trained
to read, write, and calculate; we learn foreign languages, the geography of Greece, the names of our
congress people. We're trained to do our jobs. But
when it comes time to take care of our parents or of
ourselves when *we're* old, we're completely unpre-
pared. We're babes in the woods. Dopes." The room
was quiet for half a minute.

"How can we do it differently?" Sophia asked, finally. "I mean us, right here in this room. How can *we* grow old gracefully and not have our last years be grotesque? I mean, grotesque for our children as well as for ourselves. "

"I don't want my children to have to go through what we are with our parents," Lenore said.

"So I repeat my question," Sophia said. "How are we going to do it differently?"

Chapter Two

[February, 1975]

"Let's do our own," Lenore said.

"Our own what?" Tuck asked, his voice muffled by depression and by the coffee table on which his head lay.

"Our own retreat," she said, "or retirement home or whatever you want to call it. For when we're old."

"That won't require much patience," Sophia said with a laugh. Like nearly all people around the age of sixty, Sophia often kidded about being old. Joking was a way of testing the waters of old age, like sticking in one toe at a time.

"Only, for God's sake, let's not call it a nursing home," Lenore went on. "Let's call it what it should be: home."

"You mean, like an *old folks home*?" Zoë said laughing..

"Come on, I'm serious."

"It's too late for some of us," Bentley said. "Our parents are already gone."

"No," Lenore said, "I mean let's build a home for *us*—for when we'll need it. And we will, you know. I'm saying let's buy a place and then someday move into it together."

Tuck perked up. He looked at Lenore to see whether she was serious.

"What shall we call it?" Zoë asked. "Trail's End? The Last Roundup?"

"No," Bentley shouted. "The Big Sleep." Everyone laughed.

"Or let's dedicate it to William Faulkner and call it As I Lie Dying," Sophia said.

Even with her commanding size and the aura of authority gleaned from thirty years of presiding over classrooms, Lenore was having trouble breaking through the group's hilarity. "Wait, wait, wait, people! I'm serious! Instead of waiting for our families or the State or whoever to place us in some institution called Sheltering Oaks with a faux stone façade and a little fake fountain out in front, let's find a place where we would actually *like* to live out our lives. And then call it Trail's End if we want to, but the point is, we can name it ourselves."

"Well I certainly am not going to live in someplace called Trail's End," Pamela said. "Or The Big Sleep."

"You're right," Bentley said. "How about Senility City? Or Alzheimer's Acres?"

Tuck got the giggles. "Senility City!" He couldn't stop laughing. Finally he was half-sitting on his chair and half-kneeling on the carpeted floor, slapping the arm of his chair with one hand and coming close to sloshing his wine in the other. The others watched, fascinated.

Finally Lenore managed, "Okay, Tuck, everyone, I just had the best idea you've ever heard and everyone thinks it's hilarious. I'm going to make one more pitch. Here's the plan. We go in together to buy a place big enough for all of us. We find a really wonderful house. We fix it up. We landscape it. We garden. Maybe we rent it out for the next twenty years until we need it, I don't know. In the meantime, we find the best doctor in the land to minister to us when the time comes. The best staff. The best cook! We set up everything just the way we want it. We decorate the house, especially our private rooms. And then, when we're ready, we move in together. Simple."

"Not bad, Lenore," Tina said. "Not bad at all."

"Doesn't that sound good?" Lenore asked, nodding her head, agreeing with herself.

"It would take an awful lot of money to do what you're talking about, Lenore." Bentley said. "Buy a house big enough not only for us but for live-in staff? Fix it up, decorate it, landscape it?"

"But think of the alternative," Sophia offered. "We're going to give someone that money anyway. It's all going to come out of our pockets anyway," she said. At what: $3,000? $4,000 $5,000 a month for a nursing home? That's $35,000 to $60,000 a year. And that may go on for years. Let's say we each live for five years in nursing homes, that's $200,000 to $300,000 we go through during the last five years of our lives in places that we're certain to hate!"

"Let's get a dog!" Zoë said. "I'd like a nice little dachshund."

"I don't like dogs," Pamela said. "If we had a dog, there would be dog-hair all over everything, and the house would smell like dogs."

"Dogs smell better than what nursing homes usually smell like," Zoë said. "Usually they smell like pee."

"Well, that does kind of bring things back to earth," Bentley said. "I wonder if our nursing home, I mean, our *home* has to smell like pee. I'd prefer one that doesn't."

"This conversation is revolting," Pamela said.

"Better get the subject of pee out on the table right now, while we still have good sense," Bentley answered. "What can we do about it *after* we get dementia? It'll be too late then."

"Bentley!" Pamela interrupted. "You're making me sick."

"But anyway," Lenore bravely resumed, "of course we can have a dog. We can do anything we want. I guess the principle is that we make decisions like that by voting. And we make as many decisions as possible now, so we know exactly what to expect when we get there."

"I'll tell you what I don't want to do in The Last Mile, or whatever we're going to call it," Zoë said, "and that's to sit there drooling on myself as I watch some 36-inch television."

"I'm with you there, Zoë!" Tuck said. "If I'm going to drool, I want to do it while watching some babe in a bikini!"

"Now you're making *me* sick," Bentley said. The friends laughed, knowing that Bentley's preference was for men.

"What I'm getting at," Zoë said, "is that we should have something to do other than watch television, something to keep what's left of our minds engaged."

"That's what I was getting at, too," said Tuck.

"I vote on a German shepherd," Sophia said, "one of those marvelously trained dogs that can practically answer the phone; one that runs and gets the doctor if you're having fibrillations."

"Pamela," Tina said innocently, "haven't you read those articles about how dog hair is far cleaner than human hair? It turns out that people hair has thousands of little barbs that collect all kinds of stuff. Dog hair is smooth and everything just slides right off." Pamela was regarded within the group as being a difficult person, but its members had endured her so long—from the beginning, for fifteen years—that her often sour comments were familiar ground and went largely unnoticed. A few in the wine-and-garden group actually looked forward to what she might say next. However, they were not above teasing her from time to time.

Pamela said. "I've never read about any such study."

"But there's a preponderance of very convincing anecdotal evidence pointing in that direction," Tina insisted. "Dogs are cleaner than people and they smell better, too. That's another thing they've found out."

"What would you like to look forward to, Pamela?" Lenore asked. "What would your ideal home be like if we were to pull this off?"

"I suggest that we select a very beautiful old mansion," she said without hesitation, "and that we call it, simply, The Mansion. I picture a grand entry and a curving staircase, though the oldest of us may prefer to use the elevator to reach the upper floors. I picture a view of the garden from my room. When our eyes grow too dim to read, we will have young people read to us, loudly, if necessary. A string quartet will play for us on Thursdays. Beautiful men will escort us into the dining room in the evening."

"That's where you and I come in, Bentley," Tuck said.

"Our chef," Pamela continued, "will prepare appealing foods that will help us keep up our appetites. Of course, we will prepare the menus ourselves. Our gardener will supply the kitchen with fresh vegetables. And, speaking of the garden, I suggest a network of meandering garden paths so inviting that even older people will be enticed to walk them daily for exercise and pleasure. No, rather I *insist* on meandering garden paths. I feel they are essential to growing old gracefully."

"No, rather I insist on meandering garden paths," Pamela said. "I feel they are essential to growing old gracefully."

"They would complement our meandering minds," Zoë agreed.

"Well," Lenore said to the group, "we can see

right now that Pamela is going to keep our standards up. Gorgeous men, huh? To lead us to the table."

"We could hire college boys," Zoë said. "They work cheap."

"That's the easy part," Sophia said. "But Pamela's vision sounds pretty expensive. We're really going to have to confront the money problem."

"Uh oh, Sophia is going to bring us back to earth," said Zoë. "Money. That's one thing that could stop us, and I can see another. This may be the fatal flaw that we won't be able to get around."

"Oh, Zoë," Tina said, "give us another half hour of dreaming before the fatal flaw, okay? This is fun."

"I'd better hear the bad part now, before I get too excited," Tuck said. Others agreed.

"Okay," Zoë started, "what about our spouses? Remember them? We're all friends here, but even if we like each other and we like each other's spouses, will our husbands get along with each other?"

"And wives," Tuck said. "My wife. Don't forget Weezie. She'll probably be easy. She likes nearly everybody. But I think it would be a big mistake for me to go home and announce that we have her future all figured out. It's just human nature to resist."

"And here's the other thing," Zoë said. "What if they all say yes? Will there be room for everybody? What is the right number of people to make this work, or the greatest number or the least?"

Several of the wine-and-garden lovers bowed their heads in thought. Tuck rapped his forehead with his knuckles. It made a disconcerting sound, like thumping on a melon.

Finally Lenore said, "I think it's time to have a party or a picnic and invite our 'others.' And maybe we shouldn't mention to them what we have in mind just yet. I mean, let's see if they get along with each other. If they do, maybe we can bring up the idea slowly."

Tuck, married for thirty years, said, "Well, I can get Weezie to the party, but after that it's up to you. She reads me like a book. From the minute I say 'Honey?' she's going to wonder what I'm up to."

"Don't worry, Tuck, leave that to us. You just bring her along," Lenore said. "What about you, Bentley?"

"Well, I'm not exactly going steady at this particular time. But you all realize what kind of person I would bring to a party, don't you?"

"I'm sure we will all like anyone you bring," Lenore said.

"Well, then, I'm in."

"And as for the optimal number of people in our home," Tina said, "we're just going to have to put our thinking caps on, right? We'll figure it out."

Zoë said, "Yikes, look at the time!" Lenore did and it was nearly 11 o'clock, an hour later than the group's ordinary break-up time.

Lenore asked, "Who's on the party committee?" Zoë and Tina said they would help.

"But where will we have our party?" Tina asked.

"How about Tilden Park?" Lenore suggested.

"The weather is gorgeous," Sophia said. "It'll be wonderful in Tilden Park."

"Tony's allergic to the eucalyptus trees in Tilden Park," Tina said. "They're in bloom now. But I'll tell you what, put the right beer in his hand and he'll forget all about his hay fever."

"What kind of beer does he like?" Tuck asked.

"Anchor something," Zoë said.

"Anchor Steam Beer?"

"I think so."

"He's got it," Tuck said. And then, after several of the friends finished the wine in their glasses and after a few backs were patted, everyone rose, thanked Lenore and headed toward the door.

On her way out, Pamela could be heard saying, " I don't like dogs. I'd like a nice cat, though."

Zoë, already outdoors, could be heard saying, "Do you know what a litter box smells like, Pamela? It can make a whole mansion smell bad!"

Lenore followed them to the door and called to their retreating forms, "Now drive safely, everyone. Be careful." Back inside, as she gathered the empty wine glasses and two empty bottles, she wondered, "Do you suppose they're at all serious?" And later, in the kitchen, she asked herself, "And me? Would I really do it?" She didn't know.

Chapter Three

[February, 1975]

Zoë's husband, Tony Androtti was a dentist who had probably chosen the wrong profession. He was an excitable type—that's what his mother had called him even before he had turned thirteen—in a field that called for nerves of steel and a calm, steady approach to life. Rather than instill confidence in his patients, he scared the hell out of them by grumbling and even swearing when things got sticky and their root canals were going badly. Even his body was wrong for dentistry, or at least it bothered some of his patients. He was a burly fellow with a big chest, and some of them assumed that he was going to hurt them. That's not to say he wasn't a good dentist. He was. But he did get excited. However, by the time he had been welcomed to the picnic by a bunch of really nice friends of Zoë's and had drunk a beer and joined the group of four men who were seated on logs around a little fire in Tilden Park, he was in a pretty decent mood.

Like Tony, these guys were married to members of the wine-tasting group, as he found when he introduced himself and they all stood up and said their names. They, too, were holding bottles of Anchor. "How's it going, guys?" Tony asked them.

"Well, that's what we were just talking about," said a tall, thin fellow who had just introduced himself as Owen Holt. He had a plume of hair on the top of his head that stuck straight up and reminded Tony of an ostrich. "We're all agreed that we haven't been treated this well since before we were married." The other guys laughed. Owen, like his wife, Lenore, was a professor at Cal, in engineering, and, at 61 years old, he was tired of theory and of teaching. He longed to tinker, fix, restore, invent, fabricate. He was ready for a hands-on life.

Tony grinned. "You know, you're on to something there. What do you suppose these women are up to?"

"That's what we were wondering."

Harvey Boatman, Tina's husband, spoke up. He was an affable-looking man with silvery hair atop a handsome brown face. "I think they're plotting to take us along with them on a museum tour through Europe," he said, "and we're getting buttered up. Something like that." Even though the weather was balmy and beautiful in Tilden Park, Harvey wore a sweater and leather-soled wingtips. Tony wondered whether he might have just come from work but thought it wasn't likely since today was Sunday. In fact Harvey Boatman was simply a natty dresser, encouraged and even guided in this department by his wife.

"We're getting buttered up all right," Will Fletcher said, "but I don't think they'll ask us to go to Europe with them. They would rather go by themselves. The way they see it, we'd just slow them down. No, they're up to something, but Europe isn't it." Will reminded Tony of Will Rogers. Was that right, Will Rogers? Someone like that. Maybe a famous cowboy. "*Are* there any famous cowboys?" Tony wondered.

Everyone was always surprised to learn that Will Fletcher was a musician. He seemed anything but. In fact, people assumed he was a builder or perhaps an airline pilot or a retired forest ranger—in short, he struck people as a man's man. Strangely, more than one person had guessed that he was a horse-whisperer. Instead, he was a cellist in the San Francisco Symphony Orchestra.

The fire the men sat around was more convivial than practical. There was a wonderful warmth in the spring air without it. Up the grassy hill from where they sat, the women and two male members of the garden group had a serious fire going under a grill. They seemed to be preparing quite a spread.

"Well, whatever they're up to, I hope they bribe us with food," Tony said. "I'm pretty hungry. Do I see pies up there on the table?"

"Well, boys," Harvey said, "we'd better see how long we can make this last."

Tony's attention was commandeered by the pies he believed he could see sitting on the edge of a table up the hill. He squinted a little more focus into his vision and decided one of the pies might be pecan with whipped cream. At the same time, he caught a whiff of something cooking, probably nothing fancier than hamburgers, but the smell was intoxicating. While he was peering up the hill where all the food activity was, he noticed again that the women in the group were good-looking, including his wife, Zoë, with her sassy short hair. And these guys he was sitting around with, all about his age, they were good company. Tony took a deep sniff and savored the smells of cooking.

At the top of the hill, the others watched the smoke swirl from the campground fireplace as Sophia flipped hamburgers. Pamela stood off a few feet from the others and seemed bored, but she was bored by most activities and annoyed by almost any conversation. The friends knew that she was in line to inherit a fortune from her mother someday. Wishing to draw her into the group, Lenore asked, "How is your mother, Pamela?"

"My mother shows signs of living forever," she said. "And the gentleman she has been seeing is in even better health."

"Hmm," Zoë said, "your mother is seeing someone?"

"She has every right to, no matter how I feel about it. No matter what sort of person he is, it's her life—and her fortune, to squander any way she wants."

"Pamela that's terrible. How old is your mother?" Zoë asked.

"Eighty-eight. The gentleman is seventy. And he has five children."

"Oh, no! Where is he from? What's his name?" Lenore asked.

"*Tex*," she said, looking sour. "*Tex*."

"Uh-oh," Bentley said with a moan. "What do you think about him?"

"He is quite a charmer, he and his hat."

"You mean, like a ten-gallon hat?" Bentley asked.

But Pamela had withdrawn from the conversation.

Lenore said, "Listen friends, if I were eighty-eight and going off the deep end, you would stop me, wouldn't you? I mean, whether it was for a younger man named Tex Golddigger, or for someone selling annuities or whatever, you would stop me. Wouldn't you?"

"I guess *so*," Zoë said. "Or we'd stop the gold

digger. That's what a wine-and-garden group is for, isn't it?"

"Seriously, we should stick together," Lenore said. "Because we're all capable of being idiots like Pamela's mother, no offense, Pamela. If we were 'all for one and one for all,' Tex would have to get past all of us before he could do any damage." But, she wondered silently, how *could* they stick together? Was it just wishful thinking? "That's what we're here to find out," she thought. Lenore gazed at her husband and the other men sitting around the little fire down the hill. "I wonder how they're getting along," she said aloud.

After he and the guys had talked for a while longer about this and that, Tony looked up the slope again, thinking about lunch, and Zoë and all the others were watching Tony and his fellow husbands. Zoë waved at him and he waved back. A moment later she walked down the hill with a fresh six-pack of beer in her hand. It was still shedding fragments of ice from the ice chest. The men applauded as she arrived.

"Here guys," she said. They all thanked her as she passed beer around. Tony invited her to sit down. "No, you guys just have fun. Lunch is on its way. Say Owen, Lenore tells us that you had to put your mother in an assisted care home. Do you mind if I ask how she's doing?"

"Well, thanks for asking, but I don't have any good news. She wants to go home, but of course she can't take care of herself."

"I'm sorry to hear it. I wish there were a better way. Hey guys, as long as I'm up, is there anything else I can bring down for you?" No, no, they all said, and she waved and returned to the cooking.

After Zoë went back up the hill, Will said, "This has got me uneasy, guys. Or am I wrong, Tony? Does your wife always bring the beer around and ask what else she can get for you while she's up?"

"Are you kidding?" Tony answered. They were all looking kind of worried now. "There's something terribly wrong," Tony added. They all shook their heads.

Will said, "They're planning something for us."

"This has got me uneasy, guys," Will said. "Does your wife always bring the beer around and ask what else she can get for you?"

"But what?" Harvey asked, and they all gave that

some serious thought.

Strangely, Tony soon found himself talking with the others about their aging parents. It was surprising how often the subject came up these days among his and Zoë's friends. Many of his patients and staff had at least one parent experiencing tragic health problems. "A few years ago, guys like us at a picnic would have been popping off about sports or cars or something," Tony thought. "Now we talk about nursing homes."

"Zoë's right, I wish there were a better way to do it," Tony said aloud, "I mean a better way than going off to a retirement home when we can't take care of ourselves anymore." All the guys agreed. "Are there any nursing homes that specialize in taking care of groups of friends?" he asked.

"None that I know of," Owen said. "That's a good idea, though."

Normally Tony would have gravitated toward the food as soon as he became aware of the pies and the smell of barbequing meat, but today he was having such a good time hanging out with these guys that it was a while before he and the others ambled up the hill like old bulls out for a walk.

Sitting around the picnic table after polishing off the hamburgers and pickles and a wonderful mixed green salad and several homemade pies and another couple of beers, the wine-and-garden enthusiasts and their guests gave a round of applause for Sophia Fletcher, who had baked all of the pies and who had led the cooking brigade.

"I could eat like this every day," Tony said to Sophia with a contented smile.

"Then you'd better set me up in a nice big kitchen and I'll cook for you all, every day. That would be my idea of heaven." A second round of applause went around.

"Sign me up!" Tony enthused. "I wish we could."

"Funny," Zoë said, "but we in The Purple Tongue were talking about just that."

"So were we," Harvey said. "But we didn't even think about getting a great cook like Sophia."

"I did," Tony said.

"I'm missing something," Tuck complained. "What are you all talking about?"

Tina said, "Remember the other night in the wine group when we were fantasizing about living together in our old age so we wouldn't have to be tossed into nursing homes?"

"That's pretty funny," Owen said. "Because before lunch, some of us were talking about the same thing."

"It seems to us," Tony took it up, "as if there has to be a better way to grow old than to be carted off to a hospital or an assisted living condo or whatever. I guess we were fantasizing too, because we were tossing around the idea of getting together *before* we get old and setting up a place the way we would *like* it to be."

Will took a turn: "What Tony is saying is that a

group of like-minded people—you know, like us— should get together while we're still young," (there were titters around the table at this) "and maybe buy a big house and fix it up the way we would want it to be when we are old, and then, you know, pay a staff to take care of us when the time comes. You know?" Will's voice had lost its confidence.

"Well, honey, it's a great idea," Sophia said, "but it takes a little getting used to."

"Maybe the idea isn't as crazy as it sounds," Harvey said. "I mean, we would be surrounded by friends instead of by strangers." It looked to Tony like some of the people in his wife's wine-tasting group were getting interested. A few were nodding in agreement.

Bentley said, "Now let me get this straight. You mean a group like us goes in together to buy a big house, and they fix it up to live in when they're older? So that, instead of having to go to nursing homes, they move into their own place, with their own friends and they hire their own staff to take care of them?"

"We couldn't have put it better," Tony said.

"You know," Bentley said, "that's a good idea." Others nodded in agreement. Tony thought at least several of them were interested. He couldn't tell what Tuck's wife, Weezie, thought. He still hadn't heard her say a word all day.

"I wouldn't want any dogs though," Pamela Noonan said. "A nice cat would be just the thing."

"Wow, Pamela, you're way ahead of us," Owen said, laughing.

"Oh," Pamela said, "we already talked…"

"Oh yes," Zoë interrupted, and she put her hand on Pamela's. "We're always having this conversation. Pamela likes cats and I like dogs. But listen, you guys are really something! You just thought this up today, sitting down there by the fire?"

The five husbands exchanged smiles, and Owen said, "Well, it's a simple idea."

Suddenly Tony found himself making a speech. "There's no reason to do things the way our parents did. Maybe it's because they came from the Depression, but they had no expectations at all for their old age, or at least mine didn't. I don't think it ever occurred to them to try to have a good time when they were old. When my parents retired, they didn't have any plans. I guess they wanted to travel a little, and my dad played golf. But heck, I want to have something to look forward to when I retire, even when I'm very old." Tony was getting excited, and he was starting to gesticulate. "We should find a new way to grow old and make it an adventure. And we should start thinking about it now! Before it's too late!"

Zoë brought him another beer and opened it for him.

Hours later, after he and Zoë had said goodbye to his new friends, Tony realized that he was smiling.

Still, there was one disquieting question in his mind, just a small thing, but it nagged him. What was it, he wondered, that the group, including his wife, had been cooking up for him and the other husbands? He couldn't get rid of the feeling that he and his new buddies were supposed to *do* something. He thought he and the other husbands had somehow failed a test. But maybe they had made up for it with their idea about creating their own nursing home. Anyway, everyone seemed to be happy. They had all agreed they would get together again and try to work up some plans. Tony was especially tickled. "I think they liked my idea," he said to Zoë. She patted his knee.

As Tony drove home through Tilden Park with Zoë beside him, he could feel twigs and even small branches whip up from the dirt roads and smack the underside of his SUV. "Good thing I've got these big mud and snow tires," he thought. He loved the way his SUV handled on even the funkiest roads the park had to offer.

Chapter Four

[February, 1975]

After the picnic, everyone volunteered to be on the
committee to find the right mansion, but it was
Sophia Fletcher who got things started with a call to
a realtor, Fenton Sommers of Piedmont Realty.
Evidently, the realtor had taken notes as Sophia
described what she and her husband were looking
for, because he accurately repeated her list of
"should-haves." "So this house should have no fewer
than fifteen bedrooms," he said. "There must be an
elevator to the upper bedrooms or space to install

one. It should have a very large dining room, and all the other common rooms must also be quite large."

"I forgot to mention the ballroom."

"The ballroom," he repeated. Sophia imagined him writing down "ballroom." "The house must be on at least an acre of property," he went on "and have the potential for a garden with meandering paths. If you will excuse me, Mrs. Fletcher, in my experience at least three acres are required for meandering paths."

"Of course," she said.

"Now," Sommers continued, reading back to her from the list he had assembled so far, "you will need a garage in which to park approximately ten vehicles." A vague air of disbelief had crept into his tone. He paused and seemed tempted to say something, but he went on.

"You do not require that the property be in move-in condition. Your expectations about its condition, of course, will have a great deal to do with the cost. May I ask what you and Mr. Fletcher are prepared to pay for such a property?"

Will Fletcher sat with Sophia in her office in their Oakland home, a nice place in an old neighborhood by the Rose Garden, listening to her end of the conversation with the realtor. Books were stacked high everywhere: on her desk, on the floor, on a chair by the door. As a publisher's representative, it was her job to read enough of each book to help her sell it. She was so successful at selling books in the West Coast states that she was swamped with business and could barely break away from her life on the road to spend time at home. One of the reasons that she was so intrigued by the idea of pitching in with her friends to buy a mansion was that she had a vague idea that, if they pulled this off, she could finally retire and devote herself to cooking. She would have been happy as a clam cooking morning, noon and night. Her dream, her fantasy was to hire out to cook (and, in particular, to bake) sinfully fattening things for people who were on completely unrestricted diets.

When the realtor asked how much she was willing to spend, she paused and looked at her husband. She winked. To the realtor she responded, "I'm not prepared to say yet how much we are willing to spend. What would you expect such a property to cost?"

"Please don't be overly concerned with cost at this point. May I suggest that I show you what is available before we discuss price?" She had been hoping to get an idea of what the group was up against, but she sensed that, after all, she would have to submit to the whole, formal, realtor-client ceremony to find out.

"Is there anything that sounds remotely like what I'm asking for?"

"Oh yes, there are several quite remarkable properties. Quite remarkable. Of course they are not in multiple listings. Their owners have entrusted me to handle the sale of their homes privately. No fuss. No publicity. You understand, Mrs. Fletcher, that my clients would expect you not to discuss these properties with anyone other than me? I'm sure you understand."

"Of course," she said. "Of course," and they arranged a time in three days—"After suitable arrangements can be made," he said—to view the properties.

Sophia's dream, her fantasy was to hire out to cook (and, in particular, to bake) sinfully fattening things for people who were on completely unrestricted diets.

When Sophia got off the phone, she and her husband exchanged looks that communicated much. Behind them were thirty-five years of marriage. "Sounds like he's pretty stuffy," he said, making a good guess, Sophia thought, since he hadn't heard a word the realtor said. "Did he say how much a place like that would cost?"

"I got the impression," she answered, "that if you

have to ask, you can't afford it."

"Hmm," her husband said. As he was thinking, she looked at him and noticed, as she had many times before, what a good-looking man he was.

"Maybe he's right," Will said. "Maybe we can't afford it."

"Unless we really want to," she countered.

"Maybe even then we can't afford it. We'll see," he said. "But we had better talk more about what we're doing here."

"Will, let's look at a couple of places and then get together with everyone and really talk this out. The more I think about this idea, the less I understand it. Are we talking about a retirement home to move into when we're no longer working, or a nursing home we'll go to when we're on our last legs or what?"

"I don't know either," he said. "But you're right, let's look at a few houses so the whole concept is a little less abstract, and then we'll have a pow-wow with the group."

Sophia and Will met Sommers in his spacious office, wondering how it came to be that Piedmont Realty was allowed to operate in Piedmont's tiny business district. There were few businesses of any kind in Piedmont, and certainly no other realty firms. But then neither were there stores of any kind except a couple of banks, a small grocery store and a gas station. It was as if the wealthy community had decided it was above commerce except in its purest form, that is, except as it is conducted in financial institutions, where the only merchandise that changes hands is money itself. And yet, here was Piedmont Realty. Perhaps community leaders had wanted a realty business close at hand so they could keep an eye on it. After all, realtors are the gatekeepers of a community, the first arbiters of who is and is not suited to be its new members.

The Fletchers had dressed nicely for the occasion, well aware that they would be pre-qualified—or disqualified—on the basis of just such nonsense. They had parked their three-year-old Buick around the corner, irritated with themselves for being intimidated. But still, they reasoned, they were asking to see properties that could cost a good three million dollars. If they weren't rich, they had at least better not look poor. Sommers received them in his office in an immaculate black suit and a conservative blue necktie with a silk handkerchief folded artfully in the breast pocket of his suit coat. His black wingtips were impeccably polished.

"How do you do Mrs. Fletcher, Mr. Fletcher, so pleased to make your acquaintance. Tell me, would you care to relax in one of our conference rooms for just a moment while we get to know each other?"

"Yes," Will said, "that would be fine, and that would give some friends of ours a chance to catch up with us. These are old friends of ours who would like to tag along. Would you mind?"

Sommers took the news in stride and said,

"Certainly not." In the conference room, which was dominated by a gleaming table made of an obviously expensive and rare wood, he asked where they lived now.

"In Oakland," Sophia responded. As her home address was not exactly the most prestigious, her answer was purposely broad.

"I see. And the property you're now seeking is for you and your family?"

Will and Sophia looked at each other. Will volunteered, not quite to the point, "Our children no longer live at home." Just then, a clerk stuck her head in the door and told Sommers that a Mr. and Mrs. Boatman were here to see him and the Fletchers.

"Ah yes, Carol, please show them in." It rarely registered on Sophia's consciousness that Tina Boatman, whom she had known for fifteen years, was African American, and so was Harvey, of course. It registered on her now, though. It was not that many years ago, Sophia knew, that they were not welcome in the self-consciously elite enclave of Piedmont, but Tina and Harvey were perfectly relaxed and charming with the realtor as they exchanged small talk. Sophia admired Tina's social ease where she, Sophia, had allowed herself to become intimidated. Soon Sommers glanced at his gold wristwatch and suggested that perhaps they had better be on their way.

Will was relieved. He knew that the next question the realtor was about to ask him was what he did for a living. He had been spared from having to admit he was a musician (a notoriously under-paid profession even on the higher rungs of the ladder) by the arrival of Tina and Harvey. Anyway, this guy Sommers was just the kind of person he was uncomfortable with. Will wondered what kind of person it took to sell multi-million dollar homes to the ultra-rich. It occurred to him that Sommers, for all his urbane gloss, probably didn't know Schubert from Shinola.

Sophia was just as uncomfortable with this realtor as Will was, but for a different reason. The jerk kept staring at her. She just hoped that Will wouldn't notice or there might be trouble.

Outside, Sophia insisted on riding in the back seat of Sommers's black Mercedes, and Will rode up front. Sophia settled so deeply into the auto's leather seats that it was a struggle for her to turn and look behind as the realtor's Mercedes left the curb, but she saw that Tina and Harvey were falling right in behind. Then she noticed that another car was pulling away from the curb right behind the Boatmans. My God, was that Tuck's car, she wondered? It *was*, and that must be Weezie, riding with him. "It looks like word got out that Will and I were going to be looking at property today," she thought. Then yet another and another car left the curb behind them. She could not identify their drivers since the caravan of cars stretched out so far behind, but there were a lot of automobiles back there. She thought that, with Sommers' long, black Mercedes leading, they looked like a funeral procession without motorcycles. Her face flushed in embarrassment.

Parked now near a house on a quiet Piedmont street, Sommers stood beside his Mercedes's open door and watched, astonished, as car after car pulled up behind his. Will and Sophia could not bear to watch, and they walked ahead toward the house. It was in a Mediterranean style, Tuscan yellow, rising two stories—wait, could it possibly be three—yes, it rose three stories high.

"Look at that," Sophia whispered to Will. But even as awe was welling in Sophia's breast, she heard disturbing, festive sounds behind her. She and Will turned and saw that Tina and Harvey were cheerily introducing Sommers to Tuck, Weezie, Lenore, Owen, Tony and Zoë. They could have been a madrigal group of elderly but game singers arriving to entertain at a daytime fundraiser. They were festive and jolly with Sommers, who looked a little flustered now or dismayed, Sophia thought, and not overly pleased.

Why, why, why had her friends convened here without warning? How could they embarrass her and Will like this? Before she started down the steps, she turned and glowered at them. She caught Bentley's eye and squinted her disapproval at him. He made a gesture of mock surprise as if to say, "Who, me? What did we do?" He smiled innocently, and Sophia's own blue-ribbon smile appeared without her permission.

When Sommers caught up with her and Will, he

mumbled, "I just hope she's not home. Maybe a maid will let us in?" With all her heart she shared his hope. But she noticed, too, that, distracted as he may have been, the realtor managed to walk so closely by her side that he brushed up against her. Rarely had Sophia been so uncomfortable.

The house, a stucco structure with a tile roof, was set downhill from the sidewalk, and the walkway to the house descended to it in a series of wide steps and landings. Ancient fifteen-foot rhododendrons and twenty-foot camelias grew on either side of the stone stairs. They would have towered in any other landscape but were dwarfed by this colossal house. Though grounded far below the street level, still it rose high on the horizon and seemed to grow even larger as Sophia and Will approached. As they walked down the stairs and neared its massive wooden front door, Sophia noticed that all of its windows were leaded in small panes.

Sommers rang the bell and looked over his shoulder as Sophia and Will came up behind him, and, behind them the others were catching up and pooling for a grand entrance.

The owner answered the door. She was poised, well-coiffed and wore an understated pearl necklace. There was no mistaking her for hired help. The lady's welcoming smile did not falter in the least as she took in the crowd gathered on her porch. "Why, Mr. Sommers, how do you do? And I see you've brought some friends." She extended her hand to Sommers

and Will Fletcher in turn, and introduced herself as
Genevieve Rutherford. Sommers introduced the
Fletchers. She invited them in and introduced herself
to each of the others as they passed through the
door. When they were gathered inside, she said,
"How nice of you to come. What a lovely day! What
sounds good: tea, cold cider, ginger ale, champagne?"
A young woman materialized, took orders from
Genevieve Rutherford and disappeared.

"Oh, let's sit for a moment before touring, don't
you think?" she suggested. Sophia and the others followed their hostess toward the left wing of the mansion, past a powder room, which Genevieve pointed
out to her guests "if you should happen to need it,
ladies." The party walked through a formal dining
room and then arrived at a sunroom at the furthest
point of the home's west wing. Antique white wicker
furniture seemed to invite the guests to sit and enjoy
the garden, visible through the sunroom's mostly-
glass walls. An old wisteria vine in full, purple bloom
framed the view of a magnolia and an old-fashioned
white rhododendron. As a servant arrived with bottles of cider chilled in ice buckets and with all kinds
of crackers and cookies, and, as he deployed them on
several tables in the room, Genevieve Rutherford
made pleasant small talk. Rarely had Sophia felt so
welcome anywhere, and never had she felt like such
an imposter. She had the sense that she was in the
presence of the real thing: a genuine mansion, real

wealth, and an honest-to-goodness, gracious and charming lady. Mrs. Rutherford would have made the Mongol hordes feel welcome had they invaded her home, Sophia thought—and that's just what she and her friends had done.

Sophia felt utterly exhausted by three o'clock that afternoon, when she and Will and Sommers reconvened in the realtor's conference room, this time without the others present. After touring three large houses in Piedmont that afternoon, trailing behind Sommers and the Fletchers in conspiratorial near-silence, Tony and Zoë and the rest had climbed back into their cars at last and gone their separate ways, leaving behind only Will and Sophia to negotiate with Sommers. Sitting at the highly polished table, all of them seemed tired. Sommers shuffled papers. "Well, what do you think? Did any of the three properties interest you?"

Will asked, "Uh, how much are they? The houses."

"Mrs. Rutherford is asking seven for the first house. The second house is fourteen. And frankly I think the third house is a bit expensive at seventeen."

Will said, "I see." Then, after biting his lip thoughtfully, he asked, "Million?"

"Certainly."

"I see."

"Well," Sophia thought, "end of story."

"Why are these people selling their houses?" she

asked, stalling, trying to figure out how to get out of this mess gracefully.

"Well, properly speaking, they aren't. Or certainly not aggressively. Really, I asked them to name a price for which they would be *willing* to sell their properties. You see, there really aren't any for sale like what you are looking for so I've had to dig them up, so to speak."

"But why would Genevieve sell her wonderful house for *any* price? It's hard for me to imagine her leaving that house behind."

"I discussed that with Mrs. Rutherford. She is a widow and would like nothing better than to continue living in her home, but she is trying to look realistically at her approaching old age. It would be a bit much, don't you think, for a widow to maintain that house?"

Sophia recalled one of the strongest impressions of her day. She and Will had opened a door in the basement and discovered an absolutely mountainous steam heater, vintage 1915, she guessed. It looked like something that would be useful in manufacturing steel. Giant gauges and valves and convoluted plumbing rose twelve feet above the floor, and huge vents shot off into the ceiling and walls of the basement. Seeing that furnace had brought home to her what must be involved in maintaining and simply heating a 27,000-square-foot house, and she was daunted.

"Yes," she admitted. "It would be a bit much for a widow to maintain." Sophia was convinced that the group's dream had just gone down in flames because of the huge price-tags on the three houses. Strangely, she felt relieved, and, now that the pressure was off, she relaxed and did what came naturally to her, she smiled her glorious smile. Her blue eyes twinkled. And she told Sommers the truth. "Honestly," she said to the realtor, "I think it's a bit much for us to maintain, too. We can't afford to buy it, and it's the least expensive of the three houses. You've been very nice to help us today and to put up with us and all our friends."

"Not at all, Mrs. Fletcher. But do call me, won't you?"

Their walk down the block and around the corner back to their Buick seemed much longer to Sophia than it had that morning.

Chapter Five

[March, 1975]

It had been splendid for the friends to stroll through mansions and swing open their three-hundred-pound doors and examine timbers in their foundations and admire the huge beams in their ceilings—and to say to themselves, "I can *own* all of this: the tennis court, the curving staircase, the leaded glass windows, the century-old terraced gardens, the attic as big as our house!" But when Lenore and Owen, Sophia and Will, Zoë and Tony, Tuck and Weezie, Harvey and Tina, Bentley and Pamela went to their beds that night, they already knew better. They would chatter for a while, the couples would, about sights they had seen, like the twelve-car garage on the Rutherford property or the complete log cabin that someone had built in back of the main house on another estate, and then one of them would think, "Wait, wait, wait." And he or she would say, "We can't afford any of those houses, even if we pool our money. Those mansions are too good to be true, and we know that if something is too good to be true, it isn't true." So when they woke in the morning, they weren't elated, they were depressed.

And then the next day word came from Sophia that the realtor had named the prices of the three mansions and the least expensive was seven million dollars and the most expensive was seventeen million. And so they all thought they had been right not to get too excited, but they *had* got too excited. It was three weeks before the friends recovered their spirits enough to have a meeting. Even so, when they finally met at Bentley's house, they were still embarrassed by how naïve they had been to think they could afford a splendid house. Bentley was feeling so low that he kept out of the talk while the others tried to get a conversation going. He went around knocking aphids off potted plants on his deck, where the group was gathered.

"Well," Lenore started, "on to plan B."

"Do we *have* a plan B?" Owen asked, surprised. An engineer, he was a step-by-step thinker, someone who liked to proceed in an orderly fashion and he was happy to hear that Lenore might have a fall-back plan since it looked like they had failed to find an afford-able mansion.

"No," she answered, "and we don't have a plan A either. We just have a good idea. Maybe we'll have to think of alternatives to the mansions we were so giddy about."

"Well, on to plan B," Lenore said.
"Do we have a plan B?" Owen asked, surprised.
"No," she answered, "and we don't have a plan A either.
We just have a good idea."

"How about old Masonic temples," Harvey offered. "They have a bunch of guest rooms and big meeting rooms and miles of hardwood floors and twenty-foot ceilings. And big kitchens, you know, industrial-sized. I'll bet they're cheap."

"Or old hotels," Lenore said. "If they're in a neighborhood that's become a little off, you know, they might be really good buys."

Pamela put the kibosh on this line of thought. "Old hotels and Masonic temples don't have meandering garden paths so you may as well forget it right now."

"They don't have gardens at all," Tuck reminded everyone. He walked to the railing that surrounded Bentley's deck and leaned on it and looked down into Bentley's garden. On the steep hillside below, there were all kinds of plants, but Australian tree ferns dominated the landscape. Viewed from above, the tree-sized ferns were the most exotic plants Tuck could imagine, far different from what you'd be looking down on from an old hotel in a neighborhood that has gone a little off.

"Listen, I'm just going to say this." That was Will. He sounded grumpy. "Either we get a place we really want or we forget it. Because if it's not something that captures our imaginations, we're just not going to do it, so I agree with Pamela. I say forget seedy old hotels and abandoned meeting halls."

"I don't know," Tuck said. "Maybe the whole thing isn't such a good idea. Or maybe it's a good idea but we can't afford it." Bentley thought that Tuck might be even more depressed than *he* was.

"There are some other problems, too, that we haven't talked about," Zoë said. Tuck groaned aloud. When Zoë, an attorney, talked about problems, everyone listened. "I foresee all kinds of difficulties concerning zoning. I'm sure that mansions like the ones we trooped around in the other day are zoned single-family dwellings. How do you suppose neighbors are going to like an old-folks' home opening across the street? They'll scream. Second, we're probably looking at a legal nightmare about how to handle the money we all would have to pool in order to buy a house together. Third, we may not have the same expectations about what it is we're creating, like whether it's something we move into when we're near death or whether we want to be there as soon as we retire, or what. And about all of us living together— are we sure we're going to like being together twenty-four hours a day as much as we like seeing each other once a month? Privacy will be a big issue. I mean, when I become incontinent, do I really want all my friends to know? And here is one more revolting thought. When we're at the end of our rope, are we really going to be in any kind of shape to enjoy a beautiful house and good friends?"

Bentley became more and more uncomfortable as he listened to Zoë's convincing arguments. He began pacing, pinching off bloomed-out flower-heads on his potted plants. "Well, how about we just solve the problems and quit sitting around with long faces?" he said.

"That's the spirit, Bentley! Let's whip this puppy," Tuck said.

Lenore said, "But who can answer Zoë?"

"Let me just toss out this idea," Harvey offered, "about what Zoë called the legal nightmare of handling money among ourselves. Maybe we could form a nonprofit corporation. Each of us would own shares in it depending on how much of a contribution we make to it. Holding ownership in the house in the form of shares would make it easy to pass our assets on to our heirs, whom we will have to think of."

Lenore began making notes. "That sounds like a good idea to me. It's simple. Does anybody care to follow up on that and find out if our project is likely to qualify as a nonprofit corporation?"

"I'll find out about it," Zoë said.

"But there's still the privacy issue," said Lenore. "That's what Owen and I keep coming back to. It's taken us years to learn how to give each other space. How will it be with a dozen of us all together under one roof?"

"I hope no one expects me to share a bathroom," Pamela said, for some reason glowering at Tuck as if he had proposed it.

Sophia jumped in. "Then let's think in terms of apartments," she said. "Every couple and every 'single' will have their own apartment within the house, by which I mean a good-sized bedroom, a sitting room and a bathroom—enough space to get away from everyone when we want to."

"So how big a place will we need?" Tony asked. "How many bedrooms?"

"Okay," Lenore said, "there are five couples and two singles. That's seven bedrooms and seven sitting rooms. Call it fourteen bedrooms. Now I would figure on at least two additional rooms for live-in staff. That's sixteen bedrooms."

Pamela interrupted. "If someone is thinking about dividing the ballroom up into little cubbies to make more bedrooms, you can simply forget it. I've always believed that the soul of a home is its ballroom."

"I think Pamela and Will are right," Bentley said. "We have to find a place so splendid that we look forward to living there. Someplace like Genevieve's house. If it's that good, we'll find ways to make it work. If we compromise too much, in the end people just won't do it." Everyone agreed, and Bentley noticed that a certain animation had finally stirred the earnest group.

"So, like Will and Bentley said, let's either do it right or not do it at all," Tuck voted.

The friends sipped their iced tea—the first iced tea of the season for many of them—and from Bentley's deck looked at the Oakland cityscape in the distance and at Bentley's garden below.

"I guess it all comes down to money," Harvey said. "With enough money, we can probably work around everything. We can hire attorneys to deal with zoning; we can buy a place so big that privacy won't be an issue; we won't have to chop up the ballroom, and we can buy a place that we can't wait to move into. If we have enough money." Bentley's guests had once again settled into lounge chairs and outdoor chairs with cushioned seats. A fine warmth in the air made the iced tea taste good.

"Okay," Lenore said, "one of you, solve all our money problems, please."

"I can at least identify the problems," Tony said. "Together we're worth a pretty fair amount of money, but we can't put our hands on it. Right? Most of us have two major assets: equity in our houses plus our savings and investments. We won't want to spend our savings or investments on a mansion because we'll need them to retire on, and we can't sell our houses since we need to live in them until we move into the retirement place. So who's got cash to spend on a big house that we won't even use for the next ten or fifteen years? That's the problem."

"That's the problem," the others chorused.

"But we wouldn't be *spending*, the money," Owen said, "we'd be investing it in real estate. What I'm saying is that maybe we should consider shifting our investments from stock or whatever into a fantastic property. And who knows, the right residential property could turn out to be a great investment. Then, when it's time to move in, we sell our houses and they become our cash to retire on."

"That's kind of scary," Tina said, "but it makes sense."

"So how much money are we talking about?" Zoë asked.

"Forget seven million dollars," Tony said. "We can find something *splendid*, I mean splendid for four million dollars. Right? I mean, we might even be able to buy one of the houses we looked at for a solid offer of four million. And, if not, we can look elsewhere. We sure don't have to be in Piedmont, though that's where the really big houses are. Or we could *build* a place for that much money. So now we're talking about $800,000 down. Divided twelve ways, that's around $65,000 per person, or $130,000 per couple. Now we know that there are closing costs and that kind of thing. So let's say we're up to $70,000 each. Let's say that we'll have to put $250,000 into remodeling and garden expenses, divided by twelve is another $20,000 each. So that's a total of $90,000 per person or $180,000 per couple. For a mansion that has been modified for our needs and for wonderful landscaping."

"That doesn't sound like a *crazy* amount, anyway," Lenore said.

"Especially when you consider that nursing homes cost an average of about $46,000 per person per year," Tony said.

Bentley was up and pacing again. He examined an oriental poppy in a planter on the deck and found a bud on one of the poppies as big as a ping- pong ball. An auspicious sign.

"But, assuming we can find the right place and can get the down payment together for it," Zoë objected, "we're going to have monthly mortgage payments to make on it for years and years before we're ready to use it—at the same time that we're making payments on our own homes."

"So let's lease it out," Owen said. "Maybe we'll have a negative cash flow, but we'll have tax benefits, too, like depreciation and tax deductions for interest payments."

"If we have to lease it, let's get the garden started now," Bentley said, "so when we move in, we'll have a mature garden." Bentley felt his mood soaring and tried to hold himself back.

Sophia said, "We could get the garden started, do any work on the house that we needed for our own use of it and then lease it with the clear understanding that the lease would end in, say, ten years."

"Well, okay," Lenore ventured, "that brings us back to the question of whether this place is somewhere we retire to after our working days are over in five or ten years, or whether we wait until we're unable to take care of ourselves any longer—in fifteen to twenty-five."

Tina looked pensive. "I think most of us won't want to give up the lives we lead until we have to. So I think living together will be a last resort. But on the other hand, if the place really is wonderful, we might move in earlier than we otherwise would, and we won't go in kicking and screaming as our parents have, but with curiosity and interest."

"That," Lenore agreed, "sounds a lot better than being packed off by our kids to someplace called

Peaceful Cedars. Don't you think?"

"I will not live in any place called Peaceful Cedars," Pamela complained. "So you can just get that out of your minds right now."

"The Last Resort," Weezie said. Weezie? Until right this minute, Tuck's wife had hardly said a word.

"What do you mean?" Tuck asked.

"Tina said living together will be the last resort. That's what we should call the house: The Last Resort."

The friends looked at each other and nodded. "That's it, isn't it? The Last Resort." They all had to try it out. They smiled. Tony patted Weezie on the back. They nodded. The Last Resort.

Lenore sighed, "I'm tired."

Bentley agreed. "Everyone's tired. But I'm encouraged. Three great ideas have come out of this. No, four. The first is what Will said. Let's do this thing right or not at all. Second, let's deal with the problem of privacy by making sure everyone gets an apartment within the house. And the other idea is to regard the project as an investment in real estate. That idea, if we take it seriously, is what's going to make this thing practical as well as visionary. And then there's the idea of forming a corporation so we can handle the money better."

"And the new name," Sophia added.

"I'm getting kind of excited," Tony said. People stepped back a few feet. By now he was known not just by Zoë but by all the friends as highly excitable.

Chapter Six

[March, 1975]

Sommers snatched his carefully folded towel, snapped it open and dried his face. A floor-to-ceiling mirror wrapped completely around two walls of his garage and he studied himself in it. He pulled a jump rope off a peg and began dancing as he spun it. *Snic snic snic snic snic snic snic snic.* He kept his eyes on himself in the mirror.

"I wouldn't mind selling those people a mansion," he thought. "Looks like they don't have that kind of money."

He dropped his rope and began working on the punching bag, starting with his left hand. *Ta de deh, Ta de deh, Ta de deh.* His head bobbed.

He picked up his pace, weaving now as well as bobbing, eluding imaginary blows. Sommers took an extra hard punch at the bag and broke his rhythm. That was enough punching bag anyway. One last round of jump rope to get the pulse up.

"But who did they think they were fooling? Ten, was it, ten or eleven friends just happen to want to tag along while the Fletchers look at houses? Suuuure. They're up to something. But what?" His best guess was that they were looking to cohabit. "Some kind of sex group," he thought. "Orgies."

Suddenly he stopped, threw down the jump rope and grabbed his wrist, studying his watch's second hand: 32, 33, 34, 35, 36, 37. Good. Times four is 148. "At forty-eight years old," he thought. "I look forty." He reconsidered. "Thirty-eight."

He was sure they planned to live together. "Well, they're up against a money crunch," he thought. He could still see the looks on the Fletchers' faces when he had casually tossed out prices of the houses they had looked at: seven, fourteen, seventeen. He chuckled. "I made Fletcher ask. 'Million?' 'Certainly,' I told him.' I made him look like a fool."

In the shower, he thought, "If they played it right, those old goats could get the Rutherford place for peanuts." He thought about it. "I'll bet old lady Rutherford wants out." He pictured the 1915 steam-heat furnace in the Rutherford mansion that towered twelve or fifteen feet above the basement floor. "Imagine having to keep that monster alive. Seven million? Hah! She probably would *give* it away to get out of having to feed that goddamn furnace." Sommers dried himself and peered closely at his sideburns in his bathroom mirror. Signs of gray. He popped the lid off a bottle, and when he saw it was empty, he broke the seal on a new bottle of five-minute Grecian Formula. "I was a Green Beret," he thought. "No gray hair in those days."

But he was onto something. An idea was nudging. "Instead of pumping up the price of the Rutherford place for the commission," he though, "maybe I should finagle a good price for Fletcher and his wife." Five minutes was up, and Sommers rinsed his hair. Black dye #9 stained his forehead, and he worked over the spots of black with a washcloth.

"I wonder what all those people are going to do in a big house, though. Some of those women looked fine. Sophia. If they're all going to be banging each other, I wouldn't mind getting in on it. Not much chance of that, though, with Astronaut Will around."

An hour later, dressed in his whitest shirt and blackest suit, Sommers was ready for a day's work, and he drove the Mercedes just a few blocks deeper into Piedmont's tiny business district He walked the last block and a half to his office in his leather-soled, jet black wingtips. This was the heart of Piedmont, nearly unchanged over the decades. He strode past a bank. At one time Piedmont had been one of the most exclusive communities in the country, closed to all but wealthy, conservative blue-bloods. Times had changed, he thought, but not much. "Good morning, Mr. Sommers," said the receptionist. He nodded and went directly to his office, and, once at his desk, to his phone.

"Hello, Mrs. Rutherford. This is Fenton Sommers with Piedmont Realty."

"How do you do, Mr. Sommers?"

"Quite well, thank you. Mrs. Rutherford, I'm wondering whether you have thought further about how much you would like to ask for your house?" Without doubt, Genevieve Rutherford's house was one of the most spectacular in Piedmont, maybe the most spectacular. But he was aware that sometimes the owners of such homes were people of old wealth, which was not always to say *current* wealth.

"Mr. Sommers, I was quite overwhelmed by size of the, uh, party you brought by to see the house. I had no idea…"

"Nor did I, Mrs. Rutherford."

"What do you suppose they were all *doing* here?" she asked. This caught him without a good answer. "You don't suppose they all want to *live* here, do you?" she said.

He *did* think they all wanted to live there, but he did not want to admit it. "I really can't say."

"If they all want to live here, what do you suppose they want to *do*?" Sommers thought it would be best simply not to answer. "Do you suppose they want to do something wicked? Something like having orgies?"

"What do you imagine they were all doing here?" she asked. "You don't suppose they all want to live here, do you?"

"Oh, hardly, Mrs. Rutherford! At their age?"

"Their age? They're not so old. Some of those gentlemen look pretty good."

"What I'm saying is that, at their age, it is more likely they are planning to, well, I don't know, maybe retire together."

After a rather long pause she said, "Well, for heaven's sake, I didn't even think of that." Neither had *he* until right that minute. "Well, that's too bad," she said. "No one will spend a dime for their retirement. Fixed incomes, you know."

"Do you mind my asking, Mrs. Rutherford, what plans you have for *your* retirement? I mean as your plans may relate to the disposition of your house."

"I love the old place. I'd just stay right here till I drop if I could afford to. But have you ever looked at the steam-heater downstairs? How would you like to *heat* this house, Mr. Sommers?"

"Quite," he agreed. "Mrs. Rutherford, I have an idea. I wonder whether you might have a few minutes for a little meeting at your home, maybe even a bit later today?"

"That depends, Mr. Sommers. How many people do you intend to bring this time?"

Mr. and Mrs. Will Fletcher,
916 Mariposa Place,
Oakland, CA, 94610

Dear Mr. and Mrs. Fletcher,

As you know, Mrs. Rutherford, the owner of the first house you looked at, was asking $7,000,000 for her home. I have gone to bat for you with results that may startle and please you. But first, some background about Mrs. Rutherford. First, she may not be a widow as I had always assumed. Instead, she is married to a gentleman who disappeared some years ago and has been missing ever since.

Still, for all practical purposes, Mrs. Rutherford is a single woman living alone in a very large house. More than anything, she would like to continue living in the house that she loves. But she has come to feel lonesome in it. Furthermore, the upkeep of the house is considerable for one person.

At my suggestion, Mrs. Rutherford has agreed to offer you the house for the absurdly low price of $3,000,000. I hasten to add that one

important condition must be met, though. She must be allowed to continue to live in the house until her death. She expects to occupy only a small part of it and to have only an equal amount of say in matters pertaining to decisions about the house. There are just one or two other details. The house will be sold "as is" and must clear escrow in no more than four weeks.

Mr. and Mrs. Fletcher, I can't tell you how delighted I am to bring you this good news. I look forward to hearing from you at your earliest opportunity.

Fenton Sommers

P.S. As an agent representing both the buyers and the seller, I am walking a tightrope. But just between you and me, I believe that, if you were to meet the conditions above, Mrs. Rutherford would entertain an offer of $2,000,000. You needn't mention that I said so.
F.S.

"There," Sommers said to himself. "That ought to do it," and he dropped his letter into a box in front of the tiny Piedmont post office.

Three days later, he received this letter:

The Last Resort

Mr. Fenton Sommers
Piedmont Realty

Dear Mr. Sommers,

We agree to all your conditions and to Mrs. Rutherford's conditions and hereby offer the sum of $2,000,000 for Mrs. Rutherford's house.

Do you happen to know whether she likes wine and gardening? Thank you.

Will and Sophia Fletcher

Part Two

Chapter Seven

[April, 1975]

Tina could find no words to describe the mansion that spread before them. The only thing she could compare it with was the Tower of Babel as she had imagined it in Sunday school fifty years earlier: a tower of rocks reaching to the sky. That was pretty far off the mark, though, this house wasn't made of rocks. It was faced with stucco and brick and leaded glass. But it did seem to reach well into the sky. It was like a stage-setting or a fairy-tale castle, larger than life, unreal. *And it was hers*—along with Harvey's, of course, and the rest of the group's. The realtor had hurried the sale along, and escrow had closed in record time. They *owned* the mansion! And they were coming to pick up their keys.

As Tina and Harvey descended the stone stairs that led to the massive front door, they passed Bentley, who had pulled off a few feet into the garden and was exclaiming to himself over some shrubbery. A nurseryman by trade and passion, he seemed to have gone to heaven. "Fully mature Daphne odora 'Aureo marginata!' " Bentley shouted. "Sixty years old if it's a day. I must be hallucinating. Five feet high and in full bloom. Can you believe it?" Harvey and Tina kept walking. Even though Tina was an enthusiastic gardener, her attention was riveted on the house that towered above.

"Look!" Harvey shouted. Tina ducked.

"Darn it Harvey, you scared me!" There was no doubt about it, she was tense. It had all happened so fast. One minute they had been joking about buying a retirement home together and calling it Alzheimer's Acres, and it seemed as if the next thing she knew they had stumbled onto a fabulous mansion for a third of what it was worth. Of course they had bought it "as is," and the truth is that they had wanted the place so badly that they hadn't insisted on the battery of inspections that were usually called for. They had barely even inspected it themselves because their chances of being able to buy it had seemed so remote. Now, suddenly, they owned it and she was on edge.

"No, I mean look up there!" He pointed to the highest point of the roofline. "Doves, dozens of them! They're sooo picturesque!"

"No, I mean look up there!" He pointed to the highest point of the roofline. "Doves, dozens of them! They're sooo picturesque!"

They looked more to her like pigeons, but they *were* beautiful to watch, the whole flock swooping among the gambrels and gables and mullions and all those other words Tina had never had any reason to learn till now. "I'll buy a book tomorrow," she thought. The birds disappeared behind or perhaps *into* something way up where the attic must be. The closer she and Harvey got to the house, though, the further back they had to pitch their heads to see the roofline. Harvey fell behind while he lowered his head and rubbed the back of his neck for a moment. He wiggled his head back and forth trying to work out a kink. "You should be careful with your neck," his wife told him while she waited for him to catch up.

When they reached the massive entryway and stood before the stately old door, Lenore and Owen, as well as Sophia and Will, were milling around nearby with their heads tilted slightly upward, as if they were listening to a distant sound or were sniffing the air.

"What's wrong?" Tina asked, suddenly concerned. None of the four who had reached the entryway seemed willing to discuss it.

Finally, Owen asked, "Uh, do you two *smell* something?"

Both Harvey and Tina raised their noses and began sniffing. Tony and Zoë and then Tuck and Weezie and finally Bentley and Pamela caught up with the others near the entryway and asked what was going on. Soon everyone was sniffing.

"The only thing I smell are moldy leaves," Tina said.

All heads turned downward toward the ground. There *weren't* any moldy leaves. After a while, Tuck went over to the house itself and began sniffing it like a bloodhound. "Hmmm," he said. He dropped to his knees and then to his hands and knees and crawled along as he sniffed the house near the soil line. All eyes were on him and no one noticed that the front door had swung open and Genevieve Rutherford, until recently the mansion's sole owner, stood watching Tuck.

"What's wrong?" she cried, alarmed.

Tuck scrambled to his feet, and rubbed his hands together to knock off the duff, then slapped at the knees of his trousers.

Lenore recovered first. "Well, here we are," she said brightly, as if announcing a pleasant surprise, but Genevieve Rutherford could not take her eyes off of Tuck.

"Yes," Genevieve said, vaguely. Finally she looked up at the assembled friends and said, "My, there really are a lot of you. Or I should say a lot of *us*, since now we're all in this together."

Tina had another flutter of concern. "We're all in this together?" she wondered.

"But *do* come in. I've been looking forward to seeing all of you again. I don't remember anyone's name from our brief chat before. Come in, come in." She kept one eye on Tuck, though. As he towered his way past her through the door, she said to him, "Sir, are you all right?"

"Yes ma'am," he answered like a schoolboy. "I was just..." His voice trailed off. "Please," he said, trying to steer a different course, "call me Tuck, Tuck Calhoun."

"Why, then, please call me Genevieve." Speaking to the entire group she said, "Why don't we all assemble in the sunroom where we gathered the last time.

You remember it, don't you?"

Tina had the impulse to go ahead of Mrs. Rutherford or to linger behind to assert that she was not a guest in this, her own house. Still, she didn't want to be rude, and she stuck with the group. Pamela apparently felt no such compunction and wandered off alone, most likely to stake out a claim for the choicest room. Genevieve Rutherford gave Pamela's back a worried look as she started up a curving staircase. Soon, everyone but Pamela had assembled in the sunroom.

When all were seated in the room's white wickerchairs, Tina surveyed the room. She remembered it only dimly from her brief tour of the house a month earlier. One mostly glass wall of the room looked out onto the garden. The effect was heavenly. A wonderful old wisteria, nearly finished blooming now, grew across the top of the window and down the sides, delightfully framing the whole view of the garden through the window. "How is it that wisterias seem to know exactly how to arrange themselves to show off best?" she wondered. "That would be a great skill to have." The truth is that Tina was in full possession of that talent. Her tasteful but revealing clothes, her gently curling hair and even the cosmetic surgery she had elected to have were perfect. But now she looked closer at the wisteria. Actually, this one was a bit of an opportunist, she noticed. "My gosh, it's growing right through the wall!" A large portion of the vine, which she had assumed was growing outdoors, was at home *in* the sunroom. "Hmm. Well, why not? It's probably good for the air in here. Plants breathe carbon dioxide and exhale oxygen? Something like that. Still, you would think that letting a vine come right through a wall like that might be bad for the wall." She noticed several of the others nervously eyeing the vine too but no one spoke up. Tina thought it might be rude to say anything about it in front of Genevieve, who seemed like such a lady.

"Well, why don't we all introduce ourselves?" offered Genevieve. "Mr. Calhoun and I," she started, "*Tuck* and I already broke the ice." Since she had spied him sniffing at her house, she had watched him closely. "I do hope you're all right, dear."

"Oh yes," he answered. "Uh, this is my wife, Weezie." Weezie was sitting, as it were, *behind* Tuck, as out of view of the others as possible. She smiled but seemed uncomfortable. She said hi and then was at a loss for words. Noticing her discomfort, Tuck continued, "Maybe we should say what we do. I write a syndicated garden column."

"Of course!" Genevieve said. "I have often read it. Tuck, you're quite famous."

"Not at all, but thank you."

Lenore Holt was next. She told Genevieve her name and added, "I teach literature at Cal. I don't know whether anyone mentioned that most of us here have been in a wine-tasting group together for about fifteen years. That's how we got started with this." She swept the air with one long arm, indicating the magnificent room and mansion in which they sat and the gorgeous landscaping visible through the windowed walls of the sunroom.

Genevieve looked puzzled. "You got started with this" (she swept the air with her arm just as Lenore had) "in a wine-tasting group?"

"The Purple Tongue," Lenore offered, as if that explained everything. "And gardening, too. After our tastings we talk about gardening." Noticing Genevieve's continuing bafflement, she added, "We decided to find a better way to grow old, and," for the second time that morning she told Genevieve, "here we are. I hope you like wine and gardening and that you will join us. This is my husband, Owen Holt." Lenore, sitting beside him, took his hand.

"I also teach at Cal," he said, smiling. "I teach queing theory in the school of engineering."

Tina spoke up. "I'm Tina Boatman, and before I go on, I just want to thank you, Genevieve, for making the house available to us. We were really touched by your kindness."

The others added applause and some *"Here, heres!"*

"Not at all, dear," said Genevieve Rutherford. "It was really quite selfish of me. I've wondered for years how I could manage to stay here in this house when I become old, without absolutely rattling around in it. And now I have you all to share it with!" The truth is that Genevieve was one of the two great unknown factors as far as the group was concerned, and the house was the other. It seemed possible that either might suddenly reveal a fatal dark side.

"We're all in this together," she had said. That resonated in Tina's mind. What did it mean, she wondered? Well, no one could deny that Genevieve had wonderful manners, and she certainly looked good. She was in classic Dior clothing and highheel shoes, and her silvery-blond hair was swept upward and crowned by three large curls above her forehead. She wore a simple, tasteful string of pearls.

"Well, it looks as though you'll still have it for yourself for some time," Tina said. "I'm sure we'll have plenty of work to do at first, getting it ready for later, when we'll need it. I'm afraid that things will be disrupted for you for a while, but, after that, things should quiet down. And then eventually, of course, we'll all come here to live."

"Any time, dear, the sooner the better. I'm so sorry that I can't offer you tea. Of course I dismissed Mrs. Crandle who has worked for me for so many years. And the gardeners. And dear Mr. Kleinpeter, my handyman. The cleaning lady, I let her go as well."

Several of the group's members exchanged concerned looks. Finally Bentley spoke up. "Do you mind my asking why you had to let them go, Mrs. Rutherford? Genevieve."

"Why, not at all. Am I not right in thinking that we are now a corporation? A nonprofit corporation?"

"Technically," agreed Zoë. She had set up the corporation herself. "We each own more or less equal shares in it, meaning that all of us, including you, share roughly equally in owning the house. But we're a corporation in name only. I mean, we're not manufacturing steel or anything."

Genevieve laughed. "But affairs concerning the house will be decided by vote? Yes. Well, you see, since the upkeep of the house and garden is now a shared expense, it is up to the group to decide whether to retain a staff. And to pay a staff. Am I correct?"

"You're perfectly correct," Zoë said. "I just didn't picture having to make decisions like this one so soon!" She laughed and looked around at the others and they laughed too, though without much mirth. Already they had to decide whether or not to retain a staff. A lot of decisions were going to have to be made, starting right now, and they would all involve spending money.

"Well, perhaps we should finish our introductions first," Tina offered. "I'm a clinical psychologist with a practice in Berkeley." Several in the room tittered and all the folks in the sunroom knew why. Piedmont, Oakland and Berkeley all shared the east side of the San Francisco Bay and, essentially, they bordered each other. These communities had clear opinions of each other, just as neighbors always do. In Piedmont and Oakland, it was believed that the citizens of Berkeley were crazed politicos. The city was sometimes referred to as Berserkeley, hence the titters about Tina's psychology practice there.

Oakland was considered by people from Piedmont and Berkeley to be a crime zone. Piedmont was known as snobbish. Just as there is a grain of truth in most prejudices, so was there in these.

"Harvey and I live near here, on La Salle in Piedmont," Tina continued. Except for her light brown color, Tina perfectly fit the Piedmont mold. Her political preferences were conservative, her teeth were heavenly white and her hair was artfully arranged and professionally maintained at least twice a week. Thanks to a medical regimen she had not a wrinkle on her beguiling face. She was so socially adept that her fellow Piedmont wives did not resent her for her good looks.

"And this," she concluded, "is my husband, Harvey."

"Genevieve, this house is sooo…" Under a coffee table, Tina ground her high heel into Harvey's shin. She believed that she had to keep a lid on Harvey at all times. He was a loose cannon, she thought, ready at any moment to say something inappropriate, so she insisted that he keep his remarks rather stock. "Yes," Harvey concluded, fighting back the pain, "it's so nice to see you again." Harvey too was quite acceptable in Piedmont if not quite as perfect a fit as his wife. The Piedmont matriarchy judged him to be sufficiently under Tina's control. He frequently wore the colors of his alma mater, Stanford, and in particular a cardinal-red cashmere sweater. Several times he had been elected president of

Piedmont's branch of the Rotary Club.

A time came when there was a silent moment in the conversation. Genevieve broke it. As if talking to herself, she quietly asked, "Where are you all going to *fit?*" Despite her bravado, clearly the woman was worried. Surely, until recently, she could not have imagined sharing her house with twelve others.

"Of course that's what we're all wondering ourselves," Lenore said. "Before we go we would like to look around and see if we can come up with some ideas about that. But in a 27,000-square-foot house..."

"I'd be happy to pitch my tent right here in this room," Bentley said. "I love it." He looked excited and the room really did suit him. Surrounded and even smothered by verdant landscaping seen through its many windows, the sunroom was a gardener's paradise.

Genevieve seemed unsure. "Yes, you would have to, I'm afraid."

"I would have to?"

"Pitch your tent. It often rains in this room." As a therapist, Tina had often been called on to judge the mental competence of elderly people. "How sad," she thought. "She's slipping, and she's not much older than the rest of us." She thought it best to change the subject.

"Bentley, why don't you..."

"Just a minute, Tina," Tuck interrupted. "Genevieve, it rains in this room? Do you mean the roof leaks?"

"Oh my, yes."

"And does the roof leak any other place?"

"Yes, it does. You *are* feeling better now, aren't you?"

"What do you mean?"

"Frankly, you seemed quite ill when you arrived. Don't you remember?"

Tuck blushed. "Actually, Genevieve, I was sniffing the house."

"My goodness!"

"It seemed to us like the house smelled bad, like mold or something."

Genevieve pulled herself a few inches taller. "Well, you needn't be rude!"

"Right," said Harvey, "there's no call to be offensive here. You know, we're all going to be living under one roof." Tina let her husband's remark go. She wondered if she had better say something about the wisteria.

"But, I meant no offense at all. I was just worried about the roof," Tuck protested.

"Please, Tuck." Weezie patted his forearm. "I knew it wasn't wise for you to get down on the ground and crawl around like that. That's the kind of thing that upsets people." That was the longest speech the others had ever heard her make. Tuck looked at his friend Bentley for support, but Bentley averted his eyes.

Hoping to change the direction the conversation

had taken, Tony spoke. "Genevieve, I'll just introduce myself if you don't mind. I'm Tony Androtti, a dentist, and I'm looking forward to having a good time here with you and all my friends. That's what it's all about isn't it, a little fun every day, a little joy?"

"You have a marvelous attitude," she beamed and then directed a frown at Tuck as if to say, "unlike some people."

"And this is my wife, Zoë."

Zoë gave a quick nod toward Genevieve like a sparrow pecking at a seed. "I'm an attorney," Zoë said, "specializing in the interests of children."

"Good! I'm so glad that *someone* does." Again Genevieve glanced at Tuck with a stern frown.

"We would like to encourage you to join our group, Genevieve," Zoë said, "Can you come to a meeting next Tuesday?"

"Why of course! What are you…"

Just then Tina heard a sound that froze her in her chair, the piercing scream of a woman, and it became even more frenzied.

All the men leaped to their feet and began running into each other. Only Will Fletcher seemed decisive, and he raced for the staircase that led to the upper floors. The other men fell in behind him, and by this time the women too were surging up the sweeping staircase. The screams did not let up for an instant and they were joined by a distant thumping and banging.

Chapter Eight

By the time the group spilled up the stairs onto the second floor, the screaming had stopped. Will ran down one wing of the wide hallway shouting, "Who needs help, who needs help." Tony ran down the hallway in the opposite direction waving his arms excitedly, taking up Will's cry of "Who needs help?" No one answered.

When Genevieve reached the second floor she panted, "Through that door there's a staircase that goes to the attic," and pointed to a door across the hall. "I believe I'll just wait right here."

"Genevieve," Will huffed, "you don't know who

would be screaming, do you? I mean, that's not usual or anything?"

"Heavens no!"

"Thank God. Okay, let's go!" and he charged up the narrow stairs with some of the hardier folks surging behind in single file. A door at the top was open and before he reached it he could see daylight pouring through it as if from a skylight. When he burst through the door he was instantly smashed in the face and he fell sideways to the floor. Bellowing in pain and fear and blinded by both, he hiked his arm over his head to ward off whatever might come next, and in a horror-stricken voice he screamed to those stomping up the stairs behind him, "Go back, go back!" He could hear footsteps stop, then retreat in a stampede. It sounded to him as if someone was tumbling down the stairs.

In the room where he had fallen, Will could hear sounds of a struggle—running, grunting, swearing, *flapping*. When nothing hit him again, he began trying to open his eyes. Dimly he perceived someone, a woman, taking roundhouse swings with a broom, one of those big, straw brooms he associated with outdoor use. My God, it was Pamela and the air was full of birds and bird feathers!

"Pamela!" he yelled, squinting into the tumult.

She turned and shouted, "Quick, Will, get up and find a stick or something. We have pigeons!"

Will had no heart for it. He could hardly breathe, and a humid, hen-house smell made it seem unwise to try. Still, Will struggled to his feet, then had to duck as the battle headed his direction.

"Make yourself useful!" Pamela shouted at him.

A pigeon that was fleeing Pamela's broom collided with Will's head. He had ducked in time to avoid a full-on collision, but the pigeon got tangled in his hair. He was horrified to feel its wings flapping frantically about his ears, but even more, Will was afraid that Pamela would slam him again with her broom. He ripped the bird out of his hair and backed away from the battle, inching toward the still-open door that led downstairs. Near it now, he turned and hurled himself toward the open door but smashed face-to-face into Tony Androtti, who had just arrived at the top of the stairs. Instinctively the two grabbed each other to keep from going down, and they danced around like bears before regaining their balance. Will quickly juked around Tony, flew through the door and down the stairs.

Down in the hallway on the second floor, the women were tending to Harvey, who was on his back, clutching his shoulder. Sophia was among the nurses. "Looks like he bruised his shoulder," she said to Will. "He fell down the stairs."

"What about me?" Will thought. They all rushed to Tony though, when Tony stumbled back down the stairs with a bloody nose.

"It's Pamela," Tony gasped, holding a bloody hand to his nose. "She's up there." He pointed up the stairs, though surely everyone knew where she was.

"She's fighting with these giant birds." Tony made big flapping motions with his burly arms.

"Why the devil are there birds up there?" Tuck puffed. Everyone turned toward Genevieve.

"They *live* there," she explained, as if they were all simple-minded. "They're *pigeons*."

"Why the devil are there birds up there?" Tuck puffed. "They live *there," Genevieve explained, as if they were all simple-minded. "They're pigeons!"*

But now Pamela descended the stairs. She was quite flushed, and she had really horrid-looking white spots and stains all over her clothes and in her long straight hair. She held the handle of a broom as she might an M3 rifle, with its hefty straw-end on the floor. She gazed fiercely at her damaged friends, who fell back from her gaze.

"I won't have it! I'll not have *birds* living in my

house! Someone has to set some standards, and this is where I draw the line! And I can't imagine why you are all standing around when there are still birds in this house!"

The group fell back another step or two.

"How are they getting in and out?" Tuck asked.

"You can just come and see for yourself," Pamela snapped, and she stomped back upstairs with her broom.

Cautiously, Tuck and most of the others ventured up the stairs, while Harvey lay wounded on the hall-way floor in his cardinal-red cashmere sweater and Will and Tony sat side by side on the stairway that led back to the first floor, holding their poor battered heads in their hands.

Upstairs, in the attic, the air was still thick with pulverized bird dung and pigeon feathers, a combination that made throats close involuntarily. Feathers slowly floated toward the pine floor. Except for Pamela, those who had handkerchiefs reached for them and held them to their faces. Pamela stood alert in the middle of the sizeable attic, her broom on her shoulder like a baseball bat, ready to swing, but because of the air's heavy particle content and a con-fusing pattern of blinding shafts of light from above, it was hard to tell whether Pamela had already ousted all the birds. Where were the laser-like beams of sun-light coming from? Members of the detail traced them to a corner of the room near the roofline. Tuck, one hand covering his mouth and nose with a handkerchief, cautiously advanced toward their source, steering clear of Pamela. Looking upward, he failed to see the pigeon until he stepped on it with a sickening squish. He leaped sideways, setting Pamela in motion, but she recognized him in time and forbore from whacking him. The bird was clearly dead, now, and probably had been dead, he comforted himself, even before he stepped on it. Pamela's work, he guessed.

Now from his vantage point in the corner of the room, Tuck could see gaps between the wall and the roof, large enough for a turkey to fly through. Daylight poured in, lighting up the airborne, atomized pigeon droppings and stirred-up dust. "There's the smoking gun," he said.

Back downstairs in the sunroom where the group reconnoitered, Tina thought that, under the circumstances, she had better mention the wisteria. After she helped Harvey into a chair—he groaned and held his shoulder—and when everyone had settled down, she asked whether anyone else had noticed that the wisteria was growing *indoors* as well as out. All of them looked uncomfortable. "Of course they noticed," Tina realized. "They too were in denial and were unwilling to mention it in front of Genevieve." The vine had wondered into the room—some time ago, evidently, judging from its size—through an impressive gap of about six inches that was somehow involved in the structure of a window frame. Those who were methodical traced it from its point of penetration, along its horizontal path across the bank of windows, and finally to the floor where it had claimed the arm and leg of a white wicker chair. It would have been impossible to move the chair without hacking it free from the vine.

Tuck cleared his throat again and began, "Well, we have some problems here."

Genevieve had stopped glowering at him, perhaps because it was becoming clear that he had had ample reason to sniff the house.

"We know that rain is entering the house in the attic and in the sunroom, and those are the only rooms we've been in."

"Well *I've* certainly been in more than two rooms. I've been all over the house," Pamela said.

"And?"

"And water has been entering the house anywhere it wants to."

Tuck closed his eyes briefly before he went on. "We knew we were taking a chance when we bought the house 'as is,' without an inspection. But…" Tuck shook his head, then his shoulders slumped forward and his neck bent. It looked to Tina as if he might be heading for one of his spells of depression.

Owen spoke up. "Yes, we did know. But remember, our thinking was that even if the house has serious problems, it would still be well worth the money. The *lot* is worth what we paid for the whole thing."

"That's how I saw it too," Genevieve said.

"No, no, no one blames you, Genevieve; no one is complaining," Tuck said, being careful not to get on Genevieve's bad side again. "It's just that I now begin to see what was wrong with our reasoning."

"What?" asked Bentley.

"It's just like what happens when you try to restore a car. New, the car may have cost $15,000. But if you were to buy each part separately to restore it, altogether the parts might cost $95,000."

"That's true," Tony agreed.

"So this house is like that, too. Maybe it's worth $4,000,000 or even more, but if you have to restore everything, it might cost $15,000,000." Tuck spoke in the dull monotone of gathering clinical depression.

"Tuck," Lenore said. "Get a grip! We're certainly not going to have to replace everything in the house!"

Just then a summer breeze whipped up and rustled the leaves of the wisteria, both indoors and out. A distant but impressively loud bang rang out from upstairs. Harvey, clutching his shoulder, groaned.

Genevieve, in a tone of long-standing resignation, muttered, "It's probably nothing too important."

His face looking badly discolored, Will said, "We'd better call for an inspection and find out what we're up against."

"The first thing," Sophia suggested, "is to get an exterminator out here to get rid of those pigeons. They'll be coming back."

"An exterminator!" Genevieve cried. "For heavens sake!"

"Sometimes exterminators don't actually *extermi-nate* pests, Genevieve," Sophia assured her. "Sometimes they just chase them away. Maybe the pigeons will go live in a park somewhere."

"Well, it's not like the pigeons are *hurting* any-body," Genevieve protested. Zoë barked a nasty little laugh. Harvey, Will and Tony all moaned piteously.

"Listen," Lenore said, "I don't think we should panic."

Tina was grimly amused. "Here comes General Lenore to rally the troops," she thought. "Our tower of strength."

Lenore went on in a confident voice, "We'll just have to make some repairs. Tidy up a bit. Maybe put up a new roof. Fix a little dry-rot. Foundation. Electric. Plumbing. Stucco. Floors. Sewer. Gutters. Ducts. Drains. Paint. Weatherproofing. Carpeting. Furnace. Retaining walls. Windows. Glazing. Grout. Tile. A few things like that. But we will take them one at a time."

Tuck didn't look any cheerier.

"I'll order up an inspection, okay?" asked Lenore. "And then we'll have another meeting. Okay, every-body? One step at a time, right? We'll just take it one step at a time."

For some in the group, Lenore's metaphor sum-moned up associations with twelve-step recovery programs, and that, in turn, reminded them that they would rather be home right now having a nice glass of wine. But for Tuck, "one step at a time" summoned up a memory of having stepped on the pigeon.

Just before they left, Genevieve gave them all keys to their new old house and told each one, "Congratulations" with a big smile, apparently without irony.

Chapter Nine

[May, 1975]

Minutes

Board of Directors of "The Last Resort,"
A nonprofit California Corporation

This meeting was called to discuss the findings of a pest report and a home inspection of that real property known as 1 Upper Terrace, Piedmont, CA. Present were Lenore Holt, President; Sophia Fletcher, Vice President; Tony Androtti, Treasurer;

Tuck Calhoun, Secretary; Bentley Fairbanks, Weezie Calhoun, Pamela Noonan, Harvey Boatman, Tina Boatman, Zoë Androtti, and Genevieve Rutherford. Tuck Calhoun read a summary of the Pest and Foundation Report as follows:

1.   Basically, the foundation of this 1909 structure is over-built. Enormous redwood timbers were employed for posts, joists and beams. They were found to be soundly attached to massive concrete foundations. Relatively minor termite infestations were found and must be corrected. Cost $13,345.

2.   The structure is sinking. It was built over soil with an unusually high clay content. The enormous weight of the 27,000-square-foot structure (enhanced as it is by the beefy foundation described above) is gradually displacing the soil and causing the structure to sink at the estimated rate of a quarter of an inch a year. Already it has sunk approximately 24 inches. The immediate effect is to place the house below grade, hence attracting runoff from rain and irrigation. The long-range effect is that the house will eventually be swallowed by the earth, much as would happen if the house were engulfed by an earthquake. (Interestingly, the house does sit directly on top of the Hayward Fault.) Subject to further engineering reports, it is the recommendation of this report that the house be demolished and replaced with a structure built on piers grounded on bedrock. Cost unknown. A short-term alternative would be to establish a French drain

around the entire structure to divert water from it. Cost: $274,000.

3. This report found an extraordinary amount of dry rot throughout the house, most of it seemingly the result of a roof that has leaked for decades. One major area of dry rot was in the attic and appears to have been caused by an accumulation, over many years, of pigeon droppings. Said droppings have destroyed a large part of one wall and much of the attic floor and the ceiling of several rooms below. Cost: $223,236.

4. The total of all costs in this report is $510,581.

Secretary Tuck Calhoun then summarized the 90-page house inspection in his own words as follows:

The inspector called the house "an aging beauty gone to seed." In particular he cited substandard wiring throughout, zero water pressure in the upstairs rooms, inoperable equipment and fixtures in the kitchen and the house's 10 bathrooms, "grave concerns" about the central heating system, a bad roof, no protective cover (paint) on the exterior walls, and "failing plumbing throughout." His personal, off-the-record comment to me was, "A half million dollars would keep the old tart happy for another thirty years. Maybe she's worth it."

The total cost for foundation and other work, then, is approximately $1,010,000. It was noted that this figure does not include expenses for converting the house to apartments for the shareholders' intended use.

"A half million dollars would keep the old tart happy for another thirty years. Maybe she's worth it."

The minutes of that meeting failed to report the effect it was having on the twelve friends. Among these effects were Tuck's obvious massive depression—when he finished making his report on the "aging beauty gone to seed," he folded his arms on the table and laid his head on them. And Zoë burst out angrily, "The sexist bastard! So he calls our house an 'old tart?' " She was steamed. "Who asked him, anyway?" she demanded.

"We did," Tuck explained, head on his arms. "And we paid him $750 for his opinion."

"So what's a million divided by thirteen?" Lenore asked.

"Serious money," Owen said.

Tony Androti spoke up. "That's $77,000 per

person."

"Outrageous!" Zoë shouted. "That's more than $150,000 per couple. That's obscene!"

No one knew how to respond. Owen certainly didn't. The group had gathered at his and Lenore's house, and they sat at the long dining- room table so familiar to the wine-tasting group. The air in the room was still and warm, just as it was outside.

He and Lenore had counted on having to spend additional money on the house, but this was a bit much. The group had bought it for $1.75 million cash, a ridiculously low price for a 27,000-square-foot house in Piedmont even if it did come with certain conditions such as Genevieve's inclusion in the group. Ridiculous! Even with transfer fees, taxes and so on, it had still cost only $2,000,000—for the most beautiful house Owen had ever seen, on a huge lot in Piedmont with mature landscaping. It had cost him and his wife $308,000 to buy their share of it, a bargain, but now it would take them another $150,000 to fix it up: $458,000. "Well, that *is* money," he thought. "No getting around it." Though he was trying to remain calm, Owen felt the beginnings of a panic attack. He was afraid that he might have to get up and run around the block or something, though it had been years since he had actually run and he wasn't sure he could still do it.

Owen and Lenore had taken cash from investments and savings to buy their share of the house. This next $150,000 for repairs would wipe out the last of their savings. Eventually, when they finally moved into the mansion, they could sell their present house and live on that money plus income from pensions for the rest of their lives, and their kids would inherit nearly one-sixth interest in a really valuable property. But, until that time, they would have absolutely no savings to fall back on.

Owen didn't have any idea how much money any of the others had, but from the looks on their faces, he thought everyone else must feel the pinch, too.

"Okay," Lenore finally spoke up, "what are some alternatives? Let's name five ways to deal with the problem."

"Here she goes," Owen thought. He believed his wife was the most level-headed person he knew, and a natural-born leader.

Sophia said, "We could consider bringing more people into the group to spread the expenses a little thinner. Will and I know a couple who would buy in immediately."

"Good. Okay, there's one idea," Lenore said. "What else?"

"We could do nothing at all and let the damned place fall down around our ears," Zoë snarled.

"That's what I did," Genevieve Rutherford confided. "I mean, I could have sold the jewelry, but how far would that have gone?" She fingered her pearl necklace.

That might have raised questions in the group as to whether she had suckered them into footing the bill for saving her crumbling house, but most of them had already thought that over and had come to terms with it. They had to admit that she had been perfectly honest before they bought into the house that she needed help with the house expenses. That's why she sold it.

At first they had assumed she was fabulously wealthy, assumed it because of her mansion and her heirloom jewelry, her patrician manners and her tasteful clothing. But gradually they noticed that her fox stole was showing signs of advanced age, and of course her mansion was in the same condition. In any case, goodness knows, she had not overcharged them for the property. So rather than blame Genevieve for the trouble they were now in, they agreed with her that they were all "in this together."

"Let it fall down around our ears? The idea has some merit," Tony said. "What if we *do* just let it sink? Never put another penny into it? It would still outlive us and we could spend our money on vacations to Tahiti."

"I will not live in a house that harbors pigeons!" Pamela cried. "Or falls down around my ears." She was wearing her usual turtleneck sweater and blazer despite the warm, airless atmosphere of the room. Her hair was long and rather stringy.

"You have a point. But still, that's two suggestions. What else?" Lenore asked.

"What about borrowing money against the house to pay for all of this?" Harvey said and then answered his own question. "The trouble with borrowing money is that you have to pay it back."

"Let's do the work ourselves," Will suggested.

"A million dollars worth of work?" Tuck asked skeptically.

"It wouldn't be a million dollars if we did it ourselves. Or if we did part of it, anyway."

"One thing about it," Bentley said, "is that we have ten or fifteen years in which to do it."

"I know how to operate heavy equipment, like a backhoe," Will said. "We don't have to pay $274,000 for a French drain."

"You can use a backhoe?" Tina said. "Will, you're a musician, for heaven's sake. Cellists don't operate backhoes."

"Summer job in college," he explained. "And a Bobcat," he added. "I can use a Bobcat. My guess is that we could do the job for something like twenty-five or thirty thousand dollars. Equipment rental; a hauling service to take the dirt away; materials for the drain."

The men agreed that they could all do quite a bit of work on the house themselves. Bentley, a nurseryman, and Tuck, an avid gardener, thought they could tame the garden, including the aggressive wisteria, and they knew they could count on willing help from their garden-club friends.

"There are lots of things we women can do, especially on the interior of the house," Lenore offered. "And while we're at it, we can start doing whatever is necessary to fix up our individual quarters as soon as we choose them."

"Genevieve, can we really just show up with our keys and let ourselves in?" Sophia asked.

"Any time you want. It's your house."

"Why is it that no one seems very worried about the house sinking," Tuck asked, "or that the earth is in the process of swallowing it? Or that it sits on the Hayward Fault?"

He looked at Lenore who looked at her husband, Owen. Owen glanced at Bentley and Bentley at Sophia who looked at Pamela. Pamela turned to Tina and Tina to Tony. Tony caught Harvey's eye and Harvey looked at Zoë who glowered at Genevieve. (Zoë was in a terrible mood.) Genevieve looked at Weezie and she at Will.

Finally Will got back to Tuck. "Tuck, I don't know if this is going to cheer you up exactly. But we're already sixty, you know. Our watch is only going to last so long. This house will only sink another five or six inches while we're here."

Tony said. "After that, they can tear it down and build three or four houses on the lot if they want to."

"Oh, my goodness, don't say *that*." Genevieve protested. "I would rather see the earth swallow the old tart."

"And about it lying on the Hayward Fault," Will added, "well, life is fraught with hazards. If we had good judgment, we wouldn't get out of bed in the morning. We wouldn't cross the street."

"That's the way I see it," Tuck said, his voice muffled by the sleeve of his sweater.

"So really, what's there to say?" Will added.

"You're right," Tuck replied. "That didn't cheer me up."

Minutes continued:

5. A motion was made that the shareholders of the corporation perform the necessary work to the house themselves in order to save money. The motion was voted upon and the motion was passed. It was further decided that each shareholder would place the sum of $15,000 into a repair fund, giving the corporation a total of $195,000 to work with.

6. The meeting was adjourned.

Chapter Ten

[May, 1975]

"Take it from me, ya can't let the little son of a bitch get the best of ya. Ya gotta take control." The man who trucked the Bobcat to the house on his lowboy trailor was full of advice. "Don't try t'baby it. *Stomp* on the sucker!"

Will had been pretty sure he could handle a Bobcat. He had worked with one years before on a summer job. But his confidence had waned the moment he saw this Bobcat up there on Earl's flatbed truck. He had ordered the bigger of the two models, and, instead of the cute little white Bobcat he remembered, this one was *big*. There were scars all over it where evidently it had collided with things and had maybe even rolled over.

The truck driver slammed a metal ramp out from the back of his truck and backed the Bobcat off it with alarming violence. All the while he shouted advice to Will at the top of his lungs.

"Just whomp down on them throttles and let this baby wind!" By this time Earl had barreled the tractor up to where Will was standing. Earl, who could have used a shave, looked him in the eye for emphasis and growled, "But whatever ya do, don't let the son of a bitch intimidate you." With that, Earl spun the Bobcat around on a dime—Will had to jump back to avoid the tractor's vicious front-end loader—as if he were riding a steed of which he was in perfect command. "Got that? Now let's see ya rahd this thing."

Will had been hoping for a quiet moment by himself to get the hang of the machine, but now he had to perform with Earl watching. Not only that, but he noticed that neighbors were drifting over to see what the shouting was all about, and two cars had pulled up and parked across the street, their drivers attracted by the whirling white Bobcat.

Earl surrendered the saddle to Will who now eased himself into the cab, which amounted to a metal cage with roll-bars. Instead of a steering wheel, a "stick" was before him, in the sense of a "joy stick."

He couldn't remember what it was for, but in any case, he didn't like the feeling of having no steering wheel to hold onto.

"Man, you better strap yourself into this son of a bitch," Earl said. He had a little drool flecked with chewing tobacco in one corner of his mouth, and he smelled strongly of livestock as he showed Will the straps. "You wouldn't catch me gettin' in one of these things without straps on. That's a good way to lose a leg."

Once he was strapped in, Will gently tugged at the stick in front of him. The big front-end loader whipped into the air, causing the Bobcat to lurch and Earl to leap backwards, his hands thrown up before him as if they could protect him from a 2,000-pound tractor. Seeking to correct his mistake, Will nudged the stick the other way and it slammed to the earth with a sickening wham.

Will searched for Earl, hoping he was all right.

"Jesus Christ, boy!" Earl yelled, "take it *easy* on that thing! Ya made me swaller!"

Will could see that, not only had more cars gathered across the street, but his wife and the rest of the group had come out from the mansion, where they had been working, to watch the action. Will told himself, "Will, you've been through all kinds of things in your life, and you're going to get through this one too." But he could feel the sweat beading up on his forehead.

On the floor of the cage, he could see that there

were two pedals. By this time Earl had cautiously approached Will and the Bobcat and he said, "That one there on the right makes it go clockwise and the one on the left makes it go the other way."

"Jesus Christ, boy!" Earl yelled, "take it easy on that thing! Ya made me swaller!"

"Where's the brake?" Will asked.

"There ain't no brake. If you need to stop yourself real fast, just drop yer bucket. You know how to do that good enough, I noticed."

Carefully Will stepped on a throttle with one of the new Timberland boots he had bought for the job. Earl had stepped well back from the Bobcat. It began a slow turn to the right, out into the street. With his foot off the throttle, the Bobcat stopped. Will experimented with the other throttle and predictably it turned the Bobcat the other direction. Will reasoned that, pressed concurrently, the two throttles would take him in a straight course, and he began to ease the Cat into the street, which was the only flat surface available on which to practice. He noticed that right away one of the motorists who had parked across the street started her car, as if to be ready for anything.

Once he was in the street, Will was just starting to find the balance point, the perfect balance between left and right throttle that would take him in a straight path. Unfortunately, Will's nervous left foot twitched and gunned the throttle on the left. To correct his course he stepped on the other throttle a little too hard and there began one of those situations that are easier to start than to stop. The tractor took a violent zigzag path down the street, jarring Will into losing what control he had managed to gain. He heard one of the cars across the street lay down rubber as it retreated. The other driver, still parked, had frozen at the wheel as she watched Will careen toward her Mercedes. Will could see a look of horror spread across her face.

"Just come off one throttle altogether," he reasoned, "and tromp on the other," and that's what he did. At the last moment the Bobcat left its trajectory for the Mercedes and began spinning wildly in the street, but now Will was able to lift his other boot and stop the lethal machine entirely. "Jesus Christ," he said to himself in a profane but fervent prayer. "Jesus Christ!"

Blessedly, Sophia didn't come running out to see

if he was okay. In fact he noticed that she had left the scene altogether, evidently unable to watch. "Say, fella," Earl said to him with real concern on his face, "Ya think yer gonna be okay with this thing?"

Will's first agenda was to get out of the street. Sweat was pouring off his brow, making it hard to see, but he eased the Bobcat off the road. "Uh, Earl, thanks for the lesson, but I think it's time for me to get some work done."

"Well you jist remember, buddy, don't let 'er boss ya around. Yer in command here. I guess."

"Thanks Earl. I'll call you when I'm all done, probably tomorrow." With a huge bang Earl retracted the ramp on the back of his lowboy and slowly drove off, but Will could see him checking out the Bobcat and its rider in his rear view mirror.

Tuck and Bentley had dug dozens of large old shrubs out of the ground in order to make a path for a backhoe with which Will planned to dig the French drain around the entire house. Will had rented the Bobcat so he could move the heavy shrubs and their root-balls out of the way. The garden was set down from the street and Will drove the Bobcat down the steep hill into the yard with some trepidation. Bentley and Tuck were waiting for him beside an ancient, gnarled rhododendron, its root-ball wrapped in burlap.

"You'll go easy with that thing, won't you?" Bentley hollered above the clatter of the tractor's diesel engine.

"Yeah, yeah. I'm getting better." He feathered the throttles forward, dropped his bucket fairly gently, and made a little run at the rhododendron so as to slide his loader under the big plant. As he raised his bucket, the old shrub settled back into the loader. "Must weigh 300 pounds," Will thought. Now he pivoted by depressing just one of the throttles. Pointed back uphill now, Will raised his loader about eight feet off the ground, high enough so it didn't block his vision and he could see where he was going.

Slowly, slowly he started climbing back up the hill. Tuck walked beside the tractor, looking dubiously at the shrub suspended high above ground, all the while murmuring encouragements like, "That's it Will, that's it. Come on along now, easy does it, easy does it," as if trying to gentle a frightened horse. The Bobcat, though, wasn't pulling the hill. It had bogged down when the going got a little steeper, and it simply wouldn't move forward. "Shit!" Will swore quietly. Sweat from his forehead stung his eyes so it was nearly impossible to see.

He remembered Earl's advice: "Don't try to baby it, *stomp* on the sucker!"

"I'm going to take a little run at her, Tuck. You guys stand back a ways." Was he sounding a little like Earl, he wondered? So he backed down to where the slope was gentler and gunned the engine, both new boots on both throttles all the way to the metal. The Bobcat spurted up the hill like a wounded beast, though soon it began to lose momentum and arrived at a point of stasis. Will held his breath, caught, he believed, between making it over the hump or sliding back down the hill, but he was wrong. Instead, the Bobcat rolled over on its back and the engine died.

"Do not move a muscle, Will," he told himself. "Don't so much as blink." Because, on his back now, he was peering straight up at the loader that still, though barely, held a three-hundred-pound ball of earth and gnarled shrub. It was directly above him. Will was dimly aware of a woman screaming, and he was distracted by the memory of Pamela smashing him with her broom. "For God's sake," he snarled aloud, though he didn't know at whom, "pipe down!" and the screaming stopped. "Keep your head, old boy," he told himself. "How are you going to get out of this?

"I think I got the bucket too high and it threw the weight to the back. If I can lower the bucket, maybe it'll come upright. I have to start the engine." He realized that he had never started the engine before. Earl had delivered it with the engine running. "Do I have to put it in neutral or something?" he wondered. He didn't know and he did the only thing he could think of doing, which was, gently (as if that mattered) to turn the key. The engine shuddered to life, shaking dirt down into his eyes.

"Careful, Will. Easy, old boy, easy does it," he heard Tuck saying from a ways off. "A light touch now, nothing sudden."

"Shut the fuck up!" Will roared.

The engine sounded pretty good, but suddenly Will went blank as to whether to push or pull the stick to lower the bucket. Everything seemed so different to him as he lay on his back in the cage, looking up into the sky. Absurdly, he thought of his hands. The load high above him was heavy enough to snuff his entire mortal coil, but his fear focused on his hands, the hands with which he brought forth music from his cello. Holding his breath, he nudged the stick forward, and with a lurch his bucket reached even higher into the sky so that now dirt from the huge old shrub, raised above the landscape like a flag, poured into his eyes. The Bobcat rocked back a tad further. Will began thinking over his life, not his entire life but the last few weeks of it. First Pamela knocked him to the floor, and now he was stuck on his back like a bug, helpless and ridiculous, peering up into a load that could drop on him at any moment. At least he now knew to pull, not push the stick. Slowly, gently he pulled, though his gentle tugs translated to jerky, frantic movements of the loader. Lower and lower it came and dirt stopped pouring into his eyes. The tractor creaked and Will thought he could feel it beginning to come upright. Finally, with the bucket fully lowered and nearly on the ground, the Bobcat regained an upright position and so did Will.

"Now what?" he wondered. "Drive backwards down the hill," he told himself, "but how do I get it in reverse?" He figured it out, backed off the hill a ways, turned off the engine and stepped out of the cage with a murderous look on his face. On knees that buckled and trembled, he managed to leave the scene and slink around to the back of the house where he sat quietly by himself. After a while, Sophia came out and held his hand. About an hour later, Will took a deep breath, got to his feet, climbed into the Bobcat and revved it up again. This time he looked for a route that wasn't so steep.

Chapter Eleven

[June, 1975]

In the kitchen, such as it was, Lenore was cranking out sandwiches to feed the troops when two people—men or women, she couldn't tell which—walked in wearing full-face gas masks of a type she associated with World War One, the kind of gas masks with long, blunt snouts.

"Mmmph. Mmm. Mmnn," they said, which, along with their body language, suggested to her that they would like some sandwiches. When they left, packing a couple of sandwiches each, Lenore asked

Bentley, her assistant in the kitchen, if he knew who the people were.

"Oh, that was Pamela and your husband, Owen," he said. "They're working on the attic, trying to clean up the bird mess."

Lenore was astonished. "Pamela is working in the attic wearing a gas mask?"

"Well," he said, "wouldn't you wear a gas mask?"

"Yes, but for Pamela to dirty her hands at all…"

"She has gloves on."

"Still," Lenore said, "everyone sure is pitching in."

Bentley added, "Pamela really hates those birds, you know. I think she'd do anything to get rid of every trace. I told her I'd like to use the pigeon-poop in the garden for fertilizer, but she told me she wouldn't have it."

"Pamela feels pretty strongly about those pigeons, all right."

"Did you see Will out there with that big tank this morning?" Bentley asked, changing the subject.

"That was masterful!" Lenore said.

"I couldn't believe it," Bentley agreed. "He just got in that thing, spun it around on a dime, and *then* didn't he put on a show!"

"Zigzagging down the street, showing off!"

"Did you see him run off those rubber-neckers parked across the street?"

"I thought that was going too far, though, rolling it over backwards and all that," Lenore said. "That was dangerous."

"Well," Bentley said, "I guess not if you know what you're doing."

Bentley had to excuse himself so he could get to work in the sunroom, where he intended to tackle the wisteria. When he glided into the room, carrying a pruning saw and his Felcro clippers, Zoë was pacing off distances from one end of the room to the other and then making notes in a little book. Her natural strides were so far short of a yard that she had to stretch comically even to come close. Bentley wisely stifled a laugh and asked, "Whatcha up to, Zoë?"

"I'm trying to figure out where Tony and I should set up our apartment. This room is gorgeous!" It couldn't have been more cheerful. Everything in it was painted white, though a closer look at the paint would have revealed widespread, yellowy watermarks staining it.

"No heater, though," Bentley said. "But I'm with you. Living in here with this wall of windows would be like living in the garden." He peered at the wisteria that had broken and entered. "Or," he said, "it's like the garden is living in the house. Part of it is, anyhow. Judging from the size of this vine, it's lived here about as long as Genevieve has." He walked over to it and grabbed hold of the branch that had breached the house and found it to be as big as his calf. "I sure hate to cut it." Bentley could feel a fairly brisk breeze blowing through the wall where the wisteria had penetrated. "Might get pretty nippy in the winter," he thought, "and it'll bring in some rain, too." But Zoë had paced her way out of the room and onward, down the hallway.

Bentley could feel a fairly brisk breeze blowing through the wall where the wisteria had penetrated. "Might get pretty nippy in the winter," he thought, "and bring in some rain, too."

After a lifetime spent around plants, Bentley had never settled the question of whether they feel the pain of pruning and nipping and lopping. He was certain that it was best to proceed as though they were dumb as rocks with no glimmer of feeling, because, after all, they had to be eaten and controlled and, for that matter, spruced up for selling—that was his trade. But he worried about it. If someone had accused the pensive nurseryman of harboring such worries, he would have denied it. But the truth was, he couldn't cut so much as a twig from a tree without feeling uneasy. Cutting vines was particularly disturbing for him because the way they cast about for something to hug and the way they follow the course of the sun. It suggested sentience to him, or even personality.

Bentley had similar feelings about garden pests such as snails. In their case, he was certain that snails *could* perceive pain. And yet he couldn't let them eat his nursery plants or his garden. His personal solution was to refrain from using snail bait to do them in. He shuddered to imagine their slow, slimy, painful death from poison. Instead, he simply stepped on them. He stepped decisively so there would be no lingering. And he never stepped on anyone else's snails, just those victimizing his own plants. But when it came to plants, what could you do? To lop off a branch was to lop off a branch, decisively or not. The best he could come up with was not to cut unless he needed to. That's why he looked long and hard at the sizeable old wisteria branch that had chosen to live indoors. He made his decision: "There's 27,000 square feet in this house and how many *cubic* feet? There's room for all of us!"

Bentley made a list for a run to the hardware store. Tops on it was insulating material, something flexible that would shut out the weather but still leave room for the wisteria to put on even greater caliper. "Live and let live," he said to himself and whistled as he drove to the hardware store. On his way, he saw an old heap of a car on which a bumper sticker read, DOGS ARE PEOPLE TOO. Something about it made him smile.

Zoë continued marching around the mansion seeking the perfect spot for the family nest. She made drawings and recorded measurements in her note-book, and in the course of surveying gathered a solid picture of how the house was laid out. As she paced the floors, she was dimly aware of the sound of Will's big yellow backhoe doing things in the garden. From distant places in the house she heard the shriek of a Skilsaw and the sound of hammering.

Zoë was enjoying a day away from work, and she was dressed in tennis shoes and work-out sweats in coordinated shades of moss green. Everything she chose to wear looked good on her tiny frame but especially the tailored clothes she preferred in shades of toast, khaki and green. She always dressed with a plan, one that suited her.

After Zoë had paced off the dimensions of sev-eral rooms, making notes, she started over, wishing to begin at the beginning, so to speak, and to take in the interior with new eyes as if she had never seen the house before, and this time she began her exploration on the main front porch where a pair of massive mahogany doors, scarred by 75 years of weather and careless furniture movers and naughty children (now passed on) who had used them in dart games, stood guard over the house. Zoë worked the old brass latch and pushed, and the heavy doors swung open smoothly. She walked through them like a tiny queen, into a vast mahogany-paneled entryway. She could have crossed it and ascended a soaring circular staircase, but instead she chose to stay on the first floor, and she sauntered like a sightseer in a museum down a spacious, darkly paneled hallway, no longer measuring or taking notes. A cavernous room in an Italian-gothic style opened at the hallway's end, and she stood in its doorway, absorbing it. Walnut wainscoting covered the bottom few feet of the room, and aged plaster walls rose to the ceiling, where dark old beams with the girth of tree trunks ran the length of the room. The ceilings were vaulted as in old Italian cathedrals.

When her eyes finally left the ceiling, she found the fireplace. "In a pinch, we could live in *there*," she thought, peering into its cavernous depths. Above it, craftsmen from an earlier era had carved a massive wooden mantel and had supported it by columns that peaked in scrolling figures reminiscent of oversized treble clefs. The mantel itself was so wide that it would easily have accommodated an old fashioned diorama depicting a scene from nature: perhaps a full-sized, stuffed, black panther and a stuffed tapir. Instead, the mantel was bare, but Genevieve had mounted on the wall just above it three big, gold-embossed letters that spelled: "Joy." Of all the home's wonders, Genevieve's "Joy" above the mantel made the strongest impression, for there was an air of mystery about it. Was it leftover decor from Christmastime? Did it spell out Genevieve's philosophy of life? Did she have a daughter of that name? Whatever the answer, "Joy" made Zoë smile as she went about surveying her new kingdom.

Touring the room, she found that the home's architect had not relied on the fireplace alone to heat the room. A hardly-noticeable radiator, barely a foot high, ran the length of two walls. A painted metal shroud made it nearly invisible.

But her smile faded when finally her eyes focused on the floor. Very tired, mousy-colored wall-to-wall carpeting covered it. When she pried up a corner of the horrible stuff, she smiled once more. Years ago some lovely person—Genevieve's mother?—had covered up the most glorious cherry-wood floors she had ever seen, thus preserving them for her and Tony and their friends, including Genevieve.

Zoë discovered a second sunroom—as if the "wisteria room" weren't enough! French doors on either side of the living room fireplace opened into it. As long and narrow as a train-car, its walls were made up of a hundred small windowpanes, many of them cracked or broken. Through them she admired a garden conceived and planted many decades ago. Two magnolias with nearly-white trunks, their flowers now past prime, anchored the landscape. Had Bentley and Tuck found this corner of the house yet, she wondered?

The floor in this room had been spared the mousy-colored wall-to-wall and was covered with small tiles that formed a pictorial mosaic. Hard to say what it was a picture of, though. Age and use had so grayed the tile that the scene it depicted was unreadable. Could she and the others restore it?

Zoë had arrived at the end of the west wing, and she retraced her steps back through the living room and down the hallway. Just before her starting-point at the entryway, she found the door to a men's room, identified by a brass silhouette of a man's mustachioed face. She opened it, called "Hello," and then strolled into a room furnished with three old-looking coat-trees. "A coatroom," she said aloud and then wondered whether, 75 years ago when costumes looked so different and the residents of this house would have resembled actors in an Edwardian play, its architect must not have called it a cloakroom. In turn, it led to a bathroom—yes, a *men's* bathroom: A urinal with the name "Standard" baked into its porcelain was installed against one wall. Otherwise, the room was furnished with a modern toilet and a old floor-standing washbasin that dripped water from one faucet.

Out in the hall again, she walked past the entryway and, just on the other side, she found a doorway marked by a woman's long-skirted brass image. "And surely this must have been called the 'powder room' on the old blueprint," she thought, and she pictured corseted women sitting before mirrors, powdering their noses. It was composed of two chambers. In the first, dozens of small, hazy mirrors were mounted on narrow doors. Behind each door was a tiny closet, and in some were odds and ends of women's clothing on hangers: a peachy-colored silk blouse, a blue one-piece swim suit. Small chairs lined two walls. They were upholstered with a faded fabric showing scenes of spaniels and blue jays. Flock wallpaper covered the walls where closet doors and mirrors did not. It was pink and Victorian-looking, and Zoë found it distasteful. On the other hand, she was delighted by a leaded, stained-glass window in an arts-and-crafts style, illuminated by sunlight that struck the front of the house. The light cast by the leaded glass gave the powder room a nice, rosy glow that Zoë thought was flattering to her skin.

The second chamber of the powder room, not at all spacious, had in it a toilet with a water tank and a pull-chain, and a rust-stained porcelain basin with scalloped rim that stood on a porcelain pedestal. The basin's fixtures seemed original and the faucet leaked, just as in the men's room. The towels, on racks, were clean. On the way out, Zoë resorted again to her notebook and made disparaging remarks about the pink wallpaper.

Zoë wandered across the hallway to the dining room. She had surveyed it and the other rooms before, but always with a realtor or with Genevieve or friends pointing out this and that, and never alone. Now it was as if she were becoming acquainted with the house for the first time and discovering her feelings about each room. This one was gloomy though the day was bright. Oppressively dark wood covered much of the walls, and large wooden beams tic-tac-toed the ceiling. Brass light fixtures that must at one time have been fitted for gas were mounted every few feet all around the room. Genevieve's dining-room table was Gothic and dark. Uninviting chairs with high, straight backs and cracked leather seats were stationed around it. She estimated that the table could easily seat twenty-eight people. Maroon, velvet drapes on the far side of the room added to the gloom. She pulled back one of them and was bathed in bright, cheery, outdoor light. French doors opened onto a balcony so beguiling that she could picture old Hollywood romances staged here—except that its floor was covered with pine branches and decades of fallen leaves. She wondered what the view would be like from the veranda, and she stepped cautiously onto it and waded through the mulch to the balcony's edge. A very large swimming pool stretched out below, its turquoises tiles shimmering in the sun. A bath-house beside the pool was shaded by palms. A tennis court lay beside the pool, its surface as green as the gardens around it. Zoë was nearly moved to tears by the beauty before her and the astonishing fact that she owned one-thirteenth of all she surveyed!

Her peace was disturbed by a large, yellow back-hoe that came lurching into view from around the corner of the house, shattering the quiet with its clatter and fouling the air with black diesel smoke. Will—determined, brave Will—seemed to be having trouble negotiating the steep hillside behind the house. She watched him maneuver for a position from which to continue digging the French drain. "He was pretty impressive with the Bobcat," she thought, "but I don't know about that backhoe." Will had dropped his outriggers and now had a reasonably level purchase on the hillside, but when he began digging, the backhoe bucked like a bronco, rising at least three feet in the air then slamming to the ground. "Ouch," she thought. When Will finally got a load in his bucket, he raised it by manipulating a complex-looking array of levers, then swung the arm away from the ditch in a move that would have felled a medium-sized tree if one had been in the way, or punched a hole through the house if he were to swing the arm in the wrong direction. "Yikes! I'm not watching." She turned and strode back toward the dining room. Suddenly, incredibly, one of her feet went through the floor, and instantly her whole leg followed. Instinctively her arms flailed open and they and her other leg kept the rest of her body from plunging completely through the floor. But she was trapped, unable to pull herself out of the hole into which one leg had disappeared. All she could do was wave her buried leg around ridiculously.

"Zoë! Hold on!" It was Will. He must have seen her sink out of sight as she went through the roof.

"Just hold on and I'll get you down with the back-hoe!"

"Will, don't you dare! Keep away with that thing!" She could picture the damned backhoe taking her leg off as if it were a snap pea. The image was so vivid that Zoë launched herself free before Will could get any closer. Rather than risk walking back to the dining room, she crawled through the duff on her belly, like a commando. Back inside, she shook uncontrollably, but she still had all her limbs.

Chapter Twelve

[June, 1975]

Upstairs, Owen and Pamela had finished cleaning the attic floors and walls and had begun replacing wood beams that had succumbed to the cumulative effects of pigeon droppings. On the first floor, Bentley had improvised a system that allowed the old, purple wisteria to remain in its preferred place indoors but which kept the weather outside, and he was now replacing boards in the sunroom for which his weatherproofing had come too late. In the dining room, Zoë had taken a stiff drink from a flask in her purse, and, after consultation with Genevieve, was getting rid of the velvet drapes that had entombed the dining room for a half-century. In the yard, Will was trying to control his backhoe when he glanced up and saw a stranger watching him work. The gent, who was straining a couple of shirt-buttons at the belly, was smoking a pipe or at least holding one in his mouth. He stared so fixedly at Will that Will shut down the engine and said, "Hi."

Approaching the tractor, the man pulled the pipe from his mouth and asked, "Sir, do you live here?" in what Will thought was an aggressive tone of voice. The question caught Will off-guard, so he was cautious in his reply.

"Not really."

The gentleman cocked his head in a show of skepticism. "Not really, sir?" He said "sir" as if what he really meant was "cur."

"Uh, not at the present time."

The stranger considered. "Do you have a permit to displace that earth?"

Earth? All kinds of thoughts flew through Will's head. Was this some kind of Earth First! environmental activist? He didn't look like one, but it sprang into Will's mind that his digging might be endangering a toad or something. He thought he should be careful. "Me?" he asked.

"*Sir!*"

"Have a permit? Uh, not really."

"Not really," he mocked. "Well it looks to me like

you've displaced more than six cubic yards of earth. Much more."

"Just who are you?" Will took a meager offensive.

As if that were precisely the question he was waiting for, the fellow whipped out a really impressive badge and held it up for Will to see. "I'm William Whistle with the Piedmont Department of Building Permits. Sir, unless you have a permit to displace more than six cubic yards of earth you are in violation of section 6, article 15 of the Building Code." Somehow the fellow looked sour and self-satisfied at the same time. He handed Will a business card.

"I need a permit to dig a ditch?"

"Section 6, article 15."

To buy time, Will studied the man's card. Sure enough, City of Piedmont. Then he studied the man. About Will's age, sandy-red hair but not much of it. Hideous checkered slacks. "What do I have to do?" Will asked.

"You have to quit digging immediately and then begin the procedure to apply for a permit. You may be required to fill in all the work you have completed."

Just then the bright sound of hammering rang cheerfully from the attic far above, though almost instantly it was drowned by the scream of a Skilsaw. Inspector Whistle shaded his eyes and peered upward at an open attic window, then consulted papers on a clipboard that he held in the hand that wasn't wrapped around his pipe and said, "My records show that this property is owned by The Last Resort, Incorporated. Are you building a resort, sir?"

Will thought it best to dismiss *that* idea with a hearty laugh, which he summoned forth. "Ha, ha, ha! I guess that's what it sounds like. The Last Resort! That's good! But no, we're not building a resort. Ha, ha, ha!"

Inspector Whistle didn't share Will's mirth. "Who *does* live here, sir?" he asked.

"That would be Genevieve, Genevieve Rutherford."

"Where would I find this lady?"

"I can take you up to the house," Will said, and he led the way over giant mounds of "earth" he had created with his backhoe during the past week and through the garden. Here and there Will and the inspector had to leap over the wide ditch he had dug. In the front yard now, Will made for the porch, followed by the inspector, but Will spied Tony and Harvey laboring down the stone steps with a load of 2-by-4s on their shoulders and a big sack of sixteen-penny sinkers perched on the Douglas fir. Will and the inspector were on a path to converge with Tony and Harvey.

Will turned without warning, stopped and planned to explain to the inspector that maybe it would be easier to use the back door, but the inspector, whose trajectory had not changed, smashed into Will with surprising force. Inspector Whistle, who was a head shorter than Will, then tried to go around him, but Will quickly sidestepped and stopped the inspector's forward motion.

"Oh, sorry there! Clumsy of me!" Will shouted. The inspector tried to get around Will's other side, but Will interceded again, this time having to hurl himself in the inspector's path. The inspector was fairly agile though, and, after a head-fake and a 360-degree spin he was around Will and was pouring on the steam toward the front door. Will thought the inspector must have caught a glimpse of Tony and Harvey and their lumber. Either that, or his instinct for code violations was awesome. They all arrived at the front door at the same time.

"Hey Will," Tony puffed, "could you get the middle? Man, this stuff is heavy!"

"Uh, sure Tony," Will said. "Say fellows, this is Mr. Whistle. *Inspector* Whistle from City Hall. You know, building permits and all that." Will slipped his shoulder under the load of lumber and added, "And this is Tony up ahead and Harvey behind me." Tony and Harvey shot startled looks at the inspector, who returned their looks with a thin smile.

"I guess you'd like me to open the door for you?" William Whistle asked.

"Thanks, Inspector," Tony said. Once inside the huge hallway, Tony asked, "Say, Will, where would you like us to *store* this lumber?"

"Why, right here in the hall, I guess. Put 'er down right here, boys. We'll take it back out to the truck in the morning." As the three lowered their burden, the inspector wrote something on a notebook clamped to his clipboard. With his lips pulled up to accommodate the pipe in his mouth, the inspector's teeth were quite yellow. He wore a short-sleeve white shirt with a blue collar. The inspector's arms were heavily freckled and lightly covered with red hair.

"Do you gentlemen live here?" he asked Harvey and Tony.

"Yes," said Tony.

"No," said Harvey at the same time.

"Yes?" the inspector shot back at Tony.

Tony appeared to have suddenly sickened. He looked pale. "Yes," he mumbled, "I live right here in Piedmont."

"I'm asking whether you live here in this house."

"Oh," Tony said understandingly, with the voice of someone who was cooperating fully.

"I told the inspector that Genevieve lives here," Will volunteered.

"You got *that* right," Harvey said—inappropriately, Will thought.

"Gentlemen," the inspector barked, "are you building a resort?"

At this, Tony and Harvey seemed genuinely startled.

"What sort of resort," Harvey asked.

"*Any* sort of resort." He was scowling.

"Oh," Tony said again, helpfully.

William Whistle turned to Will and said, "Would you take me to the lady you said lives here, sir?"

"Of course, Inspector. Harvey, do you know where Genevieve is?"

"She's in the kitchen with Sophia, cooking for the troops," he said, and then wished he hadn't.

"Genevieve Rutherford, Sophia Fletcher, this is William Whistle. Inspector Whistle is from the City of Piedmont, with the Department of Building Permits."

"Why, how do you *do* Inspector Whistle?" Genevieve said enthusiastically. "I can't tell you how much I enjoy your work!"

"How's that, ma'am?"

"Enjoy your work at City Hall. My hat is off to you and all the others, sir. You're an unsung hero!"

"Well, I guess so. Thank you, ma'am." The inspector stood a little straighter. "But I would like to ask you a few questions, ma'am."

"Why, of *course*, dear. Fire away."

"Do you live here, Mrs. Rutherford?"

"Yes!"

"Well I'm relieved to find someone who does." Genevieve turned her head slightly as if to bring her good ear into play. The inspector went on, "Does anyone else live here?"

Genevieve thought a moment then seemed to take his meaning. "You're thinking about my husband, of course. Aldous. Is he still in the records? I'm afraid that he went away quite some time ago and is presumed missing. Seven years, isn't that it? After seven years, someone is presumed missing."

"After seven years he *is* missing. Presumed *dead*, ma'am, I think you say, after seven years."

"Well, that's a bit extreme, don't you think, but I'm sure you mean no harm. No, I wouldn't say he's presumed dead. I imagine he'll show up here one of these days, and then we'll just have to see. Oh, how dreadful of me! I didn't offer you a thing! After what you go through day in and day out. Inspector, would you like a sandwich? Iced tea?"

William Whistle, Will, Sophia and Genevieve were conversing in the kitchen, a room that had not been remodeled since the original wood-burning stove had been replaced in 1918.

The inspector eyed the roast beef sandwiches that Sophia had made, a great pile of them on a silver platter, but he declined to eat one. Just then Lenore and Tuck walked in and Lenore said, "Well, *I'll* have one. It'll keep me going. Maybe I'll have two." Will introduced the inspector to them. Lenore suggested that they all sit in the nearby wisteria room and urged Inspector Whistle to at least have a glass of iced tea. He declined, saying that he had to avoid even the appearance of accepting favors, but he allowed himself to be led to the sunroom.

Bentley, who was standing high on a ladder in the sunroom studying water damage to the ceiling, was startled when everyone poured into the room. Fresh sawdust was still on the floor from a repair he had just made. The inspector, who *did* seem to possess an uncanny instinct for code violations, went right to where the wisteria made its illegal entry into the house. As he inspected Bentley's work and made a note on his clipboard, Bentley peered down at him from his ladder. Everyone else had settled into the white wicker chairs with their sandwiches and iced tea.

"Bentley, come on down and say hello to Inspector Whistle of the City of Piedmont," Will said. "He's interested in building-code violations."

"I'm also interested in occupancy."

"Occupancy?" Lenore asked.

"I would like to know who else lives here besides Mrs. Rutherford." He spoke these words with unmistakable authority. Bentley, his jaw fallen open, seemed frozen on the ladder. The inspector began to prowl the room with his pipe in his mouth, more like a police inspector in a murder mystery than a building inspector. He circled the ladder and walked around between the chairs, staring at each person in turn. But, before anyone could respond, Owen and Zoë ambled into the room.

"Where are the sandwiches?" Zoë asked.

"My God!" Inspector Whistle exclaimed. For a moment he stopped pacing. "How many of you *are* there?"

"That's what I said the first time I saw them," Genevieve volunteered. "But you get used to it."

Tony asked Owen, "Where's Pamela?"

"There's more?" the inspector was stunned.

"Just one," Owen said, but then he seemed unsure and he did a quick count of heads. "Right, just one more. Pamela. She's still in the attic," he told Tony. "She says she won't come down until every trace of the birds is gone."

"My God!" Inspector Whistle exclaimed. "How many of you are there?" "That's what I said," Genevieve volunteered. "But you get used to it."

After more introductions, in which Will placed pointed emphasis on the inspector's job description, Zoë, Owen, and Tuck settled down with sandwiches and tea. Will wanted to see how Zoë, an attorney, would handle this situation.

The inspector continued to pace the room. "I must make one thing perfectly clear," he told his audience. "This neighborhood is zoned for single- family occupancy. If I find that any violation of that zoning code has taken place or takes place in the future I will be forced to shut down this operation.

"Everyone in the group looked around at everyone else with 'who, me?' faces. Zoë spoke up. " 'This operation' Inspector?"

Inspector Whistle whipped his attention toward Zoë and pointed at her with his pipe stem. "Are you building a resort here?" The room erupted in laughter. There seemed a danger that Tuck, in particular, was on the verge of getting the giggles. The inspector froze. His face turned red and his mouth took on a snarling look. He continued to point at Zoë and he resumed his tirade. "Because if you are, I will personally make sure you never build another resort anywhere in this county!" At this, the laughter became even more boisterous, and Tuck's giggles became alarming.

That was the scene when Sophia and Tony showed up looking for Pamela. "What's so funny?" Tony asked the room? That destroyed Tuck and soon he was doubled over, gasping for air and, when he could breathe at all, he was going, "Hooo, hooo, hooo, hooo!" Will caught it from Tuck. All that he had endured during the past several months, every scary choice he had had to make about buying into the mansion, every bloody nose he had suffered, every hillside he had negotiated with his backhoe and every fear he had had for his hands, and now this red-faced inspector—suddenly it all seemed so funny! Soon he was howling. Sophia caught it from Will (her face became absolutely beatific with laughter) and so it went around the room, right down to Genevieve, for whom the pain she had suffered in giving up her home and her privacy seemed for a moment not to matter.

The Last Resort, Inc.
1 Upper Terrace
Piedmont, CA 94611

To the officers and shareholders,

By the power vested in me by the City of Piedmont, I hereby declare that The Last Resort, Inc. is in violation of section 6, article 15 of the City of Piedmont's Building Code (relating to the displacement of earth), and section 8, article 3 of the same (relating to altering structural members of a residential building). I am hereby shutting down all such activity unless and until such time as the Department determines that proper applications have been applied for and granted and until all pertinent fees and penalties have been paid.

Furthermore: upon my inspection of said premises I noted activity that may indicate that multiple families are living in a house zoned for single-family occupancy. A full investigation is being launched by this Department to determine whether this is so. You will soon be asked to provide the Department with documents relevant to our investigation. We expect your full cooperation.

William Whistle, Inspector
City of Piedmont,
Building Department

[The following, neatly lettered by hand, followed Inspector Whistle's signature:]

H. w. l. l. l. b.

Chapter Thirteen

[July, 1975]

It was a sober bunch of shareholders who tried to figure out what H. w. l. l. l. b. meant.

"A title, a degree, a message, an intra-office code? Maybe a sentence, since it begins with a capital letter." Lenore couldn't think of any other possibilities. But all the meeting's attendees understood perfectly well what the rest of the inspector's letter meant.

"We've been busted," Lenore said. The others gave somber nods all around, like people who had awakened with hangovers and were not willing to risk vigorous movements of the head. "Zoë, what do you think about all of this?"

"We've been busted," Lenore announced.

The group was sitting under two large shade umbrellas beside the enormous swimming pool in the rear half-acre of the property. The pool was empty of water though not of leaves and a few dead furry things with hairless tails. The house inspection a month earlier had revealed cracks in the pool and ominous problems with the pool's plumbing. It had been so long since Genevieve had used the pool that she could no longer remember what was wrong with it—only that no one ever used it. Still, its new owners were drawn to sit beside it, just as even idle fireplaces often attract customers. The landscaping around the pool was inviting. The Bay Area's congenial climate accommodated lush-leaved banana trees near the pool, and immense palms looked down on the pool and on the umbrellas under which the somber group of wine and garden lovers and their spouses huddled.

"How much damage do you think this jerk can do to us?" Lenore asked.

"Well," Zoë said, "it looks like he'll do as much damage as he can." She thought about it. "In some ways it's not as bad as it sounds. I mean, we're *not* building a resort, and maybe when he finally figures that out he'll calm down. And about obtaining permits, well, let's pay our fines and get permits and move on. But the business about single-family occupancy, *that* I worry about." Zoë *looked* worried, too. She and Tony and the other couples now had close to a half million dollars each invested in the house, and all of them had begun to dream in earnest of living there someday, maybe someday soon. Furthermore, they had responsibilities to their children, all of whom had been outraged by their parents' scheme to cohabit. Just last week, Zoë and Tony's son, Kevin, had *shouted* at them: "Don't you *care* what happens to our inheritance? You've squandered it on a hare-brained idea that won't work anyway. Piedmont is never going to let you get away with having thirteen adults in one house!" Zoë was certain that Kevin would say, "I told you so," if the enterprise failed.

"Okay," Lenore said, taking charge, "how are we going to solve the problem of single-family occupancy? Five suggestions, please." No one said a word. The silence stretched out.

"Bribe Inspector Whistle?" Tina proffered.

"Murder Inspector Whistle?" Bentley contributed. "That would be cheaper."

"Why murder," Zoë asked, "when torture would probably do the trick?"

"Hmm," Lenore said, "this discussion is taking a pretty nasty turn."

Zoë suggested, "If somehow we could establish that we were all part of the same family…" Obviously that was a dead end too.

Pamela, who had been in the attic when the inspector had appeared and had not yet met him, took her usual contrary point of view. "Why are you all so rude about Mr. Whistle? He's simply doing the job he was hired to do," she concluded, her nose in the air. Many of those by the poolside shot irritated glances her way. The women in the group had uncharitable observations about the way she wore her makeup. The men noted her stringy hair. Though the day was exceptionally warm, Pamela wore her usual turtleneck pullover and blazer. "What did you do to make him so mad?" she asked.

"Nothing. Nothing at all," Will said righteously and then grinned.

"Well, who has a plan?" Lenore asked. "We can't just sit around feeling sorry for ourselves."

Tuck was heard to moan. Genevieve asked, "Tuck, dear, aren't you taking this a little too hard?"

"Yes," Tuck mumbled. "I'm bipolar. I always take things too hard, although this time it really *is* bad."

There was a stirring of interest and concern among the group. It hadn't occurred to any of them except Tina that he had more than one pole.

"Shall I risk a guess as to which one you're exploring right now, Tuck?" Tony asked petulantly. Tuck didn't answer.

"A plan, anyone?" Lenore asked again.

"Look," Zoë offered, "I'll submit applications to City Hall for the work we want to do, and I'll handle the red tape. In the meantime, there are a thousand things we can do."

"We can patch and paint," Sophia offered. "We don't have to ask City Hall for permission to do that."

"We can garden," Bentley said.

"We can replace busted appliances."

"We can choose our private spaces."

"Heck," Harvey said, "why don't we just sit around a little and enjoy this place. After we get permission from City Hall to do the big stuff, we might not have a chance to relax again for a long time." If there was an easy way out, Harvey was usually the one to find it.

"Right!" the others chorused, momentarily exhilarated by the idea of sitting around and doing nothing. "Let's just enjoy the old tart." Their hilarity, though, didn't last long. Soon they were back to peering dismally into the pool before them at the decaying things that littered its bottom.

"And let's just keep thinking about the problem of single-family occupancy," Zoë said. "That's all we can do."

"I just hope that son-of-a bitch doesn't get the last laugh," Will said.

A gloomy silence followed Will's heartfelt wish, then Tuck moaned again. "That's it," he mumbled.

"What's it?" Will asked.

"H. w. l. l. l. b."

"What about it?" Will asked.

Tuck said, "He who laughs last laughs best."

"The son-of-a bitch," Will repeated.

Lenore mused. "William Whistle sent us a message. He intends to have the last laugh."

Chapter Fourteen

[August, 1975]

Four weeks later, Tina and Harvey and the others received two important phone calls. The first was from Zoë who was in a rage. She had been unable to make any progress with City Hall and had *not* been granted permits for work to proceed on the mansion. "William Whistle, that little shit," she snarled, "figures we laughed at him, and he has stopped us cold." There were two issues, she explained, both of them intractable. First there was the matter of needing permits to move forward with essential work, "and

Inspector Whistle personally has made sure we will not be granted the permits. Secondly there is the zoning issue of 'single-family dwelling,' and even if Whistle didn't have it in for us, that's fatal, because the neighbors will cite it to run us out of here. That's two strikes," she said, "and we may already be out."

The second phone call came three days later, when Tina and Harvey were at home, shaking their heads over The Last Resort. The call was from Genevieve, asking them and each member of the group to show up at room 305 on an appointed day and hour for an "event" at the County Building. She refused to tell them why, saying only that she would have an interesting surprise for them.

"I wonder what she's up to," Tina mused. She and Harvey were holding hand, sunk into their feather-stuffed, peach-colored sofa. It, in turn, was standing on a tasteful white-on-white Tibetan carpet chosen for them by their interior designer. A bouquet of summer flowers made of silk was positioned on the fireplace mantel, and its colors complemented the room's drapes.

They hadn't always lived in luxury. Harvey and Tina had grown up in Oakland's black ghetto. By the age of thirteen they were sweethearts, both of them fiercely determined to dig their way out of their surroundings. Since their marriage at eighteen, they had been wonderfully mobile in an upward direction. They had bought and sold many homes over the years—each time moving up to a better neighborhood. Finally, they had settled into a prestigious house in the loftiest of all East Bay neighborhoods: Piedmont. Their success had been fueled by successful careers, by their fanatical commitment to being socially correct, and by their fierce instinct to climb.

After their last move, they agreed that they had reached the end of their ascent. Given the heights they had already reached and considering their ages, they were not likely to move up another notch in income or social circle, and they were left feeling restless, as if something important had been left unfinished.

Wondrously, magically, just when they thought they had reached their limits, the wine-tasting group's visionary scheme had given them a crack at the absolute summit of social climbing. In a matter of a few months, they went from owning one of the nicer Piedmont homes to owning, *in addition*, part-interest in one of the grandest houses in the world. Suddenly they had prospects for enjoying a stunningly enviable old age!

Now, it may be asked how two people who had been so devoted to toeing the line of convention would risk outraging the community by living in the old Rutherford mansion with eleven other people. And it might be asked, too, how they could further outrage their neighbors by cohabiting with a group that included an openly gay man. That's just what they had been talking about when Genevieve's call came, requesting their presence at an event at the county courthouse. Harvey promised Genevieve they would be there, and then they went back to their talk.

"It used to bother me, too," he said.

"What did?"

"Seeing Bentley move around so…gracefully, like a dancer. Seeing him hold a coffee cup with his pinky finger sticking out. That stuff gave me the creeps." Tina laughed. "But look," Harvey went on, "in sixty years I've met all kinds of people and Bentley is one of the best. He's someone who wouldn't harm a fly."

"That's Bentley," Tina said, "and I've known him for fifteen years. But our new neighbors will hate us even without Bentley."

"Yeah, in the improbable event that the City of Piedmont will relent and let us all live there. Which they won't. But you know what?" Harvey asked rhetorically, "the hell with the neighbors." Tina turned her head to see whether he was serious.

"The hell with them?"

"I mean, we're not going to do anyone any harm by living there. Loud parties? Hardly. Will we create parking problems in the neighborhood? The place has a twelve-car garage. What I'm saying is, we won't hurt anyone. So they'll just have to get over it."

"Harvey, at one time you would have done any-thing to keep from ruffling the neighbors."

"You, too."

Tina thought about that for a moment. "Well, it just doesn't seem so important anymore what the neighbors think. What's important now is keeping out of nursing homes."

The door to Room 305 had gold lettering on its upper, glass portion that read "Family Placement Services." Before they passed through the door, Harvey and Tina stopped to regard those words but reached no conclusion about their relevance to them. Inside, the group was assembled in a waiting room. Everyone had their eyes glued on Genevieve, who had *her* eyes on her tiny, bejeweled wristwatch.

"Ah, you're here!" Genevieve said. "How nice of you to come, my dears." Tina and Harvey found a seat. Except for the space taken by a man who was not part of the group, they filled the entire waiting room.

When they had all settled into chairs, Genevieve began in the classic detective-story way: "I know you're wondering why I have called you here. When I sold the greatest part of my house to you, I was terribly worried that I would regret having opened my doors to a group of strangers. But now…I can hardly tell you how grateful I am for the considerate way you have all treated me. I wish to thank you."

"Here, here," Owen said. "Good sport! Thank *you* for what you have done for us."

"Not at all," Genevieve said. "Anyway, I wish to adopt you."

Tuck said, "Genevieve, you don't have to do that," but then he stopped talking for a moment and said, "What?"

"I would like to adopt you. Do you mind, dear?" she asked Tuck.

"You'd like to adopt *me*?" Tuck asked.

"Oh yes," Genevieve said brightly. "All of you."

"Oh shit," Harvey thought. "Genevieve's gone around the bend." He looked at Tina, who was his ultimate authority on who had cracked or not. Tina was still studying the situation.

"Uh oh," Harvey thought. "Genevieve's gone around the bend."

Finally Will spoke up. "Uh, Genevieve, you're not much older than the rest of us. I don't know about adopting us." Harvey thought that Will had got at only a portion of the problem.

"And there's quite a few of us," Harvey pointed out. "Twelve."

"Cheaper by the dozen," she laughed.

"Well, I'm with Will," Bentley said, "you don't

have to do that."

"This is pretty creepy," Harvey thought.

"Really," Genevieve explained, "I never had children of my own. This is a happy chance for me to make up for all those childless years."

Just then, a lady opened a door, looked in at the gathered group, studied a piece of paper in her hand for a moment and read "Rutherford, Holt, Calhoun, Boatman, Fairbanks, Fletcher, Noonan, and Androtti?"

"We're all here!" Genevieve answered.

The clerk gave a long, skeptical look at the assembly and said, "Would you come in, please?"

"And children," Genevieve said to all of those in the group as they stood, "don't you think it would be nice if we were all part of one, big, happy family? So we could dwell together?"

Lenore stood up. "I get your drift, Mom. Absolutely brilliant," and then everyone followed Genevieve and Lenore into the chambers. Tuck gave Bentley a high five, but he had to lean over to do it.

Judge Barron looked up in surprise as a dozen elderly people crowded into his chambers. "Oh yes," he remembered. "The weird adoption case." Eventually his clerk managed to find enough chairs and everyone was seated and staring at him. He stared back at them over his glasses, which had slipped down his nose. "I'm older than they are," he thought, "but not by much." Now seventy-two years old, he had long ago reached and passed the age for mandatory retirement but had continued to work. No one had said a word about it. The court system was glad to have the popular Judge Barron in place to help with the workload.

"Which of you is Genevieve Rutherford?"

"I am, you honor."

He peered at her for a long moment. "And you wish to adopt these others?"

"Yes."

"All of them?"

"Yes."

"I see." He didn't. He read their names aloud. "Are you all present?" They were. "And do you wish to be adopted by Mrs. Rutherford?" They did. The judge shuffled some papers on his desk. He pushed his glasses back into place. "Uh, I see some problems. Some of you are married, right? I mean married to each other. Mr. and Mrs. Fletcher?"

"Yes, your honor," Will said. "We're married. To each other."

"And has it occurred to you that you will become brother and sister if Mrs. Rutherford adopts you?" Will looked uncomfortable. So did Sophia.

"No, sir, I didn't think about that. Actually, we haven't had a lot of time to think about it."

The judge looked at him sharply. "Is this something you are being forced into?"

"Not at all, Judge. In fact, we really like Genevieve. She's quite a lady."

The judge was puzzled. "You like her. Enough to become her son. What about your birth mother?"

"Oh, she's very old now. She's in a nursing home."

"So you're going to get a new one?"

"A new what, sir?"

"Mother."

"Oh, no. She'll always be my mother. I mean my mother will be. Genevieve will just be my adopted mother."

"And what about becoming a brother to your wife?" Will scratched his head.

"I already thought about that," Genevieve volunteered. "And it's not a problem."

"Why not?"

"It just isn't, that's all. Who is it going to hurt?"

Judge Barron thought about it and decided not to enumerate the complexities the situation might cause. "There's another problem. When adoptions involve mixed races, and in particular when African American chil...people are adopted by white people, a welfare worker or a minister must interview the child, uh, person and approve the adoption. I see three people among you who may reasonably be assumed to be African Americans."

"I'm only going to adopt two of them, your honor. The other one is Reverend Fulton. He's the minister."

The judge nodded to the young black man. "Reverend Fulton?"

"Yes sir."

"Have you interviewed the African-American couple to see if this adoption is advisable?"

"No, your honor, but I could do that right now."

The judge looked at Tina and Harvey and asked their names, and then said, "All right, Mr. Fulton, if you are a minister please interview them now."

"Okay, your honor." He rose and walked over to Tina and said, "Mrs. Boatman, do you want that lady over there to be your new mother?"

"Yes, I do."

"And are you in full control of your faculties?"

"I am."

"Thank you. Now, Mr. Boatman, do you want that woman to be your new mother?"

"Yes."

"And are you over the age of sixteen?"

Harvey laughed. "Considerably," he said.

"Sir?"

"Yes, I am."

"Thank you. Your honor, I have interviewed these folks and I find that they are suitable for being adopted by this white lady."

"Thank you." The judge made some notes, then said, "I see that all of you filled out and signed the forms provided by the court clerk. Good. But I just have to ask you, Genevieve. Why do you want to do this? I mean, if you're older than they are, it couldn't be by more than a few years. You want to be their *mother*?"

And she said, "That's the only way I could adopt them, dear. They won't let you adopt a brother or a sister or a parent. The only thing you can adopt is a child, and if you adopt a child you have to be their mother or father. Well, as you can see I am not their father. That's why I had to be their mother." The judge just stared at her and finally said, "Okay, I'm going to do it. You're all consenting adults, why not do it?' And he did.

Chapter Fifteen

[August, 1975]

So that took care of the single-family-dwelling problem, since now they *were* a single family, but they still
had the inspector to deal with. He had managed to
put a stop to every improvement of which the house
was in desperate need, including fixing the roof. The
mansion simply could not be made habitable unless
the inspector could be placated or gotten around. If
not, it seemed likely to Owen that he and Lenore, like
their own parents, could only look forward to a
coventional, lonely demise in an institution of some

kind, all because they had laughed at a pipsqueak bureaucrat from City Hall.

Owen and Lenore's parents were suffering from the usual, unhappy effects of extreme old age. Lenore's mother had Alzheimer's disease, and Owen's parents were unhappy in separate nursing homes, though a little less unhappy than when they had been in the *same* nursing home. Owen and Lenore constantly worried about them. Helpless to do much for their parents, they felt driven to see The Last Resort up and running, as if, by providing for their own final years, they might help their parents.

Goodness knows, they certainly wanted to spare Laura and Ricky from having to take care of them in their old age. Surprisingly, rather than applaud their parents' plans for independence in their old age, the two children, now in their thirties, were dead set against The Last Resort.

"I don't get it," Owen said. "Laura hates the whole idea. She won't even come by to look at the mansion."

"Ricky is just as opposed," Lenore said.

"Maybe they're in denial. They just can't stand to think about us getting old," Owen offered.

"You think so?" Lenore considered. "I think *we're* in denial."

"What do you mean?"

"In denial of what our children are like."

"Maybe we shouldn't go there, Lenore," Owen

suggested.

Lenore laughed. "See what I mean?"

"Okay, so what's really bothering them about The Last Resort?"

"The money. That's what they keep asking me about: How much we're spending on it, how we're going to get our money out of the investment in the end."

"*We're* not going to get our money out of it in the end. In the end, we'll die. They'll get our money out of it. *They'll* inherit it in the form of shares in the corporation."

"That's what I've told them, of course. But my guess is that they figure we'll become addled in our old age and give the money away or be cheated out of it."

"You mean…?"

"Yes, they're not afraid of losing us, they're afraid of losing our money."

"Hmmm," Owen said. "That has the ring of truth."

William Whistle announced by mail that he would be calling on the group that morning at the mansion. The thrust of his letter to the group had been, "Be there or beware." Now Owen and the others sat staring at the inspector. "It's funny," Owen thought, "how I never noticed all that hair in his ears." But then, the only time Owen had seen the inspector, the man had been pacing around the sunroom like

Napoleon.

Genevieve, who still treated the inspector like visiting royalty, had invited him into the living room. The room had blossomed since Zoë first paced off its dimensions. She, Lenore and Sophia had ripped out the mouse-colored wall-to-wall carpeting and had revealed a gleaming cherry-wood floor. Plaster walls that had been water-stained and yellowed with age now glimmered with fresh paint. The Victorian gloom had been dispelled and a new, bright spirit showed through. The inspector's presence damped that spirit, though, at least in Owen's eyes, even though JOY still remained over the mantel.

The inspector began, "Because of the historical nature and architectural importance of this house, and because it is in grave danger of being altered by this *family*," he sneered, "I have recommended to the board that the house be declared a historical landmark. That means that to alter even its exterior paint you must receive permission from my friends in the Department of Historical Landmarks." He let that sink in.

"Now, about your application to displace more than six cubic yards of earth for the purpose of digging a French drain around the perimeter of the house, we are taking that into consideration and will respond sometime within the next several months, more or less. In the meantime, inasmuch as you began the work without permission, you will be required to replace all the earth you have displaced."

He turned to Will, on whom he bestowed a smile.

"And now I would like to inspect the house to see what other mischief you have been up to." Owen noted that the inspector was allowing himself to gloat.

And so they took him around the house, or rather they followed as he went here and there at will and made notes on his notepad. Six or eight of the group gloomily tagged along.

That was how the inspector found her as he walked into the room, haloed like a Madonna and with her head tilted nobly toward the sky.

Finally they trooped up the attic stairs behind the inspector and landed in the attic, where Pamela had once decked Will with a broom, and there she was now, with a wire brush no bigger than a toothbrush, exorcising from a wall some particle of pigeon dropping that only she could see. Beams of sunlight played on her from a skylight and they lit her long straight hair and narrow shoulders. That was how the inspector found her as he walked into the room, lighted up like a goddess and with her head held nobly.

Pamela ignored them all, of course, caught up as she was in her vendetta against the pigeons. But William Whistle stopped in his tracks and stared at her. He found he was having trouble breathing and didn't consider it might be the steep stairs or traces of pigeon droppings still in the air. He believed that the heavenly figure before him was the cause—not that she had an actual *figure*. No, it was her aura of angelic beauty that took his breath.

Finally Pamela turned and gazed at the stranger. Behind him, the others stood still as tin soldiers and regarded what was happening.

As if he were approaching a revered priestess, William Whistle respectfully inched forward. Pamela allowed the inspector to approach. Finally she looked at him closely and then led him to a window that looked out over the garden.

"Do you see how the garden paths meander? There's simply no substitute," she said obscurely.

But yes, he saw! He saw a glorious landscape below—meandering paths lit by a glorious day.

The others turned and tiptoed down the stairs.

Sophia said to Lenore, "Send someone down to the pool with an ice bucket and a bottle of Champagne and two glasses. Quick!"

"Brie!" Lenore nearly shouted. "We need brie and French bread. And flowers. Bentley! Gather a bouquet. Cut enough for three bouquets. Genevieve, do you have vases? How about a white tablecloth?"

Down in the kitchen now, the women scurried. When Bentley came back from the garden with an armful of summer flowers, the women whipped up three splendid bouquets. Lenore sent Bentley down to the pool with a picnic basket and one of the bouquets in a vase. He spread a tablecloth on a deck table and, with the exquisite sensitivity of an artist, arranged a bottle of Champagne in an ice bucket along with two Champagne glasses, bread and cheese, napkins and the lavish bouquet. When he dashed back to the kitchen, Lenore asked him to get all the men out of the house before one of them said the wrong thing and ruined everything.

Meanwhile, the women positioned the other two floral arrangements at points in the house where they would make the most romantic impression, and now all they could do was wait. Fifteen minutes later, Pamela and Inspector Whistle were still in the attic. Lenore thought that was a good sign. Another ten minutes went by while Lenore, Sophia, and now Bentley watched the clock. The men waited nervously in Owen's car, wishing they hadn't given up smoking cigarettes. Five minutes later, Bentley and the women heard stirring upstairs and then the sound of people descending the staircase. Bentley fled to the front yard, the ladies to the kitchen.

Just as Pamela and William Whistle finally made their way to the grand hallway, walking arm-in-arm, Lenore wondered out of the kitchen. She was drying her hands on a dishtowel and pretended to be surprised to see them.

"Oh Pamela, there you are!" she said.

Pamela and the inspector seemed to be walking under water, oblivious of their surroundings. Pamela looked up dreamily and the inspector gave Lenore a distracted smile.

"Pamela, darling," Lenore said, "would you do me the biggest favor? I have to finish this," and she pointed vaguely at the kitchen, "and I won't have time to show Inspector Whistle the pool. I know that you would like to inspect the pool, Inspector."

The inspector started to raise his hand as if in protest, but Lenore interrupted. "No, no, Inspector, I understand perfectly. It's just part of your job. Pamela, would you mind terribly taking the inspector to the pool so he can look it over?" Pamela and the inspector seemed more interested in the splendid bouquet of summer flowers that graced the entryway than in what Lenore was saying. So Lenore herded them toward the back door where another wonderful bouquet was standing on the floor in a very tall, green, glass vase, and then out the door.

Once the two were launched in the direction of the pool, Lenore, Sophia, and Bentley ran to a window through which they could see Pamela and Inspector Whistle wend their way along the garden paths toward the pool. When they lost sight of the pair, they flew up two flights of stairs to the attic. From a window they saw the couple arrive at the pool, where the inspector appeared to give it a cursory glance then resumed gazing at Pamela. She turned away demurely and discovered the table that had been so beautifully provisioned and decorated with sweet-smelling gardenias. After admiring the flowers and exploring the food and drink, Pamela sliced off a small piece of French bread, spread Brie upon it and held it to the inspector's mouth for him to nibble. He took her hand so as to steady the morsel she offered, and after he had eaten the cheese and bread, he continued to hold Pamela's hand.

Soon they settled at the table, and the inspector opened the Champagne and poured it into glasses for Pamela and for himself. Lifting his glass in her direction, he toasted her in a speech that went on for some time. Finally they clinked glasses and drank. Now Inspector Whistle sliced off a piece of bread, spread it with creamy Brie and popped it into Pamela's waiting mouth.

"We forgot apples," Lenore whispered from her vantage point.

But that didn't seem to bother Pamela or the inspector. They slowly worked their way through all the food and wine, and at the end of the picnic, William Whistle pulled a gardenia from its vase and spent some time exploring the front of Pamela's pullover sweater and her blazer, presumably looking for a place to mount the flower. At this point, the inspector's head interfered with Lenore's view of what happened, but when Pamela and the inspector stood up a moment later, Pamela was gripping the gardenia in her teeth by its stem.

Slowly the couple began to make their way back toward the mansion, and their gallery flew down the stairs to the kitchen. About the time Lenore and the others recovered their breath, Pamela led the inspector back inside.

Lenore soon chanced upon them and said, "Oh, good! Did you have an opportunity to look at the pool, Inspector?"

"Yes, yes," he said, "Everything's fine." Pamela was holding the flower in one hand now. She and the inspector made their way toward the front door.

Just before he left, Lenore called after him, "You'll have word for us?" He looked back at her blankly. "About your inspection today?" she added.

"Oh yes, of course," he said. "But I don't see any problems."

"Why that's lovely to hear, Inspector Whistle," Lenore said.

Looking back at her one more time, the inspector said, "Oh, just call me Bill," and he left, as Pamela looked after him dreamily.

Chapter Sixteen

[August, 1975]

When Harvey closed his eyes at night or even during daylight hours, an image often appeared in his mind that made him uneasy—an image of a furnace as big as a garbage truck, its gas-fed firebox the size of a VW. A Rube Goldbergesque arrangement of pipes and gauges added staggering complexity to the picture. In fact, this was a fairly accurate image of the actual furnace that the group was counting on to heat the house. He had viewed it only once, but it had left him with an enduring sense of danger. Of course it was idle now, but the cold, foggy summer mornings of the San Francisco Bay Area reminded him that sooner or later the household would have to crank it up, or at least try to.

Just as people are sometimes attracted to whatever they most fear—like great heights, for instance—Harvey had appointed himself the task of dealing with the furnace, going on record that he would take responsibility for getting it to work. Of course he assumed that he could phone up someone who would come out with a monkey wrench and charge the group $300 to get the pilot light going or whatever it needed. The truth is that Harvey hated to get his hands dirty, and if plumbing was involved in this job, it was bound to compromise his manicured nails. But after he phoned every heating and cooling specialist in the book, he was astonished to find that no one would have anything to do with an antediluvian steam-heat furnace. In fact several said that they had been asked many times over the years to work on that particular furnace and had wisely refused.

"Why won't you work on it?" Harvey asked a guy named Frank on the phone.

"Are you kidding? Jesus Christ, man, I'm not looking for trouble!"

"What do you mean?"

"Look, man," Frank had said, "do I look like the kind of person who wants that kind of liability if the damn thing blows up?"

"I can't see you," Harvey said, "but I guess you're

not. Uh, what am I going to do?"

"Replace it with a modern unit."

"How much would that cost?"

"How big is the house?"

"27,000 square feet."

"Get outta town!"

"Hey, I'm not kidding." Harvey took a huge shot of pleasure in having impressed Frank.

When the furnace guy had quit whistling in disbelief, he calculated and came up with $87,430. "That doesn't include installation," he said.

Harvey was stunned.

"Either that," Frank said, "or you can work on it yourself."

For several weeks Harvey wandered how to pass the burden on to someone else—like Will, for instance. But Harvey had a sense of fairness. He was aware that Will got stuck with the rottenest jobs because he volunteered for them. This was one job that Will wouldn't have to volunteer for. Harvey would do it himself. Besides, these days Will was back at work with a backhoe, digging a French drain around the house.

About a week after Inspector Whistle and Pamela fell in love at first sight, the group had received a letter from the Piedmont Department of Historical Landmarks, saying that the department was sorry but, after careful consideration, the department had chosen not to declare the house at 1 Upper Terrace an historical monument. Of course that was marvelous news. The group was spared untold grief and expense. Soon after that, Inspector Whistle approved the group's application to perform a wide range of improvements to the mansion. Furthermore, the inspector found that it would be unnecessary for the home's owners to fill in the ditch they had dug prior to obtaining a proper permit. Suddenly they were free to move ahead. Meanwhile, Pamela walked around blushing like a teenage girl.

Harvey had asked Genevieve about the furnace, and her response wasn't reassuring. She got a worried look when he brought up the subject, and finally she admitted that she hadn't used it for "quite some time, dear." How long? After being prodded, she suggested that it must have been close to ten years since she had decided to dress very heavily in the winter and not to rely on "fossil fuels" to heat the house.

Finally the time came when Harvey knew he had to confront the monster in the basement. He decided to survey the basement first and sidle up to the furnace-job gradually. Tina said she would explore the basement with him but would have nothing to do with the furnace. All the others were hard at work upstairs—all, that is, except Pamela, who was spending the afternoon at the movies with Inspector Whistle. On their first walk through the basement they passed right by the door behind which they knew the furnace loomed, but they continued walking till they found the main attraction of the bottom floor, the ballroom.

With its hardwood floors and twelve-foot ceilings, he could easily imagine it as a basketball court. At the same time he knew chances were slim that a basketball would ever bounce on this floor. He guessed that, for Tina and the other women, the room simply was a ballroom and that they intended to keep it a ballroom. Oh well, his zest for basketball had diminished somewhat in recent years as he had found his knees less reliable and his breath slower to recover after an exciting drive to the basket.

A full-sized stage stood at one end of the ballroom. Ratty old stage curtains were pulled back on both sides of the stage. Wondering whether the curtains were velvet, Harvey reached out to feel but then stopped. Decades of dust had settled into them and he could just imagine what they would do to his hands. PA speakers stood on either end of the stage. They were so old that he guessed they might have some collector value if anyone collected vintage public address speakers.

It had been four decades since he had owned a guitar, but Harvey pictured himself playing one on this stage and amazing his friends, and he could imagine blues bands playing while he and Tina and the others danced all night. He thought it likely that Tina was imagining fashion shows and maybe informative talks by authors and educators. He liked the idea of a fashion show. He could easily visualize Tina parading her long legs in a short, tight skirt. He visualized this so clearly that he took Tina's arm and tried to spin her into a close-dance position. He didn't get anywhere, though. She was clearly engrossed in imagining museum docents or antiques appraisers addressing interested ladies from the stage, and she easily shrugged him off.

Along the wall opposite the stage there was a full-sized bar and on it were a dusty bottle of Canadian Club whiskey and a dusty, open bottle of sherry. Harvey could see some wonderful possibilities though. If somebody would just get all the dust out of here, what a great place it would be in which to entertain!

Harvey could imagine playing his guitar on this stage and amazing his friends, who had no idea he could play.

"It seems like a pity to wait until we're all falling apart before we move in," he said. "The ballroom won't do much good for anyone when we're all lying around with IVs in our arms. We'll be missing some good times by not living here during these next ten or fifteen years."

"I don't know why we can't entertain here in the meantime," Tina said. "After you get the furnace working."

Harvey frowned. He took her hint but wasn't ready to think about the furnace. He was still easing up to the job.

There were a number of rooms off the ballroom whose functions were not clear. One of them was quite rough and even had a dirt floor. It felt more like a cave than a room in a house. "A wine cellar?" Harvey conjectured.

"Maybe," Tina said, "but there's no way to close it off. You'd think there would be a wine cellar down here, but I just don't think this is it."

There was an old table in the room that might have been a butcher's block. "Did they butcher chickens down here?" he speculated.

"Hmmm," Tina said. "Maybe whole beeves." She shuddered.

"And they let the blood drip onto the dirt floors," Harvey added.

"That's enough, Harvey."

Another room whose function was not apparent opened to the back yard and had windows that were covered with heavy, small-mesh wire screen. After trading ideas about it, they agreed that the room had been for cool storage of food, maybe vegetables.

Because of the hardware cloth, the windows could be left open without animals entering.

After the two had surveyed the entire basement except for the furnace room, Tina said, "It's funny. There's something here that doesn't make sense. Or something *not* here. I feel like there's a room missing or something." But after they made another turn through the bottom floor, she said, "I guess not."

Harvey began to feel like he had done as much sidling up to the job as he could and that they had better check out the monster furnace.

"Not me," Tina said, and she made a little dash for the staircase and left Harvey to face the furnace by himself.

As Harvey opened the door, he felt as if he were bursting in unannounced on a sleeping dragon. He felt no better when he stopped in the doorway and gazed at the furnace. It looked full of potential for harm. Well, if he had to wake the dragon, where would he start? By touching it, he guessed, so Harvey approached and gently patted its nearest pipe. A poof of dust rose like a mushroom cloud, and suddenly he was gripped with the certainty that the pipe was wrapped with asbestos. Instantly he stopped breathing and examined his smudged hand. "I should have worn gloves," he thought. Soon he was breathing again because he had no choice, though for a few moments he held his clean hand to his mouth and nostrils and took shallow breaths. Harvey owned many pairs of gloves, but now, for the first time, he wished he owned a pair of work gloves.

The ice now broken, he cautiously ducked under pipes and walked to the firebox, where he peered through a dirty glass hatch into a sea of gas burners. "Well," he thought, "the first trick will be to figure out how the thing works."

He reasoned like this: "The basic function of this furnace is to heat water until it becomes steam. The steam then travels in pipes throughout the house to radiators that are heated by the steam. Then the steam, probably largely water by now, returns to the furnace where it is heated again. Simple. So…" He looked here and there, traced pipes to their sources, and said aloud, "So this goes to that….It comes out here…This is a safety feature." He was examining the largest gauge of all. In old-fashioned lettering, it read "Pressure." A needle pointed to zero, but numbers ran all the way up to 100. Above 50, the numbers were in bright red, and under the red portion the word "Danger" was printed, also in red. "So the danger is that the pressure will get too high," he reasoned. "And blow up the furnace. And me. And the entire house." Danger had sharpened his reasoning-power.

Harvey identified the part of the furnace directly above the burners as the boiler. A warning was printed on it: "Fill to line with water before activating burners." That made sense. He located a faucet handle that seemed designed to allow water into the boil-

er. "So…this handle…rusted…turn a little harder…"
Rusty water, visible through a narrow glass window,
began to trickle into the boiler as he opened the old
valve. Nothing leaked and he increased the flow.
Finally the water was up to the line and he closed the
valve. Now to heat the water. Did he really want to do
this? Harvey noticed that his hands not only were
dirty, they were also trembling. He wondered what
Will was doing.

It looked to Harvey as if the pilot light was about
the same as on a modern hot water heater. "Red button," he said, "…push…that thing way in
there…match." Sweat ran down his nose. Pfff! The
pilot light lit! Frantically, Harvey sniffed for gas
fumes. "Man, if there's a gas leak, this thing will blow
me to smithereens." He couldn't smell anything,
though. When in two or three minutes he hadn't been
vaporized, he began to think about lighting the burners. He saw what he thought was the right gas valve.
Holding his breath, he cracked the valve a tiny bit,
then a bit more, then a little more. The pilot light
seemed drawn in the direction of the nearest burner
but the burner didn't light. He opened the valve a little more, then *whumpf!* Harvey sprang backwards,
smashing his head against a pipe. He saw sparklers,
like on the Fourth of July, but was conscious of the
odor of gas and dust. Harvey's head was roaring from
the blow, yet he had not gone down, and he wondered if the roar was from something else. His vision
cleared and he saw that the burners were lit, bank

after bank of them! The roar was from them! He staggered forward clutching the back of his head and stared at the gauge, still at zero. Oh, man, he was committed now. He could feel the warmth of the burners on his cheeks.

"What now?" Harvey wondered. "What you do *after* you wake the dragon?"

He wanted to go upstairs to see whether the radiators were heating or leaking or whatever, but he was afraid to leave the furnace. What if the pressure, which was beginning to rise now, suddenly spiked? So he was trapped: afraid to leave, afraid to stay.

Ten minutes later the pressure had stabilized just below the red numbers, and he decided to risk leaving the dragon's side to check out the radiators upstairs. He closed the door to the furnace room as he left, hoping that might slow down a conflagration in case of an explosion. Listening all the while for signs of trouble downstairs, he was climbing toward the first floor when, overhead, somewhere far in the distance, he heard a sharp bang. It definitely hadn't come from the furnace room. A few steps further up the stairs he heard another bang, a big one and much closer. By the time he stepped out onto the first floor, all hell had broken loose. It sounded as though in every corner of the house heavy artillery were firing, or perhaps landing. The sound was mixed with women's screams and men's cursing. The front door had been flung open and it appeared that some had already fled the house. Others were flying down the stairs from the upper floors. Bang! Bang, bang, bang! Harvey stood stock still, turned to stone by his certainty that whatever was happening was his fault. Someone whizzed past him from the kitchen and escaped through the front door, waking him to his need to get the hell out of the house, and he made a dash for the door just as an amazing fusillade of sound struck like thunder right by where he had been standing.

Once out the door and on the landing, he saw his wife and friends standing in a half-circle, keeping a safe distance from the house, peering around him through the open door to see what they could see. They were pale. Couples held hands. An especially loud bang got Harvey off the porch and beside his wife where he, in turn, faced the house and gazed through the door to see what was happening. He stood with Tina, Lenore, Owen, Tuck, Bentley, Zoë, Tony, Weezie, Sophia and Will, who still had his hard hat on, having just leaped from his backhoe. It was as if they were watching a great ship go down. Only Pamela—out on a date with the inspector—and Genevieve were missing, and now Genevieve walked calmly through the door and faced the survivors. To Harvey, she said, "Looks like you got the furnace on, dear."

How could she be so calm, Harvey wondered.

"Now I remember why we quit using it. The radiators bang. But don't worry, dear," she said to Harvey, feeling sorry for him, "the sound nearly stops after the first half hour. Still, dear, do you know how to turn it off? It's quite expensive to operate and it's not even winter yet."

Harvey wondered how he could avoid returning to the basement to shut it down. He stared at his filthy hands and thought there was no point in washing them yet.

Tina said with a gasp, "Harvey! Did you bleed on your sweater?" She examined it from behind. "That's the second time in the last two months!"

But as Harvey was on his way back downstairs, Will said to him, "Good job getting it fired up, Harv. That thing scares the crap out of me."

"Hey, Will," Harvey replied. "No problem. Let me know if you need help on that backhoe, okay?"

Chapter Seventeen

[August, 1975]

"Watching television is bad for my health," Weezie said. She wore a simple, blue blouse, a darker blue skirt and no makeup. "I told Tuck I'm not going to do it any more." Weezie, Sophia, Lenore and Genevieve were enjoying coffee and cookies and each other's company in a pleasant little breakfast nook off the kitchen.

"Television doesn't do much for me, either," Lenore said, "but I don't remember it having actually harmed my health."

"That's because you're less suggestible than I am," Weezie said. "Also, you must not have been watching the network news programs. That's where I catch all my diseases."

"Gas?" Lenore asked. "Hot flashes?"

"You *have* been watching the news!" Weezie said.

"Arthritis?" Genevieve contributed.

"Headache, dry eyes, milk intolerance?" Sophia asked.

"Bladder urgency. Depression. Itching hemorrhoids. Pain. Persistent acid reflux. I've caught them all," Weezie said. Sophia smiled. She was happy that Weezie had finally begun to loosen up around the group. Gradually she had overcome her shyness. Weezie was a nutritionist who had worked in schools over the years and had finally "run out of steam," she said, and had retired. Several of the women in the group had noticed that Weezie didn't seem to have recaptured her "steam." She often seemed tired. Was it from having to keep up with Tuck's changing moods?

"Well," Lenore said, "it's pretty clear that the only people who watch the news are geriatric cases like us. The advertising people know what they're doing." The four friends did things with their spoons and nibbled on small cookies.

"You know, sometimes I wonder how long I'm going to be able to climb the stairs," Weezie said. She was worried. "If they wheel us into this lovely house when we're eighty or something, just how are we going to get upstairs?"

"I've been wondering the same thing," Sophia said. "Even in my present sprightly youth I huff and puff on those stairs."

"Well," Genevieve said, "I can't imagine why you all don't just move in right now. Why wait? You know, it's quite lovely living here, especially now with all this bustle."

"Genevieve, it's the most beautiful house I've ever seen!" Sophia said. "It's just that we've been thinking of it as a place for our old age."

Just then a good-looking young Latino man ambled into the breakfast room wearing a tee shirt despite a chill in the foggy summer air. The shirt was short-sleeved, of course, but the fellow had rolled up what sleeves it had so that his broad shoulders were impossible to overlook. He smiled at the four ladies and said hi to Genevieve.

"Oh, hello, dear. You're not leaving so soon, I hope?"

He grinned. "I have to get back to San Francisco."

"Well, if you must, dear. But let me introduce you to my friends. Lenore, Weezie, Sophia, this is Juan." After everyone said pleasant things, Genevieve walked outside with Juan.

"Wow," said Sophia. "Who was that?"

"I don't know," Lenore said. "They have something to do with a dance class Genevieve takes in the City."

"They?"

"I've seen several guys here like him."

"Hmm. Maybe we *should* move in now. A dance class?" Sophia asked.

"Spanish dance, I think she said," Lenore added. "Whatever that means. Flamenco?"

"Somehow I don't have a picture of Genevieve dancing flamenco with a rose in her mouth, although I can picture her dancing. She's certainly trim and fit. Almost as thin as Zoë."

"Maybe they don't *all* put roses in their mouths," Weezie suggested. "Maybe that's just northern flamenco or something."

The doorbell rang, or, rather, boomed. Lenore thought something that made a sound so much like Big Ben must be sizeable, but she had never figured out where the door-chimes were. When she pulled open the massive front door, a young man wearing a baseball cap backwards stood waiting, but a little dog with him didn't wait at all. It burst through the open door and dashed everywhere, spinning, cavorting and gamboling, and it nearly turned summersaults, giddy with happiness. "Look out!" Lenore warned, back-peddling like a tennis-player half her age, and then she stopped and laughed to see such energy and joy.

The alarmed young man said, "I'm sorry ma'am, maybe I shouldn't have let him in."

"No," she laughed, "it's all right." The dog still hadn't slowed down.

The young man with the backwards baseball cap

said, "I'm Jason, ma'am, from Monarch Laundry, here to collect the drapes for cleaning."

"Oh, yes," Lenore said, "Come in, Jason, I'll show you where they are."

"I'll be right back, ma'am. I've got to get my ladder first." The dog stayed inside, though, and Lenore, followed by the little dog, went back to the breakfast room to show off her new friend.

Genevieve had returned to the room and was sitting at the table with Sophia and Weezie. "Olé," cried Genevieve when the dog raced around the corner just behind Lenore.

"Olé?" Lenore wondered.

"Oh, he's darling!" Sophia said.

"I guess you'd have to love dogs to think so," Lenore said laoughing. "That may be the homeliest dog I've ever seen." Actually, Lenore was being polite. The dog looked like a rag mop, a dirty one, dancing and trying to be several places at once. When the doorbell rang again, the whole party went to greet the boy from Monarch. The dog was ecstatic to be reunited with him.

Lenore led Jason to a set of drapes mounted in the dining room while the dog raced along, and after that she led the boy and the dog to the drapes all around the house. The women followed along, fascinated by the little whirling-dervish dog.

The dog slowed down the boy's work, though. Every time he would take down a drape, the dog would play tug-of-war with it, growling fiercely. The game did make one a little concerned for the draperies. Jason was beginning to act flustered. He looked earnestly at Lenore and said, "Ma'am, I'm afraid he's going to tear the drapes."

"That may be the homeliest dog I've ever seen." Actually, Lenore was being polite.

"Well, don't let him," Lenore said sternly. She was getting a little worried, too. The boy didn't seem to have any control at all over his dog, and the homely little rag mop hadn't let up one bit.

Even mild-mannered Weezie spoke a little sternly. "Son, don't you think you'd better keep him from tearing the drapes like that?"

The young fellow was really red in the face now. He shot Weezie a hurt look, but he didn't do anything to stop the dog.

Just then, Pamela walked through the big front

door, and the little dog streaked toward her as if she were his long-lost mom. She stopped dead and a look of horror spread over her face. The spinning dog circled her like a dust devil, but still she did not move a muscle. As Lenore moved to help her, she thought Pamela must have been taught as a child to freeze if she were ever attacked by a dog. Since the human seemed unwilling to play, the dog began barking at her like a mad thing. Still Pamela didn't move and the dog returned to the latest curtain to come off a window and resumed playing tear-the-drape.

By now, Jason and Lenore were glaring at each other, and everything had come to a standstill except the dog, which was as excited as ever.

"*Sir!*" Lenore finally shouted at the boy.

Simultaneously he shouted "*Ma'am!*" at Lenore.

At one and the same time, they yelled at each other, "*Would you please control your dog!*"

At that, even the dog stopped, and he looked back and forth, back and forth—from Jason to Lenore and back—a little rag mop with a pink tongue.

Lenore said, "But I thought…"

Jason said, "You mean he's not…yours?"

They named the dog Buddy. After failing to find Buddy's owner, the group at 1 Upper Terrace (except for Pamela) came to agree with Buddy that he belonged in the house, and Genevieve adopted *him*, too, though not officially.

"If *we* must have a dog," Pamela said, "then I insist that we have a cat, as well. I've always found them cleaner." At the animal shelter, they discovered the perfect cat—a juvenile, fawn-colored Siamese. Pamela was outvoted on the name, though. Pamela favored 'Susan,' after Susan Sontag, but in the end they named the blue-eyed cat 'Ninja' for her aggressive ways with Buddy.

That Tuesday night The Purple Tongue held its first meeting since the fateful Burgundy tasting in the spring. The friends were finally free to move on with improvements to The Last Resort and to live together in the big house if and when they pleased. A wine tasting seemed like the right way to celebrate.

Fittingly, this was also the first tasting in the new house. The friends gathered in the dining room. Another first: The core members of The Purple Tongue invited their spouses and Genevieve to attend. Everyone was present except Sophia who was stuck having to work in Seattle and Pamela who had hardly been seen at all since she had paired off with the inspector.

The charter members introduced the others to the group's rituals. First, before the tasting began, everyone had to fork over money to the person who had chosen and had bought the wines that night (Zoë) before they got too jolly and forgot to pay. Then, when it was time to start pouring the wine, the bagged and numbered bottles went around the table clock wise and never the other way. Then each person sipped and swallowed the wines and gave them points for aroma, color, body, balance, flavor, finish and general quality, and finally scored and ranked them.

They tasted eight 1972 California chardonnays.

During the first half-hour, the tasters quietly swirled and then sniffed at their eight glasses of wine. One by one they held them up to the light for a careful look. They sipped and gurgled, sipped and gurgled, stared off into space while gathering adjectives to describe the flavors they believed they detected. On their scoring sheets they wrote words such as toast, butter, melon, weeds, acid, fruit, tropical fruit and vanilla. Those with runaway imaginations detected hints of marshmallow, a suggestion of poached egg, Eagle Brand Milk, and white chocolate, and Tony wrote down "spumoni ice cream" to describe one chardonnay. To refresh their pallets they ate small slices of bread from long, skinny baguettes and then went back to swirling, sniffing and sipping. Finally, uncomfortable with the long silence, Will blurted, "I don't like wine number..." but everyone shushed him, rather rudely, he thought: "Hush!" "Don't prejudice us!" they shouted, then went back to their silent research. Ten minutes later, just as Will was beginning to sort it all out and he had actually identified his favorite wine and his least favorite wine and all he had to do now was to rank the middle six wines, Bentley announced that he had discovered a new Japanese restaurant in Alameda that was "fabulous." Suddenly everyone was talking at once and even shouting to be heard. "What's it called?" "I was there last week." "Be sure to try their sashimi!" "Has anyone tried the little Thai restaurant on Milvia at University?" Will was astonished. How did they all know when it was okay to start talking and laughing? Lenore and Zoë shouted across the table to each other and arranged to buy and split a case of olive oil. Tony was trying to tell people about the last time he had been in Napa Valley. Will was very confused. For one thing he felt a little fuddled. He was surprised to realize that he had drunk all the wine he had poured. In fact they all had, he noticed. His friends had big grins on their faces. Tuck told a joke that he shouldn't have told in mixed company. Bentley laughed way too loud. So Will found it really confusing to rank wines two through seven. In the end he gave up and just ranked the wines on whimsy. "Okay, let's give this one second place. I seem to remember liking it." It was really hard to think when everyone was shouting and laughing so loudly and kidding each other. Something Tina said tickled him, though, and he broke out laughing.

But when it came time to announce their decisions, each taster put on a serious face and made a strong case for his or her decisions. "Wine A," Zoë announced about Will's favorite wine, "is over-oaked and almost undrinkable. It has a weedy, stinky nose. I detect that it was stored badly and may even be corked. I ranked this wine last, number eight." Will considered changing his first-place wine to last place before it was his turn to hold forth about wine A.

Tina said from across the table, grinning wickedly, "No, no, Zoë: We're talking about the first wine, wine *A*."

"I know what wine we're talking about, girl. I suppose you *liked* it."

"In fact I thought this wine," she started, but everyone broke in: "Not your turn Tina! We're moving clockwise!"

And that's how it went: organized chaos, good-natured squabbling, red faces, purple tongues, loud laughing, good advice, ritualized disorder. After he got the hang of it, Will was at ease. The only thing that surprised him was that, after his first twinge of insecurity, he found himself *insisting* on the correctness of his rankings. Though they had seemed completely arbitrary just moments before, as soon as he wrote them down he was prepared to argue passionately that he had ranked them exactly right. And that's what he did.

Genevieve hated to say a single bad thing about any of the wines and was distressed that she had to give one of them last place. Tony took a kind of anti-intellectual stance and refused to talk wine lingo, instead saying things like "This one tasted nice and refreshing. It smelled good, too." Zoë, a born noticer, was the only one who noted that one of the bottles was a half-inch taller than the others. The academicians, Lenore and Owen, announced their findings about the wines with the confidence of people accustomed to lecturing. Tuck was able to draw upon his keen sense of smell to identify many of the wines. Will had no idea that he, himself, was describing the wines as if they were music. One of them could have been a piano piece by Scarlatti. "Wine C," he said when it was his turn to talk about it, "opened with bright, clear tones. It soared and took on complexity through the middle section and then gradually faded to a lingering close."

The winner, at $7.50, was the Spring Mountain chardonnay.*

After the tasting, they left the dining room and found chairs in the living room. They were eager to share their garden discoveries with each other. "Did anyone else come across the old Joseph's Coat rose down in back of the tennis court?" Tony asked, excited. "It's a beauty! Still has a few flowers on it. Pretty thorny, though."

Will had a nice feeling. He wished Sophia could have been here. Everyone was having such a good time. He smiled at the big gold letters mounted over the fireplace mantel. JOY, they spelled. He liked that: JOY.

---

* See appendix for details of the tasting. [Ed.]

Chapter Eighteen

[September, 1975]

"You there! Be careful where you throw that!" Tuck lumbered around the perimeter of the house as fast as he could move, shouting at the brutes on the roof who were intent on destroying the garden. Commissioned to repair the roof, the vandals were hurling broken pieces of roof-slate into shrubs planted before their grandmothers had been conceived. "Stop that—stop that, you damned villain," Tuck thundered. Dust rose all around the house, generated by the broken chunks of slate as they hit the garden loam and by Tuck, who trotted around and around the house like a buffalo. The brutes on the roof seemed unable to understand him or even his body language, which would have been pretty clear to most onlookers. Accustomed to excitable homeowners, the roofers placidly continued to aim the broken slate at tender new growth in the garden.

From time to time Tuck stumbled over mounds of earth that Will had done his best to level when he had backfilled his ditch. At least the ditch was completed. With the French drain in place and the roof coming along, and with the sunroom made waterproof where the wisteria still entered the house, and with the attic wall repaired where the pigeons still occasionally tried to enter, the house promised to keep water at bay. Everyone was unnerved, though, when, from time to time, they would hear a sound at a window, particularly on the upper floors, and see pigeons gazing forlornly into their former home. Tuck always wondered whether one of them was the mate of the pigeon he had squished on the attic floor.

But things were coming along. Harvey had managed to phone an old-timer who actually knew something about steam furnaces. "I know enough not to work on 'em anymore," Slim said. "Of course I don't work on *anything* anymore. But you can ask me questions." If he had been born fifty years later, Slim would have called himself a consultant and charged $300 an hour plus expenses, but, as it was, he said he would come over and take a look for $10 if Harvey would pick him up and take him home afterwards. "I don't drive anymore, either," Slim said.

Slim was old as a mummy and gnarly as a tree trunk, but he was unafraid of the furnace. He just swore at it. "The son-of-a-bitch," he said, looking it in the eye. "It was the best ever made, but it'll eat you alive."

"It will?" Harvey asked, sorry to hear it.

Slim spat something dark onto the floor. "You're gonna have some pretty fancy gas bills, bub."

"Oh, that." Harvey said, relieved. "Yeah I guess we expect it. Shall I get the furnace going and let you hear how it sounds?"

"Hell, no," Slim said. "I've heard goddamned pipes bang before. Where do you hear the banging?"

"Well, everywhere, I guess."

"That figures. The goddamned house has settled. Tilting uphill now, or downhill, one. Either you're going to have to tilt the house the other way or level the pipes."

"Uh, what do you mean?" Harvey asked, feeling dumb.

"Tilt the house!" Slim raised his crackly old voice. "How big is this son-of-a-bitch?"

"Twenty-seven-thousand square feet."

"Piece of shit," Slim said, but his meaning was unclear. For once Harvey wasn't gloating about how big the house was. He was almost embarrassed. "You can't tilt this house. It's too big. So you'll have to level the pipes, bub."

"Okay," Harvey said, "but maybe you could flesh that out for me a little." Slim stared at Harvey as if Harvey had just proposed sex. "I mean, maybe you could tell me exactly what I have to do."

"Sure," Slim said. "Gotta earn my $10. See, the water's supposed to circulate all around the house and then flow back to the boiler. So when it's flowing back to the boiler the pipes all have to be going downhill. Follow me, son?"

"Gotcha," Harvey said. He hadn't been called son in a while.

"Now if the pipes aren't going downhill, water gets trapped in them. When the pipes heat up, the trapped water explodes. *Bang!*" Harvey jumped back. "Calm down, bub. So you have to get yourself a level and keep all the pipes that are returning to the furnace going downhill. Got that?"

"Yes, I do."

"Then I earned my ten bucks."

A week later, Harvey was well along with the job, having learned how to use a pipe wrench and having finally given up trying to keep his hands clean.

Zoë had progressed with her surveying as well. But she was puzzled. Her measurements in the grand hallway at the main entryway weren't adding up. She tried to tell Tony about it. "I don't understand," he said. So she tried to show him. They took some measurements together, and finally Tony had to agree that about eight feet of the house was missing. In fact, a space of about eight by eight feet was unaccounted for: 64 square feet. Tony and Zoë began thumping on the walnut-paneled wall. They thought it sounded hollow behind the mystery space.

Tony found Genevieve, who said she knew of no secret room that had been sealed up or anything of the kind. She doubted there was such a thing.

It seemed to Tony and Zoë and Genevieve that it would take a major commitment to break into the wall to find out what was back there, if anything. It would entail removing large sheets of old paneling, with no assurance that anything interesting was behind them. Zoë's curiosity was up, though. She and Tony and Genevieve agreed that the group should decide together what to do.

When finally the group was able to sit down together—on a Saturday, the first time most of them could spend time at the house—their favorite theory was that a body was stashed and sealed up in the wall.

"What if there really is a body in there?" Tuck asked. "Do we want the coroner over here investigating a murder? I can imagine the headlines: 'Body Buried in Wall of Piedmont Mansion. Mother and Twelve Adopted Children Deny Knowledge.' "

Each member of the group thumped on the walls and walked around measuring this and that and then came back to sit in the living room, wondering what to do about the missing 64 square feet. Buddy was curled up in Weezie's lap. Ninja was on the roomy fireplace mantel thinking about leaping from it onto Buddy.

The second most favored theory was that a walk-in safe was sealed up in the wall and that it was stuffed with money. Once advanced, that idea was impossible to ignore, for no one could say with absolute certainty that it wasn't so. No amount of reasoned argument could dispel the allure of possible free money, and the group voted to open the wall.

"Well, heck," Owen said, "I'll bet we could get that paneling off in fifteen minutes. We might not ever get it back up, but if we don't find out what's in there, I might not be able to sleep tonight." He stood. Buddy seemed to sense how this was shaping up—or maybe some animal instinct told him that Ninja was getting ready to pounce him—and he jumped off Weezie's lap onto the newly exposed hardwood floor and started whirling like a top, glad for some action.

Genevieve was less enthusiastic than Buddy. "Did you say that you might never get the paneling back up, Owen? Because that makes me nervous." She fingered her string of perfect black pearls as though they were worry beads.

Owen sat back down. "Genevieve, you've been the best sport in the world, letting us make a hundred changes in the house. You must be climbing the walls to see so much change in the house you've lived in since you were a girl. I was just kidding about not being able to put the paneling back up. What if I guarantee to get it back up some way or another if there isn't a pot of gold in there?"

"That's fine, Owen. And it's not that I'm a good

sport. All this change is exciting. We're doing all the things I didn't have enough money to do myself. It's wonderful!"

On his feet again and trailing a dog, a cat and a band of friends, Owen produced a crowbar and quickly found a gap between the wood paneling and the wall big enough to get a purchase with the bar. Of course, it didn't take fifteen minutes, it took an hour to pull back the paneling and various moldings as clouds of fine, old dust rose in the hallway. Everyone who wasn't doing the actual crowbar work was trying to get a glimpse behind the panel as it started to come away from the wall. Genevieve had found a flashlight and was trying to get a clear look at what was being uncovered.

When finally Owen and Will pulled the big old walnut panel aside, the mystery only deepened. Genevieve's flashlight played on a couple of pieces of plywood. As Owen studied the plywood, Ninja rubbed up against his legs, trying to get in the way. Buddy zipped around, and a total of thirteen adult humans peered at what surely was the last barrier to solving the mystery.

Owen and Will quickly pulled away the plywood. Behind it, a door was revealed, an old door made of ornamental wrought iron. Through it nothing was visible but darkness. Some of the women standing in back of the men believed they were missing something and complained that they couldn't see. "What is it? What do you see? What's going on?" they demanded. But Owen and the others in front didn't know what was going on, even when Genevieve managed to cast a little light through the wrought-iron door. Nothing. A hole, a shaft.

"Genevieve, what's that right in the middle? Shine your light right there in the center," Owen requested. A thick old metal cable. Two cables.

"Step up here and take a look," Owen said to those in the rear who couldn't see, and he got out of their way. "But don't open the door. I think I know what it is." Since she was taller than most of the men, Lenore had been able to see over their heads, but she took a place up at the front now, along with Pamela, Sophia and Weezie. Genevieve handed Lenore her flashlight, which Lenore shined up and down the shaft.

Finally Weezie broke the silence. "My gosh, I hope it works. I was having the dickens of a time with these stairs. Folks, we have an elevator!"

There were excited shouts of "You're kidding!" and "An elevator?" Tuck made a good point. "Do we have an elevator or do we just have an elevator shaft?" The excitement did not noticeably diminish, though. Buddy was even more frenzied than usual. The first moment there was a little space in front of the door, he made a beeline for it from across the hall, aiming to go right between the iron bars of the door. Tuck caught sight of the tiny mop of a dog making straight for the elevator shaft but there wasn't a chance in the world that the huge man could intercede in time. Several others caught sight of what was unfolding, but Buddy was as fast as a dart. Just as Buddy was about to hurl himself into oblivion, *Wham!* Suddenly he was flying head over heels sideways, at a right angle to his original trajectory, rolling and skidding, and Ninja was sitting by Buddy's side, looking bored. Whether she had purposely saved Buddy's life or had merely found a convenient time to nail him wasn't clear, but to Buddy it was. It was time to play with Ninja, and he leaped up and ran circles around her, barking, while Ninja licked her shoulder a time or two and ignored him.

After Tuck got a sheet of plywood back in front of the door to keep Buddy out, the group reasoned that the elevator must have made stops in the basement and on at least the second floor and maybe the attic. And perhaps that was where the elevator itself was right now, at one of the other stops.

"Harvey," Tina said, "remember the other day when we walked all around the basement floor? I had a funny feeling that something was missing. I'm not sure why exactly, but the way our footsteps echoed and then re-echoed made me wonder if the walls were hollow. Remember, Harvey?"

"I do," he said, "and I even remember where we were when you said it. Let's go down and see what we can find."

"I think I'll just wait here," Weezie sighed. "If I go downstairs, I'll just have to climb back up."

In the basement, the friends tried to figure out where the shaft should be, but they couldn't find it. While everyone else was walking around rapping on walls with their knuckles, looking like inmates in a mental hospital, Owen and Will trudged back up to the first floor and carefully mapped the location of the shaft by measuring its distance from several fixed points, including the outside wall of the house. Back in the basement, the two methodically measured from the same fixed points and arrived at a spot on the wall of the ballroom.

Everyone imagined that the wall sounded different there when thumped on, though moments before it had been passed over. Probing revealed that the wall in that spot was made of sheetrock rather than the lath and plaster used elsewhere in the house, and soon Owen and Will were smashing through it. From the start it was clear they were in the right place. In moments a door just like the one upstairs was revealed, and behind it was another door, this one the door to an elevator car, and there it was, a simple little cage of black iron. As soon as Will and Owen had cleared a big enough area, Owen tried both doors. They worked just fine.

"We'd better be careful," Will said. "Maybe this elevator is hanging from a string." Owen took a tentative step into the elevator, then committed both feet to it, then shifted his weight around to test things further, and finally jumped up and down like a tall chimp. Outside the elevator, his audience jockeyed for position to see what might happen. If the elevator was hanging from a string, it was a strong one.

"I imagine it's sitting on the ground," Owen said. "I don't think there's anywhere below this for it to fall."

"Yeah," Will said, "but an hour ago we didn't think the house had an elevator, either. So what do *we* know?" But he climbed into the car with Owen, leaving the door open so they could jump out at a moment's notice, and they looked around. "How about we don't try those buttons just now?" Will said. He pointed to a trio of buttons that read "up," "down," and "stop."

"Okay," Owen said, and immediately he pushed the button marked "up."

"Jesus Christ, Owen! I said *don't* push it!" Will shouted in a high-pitched voice. The elevator didn't budge, though.

"Oh, sorry Will," Owen said mildly, "I thought you said to push it."

"Well, it doesn't matter," Will said politely. "We didn't go anywhere." But he was shaken.

Soon the two left the little elevator car and made way for the others. Tuck nearly filled it. Genevieve, who had worked her way to the front of the crowd that was looking in, shined her flashlight here and there in the little car. Tuck began sniffing like a bloodhound. "I smell something," he said. "Something pretty good." Ever since Tuck had sniffed out some of the problems of the old mansion, getting down on his hands and knees to do it, he had good credibility with the group when it came to his sense of smell. "But I don't know whether it's brandy or cognac." He sniffed deeper. "Brandy, I think. Courvoisier." He had fixed his attention on one wall of the elevator. "Genevieve, what am I facing? What's down here in that direction?"

Tuck was sniffing like a bloodhound. "I smell something," he said. "Something pretty good."

"Goodness, I don't know. I guess that would be the wall behind the bar in the ballroom."

"Why don't you bring your flashlight in here? Can you get in?" Genevieve, a dancer , was quite trim, and she did manage to scrunch in with Tuck, though she had to keep her arms straight up over her head, as though she were being held up. "Can you shine your light right here?" Tuck asked.

"No, dear, I can't move."

"Do you mind if I take the flashlight?" Tuck asked.

"Not at all," she said, and that's what Tuck did. Following his nose, he focused the light on one of the iron sides of the elevator car, leaving Genevieve's hands in the air.

"What's this?" he said, and, after he fiddled with something on the iron wall, he pushed open a door that had been hidden. He directed Genevieve's flashlight into the darkness behind the door. "There it is," he said.

"There *what* is?" everyone asked. "What's going on?" His sizeable bulk completely blocked their view.

"The Courvoisier," he said, and Tuck squeezed through the previously unnoticed door and disappeared from sight.

Genevieve followed him through the door, then Pamela, Owen, Lenore, Sophia, Zoë, Harvey, Tina, Tony, Will and Bentley. Wherever they were going, there was room for all of them.

Chapter Nineteen

[September, 1975]

"A *cask* of brandy?" Bentley asked.

"Courvoisier," Tuck answered. "I'm sure." He shined the flashlight around the room, and in its meager beam the explorers caught glimpses of the arm of a chair, a darkened light bulb, a tablecloth—but they were unable to picture what sort of room they were in. It didn't matter to Tuck. He was focused on the brandy, but everyone else wondered where in the hell they were.

The beam of Tuck's dying flashlight finally

touched and faintly illuminated a wooden cask about half the size of most wine barrels. It lay on its side on a tabletop, prevented from rolling by wooden shims under its flanks.

A spigot was fitted to one end of the cask, and Tuck lumbered directly to it. The others followed and gathered around to watch. He handed the flashlight to Bentley and said, "Shine it right at the spigot." And then, slowly and ponderously like an ancient oak falling in a forest, he dropped to the floor before the cask.

"For God's sake, Tuck, what are you *doing*?" Lenore shouted at him. On his hands and knees, Tuck had taken a suckling position at the spigot. "You don't have any idea of what's in that barrel. That could be rat poison!"

"Unh, uh uh umph," Tuck said, his words muffled by the tricky angle his neck had to assume in order for him to get his mouth up close to the spigot. "Uhn, unh!" Bentley, who trusted Tuck's excellent nose more than Lenore did, or who was more willing than Lenore to let Tuck risk all for the sake of science, interpreted Tuck's grunts to mean that he should open the valve, and he pulled back on the old-fashioned wooden spigot. The cask went "blub" and quite a significant shot of whatever the substance was glugged into Tuck's upturned mouth. Everyone in the dark room could hear him swallow. "Unnn!" he said and left his mouth open, apparently ready for more. Bentley gave another tug on the valve. Finally Tuck got his feet under himself and managed to rise, as ponderously as he had dropped.

"Unh, uh uh umph," Tuck said, but his words were muffled by the tricky angle his neck had to assume in order for him to get his mouth up close to the spigot.

"Courvoisier," he affirmed, wiping his mouth with his hand.

"For God's sake, Tuck, forget the brandy and tell us where we are!" Lenore said. "What the devil *is* this room?"

"I can't tell you that," Tuck said. "You'll have to ask someone else about that. Try Genevieve."

"My goodness," Genevieve said. "I'm *sure* I don't know where we are."

Lenore suggested, "How about we try to find some lights? Bentley, shine your flashlight at the walls." When Bentley found a switch, Lenore flipped it and an overhead lightbulb lit the room, though in a dim, pinkish hue. The room was not small. There were four round, wooden tables, each surrounded by chairs. Scores of racked bottles lined the walls. Tuck went exploring among them.

"Most of this stuff is whiskey, with homemade labels. Maybe it's homemade whiskey."

"But look over here," Tony said. "This is wine and it's good stuff." That interested everyone, and the group surged over to the wine racks against one wall. "Chateau Lafitte, Chateau Montrose, Leoville L'Ascose..."

"Look at the vintages!" Lenore cried. "1928, 1916, 1912. Nothing after 1928!"

"Nineteen-twenty-eight was still Prohibition," Zoë pointed out. "Look at that light fixture." A red, glass shade covered the single dim bulb overhead. "This room was designed for cozy, private drinking. That's my guess."

"But why have a bar in here when there's a big, elaborate old bar out in the ballroom?" Tina asked. "And why seal it up?"

Zoë laughed. "Maybe the bar out in the ballroom is where they served the apple cider and sassafras in 1928, during Prohibition, and they served the hard stuff in here."

"Is this a speak easy?" Genevieve said with a gasp. "All these years have I been living in a house with a speak easy?"

"I won't have it!" Pamela said. "I won't live in a

speak easy! *Think* of the type of people who must have been here, right under this roof!"

"*I* wouldn't mind," Tuck said. "Heck, I guess I wouldn't mind living right here in this room. I like the way it smells."

"Something tells me Weezie isn't going to like it as much as you do, Tuck," Sophia said.

"I don't know," Tucker said, "It has an elevator. Weezie sure hates to climb those stairs."

"Hey, you know these wines might be worth some money," Tony called to the others. He was still looking over the bottles that filled a rack against an entire wall. "Here's a 1900 first-growth Bordeaux!"

"Maybe we'd better pop the cork and see if it's still alive," Tuck said.

"Hang on," Lenore cautioned. "We'd better sit down and have a talk. We haven't even figured out where the elevator lands upstairs, or even whether it works."

"Well I'm going to go up and tell Weezie about our speak easy. That, and I think I'll see if I can find a brandy snifter."

"I guess *so*," Zoë said, "or you'll wear out the knees of your britches."

Upstairs, Tuck found Weezie lying on a sofa in the towering living room, looking very small, her coat pulled over her like a blanket and her head resting on a sofa-pillow. She smiled when he sat on a piece of the sofa that Weezie didn't cover. "Why, Tucker," she said, "you've been drinking."

"Woman, you have a good nose!" he said proudly. But he was concerned. "What's wrong, Weezie? Not feeling so good?" Just then Buddy stuck his head out from under her coat where he had been curled up asleep. He made a friendly face and gave a wag or two and fell back asleep.

"I think I caught something from the evening news again," Weezie said. Tuck chuckled but Weezie looked pale.

"Maybe it's time to go home, huh?" he suggested. A Saturday afternoon had begun to be evening.

"I'm missing all the fun," she said in a tired voice.

"Weezie, I found a great place in the house to make our apartment!" Weezie looked at him doubtfully.

"I may not like it as well as you do, Tucker."

"Hmmm, that's what Sophia said. But how could you know you might not like it if you haven't seen it?"

"I just don't want you to be disappointed and get depressed."

"But wait until I tell you about it!"

"Does it have any windows?" Weezie asked. For a minute, Tuck was stumped.

"No, no it doesn't. But it really smells good."

"Well, as I said…" Weezie began.

"You may not like it as well as I do," Tuck finished for her.

Everyone but Weezie and Tuck convened at the

house the next morning. Weekends were the only days when most of the group could be at the house together. Trapped on the road by her job, it was especially hard for Sophia to be there, weekend or not, but from time to time she would simply cancel all appointments and come home for a few precious days to be with Will and, as she said, "to cook for the troops."

"Well, it works," Will announced.

"What does?" Tina asked.

"The elevator."

"You're kidding!"

"The reason it didn't work last night when Owen pushed the button—you remember?—was that the doors were open. In fact, we didn't even have to push any buttons. Owen and I got in the elevator, closed the two doors and we took off. Pass the butter, would you please."

The friends—that's how they most often referred to themselves these days rather than as "the group"—were sitting in the dining room, enjoying Sunday breakfast together. Sophia had served buttermilk pancakes all around and had finally sat down. Buddy roamed among the diners, yipping like a coyote and even nipping at their shoes when he had to wait too long between treats. Generally, he gave Pamela special dispensation from this shakedown.

Ever since Zoë had removed the drapes from the north-facing windows of the dining room, it had become a cheerful place to gather. Something about the quality of the light that filtered into the room that morning reminded Lenore that Thanksgiving was only weeks away.

Butter and warm maple syrup went around the table. Lenore asked, "Did you find out where the elevator lands on the second floor?"

"We must have been blind," her husband said. "I don't know why none of us ever wondered what was going on up there. Anyway, it lands at the hallway, right beside the staircase. We already have the wall open, and everything works fine."

For a while everyone kept quiet and enjoyed their pancakes. "Were Sunday breakfasts important in your families?" Sophia asked the others.

"They certainly were when *I* was growing up," Genevieve said. "We kids had the funny papers spread out on the floor—sometimes right here on *this* floor—and my father cooked breakfast." It turned out that Sunday breakfasts had been family occasions for all of the friends around the big old table.

"Even when my kids were little, Sunday breakfasts were still important," Tina said. "But long before they left home that fell apart. We were too busy, even the kids." Everyone nodded.

"That's a shame, isn't it?" Will said. But the friends were having too much fun eating Sunday breakfast together to become morose.

Finally, when most of the diners had finished breakfast and were drinking coffee, Lenore said, "So where does everything stand now? I mean about the elevator and our new speakeasy?

"Well," Owen said, "the elevator works and our speakeasy is full of moonshine."

"It's also full of some very valuable wine," Tony said. "I think we should have a wine expert appraise it."

"With the idea of selling it?" Lenore asked.

"I don't think we should sell it," Pamela said. "I think we should drink it. I would enjoy having a nice bottle of 1901 Chateau D'Yquem now and then, and I noticed that we have six of them."

"Right, and they're worth about $2,000 each," Tony said.

"Yikes," said Zoë.

"I struggle with the concept of drinking a bottle of wine worth $2,000," Sophia confessed. "I don't question that the wine is worth that much; I wonder whether *I'm* worth that much."

"Well, I have no such problem," Pamela said. "If I'm not worthy of a fine wine, who is?"

Tony said, "It's just a question of whether we can afford to give up the income from the wines. Even though they were free, in a sense it'll cost us maybe $50,000 in lost revenue to drink them."

"One of the problems is that there is no way of knowing whether these wines are alive or not," Tony continued. "If we open a bottle of wine and it's no good, then it isn't worth $2,000 anymore. It isn't worth two cents. In fact, the whole collection becomes suspect if just one or two bottles are bad.

Maybe it's better not to know."

"I like the idea of neither selling nor drinking them," Harvey said, "but just keeping them in the wine cellar. I guess that would be about the ultimate collection of wine."

"We may as well find out what the wine is worth, okay? And then we can decide," Lenore suggested. "Tony, will you have them appraised?"

"Sure, I know just whom to call." The coffee went around the table again, and most people warmed their cups with it.

"Has anyone heard how Weezie is feeling?" Tina asked. No one had. "I'll call Tuck after breakfast and see if she's okay."

"Well, what else is on the agenda?" Lenore asked.

"Genevieve, what's the story with the car in the garage that's always kept covered up? Not only is it covered by an old canvas tarp," Owen said, "but it's wrapped up like a cocoon in sisal rope."

Genevieve looked blank for a moment. "Oh, it's no good, Owen," she said. "It's been wrapped up like that since my father was alive."

"What do you mean it's no good?"

"He said it didn't work, and that was forty years ago."

"What kind of car is it?"

Genevieve had to think. "It's a Jaguar, dear, but it's very old."

Owen's eyes brightened and he leaned forward in his chair. "An old Jaguar? Do you mind if I look it over next time I'm here? Or maybe right after break-fast?"

"Certainly not. But don't be disappointed."

Lenore thought to herself, "There goes Owen. We won't be seeing him again for the next three months." She knew he wouldn't be able to sleep at night until he had the Jaguar purring like a...like a jaguar. But Lenore had an idea and she spoke up with it. "Listen everybody, what do you think about having a big Thanksgiving dinner here and inviting our families?" She glanced at Bentley, Pamela and Genevieve, the members of the group who were single, and added, "Or anyone you would like to invite."

"That sounds like fun," Will said. "Unless you have to cook. Then it sounds like a lot of cooking."

"I'd love to do it," Sophia chimed. "Besides, we have a lot of cooks. You might even peel some potatoes, Will. That would help."

"What if I just keep opening wines from the cellar? How many of those bottles of 1901 Chateau-whatever-that-was do we have?"

"That's a good idea about having Thanksgiving here, Lenore," Tina said. "Our kids, Harvey's and mine, have been consumed by worry and suspicion since we bought into the house. Maybe meeting everyone and seeing the house would ease their anxiety."

Will asked, "How many people can we seat in here?" He eyed the long table that was unchallenged by the eleven who were seated at it that morning.

Genevieve said, "There's another table in the attic just like this. Fortunately, it's been covered up all these years." Pamela stirred. Lenore guessed she was thinking again about the hated pigeons. "It fits right next to this table, and between the two we can seat about sixty people."

"An intimate little Thanksgiving dinner for sixty, huh? Let's do it!" Sophia said, and her blue eyes sparkled.

Chapter Twenty

[October, 1975]

"The thing that's stopping us is closet space. Every time I think Zoë's got a place picked out, she says there's not enough closet space and we have to start pacing all over the house again." Tony was explaining his problem to Harvey, who seemed to understand perfectly. "I tell her, 'Zoë, all you'll need when we come here to live is a raincoat and a bedpan,' but she doesn't think that's funny. I mean she *really* doesn't think that's funny."

Harvey nodded sympathetically. "Tina has

already made a list of what she's going to need, including her favorite china. 'China?' I say. 'You're going to bring our china?' That woman can look pretty steely-eyed, Tony."

The two men thought about things for a while, shaking their heads and sighing.

"Zoë looked me right in the eye and told me this place isn't big enough," said Tony. Harvey ran his hand through his gray hair in wonder. "I told her there are 27,000 square feet for thirteen people; that's 2,000 square feet for her and 2,000 square feet for me."

"What did she say?"

"She said if that's so much space maybe I should give up some of mine for the linen she wants to bring over."

"The linen?" Harvey weighed that. "We're going to have to come up with something," he said. "But I don't know what." He and Tony sat in the living room, close to the fireplace, though no fire was lit. The hot days of September were past, and this October evening was cool and even a little breezy in a house that was built long before double-paned windows and thick fiberglass insulation were code. But still the house wasn't cool enough yet for a fire.

The friends sometimes found themselves drawn to the house at odd hours. They came after dinner to admire the work they had done earlier in the day, or they came to scout for the suite of rooms they would settle into when the time came. Sometimes they showed up simply wondering if anyone else was around. Tony and Harvey were sharing a bottle of wine, a $10 bottle of zinfandel and not the primo stuff down in the speakeasy.

"What do you think about using some of the common space to store clothes and china and linen and all that?" Harvey said. "The ballroom or the attic or something."

"You mean like one gigantic closet?"

"Yeah," Harvey said, "or maybe with partitions or something."

"Man, I'd say let them hang clothes in the living room if that's what they want." He looked around at the magnificent fireplace and peered up at the towering ceiling and added, "But the attic sounds better. I think that's a good idea."

"Yeah. I'd like to get on with choosing up our private spaces."

"I'll drink to that," Tony said, and he did.

A few days later, Tony and Harvey found Will and Owen sitting out on the back porch and asked if they had any ideas about closet space for the women. What did they think about using the attic as a gigantic common closet?

"My guess is the women would want something more private," Will said. "They're not going to want to share a closet, no matter how vast. But anyway, Sophia is talking the same way, like there's just not enough space in this undersized little house for her clothes. Pretty amazing. One night she cried, talking about it."

"So we have to do something," Owen said. The four men sat on the steps of the back porch, looking out on the garden. From time to time they caught a glimpse of Bentley through the trees and shrubs as he worked in the garden.

"I'll bet Bentley is just as upset about closet space as the women are," Tony said. "He's a pretty natty dresser. He even looks good when he's working in the garden."

"Not a single one of them, including Bentley, has been willing to choose a living space," Owen said. "I'd like to get on with it!"

"Okay," Will said, "if the rooms have small closets, either our wives are going to have to hike to some large common area like the attic for their clothes, which doesn't sound too likely, or we're going to have to figure out how to deliver their clothes to them."

Harvey laughed. "Did you see the ads for that auction of machinery from bankrupt laundry businesses? I wonder if they have any of those moving laundry racks for sale, the ones in laundries that bring all the shirts around until yours show up?"

Harvey had a game he played in laundries. When the clerk pushed a button and all the clothes would begin parading through the room on a moving rack, he would try to spot his clothes before the clerk did. The cleaners always won the contest, though, because the shirts Harvey had purchased so carefully and, he thought, with such good taste were surprisingly like all the other shirts on the rack. To his annoyance, he often mistook several red cashmere sweaters for his own before the rack stopped moving and the clerk grabbed his. Though each such humbling laundry-experience left Harvey irritated, the next time he picked up his laundry he would test himself once again.

But now he was wondering how those moving laundry racks might help him and the guys solve the closet problem in the big house.

Will, at least, seemed to be following his line of thought. "Well, we would need about six or seven of those racks, one for each of the fancy dressers. But I don't quite see how we could get a rack to each of the rooms."

Owen, the engineer, laughed. "Okay, what about this? All the clothes are stored in the attic. Each couple's clothes are on a separate, moving laundry rack. But instead of going around in circles, these racks would go right through the attic floor, directly into the closets in the bedrooms downstairs. Right? We could configure the racks any way we want. For instance, they could move up and down just as well as around. So they drop down into a closet through the closet's ceiling and deliver whatever clothing has been requested. Okay, you tell me why that's crazy."

"Maybe it's not crazy," Will said. "In one small closet you could see an acre of clothes, a few at a time, as they pass through the closet back up to the attic—where they are kept carefully mothproofed, by the way."

The four men looked grave. They were wondering whether, if they pursued this idea, they were going to wind up looking like heroes or goats in the eyes of their wives. The laundry-rack idea seemed kind of nutty.

Perhaps they were wondering whether, if they pursued this idea, they were going to wind up looking like heroes, or goats.

Looking out of a kitchen window at the four men sitting on the back porch, Tina said to Sophia, "I wonder what they're up to. Those guys look worried."

Sophia studied the situation and said, "They've got *something* on their minds. I hope it's something good."

The women were experimenting with turkey dressing. Faced with cooking dressing for nearly fifty people in another five weeks, they thought they had better decide early how they wanted it to taste. One school of thought was that, no matter how over-worked the old standard recipe might be, it was what people expected, and most of them would be disap-pointed with anything different. The other school had it that this was a wonderful opportunity to try something interesting for a change. Sophia and Tina, of this latter mind, were fiddling around with recipes involving oysters, water chestnuts, cranberries, corn-bread and even jalapeno peppers. But mainly they were worried about Weezie.

Weezie was sick. Tuck had called that morning with the disturbing news that she had been diagnosed with heart fibrillations. Atrial fibrillation, he called it.

Tina knew something about atrial fibrillation. "It has to do with arrhythmia. That sure could account for her not liking to climb the stairs. One of the symptoms is exhaustion." She went on to describe all kinds of things Weezie might have to go through, from merely annoying to life-threatening. "The dis-ease can be treated with medicines," she said, "or with a pacemaker or sometimes by an operation."

"Well, I don't hear much good news there," Sophia said. "Poor Weezie, and poor Tuck. We can guess how Tuck's feeling right about now."

"Depressed," Tina said. It was she who had talked with him that morning. "They have a lot to think about. My guess is that they don't have a lot of money, especially since Weezie retired. Tuck's earn-ings from garden writing can't be very much."

"Not only that, "Sophia said, "but I imagine they mortgaged their house to buy into this place. So they probably have to make giant house payments."

While the women were chopping and dicing and feeling bad about Weezie and Tuck, Sophia took a moment to peer out the kitchen window. "Owen's drawing something on a piece of paper that they're all looking at," she said. "I think they're going to surprise us with something."

"Maybe it has to do with that Jaguar Owen's started working on," Tina mused. "He thinks he can get that old car running."

Outside, the men had agreed on an approach to the laundry-rack project. Owen would attend the auction of equipment from defunct laundries and see if he could buy a moving laundry-rack, cheap. The men would then attempt to install it, sending the rack through the floor of the attic and into a closet below. If they got one to work, they would ask their wives whether they wanted their own. In the meantime, they agreed to keep mum about the project. If the scheme didn't work, no one need ever know what a harebrained idea it had been.

Even though they now had a plan, the men continued to look glum. They were talking about Weezie and Tuck.

"I didn't pay too much attention when Weezie said she didn't like climbing the stairs," Tony said. "Weezie has always seemed to hang back a little from what the group was doing."

"I always thought she was just shy," Owen said, "kind of slow to warm up to people. But now I wonder if she's been sick all the time since we've known her."

"My old ticker has had a few moments where it's fluttered and felt like it was flapping around," Will said. "That's a crummy feeling. You always wonder whether it's going to remember how to beat like hearts are supposed to."

"I don't know why Tuck and Weezie don't just come over and start living here right now," Harvey said. "There's always someone here these days, someone who could help keep an eye on Weezie."

In the kitchen, Sophia was saying, "I think Weezie and Tuck should move in here right now. That's what the house is for."

And at Summit Hospital, Tuck was saying to Weezie, "I don't see why we don't move into the big house now. If we did, we could sell our house and darned near be fixed for life; or at least we could get by on my income."

"Well," Weezie said, "the idea of going back to our place and sitting around all day doesn't sound so good to me. I miss Buddy and Ninja. And I never got a chance to use the new elevator. Or the speakeasy. We don't have either one at home." Weezie, in her hospital bed, was surrounded by vases of flowers, all delivered within a couple of hours from the time Tuck told the friends about her health problems.

Tuck had spent most of the past week alone at

home in a deep funk or by Weezie's side in the hospital in a deep funk, his head resting on various coffee tables and desks, Convinced now that she might survive, he was pulling out of the dumps.

"To tell you the truth," Weezie continued, "I miss the friends, too."

"They're going to put on a Thanksgiving dinner at the house," Tuck said, "and invite the kids, grandkids, everybody. Of course Tina said you'd better mend fast so you and I can be there."

Weezie thought for a while. "I'd be embarrassed to move into the house so much before anyone else. Do you think they would mind?"

"I think Genevieve would be thrilled if you were there. She might not even mind my being around. We got off to a pretty rocky start, though."

"Tuck, you're her *son*." Weezie smiled. "Of course she would like you to be there."

"I'd sure like to spend more time in that garden," he said. "But in the meantime I'd better go home and write a column. We're going to need some money coming in."

IN THE GARDEN
WITH TUCKER CALHOUN

Just Bought a New House with an Old Garden?
*Think twice before you pull the plug
on that 90-year-old shrub!*

*Every time I begin feeling smug about my vast knowledge
of plants, I wind up with egg on my face. The other day I took
a walk in a neighborhood that's new to me, and I discovered
three species of trees that I swear I have never seen before. At
home after my walk, I pulled down a reference book and
matched up one specimen's serrated, heart-shaped leaves and its
cluster of pendant, white flowers with pictures in the book.
This tree—a beauty!—turned out to be a silver linden. Am I
the only person who has not knowingly seen one before?*

*Tillia tomentosa. That's the Latin. The trees are native to
Europe and Western Asia and perhaps they grow like weeds
in parts of America. But here in the West? I don't think
they're planted at all. They should be, though, for their fragrant
blossoms, dense shade and heart-shaped leaves.*

*Silver lindens are in bloom right now, and of course that
helped me identify the specimen I came across. But to find out
what the other two trees are, like some freshman botanist I will
have to take my furtively snipped samples to a nursery and lisp
like a schoolboy, "Would you please tell me what these are?" I*

have already petitioned my most reliable source of plant-knowledge, my nurseryman buddy Bentley Fairbanks of Fairbanks Nursery. I was secretly thrilled when he was no more able than I was to identify them.

When I bought a house recently, of course I acquired a new garden as well. A new old garden, first planted ninety years ago. After poking around in it for a couple of months now, I'm staggered by how many gaps it has revealed in my knowledge of plants. I draw a complete blank on some of the plants I have discovered in it. And others that I thought I knew well display properties that astonish me. For instance, among the shrubs in the garden are five antique Daphne odoras that are two feet higher than I ever would have believed they could become— about five feet each!

As I learn more about plants during my permanent field trip to my own garden, I will share with you any tidbits of information I come up with. For now, I would just like to take credit for one small thing. This time I have not plowed into my new garden slashing and burning, hacking and uprooting as I would have—and often did—in my youth. Instead, I have respected plants that were born thirty years before I was and that apparently have had such merit that four generations of homeowners have spared them. By this time in my life, I understand that some of the plants that have become "mine" won't fully reveal their beauty until winter or spring. Pull the plug on them in the fall, and I will never take full measure of their worth. As it is with people, sometimes we fully appreciate plants that have touched our lives only when we contemplate what life would be like without them.

Chapter Twenty-One

[October, 1975]

"Lenore, dear, I wonder whether you would do me a very big favor?" It was about 9:30 on a Saturday night when Genevieve asked. Lenore was at the house just to see who was around.

"Of course I will!" she said. "What can I do?" Lenore was surprised to see Genevieve looking quite flamboyant, really, with rather startling makeup and a blouse as red as a bullfighter's cape.

"Well, I *would* like to go to San Francisco to dance, dear, and I'm afraid I've lost my nerve for driving. Other drivers have been doing perfectly irresponsible things to my car and I'm a little intimidated right now."

"Let's go," Lenore said. But in the car as she drove Genevieve past the soaring old mansions of Piedmont and through the ramshackle and largely unoccupied Art Deco storefronts of downtown Oakland onto the freeway and then onto the Oakland Bay Bridge toward San Francisco, Lenore grew puzzled. "Genevieve, do you really have a car? You know I never thought about it before, but I don't remember ever seeing you drive, and I didn't know you had a car."

"Well, I drive a little. You must have seen my car parked on the street by the driveway."

Yes, she knew the car, an ancient, murky Volvo, but it was such a battered and dirty old heap.

"I don't like to drive down the driveway because it's so narrow," Genevieve explained. "When Aldous left—that's my husband, dear—when Aldous left I didn't know how to do anything. I certainly didn't know how to drive. But later I had a friend who taught me. He's a policeman and he's been very nice to me."

"A policeman taught you to drive?"

"Oh, yes, and he bought me that car, too. He said it was the safest car on the road. And then he showed me which lanes to stay in when I went to San Francisco." Genevieve pulled a mirror out of her little sparkly gold purse and applied more red lipstick.

"He showed you which lanes to stay in?"

"So I wouldn't have to merge with traffic or do anything dangerous. If I were you I would move over one lane to the left."

They rode in silence for a few moments. "So you have a dance class?" Lenore asked.

"Oh no, I'm just going dancing."

"How will you get back, Genevieve?"

"I always manage, dear. Now turn right."

"Genevieve, this is the Mission district! Is this where you're going dancing?" Genevieve was fluffing her hair up and straightening her bright red blouse. "I can wait for you until you're finished. I'll just park right here," Lenore offered.

"No, no, I'll be fine. Just let me off." Lenore gazed around at the busy nightlife on the sidewalk. It seemed as if hundreds of young Hispanic men and women were cruising by, walking arm-in-arm, laughing.

"Genevieve, I'm worried about you. Phone me if you need help, will you?"

"Of course I will. But I'll be fine." Outside the car, Genevieve straightened her swishing, gored skirt, hung her little gold bag on an arm and ambled toward one of the doorways. A window next to the door advertised, Big Dance Tonight! in lurid colors. Nearby, a young man spoke to Genevieve and she flashed him a smile. Lenore shuddered and eased into the traffic. She pulled back over to the curb, though, after a car actually lurched and jumped and hopped around her automobile. Like Genevieve, for a moment at least, she had lost her nerve for driving.

In a surprisingly short time, Ninja had grown from a rangy juvenile to a filled-out, buff young adult. Her mew had become a throaty meow and her eyes an even more intense blue. In short, she was ready for action. Like Bentley, she spent most of her time in the garden, though it was the garden's fauna rather than its flora that interested her. That and Bentley himself.

Bentley knelt over a hole he had dug and he lowered a variety of viburnum called "Mariesei" into it, and as he pulled loamy earth into the hole and firmed it around the shrub's root ball, Ninja rubbed against the heels of his boots and against his back. When Bentley had finished planting the shrub, he turned and scratched Ninja's chin with two fingers and then sat down and leaned against a tree. Ninja invited pets by strolling across Bentley's lap with her tail hoisted like a flag.

From his shrub-high view of the garden, Bentley surveyed what he and Tuck had accomplished and he was pleased. He could visualize the garden as it would look next spring and even as it would look in fifteen years.

What he had trouble picturing was his own future. He had trouble imagining how his life might be different from the way it was right now. Of course the news was not all bad about his present life. He was excited by what was going on with him and his band of friends—their experiment with communal living. He had the sense that it might save him from an eventual lonely demise, and he enjoyed the garden of which he and Tuck had become the guardians. But he dreamed of being in love.

Women adored Bentley. He dressed like dashing heroes in romance novels, even in the garden and at work in his nursery. On his slender frame he wore laundered khakis, dark turtleneck sweaters and crisp blazers on cool days, and Armani alligator belts and alligator boots. Women fell in love with him—not that he cared. Many men had adored him as well, but his last great affair—with a five-star Chinese chef who taught him to talk dirty in Cantonese—had ended sixteen years before. Now he wondered whether he would ever have another chance. His forties and fifties had been lonely. They had been sad years too, for he had lost many friends to AIDS.

His loneliness was driven home by the group's plan to celebrate Thanksgiving together in the house. He thought he might be the only one of the friends there without a mate. And, worse, he wondered how well received a guest of his might be if he *were* to bring someone. He had never tested those waters before with the group.

Ninja sat in Bentley's lap and nuzzled his chin. Bentley could *feel* Ninja's purring as she rubbed against his cheek. It was hard to tell how Ninja felt about Buddy, but she clearly loved dapper, dashing, lonely Bentley.

Zoë and Tina, drinking coffee on the sun porch, were also thinking about the Thanksgiving dinner. "It looks like Tuck and Weezie will be living here by that time," Tina said. She was silent for a few moments. "When we dreamed up this crazy idea of living together in our old age, who would have thought that one of us would need the house so soon—in less than a year!"

"Yeah," Zoë said. "Kinda brings it home that there's a fine line between our age and old age, huh?"

"Not me, girl," Tina said. "I'm not old. I'm a spring chicken. And if I'm not, I'll look like one after my next nip and tuck." She patted her smooth throat with a manicured hand.

Zoë wore a pixie haircut, short as a boy's. Though she did not believe a sixty-year-old had to look boring, she had clear ideas of what was appropriate for women her age, and long hair, she believed, was not. Neither was cosmetic surgery, in her opinion.

"It's decadent, that's all," she said. "Other than that, I have nothing against it."

"Decadent?" Tina asked.

"Well, no more decadent than the Romans' tickling their throats with feathers so they could vomit and then eat more. Decadent in that sense," Zoë explained.

"Zoë, you don't have to pull your punches just because we're friends. If you're opposed to plastic surgery, just come out and say so."

"It looks good on you, but you looked good before you had it. On other people it's mutton parading as lamb—a forty-year-old head on a sixty-year-old body."

"Mutton parading as lamb?" Tina repeated, blinking. Zoë was 103 pounds of intelligence and edgy wit, much of it good-natured.

"Don't worry, you're a lamb chop, honey, and every man would agree."

"Yeah, now," Tina said, "after $20,000 worth of facial surgery. But why not? It's either that or I'm a fading rose. You painted your house when it started looking worn, didn't you? So I got a little old and worn and spruced up the old face."

"Don't worry, you're a lamb chop, honey, and every man would agree."
"Yeah, now," Tina said. "After $20,000 worth of facial surgery."

Zoë really couldn't see any ill effects at all from Tina's surgery. No weirdness, nothing inappropriate. It was the concept that bothered her.

"I mean, it *is* my body, Zoë." Tina continued. "Lifting a little flesh is something that makes me feel better, and I'm certainly not hurting anyone by it. Some people take drugs or alcohol to feel good. Or they gamble, or shoplift or have an extramarital fling. I just have a little of this and that removed or tightened or added. No big deal."

"Right, no big deal," Zoë said, "You just get cut up and then spend the next six weeks popping pain pills."

"It's my body, baby," Tina reminded her.

"Anyway, that's not what bothers me," Zoë said. "It's a matter of values. If looking young is what's really important, then you're asking for trouble, because sooner or later age catches up. The doctor says he can't do any more for you, or you run out of money or whatever. Then how are you going to feel when you become an old hag overnight? And, anyway, you're a therapist! What would you say to a patient who can't accept her age and what she really looks like?"

Tina laughed. "I'd recommend my surgeon. And if I turn into a hag overnight, I'm still going to have had seventy good years," Tina said. "Maybe more." She and Zoë laughed together.

"Anyway," Tina said, "I postponed my next bout of chopping and dicing until after Thanksgiving. I wouldn't miss this dinner for the world. Maybe my kids will finally be able to relax about our Last Resort after they meet everyone and see how nice everyone is."

"Relax? Hah! Young people don't know how. They'll just find more to worry about." The two sipped their coffee. Out in the garden, they could see Bentley sitting on the ground, petting Ninja.

"I don't know, maybe Tuck and Weezie have the right idea, coming to live here now," Tina said, "instead of waiting until they're old and sick."

"Yeah, now they're only elderly and sick, or Weezie is anyway. Sick, I mean."

"Is that what we are? Elderly? I told you, I'm not," Tina laughed.

"Having one of our friends get a serious disease makes us all seem pretty vulnerable," Zoë said. "Anything can happen to anyone at any time."

"Especially when you're elderly," Tina said. "Which I'm not."

Chapter Twenty-Two

[October, 1975]

It fell to Tony Androtti to attend the auction. The idea was to secure an automated laundry rack with which he, Will, Owen and Harvey hoped to develop a system for delivering clothes from the attic to their wives' closets. Harvey, whose idea it had been to try to find such a rack at auction, couldn't attend that night, and Owen, who actually liked to bid at auction, was spending every available hour working on the Jaguar, and he begged off auction duty.

Tony had never before bid at auction and felt like

a greenhorn. Everyone else in the big showroom seemed at ease. They moved about the room coolly previewing this item and that. They tested the action on giant mangles and peered into the inner workings of industrial-sized washing machines.

He had been told on the phone that moving laundry racks were being offered at the sale, but he couldn't find one to examine. He noticed that other previewers were holding sheets of paper on which they were making notes and circling items. He found someone behind a counter and inquired.

"Is there a list I can have?" he asked. The woman behind the counter was about his age and was chewing gum. She wore a great big ruby-colored stone on one finger. The lady gave him a blank look.

"A list?"

"Like everyone else has," Tony explained and he pointed over his shoulder with his thumb, "and they're writing on them." She looked where he pointed and then resumed looking at him with a puzzled expression. He too looked where he had just pointed and no one in sight had one of the lists. "They were walking around with lists and making notes?" Tony continued.

"You want a *catalogue*?" she said.

"I guess so," he said.

"Well, honey, do you or don't you?"

"Yes, yes, yes I do," he managed. That settled, the lady smiled and gave him one of the sheets of paper and a tiny pencil, about three inches long, which had no eraser. But by the time he had them in his hands, a bald man standing behind a lectern was banging on it like a judge and was announcing that the bidding was beginning and that item number one was a fifty-gallon barrel of cleaning solvent.

Tony knew only one thing about auctions: that any movement at all, any twitch or hiccup might be interpreted as a bid, and if he weren't careful he could wind up buying an industrial mangle. So he sat stiff as a rock as the auction unfolded. Without moving any body parts except for his eyes, he desperately searched his catalogue for some clue about the item he had come to bid on. He could find nothing, but then he was having trouble focusing his attention because meanwhile the auction went on, and items were selling every minute or two. It occurred to him that the rack he had come for might already have sold.

Suddenly the words "circulating racks" caught his attention. Could that be it? The bald man on the stage, who spoke very rapidly, was saying that the racks—there were eight of them—were to be sold as one lot. Tony couldn't see anything at all that resembled racks, but felt that he must be ready to start bidding nonetheless. He could actually *feel* adrenaline racing through his system, triggering a powerful fight-or-flight response.

"What'll you give me, what'll you give me, do I hear a hundred, do I hear a hundred, do I hear fifty dollars, do I hear fifty? What'll you give me, what'll it be, it's your call, it's your pleasure, give me twenty-five, give me twenty-five." Tony raised his trembling hand. "Thank you sir." Then the auctioneer stopped and stared at Tony for a moment. "Where's your paddle, sir? Who are you?"

Tony was having trouble breathing and wondered whether he might be in the early stages of a heart attack. "Paddle?"

"Paddle, sir. Did you register?"

"Did you register?" triggered associations he thought he had left behind years ago. Register for the draft? For Social Security? College? One semester forty years earlier, unbelievably, he had forgotten to register for classes and he had had to spend nearly four months scooping ice cream and explaining to his folks how he could have forgotten to register for college.

"Sir?"

"Uh, no, I didn't register. I just got here."

"Well, I'll let you bid," the bald man said, "but you'll have to register after the bidding."

"Thank you," Tony said.

"Twenty-five," the auctioneer said, "I have twenty-five, do I hear fifty, twenty-five, twenty-five, twenty-five, do I hear fifty?"

His heart racing, Tony thought, "I'm going to get it for twenty-five dollars, whatever it is."

"Fifty," someone said from nearby. Tony shot him a nasty look. His adversary, who wore a baseball cap, sneered at him. Tony hated him.

"Fifty, fifty, fifty, do I hear seventy-five, do I hear seventy-five?" The auctioneer looked directly at Tony as if challenging him.

"Seventy-five," Tony said. He could not keep from glancing at the ratty-looking guy in the baseball cap who had bid against him. The man's squinty little eyes were trained on Tony. Nonchalantly the guy raised his paddle.

"Seventy-five," Tony said. He could not keep from glancing at the ratty-looking guy in the baseball cap who had bid against him.

"One hundred, I have one hundred, do I hear one-twenty-five? One hundred, do I hear one-twenty-five?"

"Shit," Tony thought, growing almost faint. "One minute it was mine for twenty-five bucks and now I have to pay a hundred twenty-five. And I have a guy who's out to get me."

"I have one hundred. I have one hundred. Going

once. One hundred. Going twice. Going…"

"One-twenty-five," Tony shouted, much too loudly. This time when he looked at his enemy, the man was keeping his paddle out of sight, but for some reason he still looked as if he had won. The rest was a blur. In a daze, Tony saw the auctioneer point at him and the woman with the big red ring came over to Tony and took his name and address and asked to see his driver's license.

A few minutes later, Tony had written a check with a shaky hand and was waiting for someone to bring the rack, or, rather, the racks. But the lady told him, "Just bring your truck around to dock three," and she made a circling motion that ended pointing to the rear of the building. On his way out he noticed that the guy who had bid against him was sprawled in a chair in the office without his baseball cap. He was sitting with the auctioneer, holding a drink with ice in it, and the two were guffawing about something.

Outside, Tony was glad he had brought his SUV. It was not often he had a chance to use it the way a truck should be used. Even before he drove around to the rear of the building, he flattened the back seats of the vehicle and took a bag of books from the back and put them up in the front passenger seat.

At dock three Tony rang a bell and waited. Finally a wiry young guy came out and said, "You come for the racks?"

"Yes, I did," said Tony.

"Where's your truck?" he said, looking right past

Tony's SUV. Tony got a crummy feeling.

"Well, it's right there," he said, pointing at his sleek sports utility vehicle.

"That's it?" The wiry guy laughed. "Maybe you'd better come inside here and take a look at your racks." Already feeling sick, Tony followed him into the warehouse.

On Saturday morning Owen was working on the Jaguar when he saw a sixteen-foot U-Haul van pull up in front of the house. Tony was behind the wheel. Then Owen lost track of Tony and the truck as he concentrated on the Jag. Actually, working on the old Jaguar was turning out to be every bit as daunting as he had feared it would be. He had quickly exhausted the easy ways he knew to get cars started, and now he was beginning the process of taking the engine apart, piece by piece, with the idea of restoring the engine if necessary, or even replacing it.

Owen had enough experience in restoring old cars to anticipate the kind of trouble he might run into. "If I were smart," he thought, "I wouldn't even get started." That reminded him of Will saying, just a few months ago, that if people were smart they wouldn't get out of bed. As he disassembled and cleaned parts of the engine, he began to remember some of lessons life had taught him about restoring old, imported cars: "You finally locate rare parts," he reminisced, "only to have them turn out to be the *exact opposite* of what you need because of the left hand vs. right hand drive difference between cars designed for use in England and America. Also, the Lucas electrical parts required will *malfunction immediately* as there is an old saying that 'Lucas invented darkness.' I may find the engine entirely impossible to restore—perhaps with a cracked block—and install a new Japanese drive train. The car will then look like a Jaguar but not drive like one, nor will it be saleable. Or I might even install the body of this Jaguar over the chassis of a Checker cab. Remember," he told himself, "the old saying that a Jaguar is just a Checker cab with a good paint job."

He kept working, though, dismantling the engine one piece at a time, washing each part in solvent, wiping it dry and then deploying each part on the garage floor in careful order. In truth, he was no more likely to heed his own good advice than he was to stay in bed forever.

Owen was so absorbed that he didn't notice the parade of manpower as Will, Harvey, Tony and Bentley lugged section after section of laundry racks from the truck down the long stone stairs to the first floor of the house and then upstairs to the second · floor and then one more flight up to the attic. Then back to the truck for eight heavy electric motors— until they were panting like dogs.

"It looked like a giant erector set, or maybe model-train tracks but really big. Anyway, it took four of them to carry whatever it was," Lenore said. "And they made about six trips back and forth. I was watching from inside the elevator."

"They're up to something; we know that," Sophia said, gently chewing a fingernail. "Are they making a big model-train thingy up there? With tunnels and trees and little tin people waving at the train? Will might do something dumb like that."

"But would they really? I mean, they know they can't just take over the attic. *We're* going to take over the attic," Lenore said, "not them."

Tina spoke up. "Oh, I don't know, they might do anything. Harvey wanted to use the ballroom as a basketball court." The three women shook their heads in wonderment.

"How are we going to find out what they're doing?" Sophia asked.

"Well, let's just wait until they're doing what they're doing and we'll walk right in," Tina said. "We'd better not let this go too far."

The disassembled links of the eight laundry racks were in fact very much like pieces of an erector set. Thank God, they were interchangeable. Furthermore, there were plenty of curved pieces of track, which meant that the guys would be able to make the racks travel any way they wanted—including down through the attic floor and into the bedroom closets below. With that established, the in-house carpenters were able to start right in cutting through the attic floor. Of course it took careful measuring to find the exact place to begin cutting.

"You're sure that door is locked?" Will asked. He stared nervously at the attic door. "Because those women are going to be up here in a flash when they hear this racket." But he could see for himself that the new padlock they had installed on the inside of the door was locked. Will triggered the circular saw and lowered it to the softwood floor of the attic, cutting along a dark pencil line as sawdust flew into the air. But almost instantly a din could be heard even over the frenzied clang of the circular saw, a banging at the door. Will turned pale and released the saw's trigger. "Good lord," he said, "they're already here!"

He went to the locked door and spoke through it. "Who's there?"

"What do you mean 'Who's there?'" his wife said from the other side of the door. "Who do you think is here?"

"Uhhh," Will said.

"Open the door!"

The guys looked at one another. "Well, we can't right now," said Will, and then he added, "The door's locked." That actually seemed to stop Lenore, for a moment at least.

"Are you crazy?"

"We're working on a surprise."

"Obviously," she said. "But is it a surprise we're going to like or a surprise we're going to be mad about when we find out what it is?"

"You'll like it," he said. "If it works."

"I don't like the way that sounds."

"Lenore, why don't you give us a few days to work on this. Then if you don't like it, we'll put it back just like it was. I promise."

"Are you making a basketball court in there?"

Tony piped up. "No, we're building a resort!" Everyone on both sides of the door laughed.

Will said, "We're not making a basketball court." The men could hear the women conferring.

"Okay, you guys, but this had better be good."

"We'll try," Will said.

As they walked down the stairs, Lenore was wondering aloud whether it would be possible to see through an attic window from high up in a big old tree in the garden. "Are any of you good at climbing trees?" she asked. "I'm no good at all."

Chapter Twenty-Three

October, 1975

One morning, Lenore donned a sweatsuit against the chilly fall air, slipped on her tennis shoes, found her old wooden tennis racket and two unopened cans of balls and walked out to the full-sized asphalt court. She inspected the court's surface and found it to be sound though in need of a good sweeping and fresh paint. There was no net at all. She walked the fence surrounding the court and shook it here and there and decided that it was in good condition. One portion of the fence had been set up as a backboard with a white line painted horizontally across it to simulate a net. She opened both cans and put five balls in the pockets of her sweatpants. Facing sideways to the backboard, she dropped the sixth ball, and when it bounced up about waist-high, she smacked it with her racket into the backboard, just above the white line. The ball came back with surprising speed, and it flew past her before she was ready for it. She let the ball go and found another in her pocket. "Racket back," she reminded herself as she had so many time before, though not in recent decades of teaching and lecturing and grading during which she had not found time for a single game of tennis. The next time she swung her racket, she immediately brought her racket into the ready position and gave the ball a satisfying hit on its rebound. Twenty minutes later, when she was sweating and breathing hard, her racket contacted the ball perfectly, her arm carried through, she sprang back into position with her racket back and hit the ball again, perfectly. Lenore had found her stroke. She wiped her forehead on the sleeve of her sweat suit.

That night, Will took the stage in the ballroom, carrying his old German cello and his favorite bow. Instead of the black tie and tuxedo he usually wore for performances, he wore a crisp white shirt with rolled up sleeves, an old but reputable pair of khakis and loafers. The friends pulled chairs around the base of the stage and they clapped and whistled as he sat, then planted the cello's spike, ran his bow across a across a chunk of resin and plunked each of the cello's strings to check for tuning. Ready now, he looked at his audience and smiled, then closed his eyes and played the Bach Cello Suite No. 5 in C Minor.

Chapter Twenty-Four

[November, 1975]

"No, I *won't* go to a ballet with you and I've already told you why."

"Oh come on, honey," Inspector Whistle said, "I'll wear another shirt if you want. Whatever you like."

"And I won't have you calling me names. It's patronizing."

"You mean 'honey?' "

"Please don't, William," said Pamela.

Things had started so smoothly—it had been

love at first sight. But in no time at all Pamela had become annoyed by him. William was desperate for her approval, though he would have been satisfied if she had merely agreed to be seen in public with him. But man, she was a hard one to please. He had tried all kinds of things, first making it possible for her and all her friends to live in the Rutherford mansion. He had pulled a few strings in City Hall and signed a couple of papers, and the doors had opened for them. But Pamela had hardly noticed. Since then he had done everything else he could think of, but she barely tolerated him.

For Pamela, too, it had been love at first sight. She had looked up from her work in the attic, and a stranger was gazing at her as if she were a goddess. She had led him to the attic window and invited him to share her vision of meandering paths in the garden. There had seemed to be a made-in-heaven quality to their meeting. Though trumpets had not sounded, champagne, French bread, Brie and roses had miraculously appeared. Attention of the type the stranger was paying her was not a daily occurrence in her life. In fact, the last person she had swept off his feet was Jerry Connolly in the eighth grade. So she basked in this gentleman's obvious admiration and for a while she was actually giddy with love.

That was then. Within a few weeks, Pamela's usual high standards had reasserted themselves. William's manners, his grooming and taste in clothing, to say nothing of his paunch, she now saw clearly, fell far below those standards. Still, it was gratifying to have an admirer. Furthermore, it did not escape her that the group from The Last Resort was beholden to her for saving them from William Whistle's wrath. It occurred to her that she might put her high standards and refined taste to work to improve him. She might just be able to turn the ugly duckling into a swan.

He could understand her obvious annoyance with him. Compared to Pamela, he was nothing. She was so…perfect! First of all, she was drop-dead gorgeous, with her faultless posture. She stood perfectly upright, as straight as a board, her head held high and proud. Not an ounce of flab hung on her bones, which were alluringly prominent at her wrists and elbows and knees. Nothing round or soft marred her almost military bearing. He could *respect* a woman like that! And then, her mind! Pamela could recite whole poems from memory:

> I dreamed that, as I wandered by the way,
> Bare winter suddenly was changed to spring,
>   And gentle odours led my steps astray…

Things like that, with wonderful sounds and way above his head as to what they actually meant. Really, just knowing her had changed his life. He now aspired to be something higher than a building inspector, though for thirty years he had thought himself to be an important man.

The way Pamela talked! She sounded like a character in a classy English movie, he thought, or a schoolteacher. And the way she walked! No dallying for her. She strode forth decisive and commanding, like a general inspecting her troops.

But did she care for him or not? He had no idea! They had kept company for three months. She had let him row her around on a boat in Lake Merritt. They had walked together in Tilden Park as he had struggled to keep up. They had held hands in an outdoor theater in the Berkeley Hills as they watched a play by Shakespeare. And yet after the first several weeks she had not approved of a single thing he had said or done. Or worn.

"I will not be seen in public with you as long as you dress like that, William. That's all there is to it. Don't ask me to."

He hated to get into this again, because, try as he might, he simply could not understand what was wrong with the way he dressed, though no doubt she was right. "Is it my trousers?"

"William, what do you *think*?"

"Well I guess there's something wrong with them." He knew for a fact that they weren't too clean, but he thought there must be more to it than that.

"Look at those big checkerboard squares," Pamela said. "What do you think of that?"

Bill looked down toward his pants but had trouble seeing past his abdomen. He could see them from the knees on down, though, and she was right. His pants had large squares on them. They were held up by suspenders, which he had found over the years to be an efficient way to keep them from falling down.

His pants had large squares on them. They were held up by suspenders, which he had found over the years to be an efficient way to keep them from falling down.

"What about my shirt?" he asked, hoping to call attention away from his pants. "It's not too bad, is it?" He had seen many men wear shirts just like it, and they looked pretty good on them. It had crossed golf clubs just above his prominent left breast. Its short sleeves showed his freckled reddish arms to good advantage, he thought. But he noticed the way she was staring at his shirt. "You don't like it?"

To his relief, Pamela's harsh look softened. She

smiled and patted his arm. "William, I know what you need. And you're going to get it. No arguments, now. A makeover."

"A what?"

"A makeover. We're going to see Mr. Boris."

He was horrified. Did that mean he had to wear makeup?

"If you had a makeover I might be seen with you in public," she said. Pamela was suddenly in a better mood, cheered by her idea. But he saw trouble ahead. He didn't think he could wear makeup, though he wanted to make a hit with Pamela.

A week later, she marched him into a glass-fronted studio furnished with uncomfortable modern chairs not far from Union Square in San Francisco. The waiting room looked expensive. All the pictures on the walls were mauve and so was everything else in the room. A receptionist told them to wait there until Mr. Boris was available.

When finally he appeared, he glided silently into the room as if from out of nowhere. Mr. Boris was dark man of an indeterminable age and, without introducing himself, he leaned over and peered questioningly at William who sat fidgeting in an overly narrow chrome-and-vinyl chair. After quite some time, he said, "I see, I see," and he nodded soberly. Totally absorbed, he ignored Pamela except to say to her, while still staring at William, "Does Mrs. wish to wait here or come with?"

"I will accompany Mr. Whistle," she announced,

and she followed the two men through a door. On the other side, there was a large wraparound mirror and several clothes racks. William didn't know whether Boris was the first or last name of the man who stood him before the mirror and began to study him even more closely, from all angles. Honestly, Bill had never before noticed himself in quite the same way. He began to doubt that his powder-blue suspenders were the right color for his olive trousers. *Something* was wrong.

Mr. Boris told him to remove his clothes. William glanced at Pamela. Finally he dropped his suspenders and began to take his pants off, but this didn't go smoothly. The first trouser leg hung up on his shoe and lodged there, leaving him hopping on the other leg. As he was trying to recapture his balance a handful of change fell out of one pocket and made a really annoying sound as it hit the floor. Distracted, William had to drop his hung-up leg to the floor to keep from going over entirely, but he counterbalanced by waving his arms in the air. Mr. Boris stepped back a few feet as if to give him personal space to work this out. Of course William could see exactly how he looked during his entire attempt to disrobe since his image was reflected countless times from the front and both sides, and seeing himself in the mirror was confusing him pretty badly as he tried to re-establish his balance and get his damned pants over his goddamned shoe with everyone watching him. But he wasn't going to get flustered, he told himself.

"Do you have a chair?" Bill asked. He stood in boxer shorts and a pink golf shirt, his pants on the floor, still clinging to his shoes. When his question drew nothing from Mr. Boris but a blank look, he added, "For me to sit in?"

Understanding dawned on Mr. Boris's face, but he pointed to Pamela and said, "Mrs. sit." She was occupying the only chair in the room. She rose reluctantly. When no one brought the chair to him, Inspector Whistle was forced to hop over to it with his pants dragging behind. More change scattered on the tile floor. The entire scene was distasteful to Pamela, and she backed away from William as far as she could.

Seated now, with some difficulty he worked his pants over his shoes and freed himself. But when he looked up he noticed that Mr. Boris was staring at Pamela. Indeed, Mr. Boris began to approach her, gliding silently, and he circled Pamela, gazing at her from every angle. Pamela clutched her purse tightly but otherwise stood perfectly still as she had when Buddy had barked at her.

After some time, Mr. Boris said softly, as if to himself, "Yes, yes, I see." And then he said, "Mrs. stand," and he pointed to a spot before the mirror. Stiffly she took the spot as Bill sat and watched. For a while longer the Russian circled her. Finally he said, "Mrs. take off blazer and turtleneck. Skirt, too."

"Why, I certainly will not!" Pamela said.

"Whatever in the world are you doing?"

"Mrs. need makeover too. I make half price for you."

"*I* need a makeover? You're saying *I* need a makeover?" Pamela sputtered.

Mr. Boris glided once more around her and said, "For sure."

"Half price? I'll pay," Inspector Whistle offered, but when Pamela shot him a look he wondered whether he had said something wrong.

"He has to wait outside," she said, pointing at William.

"No, no, same time better," the makeover artist said, and to William he said, "You come," and indicated a spot beside Pamela, before the mirror. Bill left his pants on the chair and walked around the change he had scattered on the floor and took his place. She gave him one more withering look but then doffed her blazer and turtleneck, then her skirt. William caught his breath. She was magnificent standing there like a ramrod, straight as an arrow with no protrusions of flesh to mar the effect. On the other hand, he sensed and then actually began to see one taking shape on himself, a protrusion. Fortunately, Pamela was looking straight ahead into the mirror and not at him at all. For his part, he could not stop staring at her breathtaking body though he was aware of the problem that was creating.

"Shirt off now," Mr. Boris said to him. Well, that was tricky, because the shirt was the only thing keeping the lid on this thing, so to speak. Understandably, he was slow to take it off.

Beside him Pamela said sternly, "I did it, William. So must you." To make matters worse for him, she was now looking at him in the mirror to make sure he complied. William bent at the waist, hoping to pull himself in as he slipped his golf shirt over his head. But when he straightened up he noticed with horror a flash of flesh in his shorts, a narrow but significant breach that immediately showed signs of widening.

"Color!" Mr. Boris exclaimed from behind him, and the artist began to throw swatches of fabric over his shoulders, and then, thank God, Mr. Boris spun a good-sized cloth around William's waist and tied it in place like a sarong. "I do color now." Each piece of fabric was a different color. Soon Mr. Boris had similarly draped Pamela, and William's crisis was over.

After Mr. Boris had made notes about colors, he separated the two, sending Pamela into a washroom to remove her makeup—all she wore was lipstick— and Bill into a dressing room to don a rubber article something like a wetsuit with one big hole in it and two smaller holes. "What is this?" Bill asked.

"Is how you call? Girdle," Mr. B said, and it was. The damned thing was as hard to put on as his trousers had been to take off, and he was barely able to breathe when he had it fully installed. Still, looking downward Bill could get a clear shot at his upper thighs for the first time in memory. Mr. Boris looked him over and said, "Is good," but William refused to leave the dressing room in the girdle. So with the two still in the dressing room, Mr. Boris carefully measured nearly every inch of Bill's body, taking meticulous notes.

When Pamela came out minus her makeup, Mr. B peered closely at her face, then wrote in his booklet. Finally he made notes about her various diameters and circumferences and sent the two packing.

"I very busy now because of Thanksgiving. Everyone want now, tomorrow, yesterday! We finish you Wednesday, day before Thanksgiving. Clothes, hair, makeup, everything. Shoes. Everything. I write." He wrote a time and date in his appointment book and gave the couple a copy. As they all shook hands, William noticed that Mr. Boris wore a gold chain around his neck. "I like that," he thought. "I hope he sets me up in one of those."

Later, as they walked up Powell Street toward William's car, Pamela said, "For goodness' sake, William!"

He said, "What," but he didn't want to know.

"At your age!" This time he didn't even ask.

"You'd better not get any ideas, William. Just because you got my clothes off once doesn't mean you can do it again. Don't even give it a thought." But he thought maybe after he got his makeover he might give it a try. He'd have to figure out how to get that damned wetsuit off, though. That was going to be a problem.

Chapter Twenty-Five

[November, 1975]

Shortly before Thanksgiving, the male members of the Last Resort announced that they had a surprise for the women, and they called for a meeting of all the friends on a Sunday morning to present it. Everyone assembled, including Weezie and Tuck. This was the first time the friends had seen either one since Weezie had gotten sick. When she walked through the door, Buddy raced up to her, gave her a sniff and went berserk. He cried, he barked, he whirled and leapt, and after that he didn't leave her side. Weezie was pale and she moved slowly, but she was clearly happy to be back.

"I don't know what the guys have in store for us," Lenore told her, "but they want us on the second floor at 10 AM sharp." Everyone in the vicinity was patting Weezie or shaking hands with Tuck.

"Well, good," Weezie said. "That'll be my first chance to ride the elevator." Buddy cried when she and Tuck squeezed into the elevator, and Weezie picked him up and held him during a slow, creaky ride. At the landing on the second floor, they found a hand-lettered sign that said, "THIS WAY." An arrow on the sign pointed down the hall to the left. The two laughed, and Buddy jumped out of Weezie's arms and ran ahead.

Many of the friends were already assembled in the hallway outside a closed bedroom door on which a sign read, "HERE." Genevieve, Sophia, Tina, Zoë, Lenore and Pamela were all there when Weezie and Tuck arrived. Lenore said, "Everyone who isn't out here is inside that room. Hey," she addressed the crowd, "why don't we just go in?"

"They've got the door locked," Tina said. "They say it's not ten o'clock yet."

"Right," Zoë said, "it's 9:58. C'mon you guys!" she yelled through the door. "Open up!"

"Two minutes!" Harvey was heard to say from the other side of the door.

This gave Lenore time to say to Weezie, "I'm so glad that you're coming to live here now, Weezie.

Have you figured out yet where you're going to stay?"

Weezie's brow furrowed a little. "It's pretty hard," Weezie said. "Besides, we're all going to have to decide together. Tuck and I can't just come in and take whatever we want just because we're first."

Just then the door to the bedroom opened and Buddy bounded in, with Tuck and the women just behind. The room was already fairly crowded with Owen, Will, Harvey, Bentley and Tony, and of course it became completely packed when the others squeezed in. Despite the exhilarating crush and a carnival atmosphere in the air, Lenore was disappointed. There was nothing to see except each other. No work of art, no furniture, no creative painting job or stunning décor, no invention. She didn't know what she had been expecting except a surprise. No surprise here.

Zoë was the first to speak up. "Great, guys. Really great. I'm genuinely underwhelmed."

"The ceiling!" Lenore thought, and she threw her head back to look at the ceiling. Nothing there but some paint that needed retouching.

"The closet!" Genevieve said. "Is there something in the closet?"

"Well, take a look," Tony suggested.

She stepped to the door and the others jockeyed around the door to see inside. "Why, there are clothes inside! How nice of you men to hang them up. Yes sir. Hung them right up in there. By yourselves." Genevieve's kind words sounded strained.

"Okay you guys, what's going on?" Zoë sounded pretty annoyed. "It looks like maybe you made some unusual kind of clothes rack in the closet. Is that the surprise?" Buddy began to whine, as if disappointed. He looked from Zoë to Tony and back.

Tony said, "Well Genevieve, press that button," and he pointed to one inside the closet door."

Lenore had the sudden sensation that she was being attacked by a closet, a feeling she had never, ever before experienced.

"Will something hurt me, dear?" she asked.

"Genevieve!" cried Tony, aggrieved.

"All right," and Genevieve reached for the button as the others closed in to see. With no warning whatsoever, the clothes jerked into movement, all of them! Lenore had the sudden sensation that she was being attacked by a closet, a feeling she had never, *ever* experienced before. She and the others fell back, instinctively shielding their faces with their forearms.

They recovered quickly, though, and pressed back toward the closet to see what was happening. *The clothes were actually disappearing into the ceiling of the closet! And other clothes were descending from the closet ceiling and taking their place!*

"Harvey! What are your clothes doing in that closet?" Tina asked, not much to the point. Harvey's red sweater had dropped into view and was already on its way up and out as a couple of his blazers marched forward and then moved on.

"Genevieve," Tony said, "let off of the button." The whole thing came to an immediate halt. Clothes swung back and forth for a moment and then settled down.

"Jesus, Tony!" Tuck roared, "What did you guys do?" He had been tall enough to stand in the back row and still see all the action. The women were standing and staring with their mouths open.

Over six feet tall herself, Lenore had missed nothing either. "I know what you boys did. You just removed the last big stumbling block."

Lenore's husband winked at her and said, "Come on and look in the attic."

In the attic, there was Harvey's same red cashmere sweater that had just run its course through the closet downstairs, immobile now, and a familiar-looking blazer, frozen in place just as it emerged from the floor. They were hanging from a monorail track that emerged from the floor, ran the length of the enormous attic, doubled back and finally plunged back into the hole in the floor and into the closet below. Though only thirty or forty pieces of clothing hung on the rack, clearly it could have held hundreds of dresses, skirts, scarves, sweaters or even mink coats.

Will pointed out a huge pile of unused track parts that were stacked in one corner. "We have eight motors and a bunch of track. That means we can make a rack for whoever wants one."

"And we can store an unlimited amount of clothing up here," Harvey explained, "and we can keep it all mothproofed or whatever."

Lenore had seen the full implications right away. By now, everyone understood what this meant. Sophia said, "So I can stand in my closet and have any piece of clothing I want delivered to me."

"Yeah," Tony agreed.

"Wow," Zoë said. "Sign me up!"

"I think I'd like to have that room right down there," Pamela said, pointing at the hole in the floor above the room they had just come from. "Just put my name down for that one."

"Well, maybe it's time to choose up rooms, folks," Lenore suggested. "Weezie and Tuck *have* to." She looked around and for the first time noticed that they hadn't made the trip up to the attic.

"I'd like to take a couple of hours to look around before we choose," Sophia said, and the others said they would too.

"How about we get together about two o'clock to see if we can choose? Shall we meet in the sunroom?"

"That's a good idea," Zoë said. "But listen, you guys, I don't know how we can thank you enough. That was brilliant!" There was enthusiastic agreement among the other women.

"You don't have to thank us," Will said. "We just wanted to get on with choosing up rooms."

"The only thing I don't understand is why you put the rack on the floor," Zoë said.

The men looked at each other. "Uh, instead of where?" Owen asked.

"Instead of in the air," Zoë said, "so we could still use the floor to store linens and things." The men looked up. When they continued looking blank, Zoë went on, "Couldn't you hang the racks from the rafters? Instead of putting them on the floor?"

Finally Will said, "Yeah, we could…"

"But?"

"But we didn't think of it." Will smiled.

As everyone was filing down the narrow attic stairs, Pamela spoke to Lenore. "Did someone write my name down for that room?"

"Oh, for heaven's sake, Pamela, we can't go choosing up rooms on the basis of first dibs!" Lenore had finally lost patience with her. "Besides, Weezie and Tuck are going to need a place right away, and that room is the only one that's ready." Once Tuck and Weezie decided to move into The Last Resort, they had started the process of selling their own home.

"They're not the only ones," Pamela said. "I need a place too."

"You do?"

"My mother has announced that she is going to marry *Tex*," she whined, "and Mother has asked me to leave her house."

"And your inheritance?" Lenore asked, alarmed for Pamela.

"If you must know, everything will go to her *husband* upon her death. In the parlance of the gutter, I'm flat busted," Pamela said, and she raised her nose a degree higher.

Lenore suddenly felt guilty for having been mad at Pamela, but she couldn't help glancing at Pamela's chest, and, for once, she agreed with her completely.

Chapter Twenty-Six

[November, 1975]

Genevieve Rutherford had met Aldous, her husband, thirty years earlier at a ski lodge near Lake Tahoe, not long after she had inherited the mansion from her mother. Though he had called himself a ski instructor, she never actually witnessed him instructing anyone. She thought he was a ski bum but she didn't care. Aldous Tilford was the most beautiful man she had ever seen. And, oh, how he could dance! No flinging himself around on the dance floor like so many other young men. Dancing with Genevieve in the ski lodge,

Aldous moved smoothly and deliberately, like a panther.

After dancing, he had guided her to the quietest table in the lodge. Over an Irish coffee, he told her that he had renounced worldly goods, except for things that seemed to come his way: expensive gifts (like his skis, for instance) from grateful ski students. Hearing that he had vowed to live a life "uncluttered by objects" made Genevieve feel bourgeois and shallow, for, as she shamefully confessed, she had recently inherited a huge mansion near San Francisco and a good deal of other material possessions, including money. Aldous assured her that she should not feel bad. "It is your karma to possess 'things.' It is your special burden," he said. "But beware that you are not owned by your possessions. Rather than being possessed by your house, share it. Rather than being owned by your money, give it away. Genevieve," he said, looking deeply into her eyes, "I have given up far more than you may ever realize, and I am a better man for it." Genevieve was astonished that Aldous was so insightful about her situation and knew what she should do to free herself from the guilt of being undeservedly rich.

After several days and nights of skiing and dancing and talking into the early mornings, he told her that he might be willing to give up his ski students for a time in order to be with her in the Bay Area.

Aldous was so dark a man as to seem sinister to some people, men especially. He had dark skin, black hair and the bluest eyes imaginable. He was of below average height, which made Genevieve want to hold him. Thirty-five-year-old Genevieve, well protected by her parents until they died, took his hand and held it to her lips, looked into his eyes and said, "Aldous, dear, come to me in Piedmont and teach me how to live…and how to make love."

Five days later, he called from Oakland's Greyhound Bus Depot and asked if she could pick him up, "Or I can hitch," he said. They were married by a justice of the peace in Reno, Nevada five weeks later.

During the years after the War, Aldous became tight with a group of free thinkers in Berkeley and San Francisco and changed his name to Free Love. "Free love," he was fond of saying: "I preach it and teach it." He did, too. Many young people were enthralled by the handsome man who introduced himself as Free Love. He shared with them his vision of society. He was working, he told them, to found a community whose streets would be named Breast Boulevard, Sex Drive and, of course, Free Love Lane. But mainly what he shared with people was their wives and girlfriends and in some cases their boyfriends and husbands.

In the meantime, Genevieve felt like a hopeless prude, but the truth was that she just couldn't loosen up and enjoy free love. It's not that Aldous kept her home. He would have been happy enough if she had tagged along from one bed to the next, but she preferred to rattle around in the old Piedmont mansion by herself. Of course sometimes Aldous filled the house nearly to the ceilings with partiers, supplying them with enormous quantities of booze, paid for out of Genevieve's slowly dwindling stash of money. Those parties were legendary. A famous swing band once played for hundreds of drunken, naked revelers in the ballroom. Everyone loved the parties except Genevieve and her neighbors. The neighbors pulled down their shades and locked their doors. Genevieve gathered a mattress from a chaise lounge, a pillow, a flashlight and a book and locked herself in the furnace room, the only room in the house in which strangers were not copulating.

Eventually word got around that, besides sharing his vision of a free-love society, Aldous had also shared certain diseases with virtually hundreds of people in Berkeley and San Francisco. Many of his followers dropped out of his circle, took the cure and tried to put their lives back together following their divorces, alcohol burnouts and nervous breakdowns. As some of his former followers believed in later years, rather than set people free from the uptight mores of society, Free Love had cut a wide swath of destruction through a sea of idealistic youth.

Of course Genevieve had to take the cure, too, and for once she found herself blaming Aldous rather than herself. As the years advanced, the climate cooled between them. For one thing, she had become alarmed at how much money Aldous had spent.

Though she owned the mansion free and clear, taxes and upkeep still cost a ton of money. She could foresee the day when she simply wouldn't have the money to keep the house.

For his part, Aldous had begun to complain of boredom. Once again known as Aldous Tilford, and with no followers now and no friends, he became restless. Soon he began hitching rides up north to the ski country where, he said, he was trying to reestablish a business as an instructor.

Over forty now, and left alone in the big house with plenty of time to think, Genevieve finally admitted to herself that she had married a fortune hunter.

He had gone through a great deal of her money, and she had let it happen. Between them, they had no income except for the sporadic return from securities she had inherited. She was without friends, and most often Aldous was absent. For the first time, Genevieve began to think about herself. What did *she* want from life? What would she do if she were on her own, as, indeed, she essentially was? During the next five years, while Aldous came and went, seeking his own happiness, Genevieve slowly came to an understanding of her needs. They were simple. She loved to dance and she preferred dancing with handsome men with dark complexions. Beyond that she loved her house, the old Rutherford mansion, and she loved her garden. She wished to live in the house and enjoy the garden with friends.

One day Genevieve realized that her husband had

been gone for a very long time—nearly a year. She made inquiries and found that he hadn't been seen in Bear Valley for at least six months. No one knew where he was. After he had been gone for about two years, she decided that he might not ever return, and she decided that it was time to get on with her life. The first substantial move she made in response was to turn off the enormous furnace, once and for all. Shutting it down (and making sure she had plenty of warm sweaters) was part of her plan to cut overhead expenses. Along those lines, she began to defer maintenance of the old house, preferring to ignore problems rather than spend money to have them fixed. And, finally, at the age of forty-two, she began going to dances and picking up beautiful Latin men who pronounced her name "Jen ne vyay vay."

"Why not?" she asked herself. "Why not?"

Genevieve had told the group that she was going to Modesto for three days to attend bullfighting there, and of course they had been aghast. "It's an interest I acquired in Spain about twenty years ago," she had explained. "It's not at all what you think." That had been the truth but not the whole truth. "Frankly," Genevieve thought as she gunned her ancient engine and watched dark smoke billow from its rear, "my twelve adopted children are wonderful people, but such prudes!"

As she urged her old Volvo sedan up the Altamont pass, she reminisced about her sojourn to

Spain. She had gone there to pursue an interest in Latin men. During her marriage—well, technically, she supposed, she still *was* married—she had dutifully held her interest in check. But with Aldous gone off to God-knows-where, what was she saving herself for? So she went to the Mecca for Latin men, Spain. She knew only a few words of Spanish but packed her suitcase anyway and decided not to worry.

Her man-hunting in Spain started out badly. While she may have been able to snag old geezers, it was not on them that she had set her sights. She preferred the supple, virile twenty-somethings, the young men who could dance all night, but the knack for corralling them had eluded her. She had begun by staring wantonly at would-be victims in bars and dance halls. They seemed to believe that something was wrong with her and were obviously made uncomfortable by her fixed gaze. They had moved on as quickly as they decently could. She had actually fondled one dark young fellow in a bar, but evidently this had scared him to death and he fled. Minutes later his father, a man somewhat younger than she was, she noted, had shown up waving his fist and making threats in Spanish that luckily Genevieve couldn't understand.

Several times she had played damsel-in-distress, but she merely learned that young Spanish men are commendably polite. In one instance, a fine-looking young fellow had helped her cross the street as if she were blind and a hundred years old. Another handsome Spaniard had wanted to introduce her to his mother, with whom, he was sure, she would be great friends.

As Genevieve drove past miles of towering windmills on gusty Altamont Pass and finally veered south onto I-5, she recalled the moment of her breakthrough. In Madrid, in a dance hall, she had struck out again, and finally she had given up and headed toward the exit. One of the dark gods she had seen but had not made contact with walked in her direction, and as they passed, she smiled slightly and winked. That was all. But she hadn't walked another ten feet before he caught up with her and, smiling, asked her in English whether the *señora* had something in her eye.

"Why, yes, I believe I do, dear. Would you mind looking a little closer and telling me if you see something?"

After that it was easy. She simply winked. Why hadn't she known about that before, she wondered?

She adored the way they said her name: Jen ne vyay vay. How lovely!

The countryside through which she drove had flattened out, and now she began to notice irrigated farmland and orchards. On her ancient car radio she found a Spanish-language station that played popular Mexican dance music. Ahead of her the November sky was dark and she wondered what would happen to the bullfights if rain blew in.

A few days after she had learned to wink, she

attended her first bullfight. Young Latin men had been *everywhere* in the old wooden stadium! She had rarely been so excited. There had been the bullfighting itself, of course. It had been rather distressing. But the bullfighters!

After that it was easy. She simply winked. Why hadn't she thought of that before, she wondered?

Late in the evening, the crowd roared when the next matador's name was announced. This was to be the last fight, the climax of the night, and clearly this matador was the crowd's favorite, a master, though no more than thirty years old. He bore himself with the machismo of a flamenco dancer, defiant of fate. She could not take her eyes from him. From her first-row seat just above ground level, she smelled dung and urine mingled in the dusty air, and when a huge black bull was released into the arena, she could feel her bleacher seat tremble. Trumpets blared.

The bull wheeled and for a moment stood fast, seeking the enemy, blowing. Then he focused and charged. As the bull hurtled closer, El Matador feigned unconcern. He looked away from the bull, bowed to the crowd and as the bull thundered upon him, he gracefully flagged the bull by, as if directing traffic. As the bull's momentum carried him on, the matador walked away, his chest up, his back to the bull.

On the next pass, the matador bit the bull with his sharp pic, enraging him further. Time after time the bull narrowly missed the matador, and gradually the bull's rage became frustration and finally desperation. But if the bull was wounded and made desperate by the matador's pics, he also seemed more dangerous now, lunging without the predictability of his earlier charges. And finally something happened. Genevieve could see a moment of imbalance, a stumble, something not quite right at the critical pass, and the matador spun to the ground. The crowd gasped as the matador kept rolling, rolling away from the slobbering black bull that had turned quickly and was charging at the bullfighter now with his head down. The matador was up and running, running for his life toward the nearest wall, running straight for Genevieve.

She would never forget the smells and the sounds of the next twenty seconds, the sharp scent of rage and livestock, the gasping for breath that seemed l louder than the crowd's screams and finally the Whumpf of an eighteen-hundred-pound bull hitting the wooden wall under her just as the matador had cleared it. Nor would she forget the matador's terrified face as he landed nearly in her lap. Genevieve reached for his forehead and smoothed it, and with her thumb she wiped sweat from one of his eyes.

"Are you all right, dear?" she asked softly. Those in the bleachers around them stood and watched hushed, as she cradled him. The matador trembled as he searched her face. "You're very brave, darling," she said. The matador closed his eyes for a few seconds, took a deep breath and turned back to the arena. Below him, the bull lay convulsing in the dust, his neck bent in a sickening angle, panting and gargling blood. Genevieve's matador dropped to the arena floor and walked purposely to where he had fallen. There he retrieved his sword, returned to the prostrate bull and put him out of his misery with a single, powerful thrust of the sword between his ribs, into his heart. The huge, pathetic bull sounded one last moan and died. The crowd cheered the matador, who left the field without either pride or shame. He had survived.

And now, eight years later, he was in Modesto, Genevieve's matador, to teach a master class in bullfighting. She had been the first to sign up. Afraid that a woman might not be allowed to take part, she had signed her application "Gene Vieve." The surname had a nice Latinate ring to it, she thought.

As she drove into the outskirts of Modesto, she daydreamed that fighting a bull might be rather like handling some of the young fellows she danced with in Mission Street dance parlors on weekend nights. Genevieve turned up her radio and cruised on into downtown Modesto, looking for a nice old-fashioned hotel from which to stage her conquest.

His years of bravery had cost Maximo Orosco dearly. He entered the county-fairgrounds corral in which his students awaited him as if walking on glass. The students stood and applauded with adoration. One could only imagine what scars were hidden by his long-sleeved silk shirt and loose-fitting white slacks. He held his head up, though, and his hair was black. Genevieve watched, enthralled, and noticed everything.

"Friends," he began, and he addressed them in an accented but dignified English. "Haven't we all at some time in our lives looked up to find that a bull is looking us in the eye? We have come here to pick apples or mend a fence. And suddenly we see that there is a bull with balls a mile long and he is going to get us. Perhaps we are twelve years old and weigh ninety pounds, and the bull weighs two thousand pounds. It has happened to many of us. This is a moment when we may wet our pants." Everyone laughed. "We are so little and he is so big.

"But that is not the only time when we may be

scared. We might be held up by a bandit whose pistol has a barrel this big! We may be in an airplane and suddenly we have dropped five thousand feet. We may be dying. That is scary, huh? Dying? Yet we all have to do it. Every one of us. Some of us will meet up with a bull in a field, but *all* of us will die. What can we do? Even if we weigh 200 pounds, we are small when death is looking us in the eye.

"We can run like hell, right? But what can we do when we can't get away? Because sooner or later we will not be able to get away from the bull or the bandit or death. Maybe we will be afraid. You bet we'll be afraid. What can we do?

"Well, we might try some tricks." The matador grinned. "We don't have to be idiots, do we? Not me!" Genevieve was the only female in the master class, and she laughed and smiled just like the boys and young men.

"If we can make that bull run right past us and look like a monkey, well, that's okay, right? That's what I would do, play a trick." The matador grinned and so did those who hung on his words. "I'm going to show you how. Don't worry, I'll show you how." Then Maximo Orosco looked serious. "But if your trick doesn't work and you have to die...I will show you that too. I will show you how to die and be a man. Because what else is there, in the end? When tricks don't work. There is only you and Death, and if it is your time to go, so be it, you will go as a man. I will show you how to look Death in the eye."

The young men in the matador's workshop looked solemn. Genevieve thought they would have followed him into death, and she would have, too. An assistant passed out capes to the students and seemed embarrassed when he came to Genevieve, but he was very polite and asked if she wanted one too. "Yes, dear," she said, "I'm going to fight the bull, just like you."

"Not me," he said. "I'm scared of bulls."

As the first day of the three-day class came to a close, the matador finished showing Genevieve how to hold her cape and than said to her, "Señora, of course I recognize you. You once wiped the sweat from my forehead and told me I was very brave. I did not feel brave. I felt surprised to be alive. How can I thank you?"

"Well, dear," she said, "what are you doing for Thanksgiving?"

Chapter Twenty-Seven

[November 1975]

The wine man from Christie's said to Tuck, "Just hold the flashlight for me, would you? Right there. Don't want mega-lumens blasting *these* babies. Did you say turn of the century?"

"Some are older."

"Shine there. Jesus Christ! Look at this." The wine man took a soft-bristled brush out of a pocket and lovingly brushed dust from a bottle's label, like an archeologist slowly unearthing an ancient Grecian urn, one speck of dust at a time. "A hundred-year-old first-growth Bordeaux." His voice trembled. He lifted the bottle but kept it horizontal, and he gazed at the sediment that had settled along the bottle's bottom side. Then he lowered the bottle to its rack and whipped out a notebook in which he made an entry. "Fantastic," he muttered. Tuck was beginning to think they might have something here.

At the end of two hours, the flashlight was dim and the wine man had finished his inventory. But before they left the room, Tuck called the expert's attention to the small barrel of Courvoisier. "Nope, has no value. It's not in a bottle. No vintage. Drink it. Enjoy." Tuck secretly grimaced when he heard "enjoy." Along with "no problem" and "have a nice day," "enjoy" was probably his least favorite thing to hear, at least among the words that were usually uttered with good intentions. Still, he was glad to hear the "drink it" part. Ever since he had sampled it while on his hands and knees, he had been longing to get back to it.

"Going to have to crack open a bottle of wine, though," the wine man said. "See if it's alive." The fellow seemed so eager to start popping corks that Tuck wondered whether the spirits specialist might be motivated by thirst rather than the necessities of his work.

"Well, what do you want to open?" Tuck asked.

"Heh, heh, how about this 1896 Chateau Lafitte?" Tuck hesitated. The guy seemed too damned eager. "Christie's will have to stand behind this wine," the wine man said sternly. "Reputation's at stake."

"Do you have a corkscrew?" Tuck asked.

"My God, man! Can't do that. Have to decant it."

So they rode up in the elevator while the expert, his hands shaking slightly, Tuck noticed, held the bottle on its side to keep sediment from billowing back up into the wine. In the kitchen, Tuck found Sophia and Lenore and asked for a decanter. Though they both felt sure there was one somewhere, they had trouble going right to it. In the meantime, the wine guy urged them on, weary of cradling the bottle.

Upstairs, here in the light, Tuck noticed how pale the man was, as if he had spent his life in caves, or at least his adult years. "Do you feel okay?" Tuck asked.

"Well, frankly I'm getting damned tired," he said, sounding peeved now because of the delay. Lenore sent Tuck to bring a ladder so as to explore an upper cupboard. Back in the kitchen, he set the ladder up where instructed and Sophia found the decanter right away. It took rather less time to find four wine glasses, which the Christie's man insisted the women wash even though the glasses were already clean. "Dishwasher detergent residue," he explained. When the glasses had been washed, the wine guy refused to use the corkscrew that Lenore offered and insisted on the one he was carrying. Unfortunately he was unable to get at it in his trouser pocket because of his two-handed grip on the wine bottle and had to ask Tuck to have a go at it. "Right front," he instructed. Tuck couldn't even get his beefy fingers in the man's pocket though he tried for quite some time. "For God's sake, please hurry!" the man said. By this time his hands were beginning to tremble quite radically. Finally Sophia had to fish for it as the man bent slightly and did all kinds of moves to loosen the tension in his pocket that made the procedure so tricky. Within eight or ten minutes, though, Sophia had fished out the corkscrew, which Tuck thought looked an awful lot like the one the women had proffered a quarter of an hour earlier.

With exquisite care, the wine man tilted the bottle just enough so the wine wouldn't pour out as he extracted the cork, and when the cork was out he had Tuck shine the flashlight's dim beam through the bottle's neck so he could monitor the sediment as he poured wine into the decanter. His hand was now steady as a surgeon's. As soon as the wine was decanted, he poured a small amount for each person and began to peer at the wine in his glass. At first he held it at arm's length while he gazed at it, then he brought it to within a few inches of his eyes for a close-up examination. Soon, though, he began to sniff. Tuck and the others were alarmed when the man moaned as he sniffed the hundred-year-old wine. In ecstasy? Grief? It was hard to say. It rather distracted Tuck from his own experience of the wine. "There's not a hell of a lot to smell here," thought Tuck, who could smell a mildewing house from a block away or a keg of brandy through a double wall. Certainly there was nothing in it that smelled like fruit. Instead it had a kind of floor-wax bouquet. Or did the smell remind him of very old leather shoes sensed from a great distance? In fact, even as he inhaled the wine's faint aroma, it seemed to weaken. He wasted no more time and put the glass to his lips. Barely perceptible in the ancient wine was a mildly pleasant suggestion of water in which a rose petal or two had been soaked, many years ago, and then it faded.

Barely perceptible in the ancient wine was a mildly pleasant suggestion of water in which a rose petal or two had been soaked, many years ago.

Disappointed, he was startled when the Christie's wine connoisseur quit groaning and said, "Well, that's what makes life worth living!"

Tuck stifled his impulse to say, "It is?" Sophia and Lenore also wisely kept quiet and managed to assume looks of innocence.

"Heh, heh! Just drank a $3000 bottle of wine!" the wine man said. "Dead and gone now, of course. But for about twenty seconds, heaven! Heaven! The full force of my company's reputation behind it. Nothing less!"

Tuck had mixed feelings about having drunk a $3,000 bottle of wine, though his part of it only came to about $750. The others were just going to have to take Tuck and Sophia and Lenore's word that they hadn't missed anything, except the $3,000 they could have sold the bottle of wine for.

On the next day, the Christie's wine expert faxed a list of the wines he had inventoried and the prices he expected them to fetch at a special wine auction coming up soon. Lenore, Pamela, Zoë and Tony were on hand to read the news. He had inventoried a total of 119 bottles not including the "test bottle," and they had an average value of $2230 each for a total of $265,370 minus a commission to Christie's for a grand estimated total of $212,296. Of course the actual total could go one way or the other, he warned, and there were no guarantees.

"Is he kidding?" Zoë exclaimed. "$212,000?"

"Looks like we'll be able to afford the fancy Thanksgiving dinner," Tony grinned.

"I guess *so*," Zoë said. "Of course we haven't voted yet whether to sell the wine or drink it."

"Well, I vote we sell them," Pamela said.

"Good," Lenore said. "I think that makes it unanimous."

"And then split up the money," Pamela added.

"You mean in cash? We each take away…" Tony shook his head. "Whatever that would be: $15,000?"

"How long before we get it?" Pamela asked.

"I don't know if we should do that, Pamela. I can think of good ways to use that money on the house," Tony said. "Like all the expenses for making the rooms into apartments, including our new closet system."

"Or it would restore the swimming pool and pay for the new roof," Lenore said.

"Well, I'm going to take *mine* in cash," Pamela said in a huff. The room was silent. The friends were drinking coffee on a Saturday morning in what they had come to call the wisteria room. Several in the group believed that the air in the wisteria room was healthy because of its resident vine.

After a while Lenore said, "Pamela, I'm sure that will have to be voted on."

"Fine, you can vote to do whatever you wish with your money," Pamela said, "but I'm going to take my money out."

"We make decisions and settle disputes by majority vote, Pamela," Tony said. "Besides, it's not your money and it's not mine. It's income for the corporation. If we were to take money out personally, we'd be piercing the corporate veil."

"Blah, blah, blah," Pamela spat back. Then she slammed her cup down on the coffee table and stood up. "Well, I'm not going to beg. But I need that money! And it *is* mine!" Pamela's face grew red and tears came to her eyes. Without ever really looking at anyone in the room, she stomped out, and a moment later those she left behind could hear the huge front door slam.

"Wow!" Zoë said.

"The last I knew, Pamela wanted to *drink* the wine," Tony reminded them.

"She's broke now," Zoë said. "Things change."

"And she has a right to change her mind," said Lenore, always judicious, "but she doesn't have a right to take the money."

"Listen," Tony said, "I don't want to be rude, but, honestly, I can't understand why you've kept Pamela in your wine-tasting group all these years. Fifteen years? And then brought her into this? She's not very congenial. In fact, she's disagreeable most of the time. She's stuck up and she seems to contribute nothing. Am I wrong?"

Zoë and Lenore looked at each other and finally Zoë conceded, "Good question. You'd better ask Lenore."

"She's not usually so bad," Lenore hedged.

Tony said, "Okay, I'll keep out of it."

"Oh, come on, Tony, don't give up so easy. It was a good question. Lenore, why *have* we kept Pamela in the group all these years?"

"Well, she's a known quantity. Good or bad, we know what to expect from her."

"Mainly bad," he said.

"Tony! Lenore's right. We're used to her. Beyond that...Lenore, what is it that we like about her? Can you remember?"

"She does have high standards. The table setting has to be just so; she doesn't appreciate anyone wearing jeans; she expects the garden to have meandering paths, and she certainly won't have pigeons living in the attic." Lenore laughed.

"Besides that," Zoë added, "where would we stand with City Hall if Pamela hadn't charmed William Whistle? You see, Tony?"

"I feel bad for her," Lenore confessed. "For her first sixty years, she thought she would inherit a fortune. Suddenly she has nothing."

"Personally," Tony said, "I think the reason you've put up with her so long is that all of you are simply too nice to kick her out." Zoë and Lenore shrugged and Tony went on. "I don't mean that there's anything wrong with being nice. That's why I signed on, because all of you are good people. That, plus the cooking."

"The whole Pamela thing does bring it home that you have to be careful whom you elect to spend your life with," Lenore said. "It's not the same as signing-up a member for a wine-and-garden group, is it?"

"Has it occurred to anyone that she'll sic Inspector Whistle on us, and he'll find some way to shut us down?" Tony asked.

"That's a thought," Zoë said. "But why would she

do that if she's going to live here too?" For a while, they all thought about that.

"Hmmm," Lenore said. "Well, talking about cooking, Tony, something tells me that Thanksgiving dinner is going to be eventful."

"It sounds like we're going to do some pretty fancy eating," Tony said. "I can't wait."

"And some pretty fancy cooking," Zoë answered. She and Lenore exchanged looks and shook their heads as if they were already exhausted.

Chapter Twenty-Eight

[November, 1975]

In the past year or so, people had begun responding to Bentley with less enthusiasm than in his younger years, and with a heavy heart Bentley noticed the difference. They were treating him—well, like a graceless old man. He ascribed it to being sixty and he tried to shrug it off. But then, about a month before Thanksgiving, he had finally come to realize that he had been walking around like a tin man. He could barely turn his head far enough to his right to see the side-view mirror in his car, and he couldn't imagine being able to look over his shoulder in either direction. He had a perpetual stiff neck, and he had headaches every day. In retrospect, he believed that he had been in that condition for at least a year and maybe much longer. During that time, he had worked hard in his nursery business and in the garden at the Last Resort, but now he realized that he had been taking less and less pleasure in working.

And finally he had noticed that he could barely walk. "Strange," he thought, "how much pain we can tolerate without being aware of it." When he rose from bed each morning, not only did his neck bother him, but his feet hurt so much that he could hardly walk two yards into the bathroom. When he became conscious that this was so, he probed his feet and discovered that it was his heels that hurt so badly. His heels? Had he bruised them?

No wonder he hadn't been turning any heads. He had been feeling like an octogenarian and looking like one. So Bentley resolved to do whatever it would take to get over it. His doctor diagnosed his sore heels as bone spurs and his tin-man neck as osteoarthritis. The doctor sent him to an orthopedist for the bone spurs and to a physical therapist for his neck.

Today, after a month of physical therapy and after cortisone shots in both heels, he was returning to his orthopedist for a follow-up. As he walked he was conscious that his shoulders were set back, his chest was thrust forward and his head held high, and that he strode on painless feet for the first time in recent memory. And then, behind him, in the hallway of his doctor's clinic he heard, "Hey Ben, is that you?"

A thrill telegraphed up Bentley's spine. He turned. "I can't believe it! My old college roommate, is that you? Mark!" The tall man in a white doctor's smock and handsome gray hair stood grinning, and as he and Bentley walked toward one another, they spread their arms.

As Owen Holt finished teaching his graduate seminar, he found that he could hardly wait to get the hell away from the classroom and over to the mansion so he could finish up on the Jaguar. Just as he was gathering his notes and preparing to flee, a student trapped him and requested clarification on points Owen had raised during the discussion. The student's series of questions became quite windy, and Owen sneaked a glance at his watch, annoyed by the thought that daylight gave out early at this time of year, just four days before Thanksgiving, and he desperately needed natural light in which to finish the Jaguar.

Owen often dreamed about retiring. In fact, the University had made early retirement an attractive prospect and he had been tempted. After nearly thirty-five years of teaching, he no longer had the fire in his belly for engineering or for teaching. But when he had tried to imagine his life after retirement, he was disturbed by the feeling that, without the university, he would be cut loose and isolated, without community or even an identity. He would soon be a forgotten man, merely underfoot at home, which unquestionably was Lenore's domain.

Lately, though, he found himself thinking along different lines. Since he and Lenore had bought into The Last Resort, he was so impatient to get on with his life, meaning his life outside of teaching, that he no longer worried about being isolated, bored and all the other things he had feared would be part of retirement. In fact, there never seemed to be enough time these days to do the work he was looking forward to doing, and usually that had to do with the big house in Piedmont.

Like now. He had no patience for answering questions from a student who, mostly, just wanted attention. The misguided youth imagined that his professor would be thrilled to discover a student interested enough in queuing theory to ask questions about it. What actually would have thrilled Owen would have been to work on the Jag while there was still some daylight. "Smug idiot," he thought. In previous years he would have given the young fellow the benefit of the doubt. Perhaps the kid only seemed smug. Maybe the student hadn't actually cheated and charmed his way into graduate school as Owen guessed he had. But nowadays Owen wasn't likely to romanticize his students, and he muttered something to the young man about a meeting he had to attend and was out of the building and on his way to the house in nothing flat.

As Owen drove his Toyota Camry away from the University and up Ashby Avenue toward Piedmont, he reflected that there was always something interesting going on at the Last Resort, even when he couldn't be there to enjoy it, which, of course, was the problem. He needed more time to do the things he wanted to do. In short, retirement was sounding better and better to him.

Owen drove directly to the mansion's twelve-car garage where the Jaguar, covered with wool blankets, waited for him to finish the last few steps of its restoration. When he pulled back the blankets, a skylight in the garage's roof let in a few feeble rays of daylight. He gazed at the car a few moments before he began work. Owen had completely restored its engine and had lovingly removed dents and scratches from its body. Its original midnight-purple paint was marvelously preserved. All it needed now was the installation of the back seat—he had finally found one with the right upholstery in a wrecked-car lot in Reno—and waxing and polishing.

Late that night, after he had wiped away the last traces of polish from its paint and brought the auto's surface to a rich shine, he sent a postcard to each of the friends:

Would you like a ride to Thanksgiving dinner?
Make your reservations now
for Owen's door-to-door shuttle service.
"A ride you won't forget!"

While Owen was waxing and polishing the Jaguar that evening, Lenore was in the house—the bighouse, as Owen and Lenore often called it—making the bed. That small domestic chore was far more than it seemed. The act of making the bed meant that the couple had finally chosen a suite of rooms—bedroom, sitting room and bathroom—that was now theirs and theirs alone, and that, with a bed in it, their apartment was at least functional enough to spend the night in if they chose to. From this point forward, at any time and to whatever degree they desired, they could live in the house.

Like other animals, the friends seemed intent on providing for the coming winter.

When the men of the house had demonstrated the feasibility of their closet scheme and the women realized that they would have to give up nothing whatsoever in the way of clothing to move in, the logjam had broken, and Lenore and the other women had chosen their family quarters within a few days. Of course Weezie and Tuck had led the way. They had been living in the house for more than a week, and the good time those two were having—relaxing in their suite and dallying over long suppers by the fireplace—was making their friends wish for the same. Suddenly each couple and Pamela and Bentley had all secured their own, private spaces and here and there in the big old house, as the night advanced, the friends were feathering their nests. Weezie and Tuck stood together admiring the reading lamps they had installed alongside their chairs, imagining long, quiet days and nights of leisurely reading. Tuck thought that this winter he would revisit Charles Dickens. Weezie had recently discovered a passion for Agatha Christie and planned to read every one of her novels in chronological order. Bentley was pleased by the new coffeemaker he had just plugged in, and he imagined having a nice, slow cup every morning before emerging from his room. Tony and Zoë had mounted on the wall of their study a favorite painting of a Sierra landscape and they stood back to admire it. Pamela arranged books alphabetically in her new bookcase. Lenore, waiting for Owen to finish working on the Jaguar and come up from the garage, framed photos of their children and grandchildren and mounted them on their new desk. Will rigged up an extension cable for his headphones. He wanted the cable long enough to reach his easy chair so he could listen to music late at night without bothering Sophia. His project for the winter was to study the entire cello recordings of Pablo Casals. Genevieve worked at framing the certificate someone named Gene Vieve had earned by completing the Maximo Orosco Master Class in Bullfighting. Like all other animals, the friends seemed intent on providing for the coming winter, and for whatever reason— maybe because people are the only animals that know about Thanksgiving—they dreamed of having their nests in order by the fourth Thursday in November.

Chapter Twenty-Nine

[November, 1975]

The really fevered preparations for Thanksgiving began on Tuesday and were choreographed from a list created by Lenore, Sophia, Zoë, Genevieve, Tina and Weezie. Weezie had been forbidden by her doctor to take part in strenuous activity, but that did not prevent her from helping to create the master list. Pamela said that she was going to be "engaged in other activities" during the days just before the holiday.

Heeding the adage that too many cooks spoil the

broth, the others appointed Sophia to oversee the whole production. She was willing and she hoped she was able.

The men had been assigned lists of their own. "And don't whine, Harvey," Tina told her husband. "Not if you want to eat Thanksgiving dinner." Harvey didn't whine. On the other hand, he wasn't happy about having to polish silver. He knew from years of experience that he developed really serious discomfort in his knees when he had to polish silver, and after an hour of it he experienced difficulty breathing and a nearly unconquerable need to go somewhere else. That never stopped Tina from giving him the job. He would have come to dread Thanksgiving except that he loved turkey dressing so much.

Harvey developed really serious discomfort in his knees when he had to polish silver, and after an hour of it he experienced difficulty breathing.

"And bring down that big table in the attic and set it up in the dining room beside the other table," Tina said. Harvey was really annoyed at being bossed around by his wife. He had been eyeing that table up in the attic, figuring that sooner or later Tina was going to ask him to bring it down. It was a monstrous thing. Not only was it terrifically heavy, he was certain, but it had cobwebs on it, too, and the thought made his skin creep. "Dust it off before you bring it down," Tina said, as if she had read his mind. "And polish it. You can use this lemon wax."

He didn't see why it had to be polished. "I call that 'make-work,' he muttered under his breath. "That's work she's going to make me do."

Fortunately it turned out that the other guys had been assigned the same job. So on Tuesday night he, Will, Owen, Tony, Bentley and Tuck convened in the attic with a couple of six-packs. They found they needed to ease into the job with some conversation and a beer or two.

"Have you noticed how Buddy and Ninja stay downstairs with the women when there's work to do?" Tony asked.

"They're just staying close to the food source," Tuck explained.

"Remember how the women brought beers to us at that picnic?" Tony asked. In a falsetto he imitated: "Oh, here, guys, let us bring you a couple of brews! Are they cold enough? Save room for pie, though." They laughed.

"We're paying for it now, guys," Will said, and then after a little while he added, "Pass me the lemon polish, will you?" Pretty soon the gigantic table was looking good. It took the whole crew to bring it down two flights of stairs to the dining room.

On Wednesday, the day before Thanksgiving, Bentley stayed home from the nursery to pitch in with the preparations. The women sent him into the garden to cut flowers for bouquets. He didn't argue, nor would he ever have argued with them, but the truth is that Bentley really hated to cut flowers. His intuition told him that the plants *felt* his clippers' steely bite. He was able to pull weeds and to prune roses and mow lawns, but those were cases where doing so freed other plants to grow better or encouraged new growth. Harvesting flowers to decorate a house was another matter, he thought. It is true that he had complied last summer when the women asked him to cut flowers for William Whistle's seduction, but the experience had been hard on him.

Besides, he liked to view flowers in the garden, where, often, he would creep up upon them for a close look as if they were butterflies or birds that might take flight. So to fill his order for Thanksgiving bouquets, he compromised. He pruned shrubs that like a nice trim in the fall anyway, and he saved the most dramatic cuttings for the house. He took small branches from the trees whose leaves turn yellow and red even in the mild climate of the Bay Area. He trimmed pyracanthas and cotoneasters for their gorgeous displays of red and orange berries, which he justified doing because, he thought, they needed cutting back or they would soon elbow aside their garden-mates. In San Francisco's China Town, Zoë had found four-dozen tiny, celadon bud-vases, one for each place setting at the two tables. To fill them, Bentley cut dozens and dozens of rose hips that otherwise he would have deadheaded and discarded.

After hours of humane hunting and gathering in the garden, Bentley carried his harvest, much of it already in buckets of water, into the sun porch where it nearly filled the room. Just then Sophia, who had been cooking for many hours, staggered into the wisteria room for a break. When she saw in the colorful cuttings and trimmings and prunings, her weary face slowly recomposed itself into a smile that revealed her true, kindly, humorous self. Bentley was astonished when Sophia threw her arms around him, and when she left off hugging, he was alarmed to see tears in her blue eyes. "This is a nice, nice woman," he thought, "who has been working far too hard in the kitchen."

But the smile was still on her face, and Sophia said, "Thank you Bentley. For the first time since we started this crazy dinner, I think it's going to be all right."

In fact, Sophia and the other cooks had started preparing the crazy dinner three weeks earlier, beginning with the stock for the gravy. They had begun by boiling turkey parts in an enormous pot purchased for the occasion. "We may as well buy utensils to cook for a bunch of people," Lenore had said. "When we all live here, we'll be cooking for twelve or thirteen." The big pot full of turkey bones and meat and innards was busy boiling and reducing down to a tasty broth.

"Or someone will," Zoë had said. "But not me. After this, let's hire a cook."

Three weeks later, on the day before Thanksgiving, they all wished they *had* hired a cook or a team of cooks to feed the forty-eight guests they expected. Besides the thirteen core members of the group, they expected Pamela to bring William Whistle, and they believed Pamela had invited her mother and her mother's fiance, Tex, evidently to try one last time to get into their good graces. They knew Bentley was going to bring a friend! Genevieve had intimated that she had a *special* guest coming! All of the friends had invited their children and, of course, their grandchildren. And, finally, several of the friends had parents who were able to attend—God willing.

The parents were the source of a lot of anxiety among the cooks, for in most cases they were borrowing their parents from nursing homes for the occasion. So in addition to cooking and serving and doing all the other chores that hosting a huge dinner entailed, they had to worry about keeping their parents from wandering off into the neighborhood.

As Lenore, Zoë, Sophia, Genevieve, Tina and sometimes Weezie—as her energy allowed—diced, sliced, chopped, peeled, rolled, mixed, folded, whipped, measured, and cooked, Lenore said, "I'm so happy about my mom being here, but I don't know what might happen."

"What do you mean?" Tina asked.

"You've all met my mother," she began.

"She's in better shape than *we* are!" Zoë said. Everyone chimed in her agreement. "How old is she now?"

"Well, she *was* in good shape. She's 93 now. Remember when I visited her at my sister's in Florida? I never told you what happened. I thought she had some kind of fixation with *keys*. Every time I put my keys down, I noticed she was staring at them. Then she would pick up the whole bunch and look at each key as if she were searching for a message in it."

"What do you suppose was on her mind?" Tina asked.

"My sister had been telling me that Mother was showing signs of Alzheimer's and was acting strange. But to see it in person…It was giving me the willies to watch her with those keys," Lenore said. "Every day I would take her out for a ride, and she would watch the keys when I unlocked the car door and then as I put them into the ignition. And when we got back to the house she would follow me around until she saw me put them down."

"Did you ever ask her what was going on?" Sophia asked.

"Well, I didn't think of that. I was too spooked," Lenore said. "But I found out anyway."

"What was it?"

"On the third morning I was there, my sister came into my room wondering if I had seen Mother. When I said no, she asked me if I had my keys. I said sure, but when I couldn't find them, my sister jumped up and said 'Let's go!' So we ran down the stairs to the garage. There was my car, easing backwards out of the parking space. My sister raced over to the driver's door and banged on the window. I stepped in back of the car and banged on the trunk until the car stopped. Mom was driving it, of course.

"As we brought her out of the parking garage and up on the elevator she told us, 'I got out of the house just fine, and I got the car door open. What slowed me down was trying to find the ignition key. It's the one with the square handle.' Still, she seemed pretty pleased with herself."

"Where do you suppose she wanted to go?" asked Sophia.

"Well, about a month later I found out. I got a call from my sister that Mother had escaped again, this time on foot."

"Oh, Lenore," Weezie said. "Well, I'll bet she didn't get far, not at 93."

"They couldn't find her. First my sister and her husband raced all around the neighborhood in their car. Then they called the police. Apparently it happens somewhere in Florida every two and a half seconds—an elderly person goes missing. So the police put out an all-points bulletin and they still couldn't find her."

"What did they do?" Sophia was shocked.

"They sent out police helicopters. Two of them."

"You're kidding!"

"No," Lenore said, "I'm not kidding. My sister and brother-in-law could see the helicopters circling the city—and there's more. When the helicopters couldn't find her, they sent out bloodhounds."

"Yikes!" Zoë cried. "*Bloodhounds?*"

"My sister had to get, you know, an article of clothing for the bloodhounds to sniff. And that's what did the trick, the bloodhounds found her."

"Where was she?"

"Four miles away, walking. When the police stopped her, she told them that she had gotten a pretty good head start, but what had slowed her down was stopping to eat. She said that next time she would pack a lunch."

"Where was she going?" Tina asked.

"She told my sister she was going home," Lenore said. "As nearly as anyone can figure, 'home' must have meant Indiana, where she lived about thirty years ago. She was on her way to Indiana. She told my sister she had a gentleman there she was going to marry. She said he was much younger than her."

"I guess *so*," Zoë said. "It'd be pretty hard to find

someone her age. And if she did," she added, "it'd be pretty hard for him to keep up with her."

"And she's going to be here tomorrow?" Tina asked. When Lenore smiled and nodded, Tina said, "That's pretty exciting. Maybe Buddy can find her if she wanders off."

"You mean if she *escapes*," Zoë said.

"Yeah," Weezie said, "and it's pretty exciting that Tuck's dad is going to be here, too. I think I'd better warn you that he can be pretty hard to take."

"That's right," Sophia said, "Tuck told us about him. He's the one who's so grouchy."

The kitchen was arguably the most beautiful room in the house. It was hard to say whether it had ever been remodeled. If so, it had not been touched during the decades when kitchens were routinely ruined by the people who remodel kitchens, such as the 40's, 50's, 60's, or 70's. Its supreme edifice was an enormous black stove with brass knobs and handles, a double-oven affair as big as a caboose. Its roaring burners shamed the output of modern "commercial" stoves found in expensive homes. An enormous hood, nearly as big as the stove itself, hovered over it in an ineffectual effort to siphon off the intoxicating aroma of eight pies baking in two ovens.

By three o'clock on Wednesday afternoon, Sophia decided they could not wait any longer to start setting the table. Luckily, the issue of whose silver would be used for the dinner was solved naturally and without dispute. No one had a setting for forty-eight people. Lenore, Tina, Zoë and Sophia each had twelve-person sets, and all were put to use. Sophia guessed that setting the tables would take about two hours, but at six that evening, Genevieve, Lenore, Sophia, Zoë and Tina were still composing the tiny vases of flowers at each setting. Even to their tired eyes, Bentley's rosehips along with odds and ends of greenery looked splendid in the tiny vases.

In another hour or two they would go home and rest so they could be back at the house by 6:30 in the morning to put the turkeys in.

Chapter Thirty

[Thanksgiving, 1975]

"Jesus, Dad! Let's just get in the car and go over there. Why do we have to wait around here for a ride?"

"Keep your britches on, Robert," Will Fletcher told his son. "A friend of ours wants to give us a ride in a fancy car he fixed up. He'll be along in a little while."

"What, we need a fancy car to drive to dinner?"

"Owen's been working on it for months. None of us have seen it, and I think he wants to surprise us with it."

"And why in hell did Mom go over there so early this morning, before we were even out of bed?"

"She's cooking. So we *know* it'll be good."

"Cooking for forty-eight people. Christ! We should have stayed right here and had Thanksgiving dinner at home like we always do," Robert said. His father shrugged. Upstairs, a battle raged. Grandchildren shrieked. Their mother screamed. Will himself was beginning to wish that Owen would arrive soon.

"Tell me again, Dad. Who are these people? These people you've bought a house with."

"Well, your mom has been in a wine-tasting and gardening group with six of them for about fifteen years. They're all good people."

"In a *wine-tasting group*? So you invest your life savings in a joint venture with a *wine-tasting group*?"

"Well, two are college professors, another is an attorney, one a writer—they're all substantial people."

"Did you have them investigated? Did you even do credit checks? References? Anything?" Cindy and the three grandkids, ages three through nine, thumped down the stairs just then and brought their warfare into the living room. Will was actually relieved. But Robert continued. "How much money did you put into this thing, Dad?"

"Oh, we'll talk about it some other time. This is Thanksgiving. Let's have a good time."

"Dad, I have a friend who's a lawyer. He says your goose might really be cooked by what you and Mom have done, but he knows some ways you might be able to get out of it. I know you're not going to believe me so I'd like you to talk to him." Fortunately for Will, one of his grandchildren bowled into him from behind in a move that in football would have been called clipping, and knocked him to his knees. As he tried to right himself, a granddaughter tromped on his bowing hand. But the diversion was enough for him to escape to the yard, where he hid behind an old camellia shrub and watched for Owen.

Will wasn't sure there was such a thing as "royal purple," but that's what he thought the color should be called of the stately Jaguar that glided to a halt before the house. He believed he had never seen a car so gorgeous. Owen swung open the driver's door and stepped out of the automobile with a pleased smile on his face. Will popped up from behind the camellia, shook hands warmly with Owen—man, he was glad to see him—and walked twice around the Jaguar, admiring. "I can't believe it, Owen. This thing is"— Will grouped for the right word—"classy!"

"Well, we'd better get going," Owen said, grinning. "I still have to pick up about fifteen people, three or four at a time."

When the Fletcher family had finally found a way to put seven passengers in the car, Cindy piped up, "Hey! There aren't any seat belts in the back seat!"

"What?" Robert cried. "You gotta be kidding!"

"Well," Owen said, "this is a fifty-year-old car, and they just didn't have safety belts in those days."

The grandkids were starting to whine again.

When the Fletcher family had finally found a way to put seven passengers in the car, Cindy piped up, "Hey! There aren't any seat belts in the back seat!"

"Listen," Robert said from the back seat, "there are some real safety issues here. Does this vehicle have modern brakes?"

"It has brand new brakes," Owen said.

"Have you tested them?"

Owen laughed. "No, this is our maiden voyage. But I'll drive slow."

"Well I don't think it's funny. This is my family in this car." By now the kids were really acting up, hitting one another and squalling. Cindy herself was whining, like one of the kids.

"Robert," she said, "we can't ride without seatbelts. We're going to have to stay home."

He said to her in a low voice, "We'll take our own

car, Cindy. But we're not going to stay here. We have to go over there and check this out with our own eyes. And bring a pen so you can take notes."

And that's just what they did. Will and Owen rode alone in the Jaguar, and though Will enjoyed the quiet and he loved riding in the old Jaguar, he found that he had an uneasy feeling he couldn't shake off. Besides, his knees were throbbing where his grandson had felled him.

After Owen dropped Will off at the house—man, what a sour son Will had—he and Tuck swung by The Sheltering Oaks nursing home in Albany to pick up Tuck's father. Tuck couldn't stop talking about how splendid the Jaguar was. Owen of course agreed, but modestly he turned the conversation away from his majestic restoration job. As they rode, people along the way smiled and turned their heads to watch the grand old automobile.

"How do you and Weezie like living at the house, Tuck?"

"I miss my garden at home, and that's all. Otherwise, I'm happy as a clam."

Tuck really did seem happy lately, Owen thought as he stuck his arm out to signal a left turn. "I wonder whether that means he's in a manic phase." Tuck claimed he was bipolar, though it seemed to Owen as if Tuck was depressed much more often than he was giddy with happiness.

"What's it like living there with Genevieve and Pamela?" Owen asked.

"Not much different from when we lived at home and just went over to the house. It's fine." Tuck seemed to be considering. "Pamela's kind of a pill, but that's how she's always been. Anyway, Weezie really loves it. You know, there's always someone there in case she has a health crisis."

"Well," Owen said, "that was always the idea. When we're having health problems, it'll be nice to have friends around."

"I just never thought it would start so soon," Tuck said.

"Uh oh," Owen thought, "I hope I didn't get him depressed." But Tuck was enjoying his ride in the Jaguar. When they got to Sheltering Oaks, he went in to collect his father and soon came out with an old man about a third of his size. The little old guy slowly made his way to the car with the help of a walker.

Tuck introduced his father. "Owen, this is my father, Ed Calhoun, and Dad, this is my friend Owen Holt."

Before Owen could say "How do you do," Ed demanded, "What the hell is this son-of-a-bitch?" pointing at the Jaguar they were all making ready to enter. "That thing's old as the hills. How are the brakes?"

"They're fine, I'll drive slow," Owen said, already a little sensitive about the subject.

"Well don't drive too goddamn slow. I get bored. Better drive pretty fast."

"Fine," Owen agreed.

Ed Calhoun glared.

When Harvey saw the Jaguar pull up in front of his beautiful Tudor-style home in Piedmont, his first thought was, "I hope the neighbors see this." He wondered whether he could get Owen to honk the horn as they were all driving away in the magnificent and prestigious car.

"My gosh, Owen, it's beautiful!"

"Not bad for an old throw-away, huh?" Owen smiled.

As Harvey bounced up the steps to get Tina and the kids, he sneaked looks at windows and porches from which he knew neighbors had a view of the street in front of his house. He was disappointed, though. No one was watching. "Tina," he called, once inside, "Owen's here with the Jaguar."

Tina was just then descending the stairs, dressed for Thanksgiving dinner. As always, the sight of Tina left Harvey nearly breathless. Her clothes were elegant, chic, and tastefully revealing.

"You're not going dressed like that, are you!" she barked at Harvey.

He was stunned. He had groomed himself fastidiously and had thought carefully about the suitability of each piece of clothing, including his socks and belt. He had polished his shoes and paid extra attention to his nails.

"What's wrong?" he asked.

"Aren't you going to wear a blazer?"

"I was just going to put it on," he said in an irritated tone of voice, though in fact he had forgotten all about wearing a blazer. He was relieved that Tina wasn't going to make him change his shirt or something. By the time he was back downstairs, his two children were milling by the door along with Tina, and the family was ready to launch.

Outside, Harvey introduced his son, Jason, and his daughter, Joan, to Owen. Both were uncommonly good-looking even though their stiff smiles seemed a mite unfriendly. Owen seated the son in front. As he began to leave the curb, Harvey said, "Owen," but Tina gave him a nasty look.

"Yeah?" Owen asked.

In the back seat, Tina glared at Harvey and shook her head. "Just wanted to tell you again how great the car is," Harvey said to Owen.

"Thanks."

In a whisper, Tina said to Harvey, "Do *not* ask him to honk." Then, a block or so later, she added, "Maybe someone will be out front later when Owen drops us off."

Chapter Thirty-One

[Thanksgiving, 1975]

Will and Sophia's son, Robert, helped himself to turkey, turkey-dressing with chestnuts as well as walnuts and pecans, sweet potatoes, string beans, cranberries, and of course plenty of gravy, and then he went looking for his place at the table that was reserved for adults. Cindy and the kids sat at the other big table, but he wanted to see for himself what his parents' venture in The Last Resort, as they called it, was all about.

It's not that he had been *counting* on an inheritance

from his parents, exactly, but when he realized that they had taken something like a half-million dollars out of their investments and sunk it into this crazy scheme with a bunch of other old fools, a warning buzzer had sounded. His parents might lose or spend their whole "estate," as he thought of it, and he might not ever see a penny of it.

Dinner was served buffet-style, and when he had carried his plateful of food to the table and finally found his place—marked by a name-card—he found biscuits and sweet butter on a bread dish, water in a crystal glass and, surprisingly, his own tiny salt and pepper shakers. Each place had its own miniature vase full of... Robert didn't know what. Berries on stems? Bottles of white wine were deployed around the table, and his neighbor on the right, a black lady who wasn't too bad-looking, poured him a glass and smiled at him and said her name was Tina.

He had never seen such a bunch of knives and forks and spoons, about three of each, some laid out beside his plate as he would have expected, but some in front of it. Cindy probably would have remembered whether you start with the ones on the inside or the outside. He decided on a small fork closest to his plate and bit into a forkful of dressing, and for a moment he actually stopped chewing and closed his eyes. He put his fork down so he could savor the food. For some time after that he was absorbed in his dinner. He wondered why the turkey tasted so much better than any he had ever eaten before.

He noticed that there was a commotion when some people showed up a little late, a couple of people who were actually dressed pretty hip.

"Pamela!" all the people at the table were shouting. "Is that you? And William!"

"Call me Bill," the guy said with a debonair smile.

Some of the women at the table actually got up and ran around to look more closely at the couple. They kept saying idiotic things to the lady like "Look at your hair! Your new boots, your makeup, your chestnut hair!" This Pamela was wearing what Robert would have called "chic" black, layered clothing, and she had on a pair of boots that looked like snakeskin. He wondered whether she was a model. The guy— Robert himself wouldn't have minded wearing clothes like his—the guy looked like one of those men who model clothes. He had on this three-piece charcoal suit that looked expensive and a real sharp necktie. And unlike most of the other old guys at the table, he had a full head of hair that made him look reasonably young. Robert could see the glint of a gold bracelet under Bill's perfectly starched cuff. Well, at least there was one classy-looking couple at this dinner, unlike his own parents, who always looked sort of dowdy except for when his dad wore a tuxedo for performances.

When the couple had served themselves and sat down, Pamela spoke up in an impressively cultivated voice. "I prevailed on my mother to drop by after dinner. I do hope I can count on all of you to maintain a certain decorum." She looked sternly around the table and even, Robert thought, looked accusingly at him. Well, she could count on him not to drink too much, since he intended to make notes about what he observed and then later pass the notes on to his friend, the attorney. But he wasn't so sure about the gigantic fat guy named Tuck. That dude seemed to be knocking back a lot of wine.

The fat guy asked Pamela in a booming voice, "Is she bringing Tex?"

"Yes, she is, and if you don't mind I'd like to make a decent impression."

Tuck got a kind of wicked look on his face and was about to say something to Pamela, but just then a woman, whose name-card read Lenore, jumped in and said, "Pamela and Bill, I believe you haven't yet met some of our guests tonight. First, meet Bentley's friend, Dr. Mark Witherspoon." This guy, the doctor, said hi to Pamela and Bill, but Pamela just held her head high and said "How do you do" without looking at him. But what interested Robert was that the doctor and the other guy, Bentley Fairbanks, were pretty obviously gay. So his mother and father thought they were going to move into a house with possible homosexuals. He would see about that.

After that, Lenore introduced Robert to Pamela and Bill, and Robert nodded at them.

Next came a guy who looked about 100 years old. "Pamela and Bill, this is Tuck's father, Ed Calhoun."

"You're goddamned right," the old guy said.

Pamela nodded but didn't really look at him, either. The old man kept talking, though, "This is the first food I've had in a year."

Tuck looked uncomfortable. "They've been feeding you, haven't they, Pop?" The old man glared at his son.

"Hell no." Then he added, "Buncha crap. This stuff's pretty good, though," he said, jabbing at his now-empty plate.

"Want some pie, Dad? I'm going to have one." Some of the people at the table laughed.

"Yep," said Ed, and Tuck left the table.

Lenore introduced other people around the table to Pamela and Bill, a few of whom were more or less Robert's age, sons and daughters of The Last Resort people. Then she said, "And I would like to introduce my mother, Louisamay Carter." This very old lady had a nice smile. She was smiling before she was introduced and she was smiling afterwards, looking sweetly but vaguely toward the table before her. Even Pamela said hello to her, but Mrs. Carter just kept smiling without saying anything. It seemed to Robert as if she were not completely present, as if she had gone to heaven some years ago and was now just a memory.

The black woman to Robert's right, Tina, leaned toward him, smiling, and said in a low voice, "It's hard to stop looking at Pamela and Bill. Last time I saw Bill, he didn't have that nice big head of hair," and she laughed in a throaty contralto.

Robert didn't get it. Did this Bill guy let his hair grow out? But what really struck Robert was that Tina really was a babe. I mean, she was old, but not *that* old. He couldn't believe she was his parents' age. Something about her good looks made him uncomfortable. In fact, he had to admit that from the beginning he had had a strange feeling about his parents' involvement in this commune, or whatever they called it. Was there some kind of *sex* thing going on here? Were his parents and their friends swapping wives or something? The thought made him feel queasy, as if he had suddenly learned that he was from a long line of pederasts. As he was grappling with his revulsion, Tina poured him another glass of wine and smiled again at him. He wondered what she was up to.

Now the lady named Lenore was introducing a Mexican guy to Pamela and Bill. "And this is Genevieve's guest, Maximo Orosco." It seemed to Robert as if everyone's eyes at the table were glued on this dude who didn't look much older than himself, maybe 36 or 38. Genevieve looked like she was about 65. Maximo stood up when he was introduced, and as he did, he shoved his chair back with one leg just like cowboys do in movies when someone accuses them of cheating at poker and they stand up to shoot somebody or at least stare them down. But he didn't seem mad or anything.

"Thank you, thank you. It is my privilege to be here today for this great American fiesta that I have

never known before. For you this must be a great day
to celebrate your families."

*Was there some kind of sex thing going on here? Were his
parents and their friends swapping wives or something? The
thought made him feel queasy, as if he had suddenly learned
that he was from a long line of pederasts.*

Robert had never seen anyone quite like this man.
He stood there like a rooster with his chest puffed
out as if he were proud of something even though
the poor guy looked like hell. He had scars all over his
face and even on his hands—many years of knife
fights, Robert surmised.

"I am so proud to be invited to your family to celebrate. Genevieve has told me…" and here he paused
and looked down affectionately at the lady "Ah,
Genevieve, the most perfect woman I have ever
known…" There was a pleased murmur around the
table. "Genevieve has told me that you are her chil-

dren and that she loves you, one and all. Genevieve, I salute you," he said, and he raised his glass to her and drank, and all around the table, people, including Robert's mother and father, raised their glasses and shouted 'Bravo!' and drank to Genevieve and had big grins on their faces.

"And now I drink to you too, my American friends. All you who are Genevieve's children, please stand now and let me drink to you!" The man was almost shouting now, and about a dozen people his parents' age, including his parents, rose and drank with him, and now they really shouted Bravo! The Mexican guy pronounced the lady's name Jen ne vyay vay.

"Jesus Christ!" Robert said to himself, "what's going on here? That lady is supposed to be my parents' *mother*?"

"And just one more thing, my American friends, one more thing. One day, if God is kind to me, I hope and pray...." And again he looked tenderly at Genevieve, who had remained seated, "I hope to be...your father!" The standing elders went nuts then and started singing "For He's a Jolly Good Fellow."

Robert was stunned. He felt as if he were an unwilling witness to some shameful pagan ritual.

When the commotion had died down and people had retaken their seats, Ed shouted in a surprisingly vigorous voice, "For God's sake, someone get me something to drink!" He glared around the table.

Tuck seemed worried. "Do you mean water, Dad,

or would you like more wine?"

"I mean something with some goddamned kick! I know you, Tuck. Somewhere in this place you've got some brandy!"

"Brandy?" Tuck said. He smiled. "We've got some brandy all right. I'll be right back."

"Ouch!" Robert cried, and his knee slammed into the table above it, making a horrible bang and rattling glasses all along the huge table. "Something bit me!" he yelled. More frightened than hurt, he looked down at his leg and saw an ugly little dog that was now sitting up and begging. The damned thing looked like an old bristle pad.

"That's Buddy," Tina said. "It's usually best just to feed him a little something, and then he'll go on to the next person."

"But I don't have anything left."

"Uh oh," Tina said. "Then you'd better pull your legs up or something because he'll bite harder next time. Wait, here's something on my plate."

Robert thought it best to get his legs off the floor right away *and* to feed the dog, though he found it distasteful to handle the soggy morsel of biscuit that Tina gave him. Unwilling to pass the food to the dog by hand, he tossed the scrap on the floor and Buddy pounced on it. Then someone at the other end of the table called Buddy and the dog scampered off. With his feet back on the floor, Robert looked to see who had called the dog off. It was Lenore. He noticed that Lenore's mother had left her chair, and now Lenore stood and took a shawl her mother had left behind and she offered it to the dog. Lenore and Buddy were on the floor together, and it really seemed to Robert that the lady was trying to get the dog to sniff the shawl. When Lenore's mother came back into the room, Lenore jumped up right away and hung the shawl back on her mother's chair, and her mother then sat down. As Robert watched, he rubbed his ankle where the goddamned dog had bitten him. He pulled back his sock and peered at his shin, but he didn't appear to be bleeding.

Robert could hear his kids yelling at the other table and his wife whining at them to stop. He wondered whether the dog had bitten one of them, too. "Man, this place is a loony bin," he thought, and he couldn't wait to start making notes.

Just then, the big fat guy showed up, grinning and lugging a barrel with a spigot. "Do we have any brandy, Dad? Is that what you asked?" He seemed all wound up. "Where can I put this barrel down?" he asked in the general direction of some of the old women.

A lady named Zoë answered him, "You can put it down anyplace you want to, Tuck, but brandy isn't on the menu. What're you going to serve it in? Do you have forty-eight brandy glasses?"

Tuck looked confused. "Well, my dad wanted some brandy," he said. The big guy's wife, Weezie, took pity on him though and found a chair for him to put the barrel on, and she handed him a wine glass for the brandy. Tuck tapped the barrel and handed his old father the glass. The old man gave the brandy a sip. "Jesus Christ, Tuck, how old is this stuff? It tastes terrible!" he said.

Tuck seemed to crumple. He was just able to say, "We think it's about seventy years old."

"Seventy years old! What are you trying to do to me?" Tuck sat down while his father continued to rant. Robert noticed that Tuck had sagged like a deflating blimp. Weezie rubbed his back. Robert suddenly felt exhausted. This madhouse was wearing him out. At the other end of the table his mother and father seemed to be having a wonderful time.

Soon a bunch of the old people began clearing the dishes from the table. This seemed to signal that everyone was moving to some other room and Robert headed for his wife and the kids. Before he got there, though, he met his father, Will, who had a load of dirty plates in his hands and a big smile on his face. He got as close to Robert as the dishes would allow him and whispered into Robert's ear, "Hey, kid, didn't I tell you this was a hell of a nice bunch of people? Pretty cool, huh?"

Robert stiffened in disbelief and said, "Sure, Dad, real cool," but he didn't think his besotted father caught the irony in his voice.

Chapter Thirty-Two

[Thanksgiving, 1975]

When the Thanksgiving celebrants settled down again with wine or brandy or coffee and one more piece of pie, they arranged themselves into two groups. The tribal elders gathered in the living room, and all the others—that is, their sons and daughters and grandchildren—congregated in the ballroom downstairs. One might have imagined that the two groups had purposely gotten as far away from each other as possible.

Upstairs in the living room, the thirteen princi-
pals in The Last Resort sat with their parents and
with their other adult guests: William Whistle,
Maximo Orosco and Bentley's friend, Mark
Witherspoon. Buddy settled down on Weezie and
Ninja curled up in Bentley's lap. Without the children
present, the conversation quickly swerved into a ter-
ritory the friends were comfortable with: bad health,
good health, food supplements, cures, injections,
medical procedures, emergency maneuvers and growing old. They hadn't yet touched on the callowness of
youth.

"It's strange," Sophia mused aloud, "but these
days anytime I huff and puff when I'm walking up a
hill I think it's because of old age. But then I remember that I was breathing hard on the same hill when I
was thirty. I had aches and pains in my youth, too, but
when I have them these days I blame them on being
sixty."

"I think I feel better today than I did ten years
ago," Tony said.

"I have to say," Tuck disagreed, "that being sixty
isn't as good as being fifty. My fifties were my favorite
years."

"But how do you know, Tuck, you've just barely
started being sixty?" Weezie argued. "You might really like the next decade."

"Well, Doc, what are we looking at here?" Owen
asked Mark. "What can we expect to happen to us
during the next ten years?"

"Oh, we'll be okay. People do fine until they're about 75. After that it can be dicey. The trick is to keep moving."

"Dance," said Genevieve. "Dance, dance, dance!" She smiled ferociously at the matador.

"Maybe we should find someplace in the house for exercise equipment," Tony suggested.

"I've been thinking," Lenore put in, "that maybe we should restore the swimming pool. Swimming is one of the best kinds of physical therapy there is."

"I think we should farm it," Tuck said.

"Farm it? Farm the swimming pool?" Lenore questioned, sounding skeptical.

"Yeah, fill it in with soil and farm it. You know, tomatoes, carrots, potatoes, squash, melons, snap peas, beans. That's a big interest of mine," Tuck said.

"Farming?" Lenore asked.

"Eating," Zoë said.

"Fresh vegetables," Tuck said. "Now *that's* what'll keep us healthy, fresh vegetables. Anyway, you're right, Zoë, I'm interested in eating. Would you pass the pumpkin pie?" Buddy was interested in food too and he began nipping heels under the table for attention.

Sophia said, "I think we'd better add a good dentist to the list of people we want to know in our sixties. I believe we have to keep our teeth as long as we possibly can."

"This conversation is disgusting," Pamela said. "We don't have to talk about our health problems in front of guests or even in front of each other."

"Health problems don't offend me," said Mark, the doctor.

"Health problems are all I have left," Ed said.

"Oh, *please!*" Pamela protested.

"Pamela does have a point," Lenore said. "I don't know whether we want to be sitting around the house here as eighty-year-olds talking about our gall bladders all the time."

"You can tell me about it," Ed said. "I'm interested." Tuck believed that his father's mood had been improved by brandy.

"I mean," Lenore went on, "we do want our last years to be as positive as possible. We don't want to wallow in our infirmities."

"Oh I don't know," Tuck disagreed. "Pathology is fascinating, especially our own. And it's fairly interesting to hear about your friends' problems, too. You might learn something from them that'll save your skin someday."

"But wouldn't it be better to talk about a good wine or a project we have in mind or something we'd like to do?" Tony asked. "So we can keep moving ahead and not become morose."

"Or to fight a bull," Maximo said.

"What?" Zoë said. "Fight a bull?"

"Yes, Mrs. Zoë, I like to fight a bull when I am feeling old and sorry for myself."

"You'd better be careful, son," Ed warned.

"That's right," Genevieve said, "Maximo is a bull-

fighter. One of Spain's master bullfighters. An artist!"
Genevieve took Maximo's scarred hand in hers.

"You're a bullfighter!" Sophia exclaimed.

"Yikes!" said Zoë.

"And your mother is a promising student," the
matador said.

"Genevieve?" All heads turned to her. "A promising student? Of bullfighting?"

"I find it much like dancing."

"You'd better be careful too, Missy," Ed growled.
"Those damned bulls are big. I'm going to bed now.
Weezie, I'm getting too tired."

"I'll take you upstairs in the elevator and show
you your room, Dad," Weezie said, and slowly Ed,
gripping his walker, made his way out of the room
accompanied by his daughter-in-law.

Bentley had finished his pie, and now he sat on
the floor before the fireplace, leaning back on Mark's
knees, Ninja still curled on his lap. A moderate-sized
fire in the immense fireplace, the first of the year,
dimly lit the room. Sitting side by side on a sofa,
Genevieve held hands with Maximo. Harvey had gotten his arm around his beautiful wife, Tina, and
everyone basked in the glow of the fire and the memory of the wonderful food they had all enjoyed.
Lenore's mother spoke up for the first time. "Isn't
this lovely?" Lenore patted her shoulder and stroked
her gray hair.

"Well," Will said. "Maybe what we ought to do is
have a health night. One night a week when we talk

about our health, good or bad, and keep quiet about it the rest of the time."

"But I'll tell you what I'd like," Zoë said. "I'd like an aerobics instructor to come in here once a week and get us all jumping around." Tuck groaned.

After everyone thought about that a moment, Tina said, "That's a good idea, Will. But maybe just one night a month. I'll tell you what I'd like. I'd like an aerobics instructor. Someone to come in here and get us all jumping around." Tuck groaned. Just as Tuck opened his mouth to protest the idea of jumping around, the doorbell sounded, and Buddy went nuts.

Chapter Thirty-Three

[Thanksgiving, 1975]

"You are the barkingest little dog I ever did hear." Tex wasn't tall, Genevieve noticed, but he seemed to fill the mansion's huge doorway. He swooped down on Buddy with surprising dexterity for a seventy-year-old and picked him up before the dog could even yip. "I'll tell ya what, little buddy, I could put you in my hat." Tex held him in both hands and looked him in the eyes. Instead of biting Tex's nose as Genevieve would have supposed, Buddy went limp. "You look like a wire brush, partner. Ma'am, I'm Texas Taylor and this is Talulah Noonan. We were told you wouldn't mind if we came along after dinner to say hello."

"I'm Genevieve Rutherford. We've been looking forward to meeting you and Mrs. Noonan." Talulah was as thin as her daughter, Pamela, but instead of looking military, she had the bearing and glamour of a model, even though Genevieve knew she was much older than Tex. She wore a purple blouse of French origin and *pounds* of purple jade. Her brilliant gray hair was carefully feathered. She flashed Genevieve a dazzling smile. Genevieve smiled too and said, "Come in please and let me share you with the others."

She couldn't get over how Texas Taylor stuck Buddy under his arm and Buddy just seemed to take a deep breath and relax.

Texas rubbed Buddy on the head as he and Talulah followed Genevieve down the hall toward the living room. Tex turned and walked backwards a good part of the way, to take in the splendid entryway they had just left. "Goodness gracious!" he said.

At the living room, Texas stopped and said in wonder, "Look at this!" While Genevieve had been greeting Tex and Talulah, someone had stoked the fire, and it was now kicking up a lot of light and heat. Genevieve thought it made the splendid room look enchanting. She smiled at Maximo and then introduced everyone to the newcomers. During the introductions, Texas took off his hat. When one of the men stuck out his hand for a shake, Texas put Buddy inside his big Western hat, where the little dog looked like he was perched in a nest, and shook with his free hand.

"Call me Tex, folks. This is just the nicest house I've ever seen. Honey," he said to Talula, "what do you think of this?"

"It's beautiful," she said, simply. Sophia had made room on the sofa for the couple, and she invited the newcomers to sit there with her. Pamela brought Bill Whistle to them for more introductions. "I can't believe it!" Talulah cried. "Pamela, I didn't even recognize you!"

"Mother, please don't start in about the way I look. This is Inspector Whistle. William, my mother and her friend, Tex."

Tex said, "Inspector? Are you with the police?" Genevieve thought that, in his fancy suit and with the gold chain around his neck, Bill didn't look much like a policeman.

"Building Department, sir." He didn't look like someone from the building department, either.

"Well, you're a good guy to know. Folks like you can make or break a big project."

William looked pleased. "Yes, sir, it's true," he said.

"Hell," Tex said, "I had to kill one out in east Texas. Pamela, you treat this man real good, hear?"

"Kill one, sir?" Bill said. He took a step backwards.

"Yes," the Texan answered. Tex looked at the

friends and their guests sitting around the big fire-place. "Did you all have a nice dinner?"

Will, Owen, Bentley, Tuck and Tony said, "Wonderful! Fantastic! Gorgeous!" They meant it. Evidently it sounded that way to Tex, too, because he said, "Talulah, something tells me we should have eaten here. It looks to me like there's some mighty good cooks in this room, and I don't mean the men-folk. We ate at my daughter's place," he explained to the room, "but, bless her soul, she just hasn't had enough clutch time on that stove to do it right."

"Folks, what can I get you to drink?" Tuck asked. "Wine? Brandy? Beer?"

"You have some brandy? Why, that's what I'll have," Tex said.

"Our brandy is old, Tex. I think I should warn you."

"That's good, isn't it? Isn't old brandy better than young brandy?"

"It's wonderful stuff," Tuck said, "but my dad got upset when he found out how old it was. I'm talking about maybe seventy years old, and, by the way, it's Courvoisier."

"Well, goddamn, pour me a glass," Tex urged with a grin. "I'll let you know what I think about it." Tuck went to the little keg and tapped a glass of brandy. But even before Tuck got back to Tex with the glass, Tex said, "I've been dying to ask you all what you're up to here."

Genevieve wondered who was going to answer

that one. There was what seemed like a long silence and then Will said, "You mean the house and everything?"

"Yeah," Tex said. "It interests me that a bunch of people nearly my age would shack up together."

Will laughed. "You make it sound sort of sexy."

"Well, I've heard a rumor along those lines," Tex said. "I know that's what some of your neighbors think."

"We're trying to get around the nursing home bind," Lenore said. "Most of us have parents who are going through that. We're experimenting with another way of doing it for ourselves when we reach that age."

"You mean casting lots together with a bunch of old friends, right?"

"Yeah," Will said, "that's probably the main thing, but there's more to it." He looked at his wife. "Sophia, you tell him. I'm not very good at it."

"It's what I think of as 'meandering paths,' " she said, and all of the friends laughed. "That's Pamela's vision. She looks forward to meandering paths in the garden. We all want to have something to look forward to. I like the idea of having interesting people address us about opera or Oriental rugs or anything that keeps us learning and interested."

"I can't wait to audition cooks," Tuck said. "That's what I'm looking forward to. I wish you had the time to do it, Sophia. You wouldn't have to audition."

Owen spoke up. "Zoë wants an aerobics instructor to keep us moving around. We want to retain our own doctor to check in on us and our own nurse."

Tina said, "We don't want to burden our children when we're old. They won't have to put up with us living with them, and they won't have to flail around looking for a nursing home or assisted care and finding out about Medicare and all the things people have to do to take care of their old parents."

"Well, folks, you make it sound pretty good. But heck, it's expensive, isn't it? I mean it's none of my business, but aren't you spending a lot of your life's savings on the last few years of your life?"

"Maybe I should whisper," Zoë said. "Our lovely children are downstairs trading horror stories about us right now I'll bet, but in fact it is *our* life savings, right?"

"And we're not squandering it or even spending it," Tony added. "We've invested it in a house that's likely to appreciate in value, and most of us will leave our shares of the house to our kids."

"Here's my philosophy," said Bentley.

"Let's hear it," Mark said.

"I've noticed that, when I'm depressed, it doesn't cheer me up to think that things used to be better. I live in the here and now. That's going to be as true when I'm eighty years old as it is now. If I'm miserable when I'm that old, it won't do me any good to think that I had seventy good years. Okay so far?"

"I follow you," Mark said.

"So I'd better be thinking now of things that will make me happy when I am eighty, and that's what I'm doing. That's what we're all doing."

"Yeah, but is it really possible to be happy when you're eighty-five or ninety years old and you're sick and maybe even dying?" Tex said.

"I'll let you know," Bentley said, and he laughed.

"Maybe it would be wiser not to expect too much in the last years and be as grateful as possible for the good years we had," Tex said.

"Or maybe it would be wiser not to give up too easily on being happy when we are old. Look, I'm *counting* on it being harder to be happy near the end, and that's why we're getting the garden here so wonderful that even if we can't walk, we can lie around looking at it and still enjoy ourselves. And that's why I'm willing to take chances and spend real money now on those last years."

"Damn, folks, you should go on the talk circuit. This stuff is catchy!" All the friends laughed. "Is this the wave of the future?" Tex asked. "Are all of us aging folks going to start shacking up together?"

"But not everyone can afford to do what you're doing," Talulah said. Genevieve knew that Pamela's mother could afford nearly anything, and she thought it was unusually humane of her to think of people who could afford very little. Talulah went on, "It's nice that you can do this, but don't you think that most people won't be able to?"

"If anything, it's cheaper to share a house than

for each person to pay rent or pay down a mortgage on their own place." Tuck pointed out. He poured Tex and Talulah another glass of brandy each. "And it doesn't have to be as splendid as this."

"I just read about an old sorority house for sale that sounded interesting," Tony said. "Lots of rooms and a big kitchen. People might be able to buy something like that really cheaply."

"Is this the wave of the future?" Tex asked. "Are all you aging folks going to start shacking up together?"

"Or an old hotel," Tex suggested.

"Or people can move to where property is inexpensive, like to the country or the Midwest or someplace," Owen said.

"Or to Spain," Maximo said. "In Spain you can buy a castle for five-hundred-thousand American dollars. A big one."

For some time all the people in the room sat quietly, watching the fire. Were they thinking about castles in Spain? It looked to Genevieve as though Lenore's mother was asleep. What a lovely woman she was.

"Well," Tex said, finally, "I don't know what to do. I feel like you all are onto something and it bothers me to death. Maybe I should rush out and start building places for folks like us to live in together. There's a goldmine in the idea, I can tell you that. Or maybe I should just ask you if you have any space for another couple of old folks." Genevieve couldn't imagine what was going through Pamela's mind as Tex spoke about living in The Last Resort. And William Whistle was staring at Tex with alarm.

Owen smiled at Tex and said, "Well, all the rooms are taken at the moment, but we'd be glad to let you know if we ever have a vacancy."

"I hope I'm not being rude," Talulah said, "but you must know that on the average women live to be five or six years older than men...."

"That's why Talulah chose a young man like me," Tex grinned.

"You mean, is this going to be an old ladies' home someday?" Will guessed. "Probably, but I'm not ready to roll over for that quite yet."

"I guess not," Zoë said. "You're too stubborn."

"Anyway," Harvey said, "what if our wives *do* outlive us? Even if we die before our mates, we're still going to enjoy being somewhere we love while we're still alive."

"And besides that," Tony said, "it's nice to think our wives will have a nice support group if we die first. And no, Talulah, your question wasn't rude. We know what the actuarial tables say. We men have talked about the probability that our wives will outlive us, and frankly we're considering lodging a protest or at least writing a letter to the editor. It's just not right." Talulah was amused, and she cracked a huge smile.

"But things have changed," Mark said. "Our life expectancies have become very close, and in twenty years or so there may not be any difference at all."

"You hear that, boys?" Tony said. "We may not have to write that letter."

For some time, Owen and Lenore's two children, Laura and Ricky, listened to the others without joining in.

"I can absolutely *feel* my folks' money getting away from them," Kevin Androtti said. "But here's what I don't understand. Who's taking it? If it's not your parents, Robert, or yours, Joan, or anyone else's parents here, then who *is* making off with it?"

"There's a scam going on here," Robert said, "but that's all I know for sure."

Downstairs in the ballroom, the young adults had gathered on the stage where they sat on folding chairs in a loose circle, sharing an ashtray. The smokers washed away the unpleasant taste of their twentieth or thirtieth cigarette of the day with glasses of wine poured from bottles they had found in a little room just off the ballroom. Their children raced around and played on the ballroom floor.

"It might be the old woman who claims to be our parents' mother," Robert went on, "the one with the Mexican boyfriend who's half her age. I mean, where's her husband? He just disappeared? That's what my folks told me. Is he out there someplace pulling the strings on this con game?"

"And if somehow or another Genevieve adopted our parents," Laura asked, "and if now they're all brothers and sisters, what does that make us?" She looked around at the others.

"That's just absurd!" Robert shouted. "I won't even talk about it!"

Harvey and Tina's daughter, Joan, said, "You know, there was a realtor involved in this in some way or another. I would like to know more about him."

Her brother, Jason, said, "I wonder about the so-called inspector. My folks said he helped them get permits. What do you suppose his game is? That guy sure doesn't look like a city employee. He looks like someone loaded with money."

"It sounds like we're agreed, though," Robert, said, "that somehow we're going to stop our parents from ruining their lives. It's for their own good."

"Yes, somehow," Joan Boatman said, "but I don't really know what we can do."

"I already have an attorney working on it," Robert said. "Take notes. Anytime you see crazy things going on, take notes and get them to me." He handed his business card to each of his new cousins.

Jason said to Robert, "Maybe they're all just lunatics and are throwing their money away. But one thing is for sure, and that's that we'll never see any of it if we don't stop this thing."

"We'll stop them," Robert said. "Don't worry."

With that resolve in their hearts, the sons and daughters of the mansion's owners, along with their own children, started upstairs. Robert and Cindy were the first to reach the first floor. Now in the hallway, they saw Bentley and Mark, who were walking down the hall toward the kitchen. They were holding hands. Robert made a note in a little notebook.

The party inside the living room was breaking up. Some who had cooked for three days had already limped off to bed. Others were shaking hands and patting each other's backs. Genevieve thought that this Thanksgiving had been the best of her life. Less than a year earlier, lonely, she had taken a chance. She had given up sole ownership of a mansion in Piedmont and she had sacrificed much of her privacy to cast her lot with a band of people who, for some reason, she trusted. They had taken their chances, too. She knew the others had given up savings and investments to buy into the dream. Like her, those already living in the big house had sacrificed much of their privacy, too, and all of her new friends had traded in some part of their own conventional lives for an experiment. But tonight, for the first time, she had no doubt at all that she had made the right choice, and she knew the others felt the same way. Until now they had all been testing the waters and gathering impressions about each other, but tonight, Thanksgiving night, they had begun a journey together into the future. Not all of them were living in the house yet. They had other projects to complete. But they had entertained as a family, and they had grown close. Together they would face their undeniably finite future with a good spirit.

Maximo shook hands with all his new friends, and Owen asked who might like a ride home in the Jaguar.

Part Three

Chapter Thirty-Four

[February, 1976]

The ballroom had taken on a new aspect. Zoë surveyed a half-dozen chrome and black-leather exercise
machines that now rose from a portion of the old
dance-floor like abstract modern sculptures or instru-
ments of torture. The rest of the ballroom's dance
floor was clear except for several giant, brightly col-
ored balls at rest against one wall and a number of
mats that were laid out side by side. Lying or sitting
on the latter, five women, including Zoë, stretched
hamstrings, calves, groins and glutes, not prevented

by this activity from talking.

Zoë was relating a telephone interview she had conducted a week earlier. "She said she's taught aerobics classes for all kinds of people but is especially interested in teaching seniors. I told her that we certainly aren't *seniors*."

"We're not?" Lenore asked.

"I could tell she thought we're a bunch of old hags. I hope she's not some patronizing whippersnapper who thinks she's going to come in here and pat us on the head."

"What's her name?" Sophia asked.

"Stacey," Zoë said.

"Uh oh," Tina said.

"I know. Look, if she comes in and babies us like we're geriatric cases, we can just get rid of her."

"What if she runs us ragged?" Sophia asked. "What if she's one of those college girls with fabulous buns and she works us too hard and we have heart attacks?"

"Just think of it as dancing, dear. That's my plan," Genevieve said.

For some time, the women stretched in silence. Lying on her back, Lenore, who was wearing shorts, stuck her left leg straight up like a flagpole and pulled it back toward her head with a towel she had wrapped over her foot. With her bare leg upside down, gravity worked on her skin in a rather disturbing way, Zoë noticed. Next to Lenore, Genevieve worked on a neck-stretch that Bentley had showed her. Sophia seemed unclear on the concept of stretching, if that was what she was trying to do, and did vaguely hula-like moves with her hands and arms. Beside her, Tina was wearing tights that made her legs look even longer and more shapely than usual, and she wore even more makeup than ordinary, presumably of a kind that was resistant to sweat.

"What if she runs us ragged?" Sophia asked. "What if she's one of those college girls with fabulous buns and she works us too hard and causes us to have heart attacks?"

Zoë had taken a different path about makeup. No longer able to focus her eyes well enough to do a decent job with makeup, yet too alarmed by what she saw in super-magnifying mirrors, she had engaged a specialist to tattoo her eyebrows and lids with what amounted to permanent makeup. In electing to undergo the painful process, Zoë felt she had been motivated not by vanity but by convenience and an unwillingness to spend precious time primping. Of the women living in the house—and she and Tony now lived there part-time—she was the only one who had quit dyeing her hair. Tina claimed that the reason Zoë had let her hair return to gray was that it was such a perfect shade of gray, silver-gray, and not yellowish, and that, after all, her motive *was* vanity. But Zoë simply thought it was unseemly to go on dyeing one's hair forever. She wore it in a short Peter Pan haircut that was easy to care for and which looked just right on her.

On her mat, Zoë arranged her tiny body in a hurdler's position and stretched until she could touch her shin with her forehead. She wondered about Stacey. "Well, if she doesn't show up in a few minutes, she'll be late and we'll fire her."

"For heaven's sake, Zoë, Stacey might be a perfectly nice girl." Lenore said. "Anyway, she's not late yet."

"Hello ladies!" someone called. "Which one of you is Zinnia?" They turned to see a woman whose appearance surprised them. She was perhaps seventy years old and, except for the leotards and tights she wore, didn't look much like an aerobics instructor.

"Uh, I'm Zoë?"

"Zoë!" the woman said. "That's it! I couldn't remember your name for the life of me. Well I see you're all at work."

"What happened to Stacey?" Zoë asked.

"Stacey! Is that what I told you my name was? That's so funny." The woman laughed. "That's a kind of pet name my granddaughter calls me. My real name is Alma." Alma looked around and said, "You're going to need a mirror in here." Zoë and the others lay or sat on their mats staring at Alma.

Finally Zoë said, "I guess you've been doing this for a long time."

"About forty years," Alma said.

"I didn't know they even *had* aerobics forty years ago," Zoë said.

"At first I taught tap and baton. Anyway, don't be intimidated by the way I look," she said, glancing at her thin arms. "You'll shape up in no time."

Zoë heard the elevator clank just off the ballroom and seconds later Tuck walked in wearing a sweatsuit the size of a teepee and a sweatband made from a rolled-up, red bandana that called unwanted attention to his bald pate. He lugged a suitcase and said, "I see you've all met Alma. Here's your suitcase, Alma. She asked me to carry it down for her," he explained. "Mind if I stay for the workout, ladies?" He was wheezing from the exertion of carrying the suitcase.

He had never seemed so immense. This was the first time Zoë had ever seen Tuck wear anything other than loose khakis, roomy denim shirts and a big cardigan sweater. "Tuck, this is ladies' day in the gym," she said. "We don't want any witnesses when we start doing jumping tonys," Zoë said, turning to her friends, who nodded.

"I understand, I understand," he said. He looked relieved. Tuck hadn't become a 300-pounder by being fond of exercise. He excused himself graciously. In the meantime, Alma attacked the suitcase and soon had passed out red plastic platforms that she called steps and had plugged in a portable phonograph, a vintage machine with a blue naugahyde covering. By now all eyes were again turned to Alma. The last thing she took out of the suitcase was a shower cap, and she pulled it on over her bright red hair. She selected a long-playing record from a short stack of them and, while she held the tone arm poised to lower it, asked, "Ready for our step routine?" The women scrambled to their feet and took stations at the red steps that were positioned around the floor. Looking at her students with a face radiant with *joie de vivre*, Alma dropped the needle on the L.P. and took a position facing them, just behind her own plastic platform.

When the music began, it sounded a little like a Disney soundtrack: *Bambi*, maybe. At first Zoë couldn't find the beat. But Alma began counting and that helped.

"One, two, three, four, one, two, three, and step up now and right foot first and left foot…" Zoë, who had grown up in a military family, noticed with disapproval that, though Alma called for stepping with the right foot, she actually stepped with her left, and Zoë found herself confused. She noticed that her fellow students appeared to be as confused as she was. No one was doing anything remotely like anyone else, but Alma didn't seem to mind. "Left foot four more times," she shouted, then changed her own footing after only three counts.

Zoë could restrain herself no longer and shouted over the sound of the music, "Alma, pay attention!"

Alma smiled and said, "Don't worry, Zinnia, you'll get it."

"With spirit now," Alma said, preparing her class for the floor routine, and she lowered the stylus onto a vintage vinyl featuring Harry Belafonte. "Ready now, one two three four; grapevine, grapevine, lunge, lunge, lunge. Grapevine, grapevine, lunge, lunge, lunge." The five women watched Alma in astonishment as she shot across the big hardwood floor in a series of athletic moves. Then she raced back to her starting point shouting the same incomprehensible words, smiling hugely. "This time together now, one two three four," and she raced off again, shouting instructions. This time her five students ran along behind her, each trying to do something that at least resembled her moves, but almost instantly Lenore got tangled in her feet and fell to the hardwood floor with an appalling crash. Zoë and the others skidded to a halt and ran to the prostrate ex-tennis player. She appeared peaceful as she lay on her back, eyes closed, still as a rock.

It was only when Alma twirled around and started her return trip that she saw what had happened.

"Holy Mary!" she cried and stood over Lenore's body as if paralyzed, clasping her chest just over her heart. Zoë wondered whom to aid, Lenore or Alma, who appeared to be having a heart attack. But Lenore moved, first a finger, then her whole arm, which she laid across her forehead as she groaned. Then after a while, surrounded by all the women who were now on their hands and knees, she said, "I think I'd like to sit down."

"How can you do that, Lenore," Zoë asked, "you're already lying down?" She looked at Sophia and said, "That doesn't make sense, does it?"

"Maybe she's out of her head," Sophia said. "Anyway, we could help her up and then she can sit down."

"Right," Zoë said, and she and the others stood and began trying to help Lenore stand up, grabbing her arms and pulling. They got nowhere, though, with their large friend until Lenore began to rally, perhaps tired of being pulled around on the slick floor. She rolled over onto her belly, then rose to her hands and knees and finally to her feet.

When she was fully upright, Lenore seemed reasonably sound. "I think I'll just excuse myself," she said.

Alma was terribly upset. "I've hurt you, haven't I?" She shook her head in despair. "Job one, don't hurt the patient," she said, evidently thinking of the Hippocratic oath. "I've hurt you, I've hurt you!" Now she was sobbing.

"Not at all," Lenore said. "It's my own fault. But I'm tired of doing aerobics. It's too hard." Assured that Lenore was all right, Alma struggled to control herself, and Lenore headed toward the elevator.

Still, Alma was discouraged. "I guess I really messed up my audition. I don't know how I'm going to tell my granddaughter." Alma dried her eyes and then took off her bathing cap. "You don't want me to come back, do you?"

All the women of the house shrugged and looked at each other. Finally Zoë said, "Sure we do, Alma. You're great, really you are. One of the best."

"Of course we want you back, dear," Genevieve said.

"You do? After that?"

"Sure," Tina said, "any time."

"Like when?"

"Well..." and there was more shrugging, "...I guess you should come three days a week. If it's going to do us any good," Sophia said.

"Day after tomorrow?" Alma asked.

"That'll be perfect," Tina said.

Alma rewarded them all with a big smile. "Wait till I tell my granddaughter!" Soon she had gathered her shower-cap, the portable phonograph and her little red plastic steps and packed them away in her grip. Tina helped her carry it to the elevator and Alma ascended while the others waved from below.

When they were left alone, Zoë thought that Tina and Sophia looked as gloomy as she herself felt.

Genevieve seemed unfazed. "Well, I guess we botched that," Zoë said. "I did. I'm the one who told her to come back."

"Oh, don't worry about it, dear," Genevieve said. "When she's saying left this and right that, I think I'll just do anything I feel like doing. I'm sure she won't notice."

"I guess *not*," Zoë said, "and if she does notice, she'll forget it right away."

"Maybe she cooks or something," Tina said.

"I'd like to meet her granddaughter," Sophia said. "She sounds nice."

Chapter Thirty-Five

[August, 1976]

Minutes of the Board of Directors
The Last Resort, Inc.

Present were Lenore and Owen Holt, Bentley
Fairbanks, Will and Sophia Fletcher, Pamela Noonan,
Tina and Harvey Boatman, Tuck and Weezie
Calhoun, Zoë and Tony Androtti and Genevieve
Rutherford.

Chairman Lenore Holt called the meeting to

announce the filing of a joint action suit in Alameda County against the stockholders of The Last Resort, and to discuss how to respond to that suit.

1. Lenore Holt read from the suit: "Plaintiffs Robert Fletcher, son of Will and Sophia Fletcher; Jason and Joan Boatman, children of Harvey and Tina Boatman; and Kevin Androtti, son of Tony and Zoë Androtti hereby declare their parents to be incompetent to manage their own monetary affairs and hereby petition Alameda County's Superior Court to appoint said adult children to be their parents' guardians in all matters concerning disposition of their monetary assets...

   "Said parents did enter into a financial relationship with others, vesting very large amounts of their assets in a corporation whose stated purpose was frivolous: to 'Establish a communal abode for physical and spiritual health.' ...That said commune promotes immoral and illegal activities and that it has resulted in the plaintiffs' parents squandering large sums of money to their own detriment.

   "Said adult children have documented the following: a. One of the members, Genevieve Rutherford, now 66 years old, legally but frivolously adopted the twelve other members, whose average age is 62. b. Homosexual activity has been observed on the premises between members. c. Pets belonging to the commune have willfully and knowingly been allowed to bite visitors. d. Permits to operate said abode in the City of Piedmont appear to have been obtained under questionable circumstances. One member of the commune is romantically involved with a pertinent building inspector. h. Neighbors are prepared to testify that sexual orgies are known to take place

"Said adult children, if granted fiscal guardianship of their parents, avow to the Court that they will cause the joint property of The Last Resort, Inc. to be sold at public market and that the proceeds from the sale shall be proportionally allotted to the estates of their parents and that said proceeds will be responsibly managed, maintained and invested for the benefit of their parents."

Sophia and every other parent in the group heard loudly and clearly that their children had just declared them incompetent. "Isn't it a little early for that?" she wondered, but she knew how Robert viewed his parents these days. He sometimes witnessed them struggle a little to get up out of their chairs. He noticed their deepening wrinkles and Will's graying hair, their frustration and embarrassment when they couldn't remember a word or a name. He saw the fistful of pills they took every morning. In his eyes, they were tired, slow moving, slow talking, slow thinking, too trusting and were the potential victims of a con artist.

After Tuck read aloud the charges against them, Will said, "Isn't it wonderful to know our children are looking after us, especially our money?" In all their years of marriage, Sophia couldn't remember Will ever before being sarcastic.

"Said adult children need a good spanking," Harvey said.

"Homosexual activity?" Bentley asked. "Holding hands?"

"I don't want to hear about it," Pamela said.

"Pamela! You too?" Bentley was hurt.

"Now children," said Genevieve. All the defendants in the lovely wisteria room laughed, except Pamela.

"It just hurts, that's all," Tuck said.

"What?" Tony asked. "That our children have turned on us?"

"No," Tuck said. "Why haven't I been invited to the orgies?" There was more laughter around the room. "I wonder who these neighbors are who ratted on us?"

"Well Zoë, our beloved attorney, what are we going to do?" Lenore asked.

"I'm thinking about it. Why don't we go on with the meeting and then come back to this?"

Minutes Continued

2. The following have applied to become full residential shareholders of The Last Resort, Inc: William Whistle, Maximo Orosco, Dr. Mark Witherspoon, Texas Taylor and Talulah Noonan. All but Taylor and Noonan are sponsored by members.

3. The collection of vintage wine discovered to have been concealed in the "speakeasy" many years ago was successfully auctioned and fetched a net price of $204,106, which has gone into the Corporation's general fund. Pamela Noonan objected, preferring that the proceeds be split among the shareholders. The matter was decided by a 12-1 vote and the money will remain in the general fund until members decide how to use it.

Let it be noted for the record that certain adult children of group members drank six bottles of vintage wine from The Last Resort's wine cellar at Thanksgiving one and a half years ago, without permission, resulting in the loss to the group of approximately $16,000 in revenues.

"Well, folks, I would describe this as our first crisis," Lenore said, "maybe even more of a problem than our children's lawsuit. Three of us would like to sponsor new members, and there aren't any rooms left. What are we going to do?"

Sophia was still thinking about Robert's lawsuit. She felt certain he was behind it. The most disturbing thing about it was the question she now had to ask herself: *Was* she incompetent? *Was* Will incompetent? "Let's be honest," she said to herself, "there's been some slippage. My hearing's not so good; I have to practically tie my glasses around my neck or I lose them. I get flustered when there's too much going on. I probably do trust people when I shouldn't. I don't drive as well as I used to, especially at night. And Will: What about the way he weeps and sometimes even sobs at the end of every sad movie. What's that about?"

But the group had moved on to their other problems. Suddenly Genevieve, Pamela and Bentley all wanted to bring more people into the house. "Listen," Sophia said, "no matter what else happens, don't we all agree that Genevieve should be allowed to bring Maximo into our home? We wouldn't be here if she hadn't sold us her house for far less than its market value and if she hadn't thought of adopting us. Somehow we just have to find room for Maximo."

Genevieve said. "You don't owe me anything. It's just that you'll love Maximo. I wouldn't ask if it weren't for that. Anyway, you won't really have to make room for him since I have two rooms already. I would just like to share them with him."

"Well, then," Sophia said, "I move that we invite Maximo to join the group and, since he would just be sharing Genevieve's apartment, that we not ask him for money."

Lenore said, "You all remember how we set this up in the bylaws. It will take a unanimous affirmative vote to bring in new members."

"I second Sophia's motion," Tony said. "I think Maximo's a good guy and we owe Genevieve every-thing."

"Well then, let's vote," Lenore said.

"Wait a minute," Pamela spoke up. "Before we vote, I want to know how you're going to vote about William."

"Pamela," Sophia said, "it doesn't really matter how we vote about William. The question is whether we owe Genevieve a favor because of what she did for us."

"I'm not going to argue with you," Pamela argued. "I just want to know how you're going to vote about William before Maximo or anyone else gets my vote."

"Sounds like a stickup to me," Will said. "What you're saying is that if we won't let William in, you won't let anyone else in."

Sophia liked and enjoyed almost everybody, but she thought William was a self-satisfied jerk. It was harder for her to admit that she regarded Pamela, with whom she had been in a wine-tasting group for about seventeen years now, as being just as smug as William. Could Sophia knowingly, willingly vote William into a group that had pledged to stay together until death?

"Just remember," Pamela said, "William got us in here over the objections of City Hall, and he can see to it that City Hall shuts down the house, too."

"Hmm," Will said, "now it doesn't sound like a stickup. It sounds like extortion."

Sophia could feel her blood pressure rising. After all the group had gone through together—finding the house, coming up with the money for it, fighting the objections of the neighbors and City Hall, pouring thousands of dollars into improving the house, Weezie's illness and on and on—all that and now Pamela was threatening to throw a monkey wrench into the whole thing through William Whistle. And of course the kids, hers and Will's among them, were trying to have their parents declared incompetent.

"What do you think, Zoë?" Lenore asked.

"I think we should postpone this vote about new members until we've had a chance to cool down. And about the suit to have some of us declared incompetent to manage our own money, let's just meet their suit in court and make our children look like idiots." Most of the group laughed.

"Do you think they'll get anywhere?" Weezie asked.

"Absolutely not," Zoë said. "It's completely and demonstrably without merit. *But* I'm concerned about what mischief they might do about William and our permits. It seems as if everyone has identified that as a way to blackmail us." Zoë looked directly at Pamela, who, aloof, was looking at the wall at a height a little below the ceiling.

Minutes continued

4. In regards to #1 above, the Last Resort will defend itself in court against the lawsuit. Zoë Androtti will serve as the group's legal counsel in answering the plaintiffs' suit but wishes the record to show that she advises the group instead to retain an attorney other than herself.
5. In regards to members wishing to sponsor new members, the Board voted to postpone the vote for at least one week.
6. The meeting was adjourned.

That evening, Sophia and Will elected not to spend the night at the mansion. They did not wish to run into Pamela. "This time she's gone over the top," Will said.

In bed that night, Sophia couldn't stop thinking about Robert's lawsuit. She didn't *feel* incompetent, but she had to wonder. As she lay awake, again and again she went over what she called her areas of "slippage," wondering what could be behind them. For instance, her many instances of forgetfulness—she could think of three or four examples that day alone—they could be signs of early Alzheimer's. In fact, practically every one of her failing that came to mind could be explained by the icy onslaught of Alzheimer's. It made perfect sense. She had watched, horrified, as her own mother had slipped inexorably into that disease and had finally died from it.

Strangely, it was three in the morning before it occurred to her that, in accounting for the state of her mind, "Slippage," a debit, occupied just one side of the ledger. There was another page, a page of credits under a heading that she might call "Holding the Fort." She certainly would have to enter her business in that column, a business that was so successful that it was the envy of her industry.

Sophia had worked in publishing for thirty-five years. During the last fifteen years she had been partners with two others in their own distribution business. She was responsible for selling books in the Western states. From the beginning, the business had been successful, and she and her partners had been crushed with work. Five years ago they had decided they could no longer stand the workload, and they decided to hire three others to help, thus doubling their staff. Sophia and her partners knew they would make less money but felt the loss was a price worth paying for a better quality of life. They hired new people and each of the six now had territories half as big as before. Within a year, sales had tripled. Each of the partners was working harder than ever.

Anyway, she felt that her business could rightfully claim a place in the credit column, and, with that thought, she felt the muscles high on her neck begin to relax. It was some time before anything else came to mind, but eventually she thought back to that Thanksgiving dinner when she had cooked and coordinated an elaborate dinner for forty-eight people. Could Robert do that? Could his wife do that? That was two entries under Holding the Fort.

And what about the whole Last Resort enterprise? She and Will had found the Rutherford House. They had done their share of making the whole thing happen. At an age when many others become rigidly conservative, they had had the courage to try something daring. Had it been foolish? Time would tell. "It wasn't foolish to try," she decided. It would have been foolish to let themselves grow old the same way her parents had: isolated and lonely. She made one more entry on the credit side: The Last Resort. She took a deep breath and her shoulders relaxed.

Not that Robert cared what his mother could count as accomplishments. Nor did it matter to him that his father could play Bach's Cello Suite no. 5 by memory and operate a backhoe all day for two weeks. What mattered was whether they could hold together the estate that he believed he was rightful heir to.

"Well," she thought judiciously, "screw him." She smiled and rolled over on her side. As she began to drift off, she pictured Will dropping tears at the end of a sad movie. "It's cause he's an old sweetie," she said, and she patted his hip and went to sleep.

Will was having his own thoughts about Robert as he lay awake. Robert's charge had come at a time in Will's life when he felt so at peace with himself and regarded his fellow humans with so much affection that he called all children and most girls and women "honey," and patted men on their shoulders. No matter how great a gulf in age or wealth or race or culture there was between him and them, he felt so close to most people that he treated them like family. Will was dimly aware that this impulse was somehow related to his being such a crybaby lately, and he wondered whether he had simply become sentimental in his old age.

Robert's charge jolted him to the core, not because Will doubted his own competence, but because he was totally bewildered by his son's fury. As he lay rigid and unsleeping, he was smothered by hurt and outrage. And then something nice happened. Sophia reached across the bed and gave him a pat on his bottom. How did she know, he wondered? How did she always know?

No, her timely pat didn't suddenly resolve Will's agonizing conflict with his son, but now he took a deep breath, relaxed and went to sleep.

Chapter Thirty-Six

[August, 1976]

William was on a roll. First he had discovered Pamela Noonan, a goddess—and then Pamela had insisted on his having a makeover. It was the best thing that had ever happened to him. Inspector Whistle stood at his window on the 12th floor of the Roquette Hotel in Oakland and exulted. Of all the changes in his life since his makeover, the most profound change was in the way people were treating him. With respect, even with envy. Two years ago, his coworkers used to snicker at him behind his back, and waiters in restaurants acted as if they should be paid extra just to serve him. Now for the first time in his life, he was getting some deference. And deference, William thought as he gazed out his hotel-room window onto the sleepy city street below, was a mighty addictive drug. Women turned to watch him walk by, and even Pamela treated him better than before. And suddenly it occurred to him that he might be invited to become a part owner of the old Rutherford mansion.

The activities of The Last Resort had first come to his professional attention when neighbors reported to the Piedmont Police that many people, maybe twenty or thirty of them, were tromping through the house at 1 Upper Terrace Road night and day, and many of them appeared to be living there. They believed that frenzied building activity was taking place and wondered whether the many residents had obtained permits. The police had referred the matter to the Building Department, and Inspector Whistle had personally spoken to the neighbors who had complained. One neighbor whispered that she had seen a huge man in the yard, down on all fours, sniffing at the house "in broad daylight." She thought he might be dangerous. Someone else complained about a loud altercation on the top floor of the house with men and women screaming and birds flying "right through the roof." But mainly the neighbors believed that there was some kind of hanky-panky going on, hanky-panky of the sexual type.

In the course of his career as a residential building inspector in Piedmont, he had been intimately involved with hundreds of the grandest homes in the world. He had lovingly inspected their massive old redwood underpinnings, had climbed ladders for closer looks at their slate roofs and had been awed by their colorful leaded glass windows—and he had gradually formed the opinion that they were owned by people who didn't deserve them. He, on the other hand, did, but he had to labor on knowing, bitterly, that he would never have the money to own one. In particular, he had long had his eye on the grandest and most splendid house of them all: the old Rutherford mansion.

Suddenly, astonishingly, *these* people had somehow contrived to get their hands on the place—hordes of them who tromped around night and day, sometimes on their hands and knees. It was absurd, almost as if a colony of ants had taken over the mansion. It was illegal. It was infuriating and he decided—all those many months ago—that he was going to shut it down. Then, on top of everything, the people who called themselves The Last Resort made the mistake of laughing at him. Grimly he vowed that he would have the last laugh.

He had had them in the palm of his hand and was squeezing hard when he had finally met Pamela, a goddess. To impress her he had re-opened the doors at City Hall for The Last Resort. To please her he had submitted to a makeover. And then—a new man now—he had had an astonishing insight. He could join them. With Pamela by his side, he could become a part owner of the Rutherford place.

There was a hitch. Pamela didn't yet have an apartment in the mansion to share with him. As a single member, she owned only a single room. Before he and Pamela could live together in the house, before he could enjoy the tennis courts and swimming pool, before he could walk in the garden with Pamela, one more room would have to become available, and that didn't seem possible. Also, he would have to be voted into the group and pay for his share of the house. Buying into the house was no problem. What somewhat concerned him was whether the group would vote him in. After all, at one time he had squeezed them rather hard.

He had advised Pamela to remind the group that he could shut them down at will if somehow they could not find one more room. "Let them know," he had counseled her "that a few words in the right place and I can have them packing their bags in three months." Things were looking up.

And now he had won a free trip to Las Vegas! That's right, free transportation, a free hotel room and four free drinks. William was on a roll. He had responded to an ad and, by God, the free offer turned out to be on the up and up. At any time he chose during the next two weeks he could spend two days and two nights in Vegas, free. William planned to ask Pamela to come with him, though his intuition told him she might decline. He just couldn't picture her pulling the handle of a slot machine. But one way or another, he was on his way.

And now William had won a free trip to Las Vegas! That's right, free transportation, a free hotel room and four free beverages!

His phone rang. He was in such a good mood that when he answered it he said, "Hello, baby," though he knew Pamela was likely to take his head off for such vulgarity.

After a pause, a man's voice said, "Son, this is Tex Taylor. Y'all remember me?"

William was embarrassed. "Of course I do, Mr. Taylor."

"I'd like to talk to you. What if I swing by in a few minutes?"

"That's fine, sir." Tex made William feel like a schoolboy.

"Good. Wait outside your hotel and I'll be by in five minutes."

"Yes sir." When William hung up, he thought, "Why didn't I just tell Big Hat to take a leap? That guy gives me the creeps." What the hell was it that Tex had said at Thanksgiving? Something about having killed a building inspector in Texas. But William thought then and now that he must have misheard the rich builder from Texas.

In spite of being anxious to be downstairs right on time, he stood before his mirror a few extra minutes and knotted his necktie and combed his toupee. Then he hurried to the elevator to be on time, thinking, "What does that guy want?"

Tex's long, black Cadillac looked like a hearse, and it gave William a shiver. When William got in the car, Tex didn't say a word about where they were going or about anything else. He drove in silence. Tex pulled into a cement plant on 23rd Street in Oakland and parked where he and William could watch a towering cement-loader pour concrete into a big truck. Even then Tex didn't say a word.

Eventually the cement truck was full and it drove away. So did Tex, without a word of explanation as to why they had spent the last twenty minutes watching a cement truck load up. Next stop was a downtown construction site with signs posted here and there that read TEX TAYLOR CONSTRUCTION. Again, Tex parked where they could watch the action. A guy on the job-site wearing a hardhat and holding a clipboard waved at Tex. A cement truck sluiced a heavy stream of concrete into a huge wooden form below ground level, and other cement trucks waited in line to empty their loads. Finally Tex spoke. "That there's a foundation they're laying for a thirty-story building. They'll pour another 3000 cubic yards of concrete into it before they're done." Tex turned to William. "A body could get lost in that much concrete."

"A body?"

"Yep," Tex said. "And never be seen again." William went clammy. "Son," Tex continued, "I understand you've been talking about shutting down my friends over in Piedmont if they don't let you into their home."

"Well, no, not really. Uh…" William trailed off.

"Is there someplace you might like to go? Like out of the state?"

"Well, yes sir, I was thinking of going to Vegas for a couple of days."

"How long?"

"A while."

"Quite a while?"

"Indefinitely, sir."

"Good. And I know you won't bother those nice folks again."

"I hear you, sir, I hear you."

"I knew I could count on you, son. Say, would you like to drive this thing home? It's really a hoot to drive."

Back in the hotel room after his encounter with Tex, sitting on his water bed, William opened his mail and read this letter:

Inspector Whistle,

We demand that you use the powers of your office to shut down The Last Resort at 1 Upper Terrace Road. in Piedmont. We know that you made it possible for the residents there to operate the so-called Last Resort despite the fact that they were in violation of numerous codes and zoning laws, and we know why you did it. You had a clear conflict of interest because of your romantic connection with one of the residents. We are prepared to present evidence to that effect to your superiors in the Building Department or to refer the matter to the District Attorney unless you use your influence to shut down the Last Resort. We expect to see progress in that direction within two weeks.

It was signed by Robert Fletcher.

William sat for a while after reading the letter and then stood and walked to the full-length mirror mounted on his bathroom door. He wore the clothes Mr. Boris had chosen for him, the blazer that hung so loosely and casually on his girdled frame, the silk necktie that was neither too narrow nor too wide and that seemed to suggest that he belonged to a private club, the gold chain around his neck. He liked what he saw: the new William, William with a full head of auburn hair, with tasteful alligator-skin loafers, with professionally chosen makeup applied on and near his nose to obscure the burst capillaries beneath the thin skin. "Not bad," he thought. "But Pamela, my princess, my dream, my goddess. Can I leave you? Can I really leave you behind?"

He turned to her photograph on his desk. Holding her image in his hands now, studying his beloved he observed her long, chestnut hair, long and wispy. It was thin, really, her hair, almost stringy and maybe too long for someone her age. How old was she? Better not ask, he thought. He looked closer at the photo. Was that a...a blemish on her forehead? Whatever it was, it was big and he had never noticed it before. Why hadn't she ever had it removed? Strange how thin she seemed in the photo. She had always seemed to him to be a "hanger," someone on whom clothes hung as on a model. But in her photograph she just looked skinny. William frowned.

"A free trip to Vegas," he thought, and then he began to smile. "Maybe I'll take them up on their offer. I *am* on a roll," he thought, and he went back to the mirror for another look before he packed his suitcase.

Within a week after stepping off a Greyhound bus into Las Vegas's glitter, William had been offered jobs as a suit salesman, a male model, a quiz-show host and a master of ceremonies in a strip joint. A number of people who interviewed him told him that he had the "x-factor" (the strip-joint's owner called it charisma) that made him look "Las Vegas cool." He was perfect, they said. His somewhat advanced age, he was told, was an asset. It set him apart from all the young bucks who were on the make in Las Vegas.

As a result of a job interview at a strip club, he had met two young women who were not at all skinny. Their pink flesh seemed to pop out of their clothes. Rather than *hang* on the girls as Pamela's clothes had on her, the strippers' clothes seemed challenged even to contain their flesh, yet despite their differences from Pamela, the girls looked surprisingly good to William. Discussing his future with William over a couple of drinks, the girls encouraged him to become part of the "escort community," and assured him that he could make a bundle in that line of work.

Many men whose acquaintances he made in Las Vegas confided to him that they wished they could "look just like you, Bill." In the end he assumed the professional name of Mr. Bill and established his own business of making people into near-clones of himself. He studied them thoughtfully and then provided his Mr. Bill-wannabes with the right clothes and jewelry and makeup at a 100 percent markup plus a one-time $2500 fee for "design." When he was finished with them, they all owned a share of Las Vegas cool, and they were ecstatic.

A month after he had arrived in Las Vegas, established and happy in his new life, William made three phone calls to tie up loose ends. His former colleagues at City Hall in Piedmont believed that William had been enjoying a protracted vacation. He now informed his boss that he would not be coming back. Three months later, he received a large retirement package from the City of Piedmont. Next, he phoned Tex to make it clear he was now out of the picture and had no intention at all of harming the Last Resort. He figured there was no reason to have Tex even thinking about him. And just for insurance, he mentioned to Tex that someone named Robert Fletcher, on the other hand, was trying to shut down the group at 1 Upper Terrace. "Son?" Tex said. "I appreciate the information. And I'm glad to hear you're in Vegas where the air is so good. I guarantee you'll live longer out there in the desert."

Finally, he phoned Pamela and told her that he wouldn't be coming back and that she needn't lobby any longer to get him into the Last Resort. She said, "Well for heaven's sake, William, I certainly hope you're not still wearing that ridiculous *girdle!*"

But he didn't care. Mr. Bill was on a roll.

Chapter Thirty-Seven

[September, 1976]

The first Wednesday evening of each month had been appointed health night at the Last Resort. Other nights of the month were set aside for The Purple Tongue. On fair evenings, the customary venue for health night was the veranda off the dining room— the same veranda whose floor Zoë had nearly fallen through in the earliest days of the commune and which overlooked not only the garden in the rear of the house, but the swimming pool and tennis court as well.

Weezie had arrived on the veranda early, a full hour before Tuck. All afternoon he had been plugging away at writing his garden column. Weezie, though treated with drugs for atrial fibrillation, always felt as if she had just staggered across the finish line after a marathon and was still struggling to catch her breath. Ordered by her doctors to "rest, rest, rest," she watched from the veranda as late afternoon slowly deepened into dusk and the swallows came out for dinner. They darted, wheeled, swooped and banked to catch their meals. Soon Tuck joined her on the balcony, carrying a tumbler of brandy. He hunkered beside her for a moment and kissed her on the cheek, then lumbered upright without spilling a drop of his brandy, pulled a chair to her side and sat down. A moment later Mark wandered onto the veranda and said hi. Bentley's friend was a valued contributor to the health night discussions since he was a physician and a wonderful source of information about health, both good and bad. Ninja, the Siamese cat, had adopted Mark, though Mark was not a member of the group or a resident. Ninja divided her domestic time equally between Bentley and Mark, moving from one lap to another as her mood changed. At night, late at night, no one knew what she did. She might have been a cat burglar for all any of her roommates knew.

By seven o'clock, the official starting-time of health night, all the friends were there except Pamela, who in recent months rarely spent social time with the group. Lenore, who by tradition usually opened all meetings, cleared her throat and began. But even though some of the members were eager to share news of their aches and pains with their friends, and others had been looking forward to offering free advice about helpful exercises, medicines, over-the-counter curatives and mood-enhancers, Lenore made them all wait while she began the meeting with group-business.

"Pamela has asked me to announce that William will no longer be interested in becoming part of the group and living here."

After a stunned silence, Tuck put his beefy hands together in a prayerful attitude, looked toward the heavens and said, "Thank You, thank You!" He looked more than ever like a medieval monk.

"She also said that she would no longer oppose any other member we might want to sponsor," Lenore said.

"Wow!" Zoë said, then looked skeptical. "There must be some catch."

"I don't think so. In fact, I think that she was hinting that she might be amenable to selling her share of the corporation and moving out."

"Wow," Zoë repeated. "That changes everything."

Harvey said, "That means that Maximo is in, right, Genevieve? Since Pamela won't oppose it?"

"Oh, I hope so," Genevieve said. "Maximo will be here from Spain next week. It will be so wonderful to tell him he is a part of all this."

"And that means that Mark…" Bentley said. He and everyone else on the veranda looked at Mark.

"If I could make a deal with Pamela for her shares of the corporation," Mark asked the friends, "would you vote me into the group? I'm sorry to put you on the spot, everyone, but I have to know before I talk money with Pamela."

"Why, it would be perfect," Genevieve said. "Of course we would!" Everyone agreed.

"Is Pamela in the house right now?" Mark asked Lenore.

"I think she is."

"Well then, I believe I might knock on her door and see if we can arrive at something."

"But Mark," Tina said, "don't forget to come back. We need you for health night."

"I wouldn't miss it for anything," he said, and he excused himself. Honestly, Mark didn't at all seem to mind talking shop.

"Hang on everybody," Will said. "Sophia and I have some news that isn't so great. Well, it's both good and bad. Tell 'em, Sophia."

"We got a phone call from Tex. He told Will that William has moved to Las Vegas and that he can be counted on not to try to shut us down through the Building Department. That's the good news."

"That's *very* good news," Tuck said. "We've been under William's cloud since we started this."

"Here's the rest. Someone named Robert

Fletcher—our son, I'm afraid—is blackmailing William to get him to shut us down. Robert wrote a letter to William saying, 'Close down the Last Resort or I'll blab to City Hall that you were involved with Pamela and had a conflict of interest.'"

Owen asked, "But if William has gone off to Las Vegas and has already said he won't hurt us, what's the problem?"

"The problem is," Zoë said, "that if the kids really do go to the Building Department and get things stirred up, we might be in hot water whether William is involved or not. They could open up the whole matter again, especially if a neighbor complains about something or another." The friends sat quietly on the veranda for a while as the dusk became night.

"So we're not out of the woods yet," Weezie said. "Just when I was starting to like this place." The friends laughed.

"Well, folks," Lenore said, "what are we going to do?"

Owen said, "Look, what these kids are worried about is losing control of their parents' money, right? They figure the rest of us are bent on fleecing their parents and they'll never see a penny of their parents' fortune. That, and they really do think their parents are batty and might leave all their money to Buddy or Ninja or something. So, if money is what this is all about for them, why don't you," and here Owen pointed to Will and Sophia, Tony and Zoë, and Tina and Harvey, the parents of those who were suing, "why don't you threaten to disinherit them? If they pursue this suit or they go to the Building Department to try to shut us down, disinherit them."

Will finally said, "Just speaking for Sophia and myself, we don't really want to disinherit our kids. God knows they're fools and maybe even worse, but Sophia and I don't want to hurt Robert and his wife and our grandchildren."

Tony said, "That's how Zoë and I feel about Kevin. And also, there is a chance, however remote, that the kids really are worried about us, that in the arrogance of their youth they really do think they know better than we do what's good for us and they're trying to protect us."

"Young people are conservative," Tina said, "when it comes to their parents, that is. They like to think of themselves as rugged individualists, but parents are another matter. We're supposed to act like *parents*. We're not supposed to surprise them or embarrass them. What *we're* doing here really makes them nervous."

"So what are we going to do?" Lenore asked again.

Tuck said. "I think we should tie them all up and make them attend one full health night, make them listen to news about our hemorrhoids and kidney stones."

"That's pretty harsh, Tuck," Bentley said.

"Let's bill them for the wine they pulled out of the speakeasy and drank at Thanksgiving," Zoë said.

The friends laughed. "No, I mean it. Let's sue them to recover our loss, which we sustained through their willful negligence. $16,000 plus court costs. Suddenly they will have to consider that suing their parents and blackmailing people might actually cost them money."

The group looked at Zoë. She was serious, and soon everyone was nodding. "Zoë, you're right," Sophia said. "If there's a chance that he might *lose* money, our son Robert won't like it a bit. I'll bet he backs away from this." The other parents agreed.

"Let's do it!" Tony said, speaking for the group.

"Do what?" Mark asked. He had just returned to the veranda through the dining room's French doors. Two low-wattage lights were all that kept the friends from sitting in complete darkness now in the pleasant early-autumn night.

"Mark! Did you get anywhere with Pamela?" Lenore asked.

"Why, yes, I did. She named her price and I called it. We shook hands."

"Absolutely fantastic!" Tuck said, punching the night air with his huge right arm. "I'm going to find some champagne."

Everyone stood to congratulate Mark and welcome him into the group. Buddy jumped up and started racing all around while Weezie begged him not to fall off the veranda. Generally Ninja didn't like Buddy to race around anywhere and usually she would nail him while he was at it, but tonight she merely rubbed against Mark's ankle. Bentley looked like he might burst into dance but instead he just grinned and rubbed Mark's back.

When things had calmed down a bit and everyone had settled back into their chairs, Will said, "Wait. I have to get this straight. This is happening too fast."

In her English-professor manner, Lenore summarized. "Pamela is out. Mark is in. Maximo is in. Inspector Whistle is no longer here nor there. The kids are still rattling their sabers, but we now have a plan to answer them. And that's it."

"What about Tex and Talulah?" Will reminded her. "Remember, they asked to come in, too."

"They know there isn't any room," Lenore answered. "It's a shame, though, because I have a hunch that Tex had something to do with getting William off our backs."

"Well," Genevieve began, "maybe they had better buy the house next door."

"What house next door?" Owen asked.

"I'm afraid that our neighbors over there," Genevieve pointed, "are so upset by what they believe is going on here that they've decided to sell their house and leave. Apparently there's a rumor going around that we're going to have bullfighting in the back yard."

"Hmmm," Zoë said. "Maybe we should allow other rumors to circulate. Someone might be able to get that house cheap. It's a good one, too. What about an outbreak of bubonic plague at the Rutherford place? Caused by overcrowded conditions."

"I don't think we have to do anything special, dear," Genevieve said. "The rumors are already pretty vigorous. Will, why don't you mention to Tex that that house might be for sale and we'd be happy if he and Talulah were our neighbors."

"I will, Genevieve."

Tina said, "Do you suppose that things are finally going to settle down around here? We'll be able to have health night and talk about our facelifts and sore feet and not have to worry about lawsuits?"

"Tina!" Zoë said. You're *not* going to talk about facelifts at health night!"

Tuck returned to the veranda carrying a good-sized cardboard box from which he drew champagne glasses and several bottles. He deployed and poured. "I would like to toast Dr. Mark," he began, but the doorbell began its impressive gonging and Buddy started running around again.

"It's pretty late," Will said. "I wonder who that is?" He went out through the dining room to find out, followed by Buddy who was now barking as well as dashing around.

"Mark," Tuck said, saluting him with his wine-glass, "I would like to thank you in advance for all the free medical advice you're sure to give us over the years." But again he was interrupted.

Will and Buddy came back with a stranger. Buddy was upset. He growled at the man and even nipped at his pant legs, or whatever it was the man wore.

Pajamas? In the dim light it was hard for Weezie to be sure, but it appeared as though the man wore a turban. It *was* a turban.

"Uh, excuse me Genevieve," Will said, "but this gentleman said you'd been waiting for him."

"Mark," Tuck resumed, saluting him with his wineglass, "I would like to thank you in advance for all the free medical advice you're sure to give us over the years."

The turbaned gentleman brought his hands together as if in prayer and, over them, he bowed deeply to Genevieve. Then, upright again, he said, "Hello, darling."

Chapter Thirty-Eight

[September, 1976]

Genevieve was furious, as angry as she had ever been, but she said, "Why, hello dear. Sit down." To her housemates she said, "This is my husband, Aldous," and she heard a few sharp intakes of breath among her friends, and the nervous shuffling of feet. She introduced him to each in turn. The men rose as they were introduced, and with distress in their voices they said how-do-you-do to a heavily bearded man in white robes.

When Genevieve had completed introductions,

Aldous said to the assembly, "You may call me Baba."

"Baba?" Genevieve asked.

"If you would, please," he answered. "It has been many years since I have been called anything other than Baba except, sometimes, Father."

"I see," Genevieve said. "So you have children?"

"In a manner of speaking. My flock are my children, I their Baba, their shepherd, and, ironically, their sheep. After all, we are all one, om shanti."

"Your flock calls you Father?" Tuck asked.

"Or Baba."

"You must be in the same line of work as Genevieve. We sometimes call her Mother," Tuck said.

Baba took a closer look at Genevieve.

"Yes," she said, obscurely. Genevieve had never seen Aldous dressed like a Hindu mystic before nor heard him intone like one. In the old days he had always looked good but pretty standard and he had sounded about like everybody else, even when he went by the name of Free Love. Now he looked as if he had just come down from some lone mountain cave.

Tuck sensed a fracture in Genevieve's usual aplomb, and he spoke now, hoping to give her time to gather herself. "Uh, Baba, can I get you something to drink? Tea, maybe?"

"Please, just a glass of water from the tap. No ice, thank you."

"Good, good. Water. We have *lots* of that—and

also some seventy-year-old Courvoisier that will be all gone in another couple of days."

Baba considered. "I find alcohol useful for combating the effects of malaria."

"Yes, yes, so do I!" said Tuck. "And especially for preventing it. I've been drinking alcohol for years and I've never once had malaria. Courvoisier?"

"Yes, my son, so be it," said Baba.

Tuck's obvious wish to help her and the concern for her that she sensed in the others restored much of Genevieve's equanimity. Still, she was mad. She had no desire to question Aldous about his absence for the past twenty-five years or about his return. She had no wish to see him at all or to learn whether he still cared for her or to find out what his life had been like these past fifteen years. All in all, she had preferred it when he was presumed missing.

Finally, after a long silence, Zoë asked, "Uh, what line of work are you in, Baba? And where *are* you in it? I mean, here, in the United States?"

"Madam," he replied, "I toil only at seeking the truth, and I share my findings with whoever will give me a crust of bread to eat or a mat on which to sleep. Fortunately my students in India have provided for me most generously, giving me far more than I deserve, om shanti."

"Right," Zoë said. "And now, here you are, huh? Back home."

"Ah, home," Baba said, "my heart is full." Just then the man seemed to focus on Will, squinting at him in the dim light. "Have I not seen you before? Or your photograph?"

"I don't suppose so, uh, Baba. Unless you've seen me play cello."

"No, I mean aren't you a former governor of California? Many politicians and rock stars have sought enlightenment at my humble ashram."

"Well, uh, thank you," Will mumbled, not knowing what else to say.

Tuck came back just then, carrying a tumbler of brandy for Baba and a full glass of it for himself. As Baba took the glass from Tuck, Buddy sprang out of a shadow and viciously nipped the guru's hand. Baba's full glass went airborne, dousing him with antique brandy, and he leaped to his feet, clutched his hand and shrieked, "You little son-of-a-bitch!" Baba made a sudden very determined move toward Buddy, but the friends on the veranda jumped up as one and, saying things like, "Oh, poor Baba," and "Oh, how terrible," and "Are you alright?" they managed to restrain the man before he could do harm to Buddy.

Scowling and clutching his hand, Baba sat down, and while some asked him whether the skin was broken, others shook their fingers at Buddy and said, "Oh Buddy, how could you!" and "Not good, not good!" In the meantime, Baba shook his hand and then blew on it, examined it and finally shook it again.

Tuck offered Baba his own glass of brandy. Baba peered around the veranda until he saw that Buddy was under control and then took the glass. A sip or two and he had regained his composure, though he still rubbed his hand. Genevieve looked at Buddy, who wasn't at all contrite, and thought, "Everyone is trying to help me tonight. Well, aren't they kind!"

"Oh, Buddy, how could you! Not good, not good!"

As he sat with the others in the near-darkness, Baba looked down onto the scene below the veranda. Palm trees dimly visible at the swimming pool seemed far, far away, and, in the garden, dusky, ancient shrubs and trees could have been elephants and giraffes. Baba turned in his chair and peered up at the house that rose behind them like a cliff. Finally he sat back in his chair and sighed. "Ah, home," he said again. "My heart is full." He took a sip of brandy.

When Genevieve heard Baba speak sentimentally about "home" for the second time, she stood up and asked Baba if he would like to spend the night at the house and then suggested to the group that they find a nice mat and a crust of bread for him plus some water, no ice—"but I'm going to bed," she said.

Before she could stand and leave, he asked, "So you're all living here together? Do you have room for one more?" As if wishing to forestall the answer, he asked, "Why do they call you Mother?"

"I adopted them. All except Mark, and we'll have to take care of that, Mark, won't we?"

"Yes, Mum," Mark said. Everyone laughed. Buddy had slipped out of Weezie's control and was sniffing one leg of Baba's pajama.

"Do they have a father?" he asked. That was the first sign of intelligence she had heard from him.

"A bullfighter, dear. He wants to be their father. He's very brave." From nearby, Zoë laughed.

"Well, I really am going to go to bed," Genevieve said. "What time is it?" Someone said it was ten o'clock and Genevieve nodded. "Will someone show Baba to a real bed? Aldous will be leaving early in the morning."

Baba slumped in his chair. He seemed old to Genevieve, far older than her friends on the veranda. "Maybe it's just the beard," she thought as she wound back through the dining room toward the winding staircase. "He's harmless, I guess." But as she reached her second-floor bedroom something made her shiver and she wrapped her arms around her shoulders.

Chapter Thirty-Nine

[September, 1976]

Early the next morning Bentley took a turn through the garden, inspecting it with the eye of a parent. From time to time he knelt to thrust a finger into the loamy soil to test for moisture or to pull a weed. He hunted predators such as snails and, when he found them, he dispatched them as quickly and painlessly as possible, trying not to get involved in their personal lives. On the east side of the house, he found Baba basking in the morning sun in a little open grassy spot, sitting on a stone bench.

"Ah, Bentley, how nice to see you," he said. "You rise early."

For the first time, Bentley noticed Baba's extraordinary blue eyes. They were nearly transparent, especially with the morning sun lighting them. "Good morning, Baba," he said.

After a little more small talk, Baba said, "Bentley, do you mind if I talk for just a moment? No? Thank you. Last night I really didn't have a chance to mention a thought or two I have had about life. But first, would you sit and make yourself comfortable? Here, across from me. There.

"Perhaps you know the power of numbers. They are very old," he said. "They go back through the ages, back to your childhood and beyond. The number one," Baba said, his voice droning softly like a sitar, "you can visualize it, you can see it in your mind, going back, to your childhood. You were small and there was one. One hand, one shoe, one foot. And there was two," he said, his eyes wide and very bright in the morning light, "the number two, two hands, two feet, long, long ago when you were very small. You can almost see it now, the number two, the way it looked to a small child. Its back is bent, it has a tail, and though you almost remember two your eyes are tired and you are sleepy."

Bentley was starting to feel heavy and stupefied listening to Baba. He could feel his jaw going slack. He stared into Baba's blue eyes. "And after three comes five," the swami murmured, "so hard to see, so tired now and your eyes are closing and you may let them close."

Bentley was confused by what Baba was saying and he thought he might be able to follow the guru's words better if he just rested his eyes and concentrated.

"And you may let yourself drift now and relax as you think about the number seven. And backwards now to six and deeper and deeper back to five and deeper now...." Bentley felt his head nod but let himself drift. "And now the number four is drifting deeper and deeper asleep and you are deeper and deeper asleep and floating back to three and sleeping deeply now and drifting back to two.......and one.......and now you are deeply asleep."

As if from a very great distance, Bentley heard Baba's voice assume a different tone now, more commanding. "Your Baba loves you," he said. "And you love me. You love your Baba, your father, your leader, and you will do as I tell you. Now you will listen closely..."

A half-hour later, Lenore was in the kitchen and Baba wandered in. Lenore had thought from the time she first laid eyes on him last night that he was trouble, and she was not pleased to see him.

"Good morning, Lenore. I was just looking for coffee or tea."

She was startled to notice that he had blue eyes. They were all the more remarkable for being set off by the man's dark skin and black beard. "Here's coffee now," she said and poured him a cup.

Baba looked as if he had something on his mind. "Lenore, do you mind if I talk? Sit with me on the back porch for just a moment and let me share a thought with you."

Lenore was dubious but polite. When she pulled up a chair on the big back porch just off the kitchen, Baba sat across from her.

"I have had some thoughts about life," he said. "Perhaps you know about the power of the number one. It is a very old number, as old as time…"

In the two years since they had bought the house together, the friends had stocked the shelves of the mansion's library with many of their favorite books. After breakfast, Will had gone there to read, as he often did when he and Sophia spent the night at the Last Resort.

Though he gazed at the cover of *Mr. Blandings Builds His Dream House*—a novel he loved and was in the habit of rereading every five or ten years—Will was thinking about Robert, the son who had declared Sophia and him to be incompetent. As Zoë had predicted, he and the others had agreed to drop their lawsuit and to drop all opposition to The Last Resort when they had been confronted with a bill for $16,000 for the wine they had, without permission, opened and consumed from The Last Resort's "wine cellar." So that chapter was behind them.

It had taken time, but Will had finally come to terms with his 28-year-old son's anger, and he had regained his serenity. And how had he done that? By identifying the source of his son's idiocy as youth. "People under 30," he conceded, "can do marvelous things. They can absorb languages without any effort at all; they can get through boot camp; they can give birth and live through countless sleepless nights rearing their infants." But the more he thought about Robert's shallow opinions and his self-serving idealism the less he valued them. "Until people are thirty or so, they're absolutely full of themselves. They're totally self-absorbed," he decided.

"So what's the answer?" He had considered the question for weeks and had finally come to a conclusion. "They had it wrong back in the 1960's: *Never trust anyone over thirty.* It should be *under.* Never trust anyone under thirty." And that was it. Once Will reached that conclusion, he could take a deep breath and take comfort in understanding what Robert's problem was, and in knowing that even Robert would come around once he got what Tex had called "a little more clutch time" and turned thirty.

"Will, do you mind if I sit with you for just a moment?"

"Oh, man," Will gasped. "You scared me!" He hadn't even noticed that Baba had slipped into the library.

"No? You don't mind? Thank you. I would just like to share a couple of thoughts with you." Baba settled into a chair near Will. "Have you ever thought about the number one? It is a very powerful and a very ancient number."

Soon *Mister Blandings Builds His Dream House* fell to the floor, but Will didn't notice.

Weezie was sleepy even before Baba said a word. Looking into his eyes was like floating through the air, like drifting and drifting. "Weezie," he asked, "may I talk?" But the moment her head nodded Buddy began to bark. She was only dimly aware of the sound, though, and after a while she could no longer hear him at all.

Later in the morning Genevieve was watering potted plants on the terrace when she looked up and saw her husband watching her through the French doors. She felt a chill when he walked through the door to join her.

It was mid-afternoon and all the friends still lingered at the Last Resort. Without being able to say why, they felt it was important to be there. Weezie was distressed because she couldn't find Buddy, who usually slept curled on whatever part of her was available. The last time she or anyone else remembered seeing him was that morning.

"Where's Baba?" Zoë asked. "He's still here, isn't he?"

"I don't know," Will said, "but I hope we see him

pretty quick. You know, I *like* that guy."

"I know what you mean," Tina said, as she bustled around helping to prepare breakfast.

Just then Baba walked into the breakfast room. Tuck broke into a huge smile and then into loud song. "For he's a jolly good fellow, for he's a jolly good fellow…"

Lenore stopped him. "Tuck, that just doesn't seem appropriate."

"Well, Baba's jolly good!" he said. "What do you think we should sing instead?"

"Maybe we should just bow our heads or something," Owen said. "Good afternoon, Baba."

"Hello, my son," Baba said. He looked splendid in his white robes and black beard. His astonishing blue eyes caressed them all.

"Baba, we've been thinking," Weezie whispered. She looked unwell, even more so than usual. "Tuck and I would like to write you a check for your work in India." She had a checkbook open on the table. "How should we make out the check?"

"How kind of you, my daughter. Make it out to Happy Harvest Ashram. How much is it for?"

"We thought $5,000, father."

"More would be better, daughter."

"We're going to make *ours* for $20,000, Baba," Lenore chimed.

"Then so will we!" Will said. "Or maybe more."

"Happy Harvest Ashram," Mark said. "Happy Harvest…" He seemed lost in thought. "I've heard of that."

Bong! Bong! Bong! The massive doorbell boomed and Bentley went to answer.

"We just came over to say hello, Bentley. Hope we aren't intruding." It was Tex with Talullah on his arm.

"Come in, come in! I have someone to introduce you to."

"Where's my little bitty Buddy?" Tex asked.

"We haven't seen him all morning. We've been kind of worried," Bentley said. "But come on in." Bentley led the way to the dining room. Baba was presiding over the group while they wrote checks. "Baba, these are our good friends, Tex and Tallulah. Folks, I'm proud to introduce you to just about the best friend we ever had, the man who looks out for all of us, Baba." Baba bowed his head to the newcomers. Tex took off his big hat.

"Well, by golly, look at you," Tex said. "Man! You got on some kinda outfit!"

Beside him, Talulah said, "Tex."

"No, I *mean* it! That must be the biggest beard I ever did see. Whereabouts you from?"

"Tex," Tony explained, "Baba has come to guide us."

Tex looked at Tony and then looked around at all his friends. Most of them were busy writing checks. "You need a *guide?*"

"We all need guidance, my son," the guru said.

"Son?" Tex laughed. "That's a good one. I figure I got you by about five years if not more."

"Still, Tex, maybe it would be better if you called Baba 'Father,'" Zoë said. "We do."

"Shit," Tex said, "what is this?"

"Tuck," Baba said, "show these people to the door."

"Well, heck," Tuck said, "I guess you and Talulah will have to leave, Tex."

"Heck!" Tex said, "what is this?"

Tex turned to Genevieve. "What do *you* say?"

"Maybe it's better if you just leave, dear." But Genevieve looked frightened, as if she were caught in a dream she couldn't escape.

"Are you okay, honey?" Tex asked her.

"Baba is here to guide us," she said. Genevieve was trembling.

Tex let Tuck lead him to the door. When it was open and he and Talulah were halfway out, he turned and looked back toward the dining room at Baba. Tex shrugged, shook his head, put his hat back on and he and Talulah walked away.

Inside, Mark was still muttering, "Happy Harvest Ashram," but he too had made out his check to that name, a very sizable check. "Where have I heard that before?"

Baba had gathered all the checks and was adding them up and stacking them neatly. "You have all been very kind to your Father," he said, "especially my son Will. Genevieve, now you must pack a small suitcase. It is nearly time for us to go."

"Yes, Baba," she said, weeping as she left the room.

"I have only one other thing to do," Baba said. From his suitcase, he produced a mailing tube and pulled a poster from it. He glided to the grand entryway where he unrolled it and mounted it with pushpins on the old wood paneling of the hallway. The poster was filled entirely by a large close-up of Baba's face. His bristling black beard and mustache, his hawk nose and his amazing blue eyes were much larger than life. Baba stood back and admired it. Tina went to the photo and gazed at it from inches away, looking as though she might kiss Baba's image.

The doorbell rang once again. Baba shot the door an annoyed look and said, "Weezie, you and Tuck answer that. The rest of you come with me into the dining room." He pulled Tina away from the poster and into the room with the rest.

When Weezie opened the front door, there stood Maximo.

"Weezie! Tuck! It is so good to see you!" Maximo was surprised by how pale and tired Weezie looked. "Are you well?" he asked her. "Do you listen to your doctor?" He hugged Weezie and felt that she was very frail, but when he stood back he smiled. "I have brought you something," he said to her, pointing to his suitcase, "but you will have to wait."

Tuck engulfed the bullfighter in a gigantic hug, then grabbed Maximo's suitcase and started with it toward the stairs. But then, assessing the weight of the suitcase, he veered toward the elevator, and then put the bag down and began puffing. With what breath he could muster, Tuck asked Maximo, "What can I get you to drink?" Soon he abandoned the suitcase and headed toward the kitchen.

In the hallway, Maximo felt that something was wrong. "Where is Buddy?"

"We haven't seen him since last night," Weezie answered, and she looked concerned, but Maximo wondered why she wasn't *very* concerned, knowing how much Weezie and the little dog loved each other. His eyes fell on a poster pinned to the wall of the great entryway, a photograph of a dark, bearded man, and he felt a tingle of fear that seemed familiar. He had experienced the feeling many times on first seeing the bull he would be fighting. He stepped back and planted his feet. "Who is he?" Maximo whispered.

"Our leader," Weezie said faintly, "our friend and protector." She smiled a beautiful, tired smile. "Our father."

"Where is Genevieve?"

"She's packing her bag."

"Is that man in the house?" Weezie pointed at the dining room door. Maximo was wearing a lightweight windbreaker, and now he took it off as he looked at the door. His short-sleeved shirt revealed deep scars on both arms. "Weezie, take me to them," he said softly.

"I don't know whether I'm supposed to. Baba didn't say." Her voice now sounded tense as well as very tired.

"Baba?" Maximo asked.

"Our leader." Unsure of what to do, Weezie went to the door and opened it just a little, revealing Baba's face just inside, glaring out at Weezie and the bull-fighter. The guru opened the door but stood blocking the way.

"And who is this, my daughter?"

"This is Maximo, Genevieve's friend, come for a visit."

"Maximo, Genevieve is my wife. You must leave."

Behind Baba, who was blocking the door, Genevieve said, "Maximo?"

"Genevieve!"

Just then Tuck came walking back up the hallway from the kitchen, a beer in his hand. "Hey Maximo, here's your beer!"

"Tuck, my son, show Maximo to the door," Baba said. "He must leave now." The gigantic garden writer stopped, still holding a beer out to Maximo, confused.

"Uh, I guess you're going to have to leave." Tuck went to the door and opened it, but still held out the beer to Maximo.

"You forgot a slice of lime, Tuck. Would you mind getting me a little lime for my beer?"

Tuck's face lit up. "I'll be right back," he said.

"Tuck! My son. Show Maximo to the door!"

"Just a minute Baba, Max wants a slice of lime. Be right back."

As Tuck started back down the hall, Maximo gently moved Weezie aside and faced Baba. Together, almost nose-to-nose, the two looked remarkably alike. Both were small men, dark and handsome. Baba moved aside and Maximo entered the room.

"Hello dear," Genevieve said to Maximo. "This is Baba, who has come to lead us." She seemed agitated and confused.

"I'd like to say something to you," Baba said to Maximo. The bullfighter looked around the room at Genevieve and his friends. "Please sit down and let me explain something," Baba said, and he sat down at the head of the dark old gothic table. Maximo sat just around the corner of the table from him, as if positioning himself to arm wrestle with the stranger.

"Perhaps you understand the power of numbers," Baba began. "They are ancient, older than you or me, older than nations, older than people. The number one for instance." The bullfighter wondered what the man was getting at. He had angry blue eyes, Maximo thought. "You can see it in your mind. One shoe, one hand, one foot. You learned it as a child. Think back. You were very little and it was hard to stay awake, hard to keep your eyes open thinking about the number two with its curly back and its foot. The numbers three and four, so sleepy…" Maximo liked Baba's voice and thought he would like to rest. "And five, so hard to visualize, though you try hard to see it. So hard to see and you would like to sleep now and let yourself go deeply asleep."

The moment Maximo's eyes closed he was washed by sickening fear. Something was terribly wrong. He was melting away. He was helpless to open his eyes, helpless to move while Genevieve was in danger. Maximo was more afraid than he had ever been.

"And now you are drifting, drifting and going deeper asleep…"

Maximo believed he was dying, and he thought that if he were to die, so too would Genevieve. In his imagination, a droning voice held him paralyzed as a raging bull thundered down upon him and his family, and his cape hung uselessly at his side. His cape. He felt it in his hand. "*Maximo, fight!*" he commanded himself. "*Fight!*" With that, the bullfighter leaped to his feet and thrust his thin windbreaker Tonyet between him and the hypnotist.

"Olé!" shouted Genevieve. Her shout awakened all of Maximo's instincts. Baba lunged at Maximo's throat but was distracted by the Tonyet. The bullfighter easily slipped past the charging swami and tripped him. Off balance, Baba fell to the floor and instantly Maximo pinned him down, his knee on the guru's chest.

Around them, twelve friends watched in confusion. Only the thirteenth, Genevieve, was absolutely clear-minded. She went to where Maximo held down her husband and said to the bullfighter, "You are very brave, dear," and she wiped the perspiration from his brow.

"*I've got it!*" Mark shouted. "Happy Harvest Ashram! Baba, you sell *organs!* Body parts!"

"Be quiet!" Baba growled from the floor.

"I *read* about you! Kidneys!"

"Also livers!" Mark added.

"Drifting, drifting, falling deeper asleep," Baba said to Maximo, who increased the pressure of his knee on Baba's back until he shut up.

"You sell *body parts?*" Lenore asked the guru. She was mad.

"For transplants," Baba gasped. "We've helped hundreds of people."

"There's an underground market here for body parts. But a bulletin went out about Happy Harvest," Mark said. He looked down on Baba. "Poor people in India contract to sell you a kidney, but while you're at it, you harvest a few other things as well, like their livers, for instance. Without mentioning it to them."

"Who are you?" Maximo demanded of Baba.

"He was our leader," Tuck spoke up, "at least for a while there—although I don't know why we needed a leader. We always did pretty well without one."

"I thought you left last night," Tina said to Baba, confused.

"I'm on my way out right now," the swami said, but he wasn't very convincing since he was pinned to the floor.

"Now wait, uh…" Will started.

"Aldous," Genevieve said. "His name is Aldous."

"Now wait a minute, Aldous," Will said. "What are these checks all about?" Will was examining a little stack of them on the table. "Looks like checks someone made out to Happy Harvest Ashram. Hmm. It's checks *we* made out to Happy Harvest. Why in the hell did we do that?" he asked, looking at his friends.

"Shit!" Tony said, examining a check. "I wrote this guy a check for $40,000!"

"Tony!" Zoë said. "You didn't!"

"Well where were *you?*" he asked.

"Where is Buddy?" Weezie said. Everyone stopped and looked under tables and behind doors as if they had just now noticed he was gone. "Aldous," Weezie said, "where is he?"

"Can I say something?" Baba asked.

"No!" the friends said in unison.

"Do you know about the power of numbers?"

Baba started, but then Tuck took over the job of holding down the swami. Tuck sat on Aldous's back.

"For God's sake, man," Aldous gasped, "I can't breathe!"

"Where is Buddy?" Tuck asked.

"What if I just go?" Aldous panted. "Just walk out the door. I'll tell you where that little son-of-a-bitch is and you just let me go, okay? For Christ's sake, let me breathe!"

"Where's Buddy, and where's Ninja?" Tuck asked.

"I don't know where your goddamned cat is, but that ugly little dog is in the swimming pool."

"The swimming pool?" Bentley said, and he sprinted toward one of the back doors.

Four men were now in a tight formation around Tuck and the fallen swami, and Tuck got up and let Aldous stand. Tuck lumbered over to Maximo and Genevieve.

"Here's your lime," he said, proffering a pathetic little sliver of lime that was still in his hand, "but where's your beer?"

"What's going on?" Maximo asked. "I don't understand."

"We'll tell you, dear," Genevieve said, "just as soon as we figure it out."

Chapter Forty

[October, 1976]

All Baba left behind was a large poster pinned to the wall in the grand entryway of the mansion and a few drops of blood on the old hardwood floor near the front door. Just as he had been preparing to flee the mansion, suitcase in hand, Ninja sailed out of nowhere and landed on the swami's head. In a few seconds she had inflicted an impressive amount of damage to Baba's scalp and face, though his eyes were spared. Tuck pulled the cat off Baba's head as the man screamed in pain and horror. Seconds later the friends closed the door behind the retreating guru.

The friends heard a yap. Buddy bounded into the hallway followed by Bentley. The little dog bounced from one human to the next, barking all the while. He whirled and danced.

"He was at the bottom of the pool," Bentley said. "Good thing there's no water in it. What's all this blood?"

The poster was still on the wall, and, honestly, it was hard for the friends not to give Baba's deep blue eyes a lingering look before they tore it down and threw it away.

But he was gone.

Over coffee and bagels in the wisteria room several days later, Tina, Zoë and Sophia took part in the group's continuing speculation about what had happened to them. There was consensus within the group that Aldous had hypnotized them all, though it was hard for them to admit they had been so weak-kneed.

"Well, that was touch and go," Tina said, "from what I can remember.

"But in the end somehow we did manage to protect each other," Sophia said.

"It's like I said once before," Zoë reminded them, "that's what a wine-tasting group is for."

"Tex would have taken care of us," Tina said, "but when he came by and found Baba, he just didn't know what was going on. You heard what he offered, didn't you?"

"What do you mean," Zoë asked.

"When he found out what Aldous had done, he offered Genevieve to find him and give him a decent burial."

"Yikes! Does that mean what I think it means?"

"That's what Genevieve thought it meant, too," Tina said, "but she told him she thought we could deal with him if he ever comes around again." The friends shuddered at the thought of Baba reappearing.

"Genevieve sure attracts men who have some flare," Tina said.

"Some *flare?*" Zoë said. "I guess *so*. Baba and the bullfighter. That's flare!"

"I think it happens because she's such a lady," Sophia said. "She's the real thing."

"Opposites attract," Zoë said. "The lady and the macho-men. Don't forget, she was attracted *by* them, too."

"She still is attracted by Maximo," Tina said.

"I wonder if he's finally got the picture?" Sophia asked.

"About what he should do?" Tina said.

"If the Baba episode does the trick," Zoë said, "then at least something good will have come of it."

The next night, Maximo brought four bottles of champagne to the big table and made a speech.

"My friends, I would like to announce my happiness that Genevieve has agreed to be my bride." The group as it was now constituted—Mark, Bentley,

Tina, Harvey, Sophia, Will, Owen, Lenore, Weezie, Tuck, Tony, Zoë and Genevieve—all rose (except for Genevieve, of course) and shouted their pleasure and drank a tribute to the couple. "Finally I will be one of your family, and I am proud of that, too." More cheering. "I will retire from the arena and fight no more the bulls, for I want to be alive to take care of Genevieve. For this, to live with Genevieve till the end, to be your father, to face the future without my country or my work and my fans, I will need all my courage." He sounded a little daunted by the prospect, even more than he had been by Baba.

Lenore spoke up from the table in her commanding way. "Maximo, you have a *new* country. We are your *new* family and *we* are your fans. And as for work, don't worry. You have plenty of work cut out for you." The men at the table laughed, having experienced the women's endless requests that they move heavy objects back and forth, fix this and that, improve everything, polish, paint, clip, mow, water and dig.

"You're right, Maximo. You're going to need some nerve, all right, and good knees." Harvey said.

Maximo's announcement seemed to set off a chain reaction. A few days later, Bentley and Mark told Genevieve and Maximo that they would like to celebrate their own union, and asked whether they would consider having a double wedding. Genevieve and Maximo were delighted. The two couples agreed it would take about three months to arrange a wedding, and they set the date for the first of January.

After Tex and Talulah, who were frequent and welcome visitors at The Last Resort—after they heard about the wedding plans, Tex soon asked to have a word with Maximo, Genevieve, Mark and Bentley. Wearing his big hat and holding Buddy under his arm, Tex said, "Say folks, I don't want to bust in on anything private, but Talulah and I have decided to tie the knot."

"Well for heaven's sake," Genevieve said, "let's *all* get married!"

"Well, for heaven's sake," Genevieve said, "let's all get married."

And they weren't the only ones. Talulah told the friends that her daughter, Pamela, was getting married, too.

"*What?*" Tony cried. Then he felt bad that he had sounded so incredulous.

"Yes," Talulah said. She looked tall and glamorous in high-heels. "Did I tell you that we patched up our differences? She's back in my will. She met a man who teaches martial arts in Montclair and they're going to be married. Fenton Sommers. I understand that he used to be a realtor. He gave it up to follow a calling he is passionate about: boxing. Plus he had a little trouble with the Board of Realtors," she added. "Pamela took boxing classes from him. Evidently, after her makeover she had a lot of trouble with the kind of men we used to call mashers, and she says she needed to learn how to protect herself. I guess it was just love at first sight with Fenton and her."

Everyone congratulated Talulah and asked her to pass on their good wishes to Pamela. "It's so wonderful," Zoë observed. "Pamela finally found someone who deserves her."

Talulah smiled, looked Zoë in the eye and winked.

Genevieve and Maximo, Bentley and Mark and Tex and Talulah made plans for a simple wedding. They decided on a venue. The grooms chose their best men and the brides their bridesmaids. Invitations would go out to 150 friends. Genevieve would engage a catering service for food and Bentley would book a string quartet for entertainment at a reception after the ceremony. They made plans to hire an organist to bring them down the aisle and a photographer to record the event.

The next day they scrubbed the whole plan. Their reasoning was, "Why wait?"

"To tell you the truth," Bentley said, "I had pictured sharing our happiness with a few friends out in the garden."

"Maybe a Universal Life minister," Mark added.

"Someone to play accordion," Maximo said.

"Accordion?" Tex asked.

"You'd be surprised how good they can sound at a wedding," Maximo answered. There was another long silence.

Finally Genevieve said, "You would think that at our age we could have any kind of wedding we want." She thought about it. "Sometimes people decide to stop being the CEO of Pepsi Cola Company and they make dolls for a living instead." She thought for a moment longer. "Conscientious objectors lay down their arms and refuse to fight."

"Sometimes old ladies marry men ten years younger than they are," Talulah said. "Or more."

"Sometimes two men marry each other," Mark said.

"People can do anything they want," Genevieve repeated.

"So why are we having a stupid wedding with a photographer and an organist that none of us want and 150 guests?" Tex asked.

"That's just what I was wondering, dear,"

Genevieve said.

Bentley asked Maximo, "Do you actually *know* someone who plays accordion? I mean around here?"

"I know someone in Modesto," he answered.

Tex said, "Why don't you call him and see what he's doing tomorrow, about noon."

"I know a Universal Life Minister," Mark said. "Let's go find out whether all the friends can be here."

Sunday was a nice fall day. The sun leaned toward the southern half of the sky, casting a glaring light that made dramatic shadows from the leaves of old rhododendrons, even at noon. Three couples stood together in the garden facing a minister. A cat rolled in the grass on which the others were standing and then ambled from couple to couple nudging ankles and rubbing against pant legs.

Around them stood a group whom young people would have described as elderly. One frail-looking woman lay on a *chaise longue*, smiling. Standing beside her was a grinning giant of a man who held a glass of brandy. A beautiful, long-legged African American woman stood with her arms around the waist of an affable-looking, brown-skinned man in a crimson sweater. A tiny woman with stylish, short, gray hair stood on tiptoes to see the ceremony. Holding one of her tiny hands in both of his was a barrel-chested man with thick, dark eyebrows and a shock of beautiful gray hair. A rugged, outdoor-type of fellow with gentle brown eyes stood with a woman whose face was lit with a glorious smile as she watched the wedding begin. And finally, a tall, thin man with a long neck and unruly hair held hands with a woman nearly as tall as him who had the aura of a leader. A little rag-mop of a dog sat on the grass among his people and seemed to watch as the ceremony began, though he may have been keeping his eyes on the cat.

"Look at your friends out there," the minister began, pointing past the couples to the people gathered around them. "They're smiling." The couples turned their heads and waved to their friends. "They're happy," he said, "because you're in love." The little dog gave a sharp bark, and everyone laughed.

"Why do I have such a good feeling about this wedding? It feels like the start of something. It seems like New Year's Day—a new year, a new life together. I'm happy for you. I'm happy for all of you," he said, and he spread his arms to include the friends who surrounded them.

A sparrow looking down from one of the garden's tall, old redwood trees saw that, as the minister talked, the couples moved closer together and so did their friends standing around them.

"Tex Taylor, do you take this woman to be your lawfully wedded wife?"

"Yes, sir."

"Talulah Noonan, do you take this man to be your lawfully wedded husband?"

"I do."

"I now pronounce you man and wife. Maximo Orozco, do you take this woman to be your lawfully wedded wife?"

"I do."

Genevieve Rutherford, do you take this man to be your lawfully wedded husband?"

"Yes, dear."

"I now pronounce you man and wife."

"Bentley Fairbanks, do you take this man to be yours for life?"

"I do."

"Mark Fields, do you take this man to be yours for life?"

"I do."

"Then I now pronounce you married."

The accordionist, a musician with wide experience of performing for weddings, began playing even before the couples had finished kissing. Genevieve and Maximo led off the first, festive dance.

Epilogue

[Autumn 2004]

"Tuck, dear, you're skinny as a rail."

"I *didn't* fail," he said, "I just quit writing when I got too damn old."

"I know, dear. You were quite a good writer, and you still are. You and I just wrote down everything about The Last Resort, remember? But what I'm saying is you're getting too thin. You have to *eat* more."

"I used to eat all the time," he said. "I was big as a bench."

"I remember, dear."

"Well, I don't. I can't remember a damned thing."

"You remember Weezie."

"Of course I remember Weezie." Tuck thought about it. "She was my first wife."

"Well, for goodness sake, Tuck, she was your *only* wife."

"She was my favorite one, too. I miss Weezie." Tuck wept a little. He and Genevieve were sitting in the wisteria room, blankets over their laps. "I miss them all," he said, "whoever they were. I never could get their names straight."

"Of course you could, dear. You knew their names for many years. You've just become forgetful."

"Well, I know you, Mom," he said, and he laughed. "That's what we used to call you sometimes."

"I had thirteen fine children," Genevieve said, and she laughed too.

"Say, why can't I have something to drink?" Tuck asked.

"Why, you can, dear. You can do anything you want. Your brandy's right there in that drawer."

"God, that's good news!" Tuck's chronic weakness seemed to vanish as he opened the bottle and sniffed its contents and then poured brandy into a clean snifter he found in the drawer. "You have a tot now and then, don't you? Would you care to join me, madam?"

"Why, I believe I will," she said.

Tuck handed Genevieve the glass and poured a

drink for himself. Finally he settled back in his chair beside his old friend and smiled. "Well, heck," he said, "we have a good time, don't we?"

"Don't we, dear?" She and Tuck settled into one of their favorite entertainments. They watched the old wisteria slowly take over the entire room. They agreed that on warm days they could actually see it grow.

End

Appendix

THE PURPLE TONGUE

March 13, 1975

1972 Red Burgundy........at Lenore's

The Wines:		Group Ranking
Bonnes Mares Roumier	$12.50	2
Joseph Swan Pinot Noir	$5.95	7
Clos Veugeot Grivet	$10.95	4
La Tashe Romanee Conti	$30.00	5
Echezeaux Dujac	$17.50	1
Grand Echezeaux Mugneret	N.A	3
Corton Tollot	$6.79	6

[Ed. Note: The Swan wine, from California, must have been thrown in to compare new with old-world pinot noirs. Joe Swan, from Sonoma County in California, was still learning how to make pinot noir in 1972.

Recent prices for the wines above are: 2001 Bonnes Mares $264, 2001 Swan $25, 2002 Clos Veugeot $122, 2002 La Tashe $599, 1990 Grand Echezeaux $363, Corton Tollot $107.]

Attending were: Lenore, Tuck, Tina, Bentley, Zoë, Sophia and Pamela.

THE PURPLE TONGUE

August 4th 1975

1972 California Chardonnays………..at The Last Resort

The Wines:		Group Ranking
Dry Creek	$5	8
Sterling	$6	3
Hanzel	$8	6
Heitz	$6.50	4
FreemarAbby	N.A	2
Spring Mountain	$7.50	1
Montelena	$6	5
Mondavi	N.A	7

Present were Will, Owen, Tina, Zoë, Tony, Lenore, Bentley, Weezie, Tuck, Genevieve, Harvey.

Last Resort Turkey Dressing

10 Servings

½ pound cubed cornbread
½ pound whole wheat bread
1 pound cooked lean sausage, drained and chopped
2 tablespoons unsalted butter
2 tablespoons olive oil
3 celery ribs, finely diced
1 medium onion, finely diced
4 jalepeño peppers, finely diced
10 fresh water chestnuts, peeled and finely diced
1 cup fresh cranberries, diced
1 gala apple
½ cup kumquats, finely diced
2 cups walnuts, toasted and chopped
1 tablespoon sage, finely chopped
1 tablespoon thyme, finely chopped
2 eggs, beaten
1 cup turkey or chicken stock

Melt butter and olive oil together in a large deep skillet. Add onions, celery and jalepeño peppers and cook over medium heat until soft.

1.   Add water chestnuts, cranberries, apple, kumquats, sage, thyme, salt and pepper. Toss together and transfer to a very large bowl.

2.   Combine the above ingredients with the stock and beaten eggs, cornbread, whole wheat bread and walnuts.

Butter a 3 to 4 quart casserole dish and spread the dressing evenly. Bake in a 350° oven, 30 minutes until top is brown and crisp.

A Note on the Type

Most of these pages were set in 14-point Garamond. The authors lobbied for a 14-point type rather than the smaller, more standard 10- or 12-point type because it better suited their sixty-year-old eyes. They voted for Garamond because they came across it in their word-processing software and thought it looked really good. Don't laugh. Even very important matters, such as the interpretation of your biopsy, are determined every day for less weighty reasons than these. Dr. Mark will be discussing this disturbing problem at next Wednesday's health night.